One True Love

'When I'm old enough?' said Susanne, tilting her head.

'Old enough?'

'Old enough to marry you.'

'What? Marry? Good God!'

Then he saw that she was smiling. She had caught him on the wrong foot, and he resented it. He looked along the broken curve of the cliff towards the caves. He had half a mind to teach her a lesson by scaring her with tales of ghosts and demons; then she put out her arms and pushed him, quite violently, and, laughing, pushed him again.

'I wouldn't marry you, Louis Hollander,' she said, 'if you were to go down on your big fat knees and beg me. I wouldn't marry you for all the tea in China. So there!'

About the Author

Born in Glasgow, Jessica Stirling is the author of
twenty-five heartwarming novels, many with
Scottish backgrounds.

JESSICA STIRLING

One True Love

HODDER

A CIP catalogue record for this title is available from the British Library

ISBN 0 340 83489 7

Typeset in Plantin by Hewer Text UK Ltd, Edinburgh
Printed and bound by
Mackays of Chatham Ltd, Chatham, Kent

Hodder Headline's policy is to use papers that are natural, renewable
and recyclable products and made from wood grown in sustainable
forests. The logging and manufacturing processes are expected to
conform to the environmental regulations of the country of origin.

Hodder and Stoughton Ltd
A division of Hodder Headline
338 Euston Road
London NW1 3BH

PART ONE

I

On 16th October 1845, the Bank of England raised the borrowing rate to three per cent and the market in railway shares went into steep decline. Wild speculation was replaced by panic, prices tumbled and many a fine gentleman who had got rich quick suddenly found himself poor again; Mr Neville Spencer Reeve was not among them. A wink and a nod from a friend in the City enabled him to escape penury by the skin of his teeth, but, for several years thereafter, he was obliged to devote himself to the practice of law with a diligence that had been sadly lacking during his time as an inveterate gambler on railway stock.

The fortune he had almost lost had been spent mainly on women. He had buried two wives and fathered more than his fair share of children in, and out, of wedlock. He was no model parent but had nursed too many paternity claims through the Court of Chancery to neglect his obligations entirely and had made provision for his offspring, legitimate and otherwise, by farming them out to rural schools or setting them up in industrial apprenticeships. He could not, therefore, be brought to book for irresponsibility or condemned as a man totally lacking in heart. So, late on a gloomy March afternoon, he was not unduly alarmed to experience a twinge of compassion at the sight of little Susanne Thorne, hand in hand with her aunt, tripping across the courtyard of the Staple Inn just below his window.

He stepped away from the window and carried a walnut

high chair from its position against the wall and placed it before his desk on which lay a volume of Blackstone's *Commentaries on the Laws of England* together with all the documents relating to Joshua Thorne's last will and testament.

The door from the courtyard slammed. The clerk's voice rumbled in the stone stairwell and, a few moments later, Mrs Hollander and her ward were ushered into the office.

'Madam.' He shook Mrs Hollander's hand. 'Miss Thorne, have you recovered from your ordeal?'

'I have, sir,' the girl informed him. 'Do you wish me to sit?'

'By all means. See, I've put out a special chair for you.'

'A baby chair, Mr Reeve?'

'A chair for persons who are not full grown.'

'Well, I'm not quite that, not yet.'

Susanne clambered on to the high chair, planted her feet on the sloping step and did her best to appear grown up. Reeve waited until the aunt settled before he took up his position behind the desk. He was tall but not stooped and, except when occasion demanded it, wore no wig or robes. He was, in fact, far too much a man of fashion to favour the ancient accoutrement that had accumulated around his profession, much of which was designed simply to intimidate.

'What age are you, Susanne?'

'I'm fourteen, sir.'

'Small for her age,' said the aunt. 'We'll feed her up and she'll blossom into a fine big strapping lassie in no time. Won't you, my love?'

'Yes, Aunt Bette. It's what Papa would have wished for me.'

Joshua Thorne had built up his printing business through sheer hard work and was known in the City for honesty and square dealing. He had married late in life and when his wife had passed away soon after presenting him with a daughter had employed a nursemaid, Miss Ashworth, to care for the baby. Miss Ashworth had been rewarded for her years of devoted service with a legacy of one thousand pounds and, soon after Aunt Hollander had arrived in London to take charge of Susanne, had gone off to live with a sister in Torbay. The Thornes' house in Holborn, together with the printing shop in Farringdon Street and a paper-making factory in Shoreditch, had been sold and the proceeds invested in a trust to provide Susanne with an income, until she came of age.

Reeve had first met the girl at the graveside in the cemetery in Gray's Inn Road; a waif-like figure in childish weeds flanked by the nursemaid and the plump aunt and surrounded by a pack of *faux* relatives who had calculated precisely what Susanne was worth and who had clambered all over themselves in a belated attempt to lure her away from the Scottish aunt. He had admired her fortitude and common sense then, and he admired her now.

'Do you understand, Susanne,' he said, 'the arrangements that have been made for your welfare?'

'My Aunt Bette is to take care of me.'

'Can you read?' Neville Reeve enquired.

'Of course I can read,' Susanne replied, indignantly. 'I learned at Miss Millar's Academy. I can read music too, and count and embroider.'

'My enquiry is directed not towards ascertaining if you *can* read, Susanne,' Reeve said, 'but to ensure that you are capable of understanding that which I will read to you.'

'Is it the law, sir?'

'It is the law.'

'Is it about my papa's money?'

'It is.'

'I'll try to understand,' Susanne promised.

Neville Reeve could have recited the relative clauses from memory but he preferred the girl, and the aunt, to have it straight from the horse's mouth. He opened the volume of legal commentary and read from it: ' "The power and reciprocal duty of a guardian and ward are the same as that of a father and child, except in as much as the guardian, when the ward comes of age, is bound to give an account of all that has been transacted on behalf of the ward and must answer for all losses by wilful default or negligence. In order then to prevent disagreeable contests it has become a practice for many guardians to indemnify themselves by applying to an officer of the Court of Chancery, acting under direction, and accounting annually before the said officer of appointment." '

'Is that who you are, sir?' Susanne asked. 'The officer of appointment?'

'Indeed, it is,' Neville Reeve answered. 'I have been licensed by the Court of Chancery to ensure that your aunt, Mrs Adam Hollander, receives a quarterly sum to keep and maintain you, and that she accounts annually for all additional sums spent on your welfare, no more and no less.'

'Until I come of age?' Susanne said. 'When, sir, will that be?'

Neville Reeve paused, then, by way of answer, resorted to reading from Blackstone. ' "A female at fourteen is at years of legal discretion and may choose her own guardian; at seventeen may be executrix; at twenty-one may dispose of herself and her lands." '

'My lands?' Susanne giggled. 'What lands have I got?'

'You may dispose of yourself, then,' said Neville Reeve.

'How do I do that?'

The lawyer shrugged. 'By marriage.'

'When I am twenty-one?'

How typical of a female not to interrogate him about the size of her fortune but to fix instead on the conditions of marriage attached to it. What in heaven's name were they teaching them in Miss Millar's Academy these days, he wondered, and had the law found its way on to the curriculum along with etiquette and embroidery?

'Well, no,' Reeve admitted. 'Under Scots law, you may, in effect, marry after you are above the age of twelve years. It would, of course, be better – I mean, better for you – if you did not throw yourself into an ill-considered union with some young man who may court you simply because you have money.'

'What,' Susanne said, 'if he loves me?'

'Nature,' said Neville Reeve, 'may well endow you with all that is necessary to be a wife, and the law recognises that fact. Nature, however, may be somewhat more tardy in endowing you with sound judgement. I would strenuously advise you to seek advice from your aunt before you allow yourself to be beguiled by the blandishments of a person of the opposite sex.'

'Beguiled?' Susanne giggled again, then, sobering, asked, 'Do I not need *your* consent to marry, then?'

Neville Reeve closed both eyes and wrestled with what remained of his conscience. He tried to imagine what she would look like when she grew up. Pretty, perhaps, but more likely veering to the plain, though those dark brown eyes were mischievous enough to hint that she might have more character than he gave her credit for.

'No,' he said, at length. 'No, you do not need my consent to marry.'

'Thank you for telling me,' Susanne said. 'That *is* a useful piece of information to have at one's disposal.'

Reeve placed a hand on Susanne's shoulder and peered into her dark brown eyes. 'Twenty-one years, young lady,' he said, 'twenty-one years is the age at which you will cease to be regarded as an infant, so styled in law, and will be free to do as you wish. Marriage does not enter into it.'

'It might?' Susanne insisted.

'Yes, my love, it might,' said Aunt Bette Hollander. 'There are lots of handsome young men in the Kingdom of Fife.'

The Kingdom of Fife; a tusk of land jutting into the North

Sea. The village of Strayhorn, where Bette Hollander's husband had built himself a house, did not even deserve a mention
on the map; one house, one servant, one adult son, no railway,
barely a decent road, as far as Reeve could make out; yet the
girl professed herself happy to embrace a new life in that
remote corner of Scotland, and who was he, a humble servant
of the Chancellor, to deny her?

'Madam,' he said, turning away from Susanne, 'I require
your signature on the petition of wardship. You will receive
your first quarterly payment on the first day of June, paid to
you through the Dundee branch of the Merchants and Traders Bank, with which institution a portion of the late Mr
Thorne's capital has been invested. The balance of the fund is
under my jurisdiction and will be placed to yield a maximum
return.'

'Is a signature all that is required of me?' Mrs Hollander
asked.

'That is all,' Neville Reeve answered. 'I will see to it that
copies of the documents are delivered to your hotel before you
set off tomorrow morning.'

'And your fee, sir?' the aunt said.

'My fee has been deducted from capital. It is all, I assure
you, to the letter and quite above board.'

'I don't doubt it, Mr Reeve,' Mrs Hollander said. 'Joshua
wouldn't have chosen you if you hadn't been reliable.'

Drawing the papers across the desk, the attorney flicked
open the lid of a brass inkwell and, with a flourish that
bordered on legerdemain, presented the woman with an ebony
pen-holder. He leaned over her shoulder, and pointed.

'There, if you would be so good.'

Laboriously, Mrs Hollander signed her name.

'There, too.'

Mrs Hollander repeated the process.

Mr Reeve dried both signatures with lilac blotting paper,

witnessed each sheet with his own dashing moniker, blotted them again and filed them with the rest of the Thorne documents.

On glancing up he was surprised to see tears trickling down the girl's cheeks. He was tempted to console her but the milk of human kindness had been somewhat soured by his recent reverses, and he restrained himself.

'Oh now, now,' Bette Hollander crooned. 'Oh, my poor wee lamb,' and, plucking Susanne from the high chair, smothered her with kisses.

And while this touching scene was taking place Neville Spencer Reeve seized the opportunity to stuff the Thorne documents into his enormous safe and, with a sniff of satisfaction at a job well done, locked them securely away.

Competition had reduced the travelling time between King's Cross and Edinburgh to thirteen and a half hours and the race was now on between the Caledonian and Great North Western railway companies to woo customers with comfort and convenience. The convenience of having a water closet situated between the first- and second-class carriages was greatly appreciated by Aunt Bette Hollander who, so she told Susanne, had a barometer instead of a bladder and could measure not only changes in temperature but even in altitude by her need to make pee-pee.

In the month of their acquaintance, Susanne had become used to her aunt's lack of modesty. Life in Strayhorn and marriage to a sea captain had, it seemed, imbued her with an earthiness that sat ill with her aspirations to be regarded as a lady of quality.

Aunt Bette had spared no expense in contracting for one of the well-upholstered U-shaped berths in the first-class carriage and had paid extra to have the quantities of luggage that she had acquired in the 'Metrolopus' stowed in the van. Susanne was unaware that the cost of her transportation from the Hub of the Empire to the Kingdom of Fife had been deducted from her account with the Merchants and Traders Bank, or that Mr Reeve had signed away twenty-six guineas to cover nineteen nights in the New Holborn Hotel where Aunt Bette and she had resided after Papa's house, empty of furnishings, had passed into other hands.

It was beginning to dawn on Susanne, though, that she would never see Miss Ashworth again, would never again prattle with Esmeralda Finch or Lisbeth Crouch, her best friends at Miss Millar's Academy, never sit with Papa in the library upstairs while he read to her from Lamb's *Tales from Shakespeare* or the illustrated edition of Bible stories that, at Miss Ashworth's insistence, he had provided for her instruction.

The coach lurched and rattled. The green fields of England and its dusty towns bobbed past the window, veiled by smoke from the locomotive.

Long before the train reached Grantham there was a nasty, metallic taste in Susanne's mouth that not even a sip of cordial from her aunt's silver flask could remove. After several sips from the silver flask Aunt Bette fell asleep and, lying back against the cushions, Susanne eyed the woman listlessly.

She looked, Susanne thought, more like a painted doll than a person, like one of those elaborate waxworks that, by means of hidden bellows, were made to breathe. Her plump cheeks were daubed with rouge purchased from a stall in the Soho Bazaar. Her hair hung in fat loops intertwined with tiny pearls bought from a shop at Oxford Circus. She was wrapped in a voluminous mantle acquired from a splendid emporium in Regent Street, and a new black Babet hat, crowned with feathers, danced tipsily to the rhythm of the iron wheels. There was something ungracious about her aunt in repose, something to which Susanne could not yet relate; nor was she entirely convinced that the village of Strayhorn was quite the paradise that the woman made it out to be.

She had been happy in London with Papa and Miss Ashworth, Cook and Mary Jane to look after her, and no memory of Mama to trouble her dreams. She had revelled in the little treats that Miss Ashworth had arranged: a sail on the Thames to Greenwich, a visit to the Tower, an evening excursion to Drury Lane to hear an opera sung in Italian. She had also reached an age when the future flickered with fascinating possibilities. The older girls at Miss Millar's Academy were full of talk of balls, parties and picnics, of meeting young men, falling in love and, lurking behind a veil that not even Esmeralda could penetrate, all the alarming mysteries that marriage entailed.

Then, in January, Papa had fallen sick.

In those last days Susanne had seen little of him. Miss Ashworth had kept her 'amused' downstairs and life had gone on almost as before, except that there had been lawyers and doctors and gentlemen from the Merchants and Traders Bank calling at the house, bearded, black-coated gentlemen in tall hats to which granules of snow or droplets of rain adhered.

At first Susanne had refused to accept that death had entered her papa's house. He had seemed so peaceful lying in his spotless nightgown, hair and beard combed, with nothing to indicate that anything much was wrong with him, save for a freckle of blood on a handkerchief tucked under the pillow that supported his head, and the medicines that the doctors had left on the night table.

Papa had smiled and stroked her hair. He had little enough to say, only, 'Dearest, dearest, I will soon be with your Mama in heaven, or so Miss Ashworth tells me,' and, later, 'I have instructed Mr Reeve to write to my relatives in Scotland and ask them to take care of you.'

Then, one terrible morning, Miss Ashworth had held her

tightly and everyone had cried and, late that same evening, her Aunt Bette Hollander had arrived from Scotland, breathless, but not speechless, with concern.

Grantham and Newark, Tuxford and Retford, on to Doncaster, to York and Edinburgh and, tomorrow, Perth. All the things that she had loved were being left behind, stripped away, mile upon mile, by cuttings and viaducts, embankments and tunnels. The fields were no longer shot with green. Snow lay in patches along the footpaths. Spring sunshine was swallowed up by lowering cloud that grew thicker and more constant as the locomotive puffed northward.

In vain Susanne tried to cling to the remnants of her composure, to convince herself that Strayhorn was all that Aunt Bette said it would be and that everyone there would be kind and loving and would welcome her with open arms. But, as the journey became ever more tedious and tiring, her confidence waned and she began to cry, very softly, holding her hands to her face to hide her ingratitude.

2

When the grandfather clock in the hall struck six, Buckie Hollander heaved himself from his armchair by the fire and hobbled to the window. He had been on tenterhooks all afternoon, bobbing up and down like a cork in a bottle.

He pulled back the lace curtain and peered out into the dusk.

'Nancy,' he shouted. 'Nancy.'

Nancy Bissett, the Hollanders' maid-of-all-work, appeared in the kitchen doorway. A lean, craggy-featured woman on the far side of thirty-five, she had been with the Hollanders long enough to have lost all fear of her master.

'What is it now?' she said, testily.

'I can't understand it,' Buckie said. 'Bette should have been home hours ago. Do you think there's been an accident?'

'I told you, she'll have stopped off in Edinburgh to buy things.'

'Why would she do that?' Buckie said. 'She's been in London for the best part of a month. Her last letter said that the girl's affairs were close to being settled and they would be home today about noon.'

'They'll be stuck down the road in Strayhorn waiting for Sandy Raiker to finish his ale. I thought Louis had gone to meet them?'

'He did,' Buckie said. 'Hours ago.'

'He'll be drinkin' with his cronies in the Dalriada, like as not.'

'Not tonight, surely, not when his mama's due home.'

Nancy snorted, and vanished into the kitchen.

Buckie peered through the salt-stained window but could see nothing to give him hope. The pain in his legs was heavy. He prayed that he wasn't in for another bad spell. What sort of a welcome would it be for a poor wee orphan lass if the first thing she encountered was a groaning old man? He levered himself upright, reached for his stick, limped into the hall and, taking an old pea-jacket from the cupboard, draped it over his shoulders and opened the front door.

The wind almost bowled him over as he stepped on to the wooden porch that fronted the house and peered towards the shoulder of the hill behind which lay the village of Strayhorn. A booming westerly drove masses of tarry-black cloud across the sky. Tonight, when the tide turned, High Cross beach would be swallowed up by a roaring surge and the house would shake with the force of the gale. He hoped that little Susanne Thorne, a city girl, would not be frightened by her first taste of Scottish weather.

Buckie had never met the girl but he had met her father, Joshua Thorne, Bette's second cousin, long before Susanne had been born.

Shortly after their marriage, Bette and he had sailed to London to see the sights and had been entertained by Joshua in his grand house in Holborn. Buckie had been treated to a tour of the printing shop and dinner in a chop house somewhere off Fleet Street. He had rubbed along very well with Mr Thorne and remembered him fondly. So, when a letter had arrived from a London attorney informing Bette that Joshua was close to death and that his little daughter would be left alone in the world, Buckie had urged his wife to leave for London at once and to bring the child back with her.

Buckie knew only too well what it meant to be alone in the world.

He, too, had been orphaned at an early age. His father and brothers had gone down with the *Goldfinch* in the Davis Strait. Three years later, he had set off from Peterhead in the *Penguin*, to chase the whales like his da but while he had been gone his mother and sister had been taken by the cholera and he had come home to a world as empty as an old crab shell.

The wind tore at his jacket. He tried to batten the garment around him, and dropped his stick. Just as he bent down to pick it up an enormous curly-coated Newfoundland dog bounded on to the porch, knocked him over, straddled his legs and, with a tongue as long as a grown man's arm and as pink as a coral daisy, began licking his face.

'Ajax, great heavens, Ajax, will you get off me.' Buckie wrestled with the dog and glared up at the young man who had followed the dog on to the porch. 'Call him off, Louis, for God's sake.'

Louis Hollander grinned and, grabbing Ajax by the throat, hauled him away. 'He's only demonstrating his affection, Pappy. He's saying he loves you.'

'Well, the stupid creature doesn't have to murder me to prove it. Here, put him inside, then come and help me up.'

Louis and Ajax were too full of vigour to know the meaning of restraint, and Buckie could not be angry with them for long. Louis returned, minus the dog, and helped his father to his feet.

'Have you been feeding that animal ale again?' Buckie asked.

'Of course not,' Louis said, then, 'well, just a sup to keep me company. Ajax's very fond of the barley brew. By the by, the coach from the railway station at Perth hasn't arrived. If we had a trap and a pony of our own I would have gone to Perth to pick them up.'

'Traps and ponies cost money.' Buckie tapped the young

man's shin lightly with his stick. 'Besides, who'd look after a pony? You?'

Big spots of rain whipped against Buckie's face.

Louis tilted his chin and parted his lips to taste the salt, his pilot coat wide open, his shirt plastered against his chest, his jet-black hair forming loose wet curls on his neck. Pride mingled with anxiety in Buckie as he studied his son and wished, not for the first time, that Bette had blessed him with more children.

There had been three conceptions before Louis, two after, and old Dr Campbell had told him in no uncertain terms that another miscarriage would 'do' for Bette, even if she was fifteen years his junior and still in her prime.

Louis nudged him and pointed. 'See, Pappy, here they come now.'

'Are you sure?'

'Isn't that Dr Redpath's gig on the hill?'

'It is,' Buckie said. 'Who's that waving?'

'Mama,' Louis Hollander said. 'Home safe and sound at last.'

'Late?' Bette bussed her husband's cheek. 'Lucky we are to be here at all. What a nightmare of a journey we've had of it, not least searching for Raiker in Strayhorn. If it hadn't been for the kindness of Dr Redpath we would be still be waiting for that horrid little fellow. Louis, bring in the luggage, if you please, and help the girl down.'

All eyes turned to the gig, and its passenger.

'Allow me,' Alan Redpath called out.

The hood of the gig fell low and for a moment all the Hollanders could see of the new arrival was a black skirt and gloved hands. When the doctor approached she stood up, stretched out her arms and let him swing her to the ground. She seemed slight, almost sickly. Her lips were full and the

shape of her face pert but she was weedy, too weedy, Buckie
Hollander decided; she definitely needed fattening up.

Nancy Bissett came out to welcome her mistress and cast a
wary eye over the newcomer. Ajax had no such reservations.
He bounded down the steps, tail wagging, raced towards the
child, sprang up between her arms and washed her face with
his long pink tongue.

'Don't be frightened, sweetheart,' Aunt Bette cried. 'He
won't bite you.'

'I'm not frightened,' Susanne said. 'I love dogs.'

'Well, we've that in common, Miss Thorne,' Alan Redpath
said. 'Watch he doesn't knock you over, though. He's a big
chap and doesn't know his own strength.' Susanne braced
herself and kissed Ajax on the snout.

'Aren't you going to kiss your uncle, too,' Aunt Bette said.
'See, this is your uncle, since you call me aunt. And this big
strapping lump, who isn't near as well behaved as you are, is
your cousin Louis.'

Pushing Ajax down, Susanne skipped to the porch and
kissed each of her relatives with, Buckie thought, all the grace
of a young lady who had been well schooled in manners.

'Welcome to High Cross,' Louis said and tapped his chin
with his forefinger to elicit another kiss.

'The bags, Lukie.' Aunt Bette pushed her son towards the
gig. 'Come on, you useless donkey, fetch the luggage indoors
before the rain comes down again. Besides' – she looked up at
Nancy for the first time – 'I'm hungry for my dinner. Good
evening to you, Nancy.'

'Good evening, lady,' Nancy said and stepped from the
porch to unload the luggage, while the Hollanders, Louis
included, made a great show of ushering Susanne indoors.

The Hollanders' wasn't the only house in Fife to bear the name
of High Cross. At one time, two or three hundred years ago,

there had been many abbeys and monasteries in Fife and several rude stone coffins had been dug up during the building of the Protestant church that served the fisher folk of Stray-horn. The house had been built on top of a ruined cottage that had occupied the site for as long as anyone could remember. There were three rooms on the ground floor and two on the upper. It was too dark to see much of the yard but, as she washed her face and hands at an iron basin in the kitchen, Susanne could make out a pump and the arch of a well, a scatter of hens, and some bed sheets flapping like apparitions on a length of rope fastened across the mouth of a shed.

Bette took her turn at the basin. Susanne wandered back into the living-room. Her uncle was seated in a big leather armchair by the fire. Louis, at the table, was cutting a loaf of bread into thick slices and laying the slices in a fan shape on a floral plate. The table, Susanne noticed, was set for four.

'Isn't the doctor staying for supper?' she asked.

'The doctor,' her uncle answered, 'has other sick folk to attend to. There's nothing he can do for me.'

'Are you sick, sir?' said Susanne.

'He has the gout,' Louis stated, still working the knife.

'Is that a painful affliction?'

'Do not, I beg you, ask him that question,' Louis said, then chanted, 'Gout, gout, gout, gout! O God, protect us from the gout.'

Her uncle grimaced and raised a bushy eyebrow. His big, coarse hands roved over the muscles of his legs, stroking and kneading mechanically.

Susanne was quite old enough to take a hint, and said no more.

The room was furnished, mainly, in walnut wood: a side-board, half a dozen chairs, a hanging lamp of polished brass. Plaster leaked from the painted wainscot. There were scratches on the wallpaper and grease spots on the rug, a general shabbiness that made her realise just how clean her father's house had been with its glossy banisters and gleaming fitments and not a speck of dust, let alone a stain, to be seen. She did not find the cramped room uncomfortable, though. In fact, it was warmer than any of the rooms in the tall house in Holborn, for her father had always been niggardly with coal.

Six or eight framed lithographs hung not quite straight on the brown wallpaper: wooden ships, ice and snow, great big fishes – whales, of course. Aunt Bette had told her that her uncle had been the master of a whaling vessel in his younger days.

'Blubber, blubber, blubber!' Louis chanted, as if he'd read her thoughts. 'O God, protect us from the blubber, too.'

Susanne experienced a little prickle of annoyance at her cousin who was, she thought, showing off. On one side of the fireplace hung an ancient barometer. On the other, dangling from a shrivelled leather thong, was a fat brass telescope and, monopolising the length of the mantelpiece, a model ship, intricately detailed down to the longboats that hung from its tiny tarnished chains. She asked, 'Did you catch whales in this boat, sir?'

'The *Merrilyn*,' her uncle answered. 'I owned her.'

Before his son could wax sarcastic, the old man pushed himself to his feet, lit the hanging lamp above the table and in a voice more whimsical than dictatorial, called out, 'Dinner, where's our dinner?'

Nancy stormed out of the kitchen and stood in the doorway, hands planted on her hips. 'Who said that?'

Father and son answered in unison, 'He did.'

And Susanne, knowing no better, laughed.

The dog was locked in another room. The lamp was lowered over the table. Susanne was seated between her uncle and her cousin. Nancy served broth from a porcelain tureen while Bette, with the restlessness of a person who can't remain still for long, rummaged among the luggage in the hall. She returned with a chamois bag from which she extracted a battered silver mug that Susanne recognised as one that she had used as a child in the nursery in Holborn. It occurred to her that the Hollanders still thought of her as a child and, until she proved otherwise, would continue to treat her as if she were nine years old.

Aunt Bette wiped the mug with a napkin and placed it before her.

'Nancy, take away the water glass. Susanne is used to having her own mug which, as you can see, I retrieved before it could be sold.'

'Ah yes, the sale?' Louis glanced up. 'How much did his stuff fetch?'

'That,' Aunt Bette said, tartly, 'is none of your business.'

Susanne let the servant fill the silver mug with water and dutifully took a sip or two. She had forgotten all about the nursery mug that Miss Ashworth had stored with other baby things in a chest in the attic. For the last year or so she had been taking wine at dinner; Miss Ashworth, like her papa, had been very fond of claret.

The soup was too salty for Susanne's taste. She mopped it up with a slice of bread, a mere peck compared to her cousin who finished the whole loaf almost by himself then sat with an arm draped over the chair back, looking expectantly towards the kitchen. Nancy brought in a big serving plate on which slithered a wet piece of meat. She dropped the plate on to the centre of the table. Bette looked at the meat, and sniffed. Buckie gazed at it mournfully.

'What else have you got, Nancy?' he asked.

'Fried potatoes.'

Buckie sighed.

'Flank mutton, my favourite.' Louis reached for the serving plate and a sharp-bladed knife. '*Mater, pour vous?*'

One True Love

Buckie said, 'With the potatoes, Nancy, the malt vinegar, if you please.'

'No vinegar for you,' Nancy told him. 'You know what the doctor says.'

Buckie uttered a petulant little moan and, with a nod, sanctioned Louis to place a slice of mutton on his plate. He tucked his napkin into his waistcoat, lifted his knife and sloshed the meat about in a puddle of gravy. Louis served his mother and Susanne, and helped himself to the lion's share.

Susanne cut the mutton into tiny pieces and contrived to swallow without chewing. The taste was strong, not subtle. She recalled casseroles of prime lamb that Cook had produced and the delicate sauces that flavoured them. She drank water, ate the greasy meat and greasy potatoes, and envied Louis his appetite.

For the next quarter of an hour not a word was spoken as each of the diners coped in his or her own way with the mutton and the lumpy suet pudding that followed it. As soon as supper was over, the table was cleared and Nancy laid a faded red cloth over it. Buckie settled into his armchair at the fireside, Bette, Susanne and Louis at the table. Released from captivity, Ajax bounded hopefully about, licking and whining and generally exhibiting a servility that sat ill with his size. He nudged Susanne's legs and lapped up every microscopic crumb that had found its way to the floor. That done, he claimed his space in front of the fireplace and, with a windy sigh, fell asleep.

Louis left the room and returned with an armful of papers, an inkstand and pen. He spread the papers out beneath the lamp and began to copy something from one sheet to another.

'For heaven's sake, Louis,' Aunt Bette said, 'can't you put your work aside for one evening, especially as you haven't seen me for weeks?'

'I'm here, am I not?' Louis said, without looking up. 'You know very well that my concentration is absolute and that talking doesn't put me off. Fire away and talk to me. I'm all ears.'

Susanne roused herself enough to enquire, 'What are you writing, Louis? Is it an essay?'

'Music,' Louis said. 'I'm transposing a Bach chorale.'

'Oh, you're a musician?' Her aunt had failed to mention that aspect of her cousin's genius.

'Music,' said Buckie, mildly. 'No money to be made in music.'

Louis smiled indulgently at his father. 'Bach didn't do too badly.'

'I hope you're not comparing yourself to Bach?' his mother said.

'One has to start somewhere,' Louis told her. 'Besides, it's not something over which I have much control. Music, I suppose, is my destiny.' Then, lowering his head, he concentrated on throwing more musical symbols on to the paper.

The heat of the fire, and the long day's journey, had tired Susanne. Resting an arm on the table she laid her head down upon it, closed her eyes and, after a moment, let out a little purl of breath that bordered on a snore.

'Wore out, poor lamb,' Bette said. 'We'll wake her when tea's served and then I'll put her to bed.'

Louis laid down his pen and, brushing a lock of hair from his brow, peeped at his sleeping cousin. 'All right, Mother,' he said. 'Out with it. How much is she really worth?'

'No more than we'd have been worth,' Bette Hollander said, 'if we'd invested our savings with Mr Reeve instead of that scoundrel Coburn.'

'It wasn't Henry's fault that railway stock plunged,' said Louis.

'Perhaps not,' his mother said. 'I have remarked, however, that Henry Coburn isn't living in reduced circumstances.'

'That's true,' Louis admitted, 'but old Harry has property and you'll never starve if you have property.'

'We have property,' Buckie reminded him.

'Property?' said Louis. 'Do you call this dismal hovel property? If ever we have to borrow on it, how much do you think we'll get? Hardly a penny. Hasn't it occurred to you, Pappy, that Mama and I deserve something better?'

'If only we'd invested our capital with a London gentleman like Mr Reeve,' Bette rambled on, 'we'd be sitting pretty by now.'

'You were obviously impressed by this lawyer chap,' said Buckie.

'He's a man of some authority,' Bette said. 'He'll do well by Susanne.'

'Ah!' Louis said, softly. 'And Susanne will do well by us, *n'est-ce pas?*'

'That,' said Aunt Bette Hollander, crisply, 'remains to be seen,' then, rather more flustered than usual, reared back in her chair and called out to Nancy to fetch in the tea.

Bette held her up as if she were an invalid and offered her the nursery mug filled with milky tea. She took the mug in both hands and drank while her uncle and aunt studied her admiringly, as if she were performing a clever trick. Then her aunt took a candle-holder from the mantelpiece, stuck a candle in it, lit it with a taper, shepherded her out into the hall and up the steep staircase into the room at the rear which would be her bedroom. It was not so grand as her room in Holborn but the wallpaper was a cheerful creamy yellow flowered with little blue roses and there was an iron bedstead with a patchwork quilt, a dressing-table, a chest of drawers and two chairs upholstered in faded green velvet.

'Nancy has put a hot pan in the bed,' Aunt Bette told her, 'and unpacked your clothes. There's water in the jug, towels and soap and, yes, there's your nightgown on the pillow. Don't be alarmed by the noise, dear. It's a wild night and the wind will find all sorts of things to throw about. If you're frightened call to Louis across the corridor.'

'Yes,' Louis said, making her start. 'I'll fend off the ghosts and ghouls.'

He leaned in the doorway, arms folded, watching her. He had taken off his collar and unbuttoned his vest and looked, Susanne thought, very languid and handsome in that pose.

'No such thing as ghosts,' Susanne said.

'Is there not now?' said Louis. 'Ah well, we'll see.'

'Off with you,' Aunt Bette said. 'Give the poor girl some privacy.'

Louis seemed reluctant to leave. 'Isn't she going to say her prayers?'

'What would you know of prayers?' Aunt Bette said. 'A pagan wretch like you wouldn't know a prayer if it was sung to you by angels.'

'Well, we have an angel now,' Louis said, 'an angel of our very own, so perhaps I should stay and listen. Who knows what I might learn?'

'Out,' said Aunt Bette, and closed the door on him.

Susanne took off her shoes and stockings, dress and petticoats and slipped into her nightgown. She knelt by the side of the bed, bowed her head and tried to recall the prayers that Miss Ashworth had taught her. She could think of nothing, though, except the strangeness of it all, how weary she was, and how, even at the back of the house, she could hear the roar of the sea as clearly as if it were breaking over the sheds in the kitchen yard.

She murmured the Lord's Prayer into her fists.

Aunt Bette stood behind her, nodding approval.

'I'll leave you now,' Aunt Bette said when the prayer was

over. 'See, here's a little candle in a water-dish. It'll burn for an hour and you'll be fast asleep long before that.'

'Thank you, Aunt Bette,' Susanne said. 'Thank you for everything.'

Another kiss and, without haste, her aunt left her alone, closing but not locking the door behind her.

Susanne sat on the end of the bed and listened to the storm batter against the roof. She felt both small and large, like a child and a grown-up at one and the same time. Soothed by the light of the little tablet of wax that floated in a saucer of water on the dresser she turned to the bed and peeled back the covers.

The entity leaped out, sleek and black with evil yellow eyes.

It soared from the pillow to the floor, and vanished.

Susanne shrieked and fell from the bed.

She flew to the door, flung it open and fled into the passage.

Louis's bedroom door was open, the room lamplit behind him. He had stripped off his vest and shirt and was barefoot and bare-chested.

'What's wrong?' He showed no alarm. 'Ghosts already?'

'Yes,' she gasped, shivering. 'Yes, a ghost was hiding in – in my bed.'

He stepped past her into her bedroom and with a courage that seemed almost foolhardy, knelt on the boards and peered under the iron cot. He fished about with his hand and dragged 'the entity' out by the tail. With the cat in his arms, Louis came towards her. Black fur against his pale skin seemed so unnatural that it was all Susanne could do to look at him. The cat's yellow eyes closed and opened, pure black paws opened and closed on her cousin's flesh.

'It's only our Thimble. She was sleeping in your bed. Trust her to find the warmest spot in the house. You frightened her as much as she frightened you. She's really very amiable, as a rule.'

Susanne, still shaking, forced herself to stroke the cat's forehead. The cat purred loudly and rubbed her nose against Louis's chest.

'She'll sleep with you if you're nice to her,' Louis said, 'or would you prefer me to take her away?'

'Take her away,' said Susanne.

'She'd be company for you, you know.'

'No, please – just take her away.'

Louis stepped past her, tossed the cat into his room and closed the door. He came back across the passageway and laying a hand on Susanne's waist guided her back to the bed.

'I'll leave my door ajar,' he told her. 'If you need me, I'm but a step away. Meanwhile' – he kissed her – 'sleep tight.'

'I will,' she promised. 'I will.'

She held the sheet to her chin and watched him close the door, then, when she was certain that he wasn't coming back, stretched out her legs, folded her arms over her breast and dented the pillow with her head.

The candle flame flickered. The window frame shook. Rain beat upon the slates. The sea, like a huge heartbeat, pumped waves on to the shore.

None of that mattered.

Her brave cousin Louis was just across the passageway.

She grew warm beneath the quilt and, with everything fading from her mind, sighed and settled down to sleep, eager now for the first day of her new life to begin properly.

3

The path that zigzagged up the cliff from the cove was regarded as unsafe. Bette was the only one who used it regularly. On Sundays Buckie summoned the trap from Strayhorn and, with Nancy striding out behind them, Bette and he were driven over the hill to the edge of the village and doubled back to the church. It took a half-hour by the village route but only ten minutes to scramble up the cliff path and plump Bette Hollander was, as a rule, so eager to meet with her friend Thomas Oakley that she would have tackled the cliff with a rope and grappling iron to keep her rendezvous with the minister.

She was flushed and breathless when she clambered on to the apron of grass below the wall of the burial ground that hugged the stout grey granite of Strayhorn Old Parish Church.

The building itself was ungainly – some called it ugly – with urn-topped gables and a battlemented tower in lieu of a steeple for, sixty years ago, patronage had fallen into the hands of a branch of the family Arbuthnot who were Episcopalians and consequently had queer ideas about architecture. The Arbuthnots had been generous in their endowments to the parish, however, and had recently spent upwards of two hundred pounds improving the manse, much to the relief of Effie, the minister's wife, who had become thoroughly weary of satisfying her husband's less-than-spiritual needs with drips from a leaky roof falling on her head. New slates and plaster lathes did not fill small bellies, though, and the living of Old Parish was scant by any standards.

Couched in a mellifluous baritone that could make the
reading of marriage banns sound like a new Apocalypse,
Tom Oakley's question was, therefore, pardonable. 'And
what, my dear Bette, have you brought me this gusty March
morning?'

Tom Oakley was a small, squat man. He had a round head
topped by a scroll of hair, more ginger than brown, that with
diligent combing and an application of pomade, could, so he
fondly imagined, be groomed into something resembling a
tonsure, not monkish – dear God, no – but senatorial.

Bette panted, 'I – thought – you would – be pleased to see
me.'

'I am. I am indescribably pleased to see you. Overjoyed, in
fact.'

'Have you – missed me?'

'With every sinew of my being.'

The wind filled her black cashmere cloak, and her spoon
bonnet, veil removed, clung to her head by the merest thread.
Tom took her arm and drew her into the potting shed that
leaned against one of the buttresses. The garden, part of the
church's inventory, had already been turned over and planted
with spring vegetables and the potting shed was hardly more
than a hut for tools. Dropping her wicker basket, ripping off
her bonnet and throwing open her cloak, Bette closed her eyes,
and puckered her lips for the minister's kiss.

Wrapping an arm about her, Thomas Oakley kissed her,
passionately. His lips were hard, his tongue as soft as a sea
anemone, but when he took her hand and pushed it down into
the fork of his clerical breeches Bette found no matching
softness there.

Tom murmured into her ear, 'Every sinew, I said, and every
sinew I meant. What have you brought me, my dear? What is
my reward to be?'

'For the sake of pity, Thomas,' Bette said, 'do not tease me.'

He crushed her hand between his thighs and, rocking rhythmically against her, kissed her lips once more. The wind beat upon the door like a fist. Thomas calmly walked the lady backward and pushed her shoulders against the salt-stained wood to silence the clamour. Her fingers were already fumbling at the double row of buttons that contained him.

'Greedy,' he said. 'Oh, you are a greedy girl, Bette. Is this what London has done to you, made you forget your manners?'

'Damn my manners, Thomas,' Bette Hollander said. 'Where are you?'

He brushed her hand aside and removed the last impediment.

'Right here,' he said.

'Where's Aunt Bette?' Susanne seated herself at the breakfast table and stared at the lumpy grey substance in the bowl that Nancy had dumped before her. 'Is she still sleeping?'

'Gone out,' Nancy replied, then returned to the kitchen to grind the coffee beans that the lady had brought from London.

Buckie took his hands from his knees and lifted a spoon.

In spite of the ache in his legs, he smiled and patted Susanne's head lightly. She had combed her hair and put on a clean, chequered dress and looked as sweet as a little hazelnut, and all bright and curious.

'Your aunt,' he said, 'has gone to visit her friend the minister. I believe she has gifts for his family.'

'Yes, she has,' said Susanne. 'She bought a snuff thing in the shape of a sheep's horn in Edinburgh to give to him. And a whole Dutch cheese in a wax cloth. Peppermints. And a big packet of chocolate, the kind you drink. And – and I do not know what else. Is Mr Oakley poor?'

'Poor enough,' said Buckie, 'to welcome donations to his domestic welfare. He's a minister, what you, I believe, call a vicar. Did your – em – your father, did he take you to church every Sunday?'

'Miss Ashworth took me to church. I don't think Papa believed in God.'

'Did not believe in God!' said Buckie, dismayed. 'How can a man not believe in God?'

'I don't know, sir. Papa wasn't sure what he believed.'

'Good Lord!' Buckie Hollander said. 'All a person has to do to be assured that we're the receivers of God's bounty is to look from the window.'

Susanne turned her head and gazed at the glass. She remembered the fierce arguments that Miss Ashworth and Papa had had on the subject of religion and how she would hear them at it long after she had gone to bed.

She frowned. 'Has the storm gone away?'

'Abated. It'll be fine this afternoon, though still breezy.' Buckie put her spoon into her hand. 'Eat your porridge, sweetheart, there's a good girl.'

'Miss Ashworth told me it would be fish here, nothing but fish.'

'We often have fish, it's true,' Buckie told her, 'but the boats haven't been out for days.'

'Because of the storm?'

'Aye, because of the storm.'

'Where's Louis?'

'Dead to the world.'

'And Ajax?'

'Guarding his master, I expect.'

'Lying on Louis's bed, sir?'

'Under it. By the by, you don't have to call me "sir".'

'What should I call you?' said Susanne.

'Buckie will do.'

'Isn't it disrespectful to call you by your name?'

'Nay, there's nothing disrespectful about it.'

'What is your name, sir?'

'Adam,' the old man told her. 'I was born in Buckhaven, down the coast a piece, and it's a habit sailors have to baptise you again. Buckie's not so bad. It could have been Puggy or Porker or the Dribbler.'

Susanne giggled. 'The Dribbler.'

'A fine enough fellow,' Buckie told her, 'and a grand man with a harpoon but he couldn't sup his meat without spilling it down his beard. He was, I think, somewhat short of teeth – and do you know why he was short of teeth?'

'Because he didn't eat his porridge?'

'Hah!' Buckie shouted, delighted by her quickness. 'The nail on the head. So, my lass, up with the spoon, open the hatch and shovel it in, or we might be calling you the Dribbler, too, before much longer.'

Tom opened the door of the potting shed and stuck his head out. Duty done, he was all safely tucked away, and now he wanted his reward.

Within the shed, among the spades and hoes, Buckie Hollander's wife rearranged her clothing and shakily called out, 'Is the coast clear?'

The coast, in fact, was rarely anything else but clear at that hour of a weekday morning for the older children were at school and the babies still tied to Effie's apron strings. Tom gazed out to sea. Bands of sunshine moved across the face of the deep and the swell was less violent than it had been a half-hour ago. There were reports of heavy shoals of herring out by May Island. The winter drive for the silver fish had not peaked yet and the season, so far, had been poor. Soon the boats would be pushing out from Anstruther and, if they'd nothing better to do, the fishermen of Strayhorn might even deign to join them.

Cautiously, Tom scanned the wrinkled coastline.

'Coast clear, my dear,' he called over his shoulder. 'Come along, come along, a step or two around the corner will set us free of suspicion.'

Bette stuck her nose out of the shed. Holding down her skirt and, Tom noted happily, clutching the wicker basket to her chest, she emerged and with quick, tight little steps, as if she were holding an apple between her knees, trotted round the buttress into the garden proper.

If Effie, with or without the baby at her breast, did happen to be scurrying about the yard or squinting from the kitchen window she would see only what she had seen a hundred times before: her dear husband being charming to one of the ladies who put bread on the table and beef into the mouths of her bairns. Mrs Hollander seated herself on the rustic bench, damp though it was, and primly pressed her knees together. Mr Oakley placed one foot on the bench and looked down at her, gravely.

'Did you conclude your business in London to your satisfaction?'

'I did, Tom, I did.'

'The girl, the orphan, where is she?'

'At home with Buckie, having her breakfast.'

'Is she pleasant?'

'Very pleasant,' Bette said. 'A little treasure.'

'In more ways than one, perhaps,' said Tom Oakley.

'I'm sure I don't know what you mean.'

'I'm sure you do,' said Tom.

'The extra income, certainly, will be useful.'

'A godsend.'

'I would not go so far as all that,' Bette said. 'It's the child herself who's the godsend.'

'Of course, of course.'

'You'll meet her on Sunday and see for yourself.'

'I look forward to it.'

'And us – I mean, when will we . . .'

'Reconvene?' Tom Oakley extracted a small notebook from his vest pocket and pretended to study it. 'Monday?' He looked from the booklet to the plump wife. 'Will you not be too busy?'

'Too busy doing what?'

'Looking after your protégée.'

'No,' said Bette, curtly. 'I'll not be too busy.'

'Monday then,' Tom said.

'But not standing up in that filthy shed. I'm tired of being treated like a – I mean, so off-handedly.'

'Very well,' Tom Oakley said. 'I'll come down to the shore, to the cave at half past eight. Is that suitable to you?'

'Monday's a wash day.'

'Dear God, Bette!'

'Yes, yes, Monday at the cave; half past eight.'

'Good!' Tom Oakley reached for the basket, but she held it away from him, clutching it with a possessiveness that he had not detected in her before. 'What?' he said. 'What's wrong now?'

'On top, in a brown paper wrapping,' Bette told him, 'is my gift to you.'

'Oh!' Tom said. 'May I peek?'

'No, you may not peek.' Bette Hollander gave his groping hand a little smack. 'It's a surprise.'

'Will I like it?'

'I'm sure you will.'

'I'm sure I will, too,' Tom said, generously.

He offered her his hand. She rose to her feet.

As a rule she was prudent enough to release him at once but this morning, with the wind blowing and sunlight skimming across the water, she held on. For a moment he thought she might be about to throw herself into his arms and cling to him like a barnacle to a rock.

'On Sunday . . .' the woman began.

'What?'

'Will you say a welcome to my little niece?'

He let his breath out and, with his head tilted to show off his professional profile, said, 'Of course, I will, my dear, of course I will,' then, with relief, escorted her to the end of the garden and, a minute or so later, watched her vanish over the edge of the cliff.

Behind a sandstone outcrop at the base of the cliff path Bette paused to catch her breath and wipe her skirts before she rounded the rocky corner and followed the line of shingle that led to the house. She was surprised to find Dr Redpath's gig drawn up by the porch and experienced a flutter of panic at the thought that Buckie had been struck down in her absence.

Buckie, gout and guilt had been inextricably linked in her mind since she had been forced to leave her fine house and her fine friends in Dundee. If only she had realised then that her pleasure would be so short-lived and if her ambitions for her son's advancement were thwarted not by shipwrecks or storms or a slump in the price of whale oil but by insidious changes in the constitution of her husband's blood.

At first she had treated the disease as something of a joke. Buckie had long been a trencherman of repute in a town where eating and drinking to excess were regarded as attributes of manliness. He had displayed all the hardiness associated with his trade by sneering at pain, a rebellious phase that did not last long. All too soon swellings and fevers had sent him scurrying to doctors as far afield as Edinburgh, and aches, pains, diagnoses and cures became the sole topics of his conversation.

Bored, anxious and resentful, Bette had been obliged to learn a whole new vocabulary that had nothing to do with whale oil or what style of hairpiece was in fashion but had everything to do with urates, diathesis and the so-called 'law of atavism', by which was meant the transmission of hereditary disorders. The plain fact of the matter was that her husband had flouted the doctors' advice and had continued to console himself for his misfortune by consuming quantities of red meat, pickled herring, oysters and goose liver, washed down with wine, and the decline in family fortunes was, in Bette's opinion, attributable to nothing more atavistic than greed.

'What,' she said, bustling into the hall, 'is the matter with him now?'

'What do you think's the matter wi' him?' Nancy growled. 'Didn't you hear him groanin' in the night?'

Bette bounced into the living-room and, waving her hands, said, 'What, again? No sooner do I get back from London than you start bellowing. Stop it, Buckie, you'll frighten the girl.'

Susanne didn't seem to be in the least frightened. She knelt on the rug, watching Dr Redpath mix powders into a glass of water.

Ajax was transfixed by the sight of the old man's swollen legs and Thimble, very still, very attentive, clung to a wing of the old man's chair. Everyone, Bette noted, was gathered around her husband, everyone except Louis who, of course, was far too sensible to tumble out of bed to observe another of his father's fits.

Alan Redpath had not been a practitioner of medicine for long and his patients were still suspicious of his abilities. They had trusted old Dr Campbell even after his legs had gone, and there was something too fresh and springy about the new chap to satisfy their need for gravitas.

'Who sent for you?' Bette asked.

'No one sent for me,' Alan answered. 'I happened to be in the vicinity and thought I'd drop in to enquire how the young lady had passed the night. No,' he corrected himself, 'not strictly true. I didn't like the look of Mr Hollander last evening, which is why I happen to have sedatives in my bag.'

'I passed the night very well,' said Susanne. 'Uncle, is it very sore?'

'Aye, lass, it is,' Buckie got out.

Every eye was centred on her husband's swollen feet. Not for the first time Bette cursed the gout for having blasted all her hopes and for driving her out to this god-forsaken hole where nobody cared who she was.

'What's that you're givin' him?' Nancy asked.

'Iodide of potassium and sulphate of magnesia.'

Alan stirred the cloudy liquid with a glass rod. His leather portmanteau, the colour of liquorice and shiny new, was open on the table, rows of small bottles glinting in the sunlight that brightened the room.

'Is that the sun?' Buckie craned forward in his chair. 'Aye, Susanne, you'll get out' – he winced and went on – 'out on the shore today now the – the clouds – are breaking up.'

Ajax's sad brown eyes followed the glass but the cat remained indifferent as if she, unlike the dog, had learned to tell medicine from milk.

Alan wiped the rod against his sleeve and slipped it into his waistcoat pocket. He glanced at Buckie and shook his head. 'There won't be much sunshine for you for a week or two, old chap. Bed is best, I think.'

He handed Susanne the medicine glass. She held it carefully in one hand and insinuated herself across her uncle's lap. She placed her hand behind Buckie's head, eased him forward, held the glass to his lips and let him drink, rubbing her hand across his neck as he did so, as if she were soothing a child.

'Poor chap,' she said, 'not being able to enjoy the sunshine.'

Buckie forced a smile. 'Well, the sun will still be there tomorrow.'

Bette, disgruntled, bounced off to help Nancy make ready

the sick-room and, as if a spell had been broken, Ajax bounded off upstairs to rouse his master, and Thimble, with incomprehensible urgency, fell to washing her tail.

There had been a time, now long forgotten, when the minister's wife had believed in love, when, trapped in the gloom of her father's manse on the Lammermuirs, she had dwelt in lovely ignorance of the brute realities of marriage; a border region midway between maidenhood and motherhood when the fecundity of every male over the age of twelve had seemed like an invitation, though to what she did not know.

She had been wrapped up in and protected by her father's obsession with sin and redemption, of a love that spoke its name all too often but none too clearly, a spiritual manifestation of love that had no meaning for a sixteen-year-old country girl who, when young Thomas Oakley had arrived to serve term as her father's probationer, had thus been ripe for the taking.

Now, in her thirties, Effie cared not a fig about her body or her soul, only about keeping the two together; that and feeding her children on the pittance that Tom, by one means or another, scraped from the parish.

She fell on the basket that the whale-master's wife had given her husband, tore off the dainty cloth cover and tipped the contents on to the table. The latest baby, ten months old, clung desperately to her teat, his gums tugging at her elongated nipple, his fingers clenched to her flat breast, blue eyes wide with fear that he would be separated from a sure source of nourishment.

'Cheese.' Effie rolled the object across the table. Tom caught it. 'Sweetmeats. What do we need with sweetmeats?' She despatched the parcel of peppermints by an airy route. Tom caught it, too.

'What's this?'

'I have no idea,' Tom said.

Effie hoisted the baby higher in her arms and stripped off the brown paper wrapping. 'What is it?'

'It looks like a snuff box,' Tom said, placidly, 'or, to be more accurate, a snuff horn.'

'I can see it's a horn. Is that silver?'

'I imagine it might be.'

'Is there snuff in it?'

'Here, give it here,' Tom said.

He scooped up the wrappings and the horn before his wife could object and, tucking the brown paper under his arm, flicked up the lid of the chased-silver object and, wetting a finger, slipped it inside.

He shook his head. 'No, no snuff.'

'What's she giving us a snuff horn for? I mean,' Effie whined, 'why in the name of our Sovereign Lord does she think we need a snuff horn?'

'She's a kindly soul,' said Tom, 'but I doubt if she fully comprehends our predicament. However, after a decent interval, we'll sell it.'

'What's it worth, do you reckon?'

'Two or three guineas.'

'Pop it,' Effie said. 'Pop it tomorrow.'

'I'll do no such thing,' said Tom, firmly. 'I've no wish to insult Mrs Hollander who has, after all, been very good to us these past few years. I'll keep it for a six-month and let her see me using it, then I'll sell it.'

'Two guineas would buy us many a good joint of beef for Sundays.'

'We'll have fish on Sundays,' Tom told her.

'Fish, fish, fish.' Effie rummaged among the other items that she'd poured from Bette Hollander's basket. 'I'm sick of fish, of cooking it, smelling it, eating it. I'm sick of picking bones out of my teeth and slapping the bairns on the back for fear they choke on your precious fish. Meat, I want meat, a good juicy joint to thicken my blood and improve my milk.' She held the baby, Roland by name, up and appeared about to throw him at her husband. 'Ask this poor wight if he prefers a silver snuff horn to a bellyful of hot brisket.'

'*Paaah*,' Roland squeaked in alarm. '*Paaah-paaah.*'

Stuffing the snuff horn into his pocket, Tom reached out, took the latest into his arms and let him ride on the crook of his elbow. He tickled the little boy under the chin, 'Oatmeal saps and cream of the milk for you, my lad,' he said. 'You wouldn't know what to do with a joint of beef yet.'

'Yes, he would,' said Effie. 'He has teeth.'

'Has he?'

'If it was your teat he was gnawin' upon you'd know about teeth.'

'Drinking chocolate,' Tom said, lifting up the packet. 'And, look, I think that's chicken pieces in a jar of aspic, all the way from London town. You could do something with those for Sunday, Effie, could you not?'

'Aye, I could swallow them whole, aspic and all,' said Effie, 'and still have a gap in my stomach the size of a hayrick.'

'Come now, Effie,' Tom said, less patiently, 'you're not starving, and the children aren't starving. Compared with some—'

'Don't you dare trot out your list of comparisons, Tom Oakley,' she told him. 'If I was one o' your farm girls you'd treat me with more respect.'

'My farm girls?' Tom addressed the question to his son. 'What does your mama mean by that, I wonder?'

'Mama means you tend your flock better than you tend your family.'

'I see cake,' Tom said. 'I see fruit cake in a wax-cloth shroud.'

'Yes, because it's dead.' Effie pounded the fruit cake on the edge of the table. 'Dead and mortificated.'

'Behold a tub of plum preserve, too.' Tom continued to address his son. 'I see a feast fit for a queen, yet all your mama does is complain. Complaining keeps her happy, you see. Complaining is her way of praising God for all His bounteous mercies. But if she doesn't shut her mouth very soon, I'll really give her something to complain about. Now' – he dangled the infant over the table – 'Papa's going into the study to unearth an apposite text for Sunday morning and write a marvellous address that will enchant the multitude and oblige them to give thanks for all the blessings God has bestowed upon them. And Mama' – he propped the little boy on the table top and let Effie catch him as he began to fall – 'Mama is going to make Papa a scrumptious luncheon, is she not?'

'What about the garden?' Effie said, not quite meekly.

'For the time being,' Tom Oakley told her, 'the garden can look after itself.' Then, turning on his heel, he strode out of the narrow kitchen and across the hall to the study, with Bette Hollander's love-gift tucked away safe in his pocket.

Buckie said, 'Our little friend would make a fine doctor, would she not? Her gentle caresses are easing my old joints even as we speak.' He lay rigid in the armchair, trying to make light of his pain.

'She canna be a doctor,' Nancy said. 'Girls aren't allowed to be doctors. What would you say, Captain, if she was obliged to siphon your water from your parts, eh?'

Buckie closed his eyes. 'It was only a manner of speaking, Nancy.'

'She could be a midwife, though, if her stomach's strong enough.'

Susanne glanced at Dr Redpath. 'Doesn't a midwife deliver babies?'

'She does,' Alan Redpath answered.

'I'd rather like to deliver babies.'

'She doesn't even know what her womb's for an' she wants to bring babies into the world,' Nancy said. 'It's sheltered she's been in that fine mansion in London, I'm thinkin'. She'll make some man a good enough wife, though, her and her money.'

'Nancy, that's quite enough,' said Buckie.

Alan Redpath closed his portmanteau.

Nancy, hands on hips, said, 'Are you not leavin' us any laudanum?'

'No, I'm not.'

'Dr Campbell always left the laudanum.'

'I'm not Dr Campbell.'

'He was a real doctor,' Nancy said. 'He knew how to keep pain at bay.'

'I don't believe in leaving laudanum where anyone can find it,' Alan Redpath explained. 'If the captain feels he needs it then send for me and I'll administer a dose in the proper balance.'

The argument was interrupted by a strange wheezy wail from the apartment upstairs followed by a ripple of notes that grew so strident that Susanne felt it drumming on her temples.

'His lordship's up at last,' Nancy said. 'Up, with the day half gone.'

'What is that noise?' Susanne asked.

'It's your cousin Louis composing his masterpiece,' Buckie answered. 'He claims he's at his best when he first wakes up, his head so full of harmonies he has to get them down before they drive him mad.'

Nancy stepped into the hall and opened the front door just as Ajax came bounding downstairs and shot out on to the porch.

'If you're wise,' Buckie said, 'you'll follow the dog, Redpath. The boy might keep that racket up for an hour or more before he comes down in search of breakfast.'

Head tilted back and eyes fixed on the ceiling, as if she expected an arm or a leg, or a quaver or a crotchet, to break through the plaster, Susanne said, 'What sort of instrument is it? Is it the bagpipes?'

'Lord, no!' Buckie answered. 'A parlour organ. Louis studied music in school and nothing would do but he would have an instrument of his own when he came home. I argued with his mother about the expense, but she was adamant. Nothing's too good for her darling boy, you see. So an organ was ordered. A pretty penny it cost, too, shipped from London in parts in a watertight crate. I'll give Louis credit, he knew how to put it together and bring it into tune, or whatever it is you do with a thing like that.'

The conversation seemed to have taken her uncle's mind from his affliction but the notes that poured from upstairs had an angry, unsettled quality that set Susanne's teeth on edge.

She started when the doctor put a hand on her arm.

'Come,' he said, 'accompany me to the top of the brae and I'll show you where you are and what lies about you. You'll not be out of sight of the house and will have no difficulty in finding your way back.'

'Aye,' Buckie said, 'go with him, sweetheart, for it'll be no pretty sight watching me being put to bed.'

'Won't Louis come with us?' Susanne said.

'Not him,' said Buckie, 'not when the musical mood is on him.'

The gig was lightly sprung, the pony, a Shetland, sturdy and passive. Susanne forgot about her uncle's distress, her aunt, even her musical cousin as the wonder of the ocean filled her eyes once more.

She held her bonnet on with one hand and left the other, all unconsciously, resting on Alan Redpath's knee.

She wriggled this way and that, glancing inland at the cliff-top church, at fields ploughed for sowing, at cottages hiding in trees and farms set so far back from the road that they might, for all she knew, be in another county.

Demanding and irresistible, though, was the sea: the North Sea, the German Ocean, a confluence, so the doctor told her, of the great rivers Forth and Tay, containing headlands and bays and hidden coves, fragments of land stretching out like the spidery legs of a compass to mark the line where the land stopped and an infinity of waters began, indistinct even on a whisking, cloud-tossed morning.

Alan braked the gig at the top of the hill and left the pony free to graze on the scant grasses. He helped Susanne down, offering his hand as if she were a lady. He wasn't as tall as cousin Louis, or so handsome. He had a square face with a cleft in his chin but his eyes were piercing blue, very sharp and amused and, though he was older than Louis, he was not so old as all that.

They climbed to the crest of the hill.

There was no definite edge to the cliff. It dipped down a grassy slope and slipped into the sea in a jumble of reddish-black rocks strewn with seaweed. Flocks of seabirds rode on the waves and hung on the air currents. Cowering against the back side of the hill lay the village of Strayhorn, not much of a place by the look of it, and the wall of a harbour in poor repair.

Alan said, 'Only seven or eight boats there now, though once it was a thriving fishing station.' Susanne leaned against the doctor, and followed the line of his finger. 'St Andrews lies in that direction. Beyond it, the River Tay on which stands the town of Dundee where your aunt and uncle lived at one time. Far off, too far to see, is Aberdeen where I, for my sins, studied medicine.'

'Is that where you were born?'

'No, I was born in Inverness, far to the north of here. My father's a doctor there and my brother's a surgeon in the Royal

Infirmary in Edinburgh. He has a daughter, my niece, about your age. He's much older than I am, of course.'

'Are you a Highland man?'

'Aye,' Alan said. 'I suppose you might say I am.'

'Do you speak the language of the Gaul?'

'Gael,' the doctor corrected. 'No, lass, I'm afraid I never learned Gaelic properly, though my mother, rest her soul, spoke nothing else until she was twelve years old.' He studied Susanne for a moment or two, then smiled. 'It's geography we're here to teach you today, not history. See' – he pointed again – 'out there is the Isle of May, the broad, flat one not far from the shore, where, sometimes, the fish gather in profusion and all the boats from the towns and villages round about go pouring out and the quays are slathered with fish and the merchants come from far afield to buy them up for curing and smoking. It's a sight you'll see for yourself if you stay long enough.'

'I have to stay,' Susanne said. 'I've nowhere else to go.'

Alan nodded, turned her again by the shoulders. 'In that direction,' he went on, 'lies Anstruther, a market town, and that way, Crail, our post town. If you lift your eyes a wee bit and look across the water you'll discern the shape of the Bass Rock that lies off the coast not far from Edinburgh.'

'Fife's a very big place, is it not.'

'A world unto itself,' Alan Redpath said. 'Not a world like London, though, not so much life as London, I'm afraid.'

'I must try to put London behind me if I'm to be happy,' Susanne said, 'for I'm here now and – and it's not so bad.'

They walked down the slope to the gig.

'Your – what is he to you? – Louis Hollander, I mean?'

'I call him cousin,' Susanne said.

'Well, your cousin will tell you about the nature of the things that inhabit the shore. He's better versed than I am in that respect.'

'Is he as clever as my aunt says he is?'

'No denying that he's a clever fellow and, in spite of his recital this morning, a very fine musician.' Alan put a foot on the step of the gig. 'Off with you now, Susanne Thorne.' He tapped her bonnet in farewell. 'Follow the path and you won't go far wrong.'

If she had been parting from him on one of the byways of Piccadilly she would have dropped him a pretty curtsey but somehow a curtsey didn't seem appropriate in this rough landscape.

'You've been very kind, sir,' she said. 'Will I see you again soon?'

'All too soon, lass,' Dr Redpath told her. 'All too soon.'

She gave him a smile, then, holding on to her bonnet, flew down the sandy track towards the house, eager perhaps, Alan thought, to unearth her handsome cousin and persuade him to take her walking on the beach.

4

Susanne had been used to worshipping at St Edmund's Holborn, with its trumpet tower, marble Communion table and a great deal of gilt and painted plaster. Strayhorn church, however, seemed to have been carved out of wood so blunt and plain that it was hardly surprising that several of the older gentlemen and quite a few of the ladies fell into a contemplative reverie that closely resembled sleep. The little man who had carried in the Bible, for instance, was seated on a stool under the prow of the pulpit with his head in his hands in a pose that suggested more pain than piety. He was very small, bald save for a wisp of pure white hair that sprouted like a coxcomb in the centre of his brow. His name, Aunt Bette whispered, was Angus Gamrie and he was the session clerk, though what that office entailed Susanne had no idea.

She was seated with Aunt Bette close to the front, Nancy in the gallery with the other servants. Buckie and Louis had not accompanied them to church and there was no sign of Dr Redpath, who lodged in Seameads, two or three miles away, and presumably attended church there.

The minister, Aunt Bette's friend, strode between the Communion table, the font and the pulpit, reading announcements from a piece of paper. When he paused, smiled at Aunt Bette and welcomed Mrs Hollander's niece to Strayhorn 'as a stranger into the fold', there was a general shuffling and craning of necks and some bold boy in the gallery uttered a quick, sharp chirrup that brought Mr Gamrie, glaring, to his feet.

Susanne found Mr Oakley's preaching very odd, indeed. Louis had told her that Tom Oakley was a moderate with evangelical leanings but Susanne's vague understanding of the word 'moderation' did not jibe with what the minister had to say or, still less, with the relish with which he said it.

'There are those,' he began, 'who believe that Satan was crafty in praising God and saying that he – by whom I mean Satan – would never prohibit men from sampling wholesome fruit, but this was only part of Satan's strategy for ensnaring the miserable woman, Eve.'

The minister's voice made the woodwork under Susanne's thighs vibrate and her head spin a little. She inched closer to Aunt Bette.

'Knowledge,' the minister went on, 'is supposed to confer happiness – a point one might debate – but Eve erred in not regulating the measure of her knowledge according to the will of God. Thus, daily, do we all suffer from the same disease, desiring to know more than is good for us. Eve, you see, was infected with the poison of concupiscence and, at the moment when her hand closed round the forbidden fruit, she became both the messenger and the witness of an impure heart.'

Susanne leaned into her aunt and whispered, 'What does "concupiscence" mean?'

And Aunt Bette, with something that may or may not have been a smile, answered, 'Never you mind, my dear, never you mind.'

The curricle was much grander than Sandy Raiker's cart. The horses had the lean, agitated look of thoroughbreds. They pranced and snickered when they spotted the carter's moth-eaten donkey and it was all that the little tiger, the travelling groom, could do to hold them still.

The tiger was no lad but a jockey-sized adult who, in a pink
cutaway and cream breeches, would have presented a very gay
picture indeed if he hadn't been so irascible. He danced about,
cursed and eventually punched one of the animals with a
stabbing uppercut to its belly that, oddly, seemed to calm it.

Sandy Raiker took his clay pipe from his mouth, and spat.

'Aye now, Benbow,' he said, 'you'll have your hands full wi'
them fancy blue-blood creatures.'

'None o' your damned lip, Raiker,' the tiger snarled, before
greeting Aunt Bette with grudging deference. 'Mistress Hollander, a good-day to you, and you too, missie,' he said, then
leaped into the driving seat of the curricle and steered it thirty
or forty yards along the shingle away from the house.

Aunt Bette had turned pale when she'd caught sight of the
curricle drawn up at the door. She had muttered and tutted
during the descent of the hill and Nancy and she had fallen
into a heated debate about the quantity of meat in the larder
and how long it would take to bake a beef steak pie, the answer
to that question being, as both women knew, far too long. Aunt
Bette was still muttering when she climbed down from the cart
and, with Nancy trailing behind her, ducked around the
corner into the kitchen yard.

Susanne had been thinking of Louis, hoping that Louis
would be up and about and that the musical mood that had
kept him to his room might be put aside for Sunday and he
would be eager for a turn along the beach, but when she saw
the curricle, the glossy horses, and heard Aunt Bette and
Nancy arguing, she knew that the afternoon was spoiled.

'Who are our visitors, Mr Raiker?' she asked.

'The Coburns,' Sandy answered, and spat on the ground
once more.

They were gathered in the ground-floor bedroom, a man, a
girl, and Louis. Buckie, propped up in bed, was putting a

brave face on it. He had been in torment for the past three days and Dr Redpath had been summoned to administer laudanum in the form of a sticky brown pill.

Louis was perched on a stool, knee crossed over thigh, munching hard-boiled eggs from a bowl in his lap. He topped them with an oyster knife, shelled them, dabbed them with salt from a little dish, and ate them in two mouthfuls.

The visitor had raffish side whiskers and wore a huntsman's coat with pewter buttons, a striped waistcoat and cord breeches, but his scarf neck-tie and ruby stick-pin, Susanne thought, were more town than country. He was seated by the side of the bed, leaning over Buckie, talking seriously, while the girl, balanced on a little gilded chair, watched Louis scoff eggs as if she had never seen anyone eat breakfast before.

Susanne hovered by the bedroom door; a full minute elapsed before anyone noticed her. 'Ah-hah!' her uncle called out, at length. 'Here she is now, my ministering angel. Susanne, don't be bashful. Come in and say "How-do" to Mr Coburn and his daughter. Where, by the by, is your aunt?'

Susanne managed a curtsey of sorts. 'Gone to attend to luncheon. I think she's worried about there not being enough meat.'

Buckie shrugged. 'Bette will be with us shortly, no doubt. She'll tell you herself, Harry, what transpired in London. In essence, this young lady is what transpired in London, and what a treasure she is proving herself to be.'

Embarrassed by her uncle's praise, Susanne glanced at Louis in the hope that he would say something to bring her back to earth, but Louis was too taken up with the girl to respond.

Harry Coburn's daughter had auburn hair and features so refined that they seemed to be fashioned from an expensive mineral, not humble flesh. Though a year or so older than Susanne, she wore a childish dress sprinkled with forget-menots, white cotton lace-edged pantaloons and tiny pink shoes tied with baby ribbon.

'Darsie, I'm Darsie, my dearest one,' the girl cried and, flaring her emerald-green eyes so wide that it seemed they might pop out of her head, flew from the chair and, to Susanne's amazement, threw her arms about her.

'I – I'm Susanne Thorne.'

'Oh, you are, you are, of course you are,' Darsie Coburn cried.

Harry Coburn and Buckie Hollander smiled at the warmth of the greeting between their little girls, while Louis, head cocked to one side, casually bit the top off another hard-boiled egg.

At Harry Coburn's insistence sherry and shortbread stood in for luncheon. Darsie and he were on the way to call upon the Arbuthnots and had dropped by en route to enquire after Buckie's health, and to greet the little orphan.

Precisely how the Coburns were related to the Hollanders remained a mystery but, however tenuous the kinship, it did not deter Darsie from following Susanne about and declaring affection in terms so cloying that Susanne wriggled with embarrassment. Having finished his breakfast, Louis fetched Ajax from the yard and brought him into the living-room. To Susanne's consternation, Darsie Coburn showered affection on the dog and was soon leaning on Louis's knee and whispering similar endearments into his ear, too.

Abandoned and neglected, Susanne listened to her uncle's groans from the bedroom, the tick of the grandfather clock, and the sea thumping on the shore. She heard Louis's throaty laughter, the girl's high-pitched giggles, and Aunt Bette saying, 'I appreciate that the opportunity is not to be missed, Harry, but for the time being I must harbour my resources. It hasn't been easy for any of us of late, and while the girl's income will be exceeding handy, it's not a fortune.'

'It can become one, can it not?' Harry Coburn said.

'It isn't mine to play with, you know.'

'Do you not have charge of it?'

'No, Harry, charge of the capital resides with Mr Reeve.'

'That rogue!'

'Rogue he may be, but he has the Chancellor's seal and that's good enough for me. I'll be candid with you, Harry,' Aunt Bette said, 'which is more, I fear, than you've been with me: if I did have more capital to place I'm not sure I would place it with you. You haven't done well by us.'

'The railway stock . . .'

Glancing up, Harry Coburn noticed that Susanne was eavesdropping. He gave her a faint smile then drew his chair closer to the table, lifted the sherry glass to his lips, and went on conversing with Aunt Bette in a wheedling whisper.

In the kitchen Nancy clashed pans. In the bedroom Buckie groaned. Unable to recapture his master's attention, Ajax slumped down upon the carpet and sulkily stuck his snout under his paws.

Darsie Coburn rubbed her pantalooned ankle against Louis's shin and recounted gossip about a glove merchant in Kirkcaldy, a tale that Louis pretended to find uncommonly amusing.

Susanne slipped into the hall, stepped out on to the porch and quietly closed the front door behind her.

Mr Coburn's groom was seated on a rock, smoking a cheroot. The beautiful thoroughbreds, quiet at last, nibbled the winter grass by the side of the track. Neither the tiger nor the horses paid Susanne the slightest attention and she stared at the sea and wondered if she would always stand apart, complimented and cosseted, but not loved.

She walked in a straight line away from the house.

The hill cut off sight of the village and the cliff that fell from the fold of the church shut out views to the north. She walked over dry seaweed on to sloping shingle, walked on to the trembling sand that the tide had left behind, picking her way between shallow pools and big weed-draped boulders. She could feel dampness seeping through the soles of her shoes, but walked on regardless. She stopped only when she could go no further.

Sweeping arcs of clear brown water broke from the blue-green waves that swelled from the dark blue depths. There was nothing here, no sadness, no despair, only stalking gulls and seaweed, and the ceaseless energy of the sea. It occurred to her that Adam and Eve had never seen the sea, that the knowledge God had withheld from Eve must have included a knowledge of the oceans from which He had raised up the earth, before He had even thought of making a man and, after a man, a woman.

She glimpsed the dog out of the corner of her eye and, turning her head, watched Ajax shake himself and, tail up and ears back, race along the beach towards her. She realised how young and lithe he was under all that curly brown hair, bounding and leaping as joyfully as if he had just discovered dry land. She staggered when he leaped on her, took his weight on her chest and, laughing now, pushed him down. Round and round he went, chasing his tail, looking up at her, tongue lolling, but on the rim of the beach, by the sea's edge, even Ajax seemed small, and Louis smaller still.

'Ah, there you are,' her cousin called out. 'We thought we'd lost you.'

He walked with long strides, barefoot, his shoes hung about his neck, his shirt pasted to his chest as if he too had just emerged from the sea.

It had been rude of her to leave when visitors were present. She expected Louis to chastise her, but he was grinning, grinning like a mischievous boy.

When he reached her he did nothing more severe by way of punishment than pinch her cheek.

'They've gone,' he said. 'Thank God.'

'I thought you liked them – liked her.'

'Darsie?' Louis said. 'Oh no. No, no.'

'She likes you.'

'For which,' Louis said, 'she can hardly be blamed.'

Then, laying an arm across Susanne's shoulder and calling Ajax to heel, he led her gaily back across the sand.

At the ripe old age of nineteen Louis Hollander did not consider himself a stranger to love. He adored his mother, his dog, and the beautiful Seraphine harmonium that he had carefully assembled from parts supplied by Kirkman and White of Soho Square, London. The fact that his cousin hailed from the same place as the reed organ added sauce to a friendship which was not, of course, a courtship, or anything remotely like it.

He carried on as he had always done, smoking his pipe, lolling in his chair with his legs cocked up, reading, or writing music. But, between whiles, he teased, instructed and bullied his cousin and generally engaged in the sort of rough-and-tumble that boys enjoy, for Susanne was far too young to be considered a rival, or even a threat to his dignity. He was also mindful of the fact that Susanne's 'contribution' to family finances would see him through a year of study with Professor Bertini in Edinburgh and might even provide the wherewithal for a tour of the famous organs of Europe.

Meanwhile, he revelled in the novelty of having a playmate and when the showery rains of April drove them indoors invited Susanne to hang about his room while he worked.

It was a great long glory-hole of a room where all the stuff that had accumulated over the years was stored: broken toys, golf clubs, botanical specimens, mineral samples and, resting on the bare floorboards, hundreds of books picked up cheaply on stalls in Dundee and St Andrews, books on all sorts of obscure subjects that had taken his fancy at the time. On a high old drawing-table were tobacco jars, racks of pipes, chewed pens and leaky inkstands, all buried under a litter of papers, and the only object that had a distinctive place in the chaos was the harmonium.

At first Susanne was afraid to go near the instrument and when Louis was gracious enough to play for her, stood well back against the wall. She was tempted to confess that she could read music but some instinct checked her, and she kept that little secret to herself.

Louis played with verve and authority when he was in the right sort of mood but often, too often, he was not in the right sort of mood and struck deep sonorous chords that made Susanne shiver. Now and then he would add a vocal accompaniment and Ajax would howl mournfully and the plates on the shelves in the kitchen and the ornaments on Aunt Bette's dressing-table would rattle, and Susanne would be tempted to follow her uncle's example and look for a cushion to clap over her ears.

She endured the tedium and the noise uncomplainingly, however, and before April was out had been granted the freedom of her cousin's room.

She scampered in and out at all hours, darting across the passageway last thing to kiss him goodnight or skipping in merrily first thing in the morning to haul him, protesting, from his bed. Louis would throw a scruffy dressing-robe over his nightshirt and pursue her down the passageway, growling in mock anger. Ajax would join in and Thimble would pit-a-pat after them, up and down the passageway. Nancy would mutter that the devil would take his revenge for these shenanigans and Bette, at her toilette, would *tut* and shake her head.

But Buckie, on the road to recovery, would lie back in bed

and smile at the racket, for if there was one thing in life he liked more than any other it was the sound of young people at play.

'School,' Aunt Bette said. 'We'll have to be thinking about school for you.'

'I've been to school,' Susanne said.

'Ah, but you haven't been educated,' Louis said, 'not properly.'

'Lassies don't need schoolin'.' Nancy brought in the soup. 'Learnin' gives lassies notions above their station.'

Aunt Bette said, 'I think a boarding academy might be the answer, Susanne. There's one in St Andrews that would suit very well. Mr Coburn sends his daughter there. St Andrews is not so very far away. You would be able to visit us on holidays, and possibly on an occasional Sunday too.'

'Visit!' Susanne exclaimed. 'I don't want to visit. I want to stay here with you. Louis could teach me my lessons.'

'Louis won't be with us much longer,' Aunt Bette said. 'Louis is going off to Edinburgh to study with Professor Bertini.'

'What!' Susanne cried. 'He'll be here sometimes, though, won't he?'

' 'Fraid not,' said Louis, sympathetically. 'I understand that Professor Bertini doesn't allow his students much liberty. I'll be gone for the best part of a year; longer if things work out well.'

Susanne's eyes filled with tears. Buckie leaned over and presented her with a spotless red-checked handkerchief.

'There! There!' he said. 'We're not going to ship you out, lass, not if you don't want to go.'

'Are we not?' said Bette.

'No, we're not,' said Buckie. 'If you feel obliged to have Susanne's knowledge increased then enrol her in Miss Primrose's class. She has French at her disposal, I'm told, and if she's good enough to teach the likes of the minister's children surely she's good enough to teach our Susanne.'

'How would she get to and from the village school?' said Bette.

'Walk, of course,' said Buckie. 'Good God, woman, it's not much more than a couple of miles. When I was her age—'

'When you were her age you walked ten miles, barefoot, every morning just to fetch your breakfast,' said Bette, scathingly. 'I've heard your tales before, Buckie Hollander; I don't believe a word of them.'

'Might I suggest,' said Louis, taking the tureen from Nancy's grasp and helping himself to soup, 'that before you make a decision, you consult the minister of our illustrious parish and add his opinion of a village school education to the equation.' He handed the dish back to Nancy. 'I know, Mother, that you have great respect for Mr Oakley both as a preacher and as a man. Ask him what he would do with Susanne.'

'Now there's a grand idea,' said Buckie. 'Tom Oakley's an educated chap, with Latin and Greek . . .'

'And Hebrew,' Bette put in.

'Hebrew? He's not a Hebrew, is he?'

'Of course he's not a Hebrew,' said Bette. 'He can read books written in the . . . Oh, very well. I'll ask Tom next time I see him.'

'When will that be?' Buckie asked. 'Sunday?'

'Possibly sooner,' said Bette.

The following morning Louis coaxed Susanne out soon after breakfast in an attempt to cheer her up a little. She had been nagging him for weeks to show her the Lepers' Cave but he had no great liking for confined spaces and had absorbed so many of Nancy's stories about sea demons that he still had nightmares about tentacled creatures with huge eyes and vertical mouths.

'If you're frightened,' Louis said, 'just say the word and we'll hop out again immediately.'

'I'm not frightened,' Susanne said.

'You're sulking, aren't you?'

'I'm not sulking either.'

'Is it because I'm going away?'

'What if it is?'

'Susanne, I've been stuck here so long there are times when I think I'm going mad. Besides, I have to pursue my studies if I'm to succeed in life.'

'I thought you liked me.'

'I do like you, I do.' Louis sighed. 'Look, we've no money, or not much, and Mama's counting on me to raise the family up again.'

They were under the brow of the cliff. Droplets of water fell from above like beads sliding down a cord. The shadow of the cliff cut a swathe across the sunlit beach and the sea was like polished agate. Louis put a hand on her arm and pushed her back against the rock face.

He lowered his voice. 'When my father sold the *Merrilyn* he invested some of the profits with Henry Coburn. Mr Coburn's a dealer in shares; a broker – do you know what a broker is?' Susanne shook her head. 'A broker,' Louis went on, 'is a sort of agent, a middleman. Harry Coburn got rich by investing other people's money. He has land too, of course, land under rent. But he did not do well by Mama and Papa. Thanks to Harry Coburn, our income has dwindled considerably in recent years.'

'Is that why you've taken me in?' Susanne said. 'For my money?'

'Certainly not,' Louis assured her. 'We took you because you were alone in the world – and because your papa asked us to.'

'I'm just a charity girl, aren't I?'

'Susanne – no, you mustn't think that.'

'What else am I to think, when your mama wants rid of me.'

'She thinks boarding would be best for you.'

'I want to stay here with you.'

'Well, you can't,' said Louis, voice rising. 'I mean, look, I won't be gone for ever. When I complete my course of study and start selling my musical compositions, I'll come back for you.'

'Do you promise?'

'Yes, I promise.'

'When I'm old enough?' said Susanne, tilting her head.

'Old enough?'

'Old enough to marry you.'

'What? Marry? Good God!'

Then he saw that she was smiling. She had caught him on the wrong foot, and he resented it. He looked along the broken curve of the cliff towards the caves. He had half a mind to teach her a lesson by scaring her with tales of ghosts and demons; then she put out her arms and pushed him, quite violently, and, laughing, pushed him again.

'I wouldn't marry you, Louis Hollander,' she said, 'if you were to go down on your big fat knees and beg me. I wouldn't marry you for all the tea in China. So there!'

She made to push him once more, teasing yet not teasing, and in his uncertainty he caught her and held her in a bear-hug, his chin pressing down on the top of her head. He could smell soap on her hair, his mama's scent, could feel her little stick-thin limbs under the dress, her tiny hands digging into the fabric of his pilot coat.

'And,' he said, 'I'd die before I'd ever ask you.'

'Good!' Susanne clung to him, chin jabbing his chest. 'Now, where's this famous cave you want to show me? Is there treasure hidden inside? Pirate treasure – or smuggler's gold, perhaps?'

'No,' Louis said. 'No gold, just bones.'

'Even better,' Susanne said.

Being a creature inclined to perversity Bette Hollander didn't ask Tom Oakley's advice concerning her niece's education. She went instead to the schoolhouse on the high road between the church and the village. It wouldn't have surprised her to find Tom Oakley there, however, for a small segment of the minister's day was spent instructing Gillian Primrose's charges in the disciplines of the Christian religion which, given the incredible number of divisions within the Scottish Church, was a lot less simple than it seemed.

It was mid-morning before Bette Hollander arrived at the schoolhouse, a long, low, thatch-roofed building that had been home to a herd of pedigree pigs until, some thirty years back, one of the more progressive Arbuthnots had taken it into his head to endow the village with a schoolhouse. The haunting odour of swill still clung to the place, though, and Miss Primrose's tiny lean-to cottage, so prettily decorated with roses and seashells, had no fresh water supply and no drainage and, in hot weather, reeked to high heaven.

Bette could hear the children chanting verses, though she could not make out the words. She loitered in the yard to catch her breath then went to the window and knocked upon it. The chanting ceased immediately and several small noses were pressed against the glass.

Miss Primrose appeared at the door.

'Ah, Mrs Hollander!' she said. 'If you're hoping to catch Mr Oakley, I'm afraid he's been and gone.'

'It's you I have business with, Miss Primrose, if you'd be good enough to spare a minute or two.'

There were faces at both windows and a sound within the room that reminded Bette of squabbling rooks. She knew she should have waited until the dinner hour but she was impatient to have the matter settled.

'Me?' said Miss Primrose, surprised. 'Very well, Mrs Hollander, if you'll wait just a moment while I give the children something to keep them busy, I'll be with you presently,' and stepped back into the classroom.

It was a fine open sort of morning with high fleecy clouds overhead. The breeze had the smell of spring to it and, in two or three weeks, lambs would be blethering in Arbuthnot's meadows. Bette tidied her hair, adjusted her bonnet, smoothed her skirts and generally made herself presentable, for she, like many folk, was in awe of schoolteachers.

Gillian Primrose reappeared.

She was a woman of middle height, fair-haired and freckled, with large hands and even larger feet. She was, Bette conceded, pretty in a rustic sort of way, and dressed lightly in gingham and print cotton, as if it were already high summer. She placed herself by the open door, indicated that she was ready to listen to what Mrs Hollander had to say and, while Bette outlined the nature of her dilemma, nodded as if she were already one step ahead of the whaler's wife.

'How old is the child?'

'Fourteen,' Bette answered. 'Fifteen in a month or two.'

'Schooled in London?'

'Six years at a dame academy.'

'So she can read, write and count?'

'Yes, and embroider.'

Nodding, smiling, Miss Primrose said, 'Embroidery isn't taught in our school, Mrs Hollander. I assume she speaks well.'

'She speaks very well.'

'Most of my pupils do not, you know.'

'Perhaps her presence will help to improve their diction.'

'And perhaps her diction will merely become more slovenly.'

'Oh!' Bette said. 'I hadn't thought of that.'

'She might be better suited at Mr Wishart's school in Whitfield.'

'It's too far away.'

'And expensive?' said Miss Primrose, making a question out of it.

'Well, that is a consideration, albeit a minor one.'

'She would learn Latin there, and Greek, if you've a mind to educate her properly. Here – well, I can't promise that she would learn much more than she knows already. I could, I suppose, take her in for a year but I can't afford her any special treatment, I'm afraid.'

'I need a place to put her, that's all,' said Bette. 'I mean, to give her something to do, to keep her out of mischief.'

'Is she a mischievous child, then?'

'Not in the slightest. She's very well mannered, very well behaved. She won't cause you the least sort of trouble in that respect. The alternative is to send her to board in St Andrews.'

'Does she wish to be boarded in St Andrews?'

'Frankly, no. She wishes to stay with me.'

'How long is it since her father died?'

'A matter of weeks.'

Miss Primrose folded her arms, leaned back against the doorpost and looked at Bette Hollander as if it were she, not her niece, who required an education. 'Where's the girl now?'

'Playing on the beach, I think.'

'Alone?'

'My son's with her.'

'Louis?'

'Yes.'

Miss Primrose paused, then said, 'Bring her to my house on Tuesday evening, about five o'clock?'

'Will you take her?'

'Probably,' Miss Primrose said.

'But,' Bette said, 'no promises?'

'No promises, Mrs Hollander,' Gillian Primrose said and, with a final nod, stepped back into the schoolhouse to quell the clamour within.

'Why is it,' Louis said, 'that one invariably feels the need to whisper in caves?'

'Perhaps,' Susanne said, 'we don't like the sound of our own voices.'

'How profound!' said Louis. 'Did you read that some-where?'

'No.' Susanne giggled, softly. 'I just made it up.'

'Do you dislike the sound of your own voice?'

'Not I,' said Susanne and, with a little shout, sent echoes careening from the walls. '*Pau-leen, Pau-leen, Pau-leen Thaaaw-er-en.*'

'Hush,' said Louis, alarmed. 'Don't do that.'

'Why not?'

'You never know what may be lurking in the depths.'

'Pigeons,' said Susanne. 'I'm not afraid of pigeons.'

'Bats then,' said Louis.

'I'm not afraid of bats either.'

'Have you ever seen a bat?'

'No, but . . .'

'A sea-bat,' said Louis.

'Sea-bats? No such thing I've ever heard of.'

'They're native to the Kingdom,' Louis told her, 'and very fierce.'

He had brought no lantern and the cave was dark.

Sand and shell-shingle sloped steeply upwards, moist at the cave mouth then drying to coarse powder above the scribble of weed that commemorated the autumn's high tides. The walls did not seem to converge so much as insinuate themselves one into the other, slanting up to the arch and narrowing to the back of the cave where, so Nancy had told him, there was a large chamber out of which sea creatures came when Satan summoned them.

'Nonsense!' Susanne scrambled up the slope. 'You don't scare me, Louis Hollander. Sea-bats, indeed!'

He remained in the avenue of daylight and watched his cousin vanish into the gloom. He was less afraid of Nancy Bissett's monsters than he was of death – and the cave stank of it. He put a hand on the slimy wall and drew it away again, as if the rock had burned him. He could see nothing of the girl and wondered what had become of her.

'Susanne?' he hissed.

'What?'

'Where are you?'

'I'm here.'

'I can't see you.'

'But I can see you,' his cousin whispered.

'What – what are you doing?'

'Exploring.'

'Is there much to explore?'

'Come see for yourself. You're not afraid, are you?'

'No, of course not.'

He sucked in a deep breath and crept forward. The walls closed about him. Powdery shingle shifted under his feet. He hunched his shoulders, clenched his fists and forced himself up the slope. He flinched when she touched him, as if her cold little hand was a claw, or a tentacle.

'I – I can't see a blessed thing.'

'I can,' Susanne said. 'Take my hand, silly. I'll guide you.'

He groped about, found her hand, clasped it tightly.

She led him deeper into the cave.

The floor levelled out and the raw sea stench gave way to earthy odours that were almost, if not quite, soothing. The girl rubbed against him like a cat, like Thimble, her skirts brushing his legs.

They were inside the chamber now. In the trickle of daylight he could just make out a mound of fine sand breasting the wall. There were no noises in the chamber, no crabs or scratching rats, no fluttering of wings.

Odd, Louis thought, how just a few yards from a beach that teemed with life everything was suddenly dead or, if not dead, dormant.

'Where did they find the bones?' Susanne whispered.

'Bones?'

'You said they'd found bones here. Were they lepers' bones?'

Louis didn't want to think about those poor cast-off souls, too weak to scrape mussels from the rocks or forage for seagulls' eggs; men, women, children, all scaly with decay, herded here to die.

'Louis?'

'What?'

'This is the Lepers' Cave, isn't it?'

'Yes.'

'Did they really find bones here?'

'They did. Some twenty years ago a scientific gentleman dug them up and identified them as human. They were very old, of course, two or three hundred years old, in fact.'

'I wonder,' Susanne said, 'if they found them all.' She sank down on her knees and drew her hands across the sand, as if, like a dowser, she could sense what lay buried beneath. 'We must come again, and bring a lantern next time.'

'Well,' said Louis, 'perhaps.'

Her position was that of a supplicant, back bowed, head tucked to her chest, arms stretched out as if awaiting punishment.

'Get up,' he said. 'Please get up.'

She looked over her shoulder. She said, 'Did lepers wear drawers?'

'Drawers? What *are* you talking about?'

'See.' Susanne lifted a tangled garment and held it out to him. 'Drawers, calico drawers.'

Louis reared back, crying, 'Put them down, put them down.'

'Why?'

'They're filthy, and – and you don't know where they've been.'

Susanne fanned out the undergarment and scrutinised it, thoughtfully. 'They don't look dirty to me. I wonder how they got here.'

'Washed up by the tide, I expect,' Louis said.

He was both embarrassed and afraid. He had heard stories in the Dalriada about other caves along the coast that were used by young bucks from the boats and their fancy women, but he had never given much credence to the lewd stories. Now here was evidence that some buxom lass had removed her most intimate garments and, sprawled here on the sand, had done all kinds of nasty things that he didn't like to think about. He snatched the garment from Susanne's fingers, crumpled it into a ball and tossed it into the darkness.

'Filthy,' he snarled. 'Filthy things.'

'Washed up from a dead person,' said Susanne, with more enthusiasm than awe. 'My goodness! I wonder what else we might find.'

Louis wrapped an arm about her waist and yanked her to her feet. 'Let's get out of here.'

'What's wrong with you, Louis? It's only an old pair of drawers,' Susanne protested as he dragged her towards the cave mouth.

He held her against his hip, as a mother might hold a baby, and lugged her bodily out of the gloomy chamber into the shaft of daylight. He put her down, looked at her for a long moment and then, heaving a sigh, stared out at the telescopic prospect of the sea. He wanted to be brave, to go back and pick up the garment that Susanne had found, to bring it out into the light and carry it home like a trophy, but he could not bring himself to do so.

Susanne, on the other hand, seemed to have forgotten all about her unusual find. She laughed at the gleam of a seagull as it flitted past in the sunshine, at the sleek black backs of porpoises dipping across the mouth of the bay, at the sails of fishing boats tilting and tossing, and pigeons whizzing away, hardly visible at one moment in the shadowy arch and then, suddenly, radiant in the light. It was as if she had stepped out of the darkness into a world strange and beautiful and took more delight in it than he had ever done.

'I'll race you,' Susanne said, eagerly.

'Race me?'

'As far as the brown rocks.'

'You'll want a start, I suppose.'

'No,' Susanne said, then, with a shriek, shouted, 'yes.'

And, hitching up her skirts, shot off into the sunlight, leaving Louis, the cave and the calico drawers behind.

5

Angus Gamrie not only fulfilled the onerous duties of session clerk, he was also secretary of the Sea Box Society, the Mortcloth and Benefit Society, the Poor House Trust and a school inspector, ex officio, on behalf of the Presbytery. In this capacity he had taken it upon himself to ensure that the twenty-three pounds paid in annual salary to Miss Gillian Primrose was not being frittered away.

He sat on a three-legged stool, head bowed, the coxcomb of silver hair bristling, his eyebrows as threatening as icicles. When Miss Primrose ushered Bette Hollander and her niece into the parlour he did not look up, but seemed to be searching the floor for cracks or, perhaps, pondering the problem of the minister's hand-lasted ankle boots which were 'awfy braw' for a man who was constantly pleading poverty.

The minister clasped Mrs Hollander's hand, then, linking his hands behind his back, smiled down on the little charmer, Susanne Thorne.

Mr Gamrie raised his head. 'You, girl,' he said. 'Stand up straight.'

He was small and thickset, with the bowed spine of the loom-weaver he had been before the trade expired in Strayhorn. Since then, for many years, he had been an agent for a Dundee linen draper and travelled about the county in his cart recording orders and delivering everything from bed sheets to burial shrouds. He had never taken a wife, had, in fact, never so much as courted a girl, and – so the wags in the Dalriada claimed – was so shrivelled in his reproductive parts that he had to make water squatting like a woman.

'Permit me to put the girl to the test, Mr Gamrie,' Miss Primrose said and, without further ado, put to Susanne a series of simple questions that the girl had no difficulty in answering. Mr Gamrie continued to glower while Mr Oakley pulled a ram's horn box from the pocket of his breeches and ostentatiously helped himself to a pinch of snuff. He sniffed, sneezed into a handkerchief and exchanged glances with Bette Hollander before putting the box away.

What with Mr Oakley and Aunt Bette flirting on the edge of her vision, Mr Gamrie planted before her and Miss Primrose asking her what she'd been taught at Miss Millar's Academy, Susanne felt as if she were caught in a dream and answered the teacher's questions more and more rapidly; questions on the capital cities of Europe, questions involving compound arithmetic, questions on the history of the kings of England, questions on the parables of Our Lord Jesus; questions, questions, questions coming so thick and fast that Susanne had no time to think, but simply furnished the answers that popped into her head.

'There!' Miss Primrose exclaimed, at last. 'What do you make of that, Mr Gamrie? Are you not impressed?'

'Aye, but there's a wheen more to learnin' than parrot talk.'

'She has no French,' said Mr Oakley.

'Aye, an' no Latin,' said Mr Gamrie.

'Omissions that can easily be remedied,' said Miss Primrose.

Susanne mopped her brow. She longed to be out in the fresh air, walking along the cliff top looking out at the sea or chasing along the beach with Ajax and Louis. She closed her eyes and felt empty, empty and uncaring.

'Take the girl out,' Angus Gamrie said. 'We'll decide here an' now.'

To her relief, Susanne was led from the odorous little cottage into the garden, and left there. She had no notion what was going on or what the raised voices were arguing about. Twenty minutes later Mr Gamrie stalked out of the cottage and strode off down the path. Aunt Bette, Mr Oakley and Miss Primrose came into the garden. The teacher took Susanne by the arm.

'Congratulations, my dear,' she said. 'On Monday you will become a pupil-teacher. I do hope you're pleased.'

'Pupil-teacher?' said Susanne, astonished. 'What's that?'

'Didn't your aunt explain?'

'No.'

'In exchange for helping me with the younger children, you will be taught at a higher level – without charge,' Miss Primrose said. 'I have one pupil-teacher already, Zena Oakley, the minister's daughter, and the school board won't allow me another. I've come to a private arrangement with your aunt, an arrangement approved by both Mr Gamrie and Mr Oakley.'

'I don't know how to teach,' Susanne protested.

'It's much less difficult than you imagine,' said Miss Primrose. 'I'll show you what to do, and Zena will be there to guide you. Because you aren't, as it were, one of us you will have some authority from the start.'

'How can I learn anything if I'm instructing others?'

'Oh, you'll learn, my dear,' Miss Primrose said. 'At the very worse, you'll learn how to teach, and that's something quite valuable, believe me.'

'Did my aunt put me up for this?'

'She did – she and Mr Oakley together. Class starts at half past eight,' Miss Primrose said. 'If you arrive at eight I'll show you the ropes, enough to get us all off on the right foot.'

At home in Holborn Susanne had been used to being told what to do but here in Strayhorn she had tasted freedom of a sort. The holiday was over. Now she would be obliged to make her way in the world. Perhaps, she thought, that's Aunt Bette's intention; perhaps she's sending me to school to learn how to be a worthy wife for Louis.

'Yes,' she said. 'Yes, why not!' and laughed.

Louis had negotiated for two fat young rabbits in the Dalriada and, since poaching was no longer a hanging offence, even in Fife, had hoofed it home with the catch slung over his shoulder. Nancy had been pleased with the purchase. She had recipes galore for rabbit and had the pair stretched and headless on the chopping block before Louis had taken off his coat.

Soon the smell of onion marmalade wafted through the house. Buckie, purring with anticipation, dug a bottle of burgundy from the hall cupboard. The April evening was cool, the fire banked high, the lamp lighted and the table set. Louis, upstairs, played cheerful Scotch airs on the harmonium, and Ajax and Thimble, like sentinels, sat upright and alert by the kitchen door.

Buckie bussed Bette's cheek. 'It went well?'

'It went very well,' Bette answered him. 'Have you been drinking?'

'Don't we have something to celebrate?'

'Aye, well, I suppose we do,' Bette said. 'Now where's that girl got to?'

'Where do you think?' Buckie pointed his thumb at the ceiling. 'She's galloped upstairs to tell our son and heir that she's going to be a teacher.'

'Hmm,' Bette murmured, not displeased, and, holding Ajax and the cat back with her foot, slid into the kitchen, and closed the door.

'A teacher!' Louis said. 'Well, well, well!' He sat at the harmonium, fingers resting on the keyboard. His hair, thick and unruly, clung to his neck in glossy black curls. He'd had a few jugs of ale that afternoon and was mellow and relaxed. He signalled Susanne to come to him, put an arm about her and pulled her down on to a corner of the organ bench.

'Aren't you proud of me?' she asked, snuggling close.

'Very proud, indeed,' Louis said. 'I've never heard of anyone being taken on as a pupil-teacher at age fourteen. Ewan Connover, with whom I went to school, was a pupil-teacher but he was bent on a career as a missionary and, as far as I know, is now in India, or perhaps it's China. A year instructing the young served him well, but it was only a stepping-stone which, dearest, is the point I'm trying to make. I reckon you're off to a flying start.'

Susanne leaned her head on his shoulder and smiled.

Louis drew upon a stop-knob, depressed the treadle below the board, coaxed a single throbbing note from the harmonium and let it waver along the reed pan. His cousin was as tipsy as he was, elated by the trick his mother had played, and looked, he thought, very pretty in that state.

Leaning into her, he kissed her lips.

'Oh, Louis!' she whispered. 'Oh, Louis!'

From below came a deep baying howl as Ajax grew impatient to be fed and Louis, aware of his mistake, thrust himself up from the bench and, blushing furiously, headed off downstairs, leaving Susanne in seventh heaven in the twilit room upstairs.

The bed that the minister shared with his wife had long ago become a mere adjunct of the nursery and every corner of the room was littered with baby clothes. The manse was no grand mansion but an upright, two-storey, four-roomed hovel that, before repairs had been carried out, had barely been habitable, let alone comfortable. Comfort was something that Tom Oakley couldn't live without. He had, therefore, claimed the larger of the ground-floor apartments as his own and there, behind a bolted door, found the measure of solitude that his nature required.

The rest of the house, including the bed in which he slept, was polluted with children or the mess that seven children created.

'Must we have Roland in bed with us?' Tom enquired, mildly.

'Where else am I to put him?' Effie answered.

'In the basket in the corner.'

'Morven's in the basket.'

'I thought she'd been transferred to the nursery?'

'Nightmares again,' said Effie.

'I see,' Tom said. 'What's this?' Something damp nuzzled his rump. 'Oh, Lord! It's not Wayland, is it?'

'He has a bit of a fever, I think.'

'He's wet through.'

'I'll change him.'

Tom heard the scratch of a match and a moment later the candle on the floor beside the bed flamed. Light filtered through Effie's gown, illuminating her figure; not much of a figure, really, for incessant child-bearing had pared her to skin and bone. Not for the first time, Tom wondered why he had been cursed with a skinny wife and not one of those women who, after breeding, become all plump and comfortable.

'Give him here,' said Effie.

Roland, smelling of milk, lay across the bolster, dead to the world and snoring. Wayland, however, had become more and more fretful and would not settle in the room across the landing where, in theory if not practice, Zena had charge. Tom blamed Effie, not his daughter, for retarding Waylie's progress towards adulthood, which, in Tom's narrow definition, meant the ability to use a chamber pot unaided. He groped under the bedclothes, found the child, yanked him up and handed him over to Effie who, kneeling on all fours, proceeded to pin Wayland to the floor and had the skirt, gown and napkin off him before he had the wit to wail.

Tom watched his wife work a moist rag over his son's parts and crooning – croaking more like – to soothe him, wrap a ragged napkin over his bare belly and nail it in place with a multitude of pins.

In the basket in the corner, little Morven whimpered as yet another bad dream flitted through her tousled head.

Tom lay back and placed his head on the bolster an inch from Roland's long body which was clad only in a flannel bodice and a napkin since no clean nightshirts were available. He felt the baby's breath against his cheek, soft as a caress, and, with Effie kneeling half-naked just beside the bed, found himself tweaked into a state of mild arousal. He was, alas, cursed with a passionate nature that took no account of the hour of the day, the day of the week, or circumstances that were, to say the least, unfavourable.

At any moment Effie would blow out the candle and with Waylie tucked under her arm would hoist herself back into bed. Roland would be lifted from the bolster and arranged against his mother's flank and all possibility of connubial bliss would vanish for another night.

Tom sighed, tossed back the covers and slid out of bed.

'Where do you think you're going?' Effie demanded.

'To the study.'

'Oh no, you're not.'

'Oh yes,' Tom said, 'I am.'

'All very well for you, sittin' down there in perfect peace while I'm stuck up here not able to shut an eye.'

'I'll shut your eye for you, if you wish,' Tom said.

'You would, too, wouldn't you?'

'Without a qualm.'

'All right,' Effie said, 'if you must go, go quietly.'

She watched him pad barefoot out of the room and vanish into the darkness at the top of the stairs. She shifted into the centre of the bed and arranged her small sons, one on either side.

Dry-tailed and secure, Wayland wriggled and flopped a sleepy arm across her stomach, while Roland, thumb in mouth, rested his chin on her shoulder and breathed his sweet baby breath into her nostrils.

Effie sighed contentedly.

She was relieved to be rid of her husband who would surely have expected her to satisfy his lust at some point during the night. Effie loved her children dearly, but she was terrified of another pregnancy and had never taken to those ways of pleasing her husband that he considered part of normal wifely duties. She would sleep more soundly with just her sons by her side.

In his study on the ground floor Tom draped an old greatcoat over his nightshirt and, without lighting the lamp, stood at the window and peered out at the moon snared in the beeches that lined the road between the church and the village. The first of Arbuthnot's lambs had been dropped that morning and, within a week, the fields would be alive with them. Spring did not rouse his ardour quite as much as autumn – but it was bad enough. He pressed his brow against the glass and tried to make out the shape of the schoolhouse and, tucked against its flank, Rose Cottage where Gillian Primrose lay asleep.

He knew full well that he couldn't see the cottage from the manse but lived in hope that one dark night the earth might shift and he would catch a glimpse of candlelight in the schoolteacher's window, a little spark to ignite his imagination and, as it were, bring him to the boil.

There was nothing that Gillian Primrose could give him.

She was almost as poor, if not more so, than he was. While he longed to hold her in his arms, thrust himself into her young, nut-brown, freckled body and kiss her full lips, he couldn't honestly say that he liked her very much. She was too rebellious, too saucy, too difficult to impress. He wanted her, he supposed, as an antidote to Bette Hollander whose fat little figure gave him no more than fleeting pleasure, and not enough of that. He was weary of potting sheds, coverts and caves. He wanted comfort, warmth, time to enjoy himself, things that the occupant of Rose Cottage would surely offer him if only he could win her round.

Reluctantly, he pulled himself away from the window and lit the lamp.

Perhaps, he thought, smiling to himself, the schoolteacher would see the light in his window and, sensing his need, would come to him over the fields and appear like a vision at his window.

With a *tut* and a shake of the head at such futile imaginings, Tom Oakley threw himself down in the chair behind the desk and reached for Calvin's *Genesis*, a commentary guaranteed to soothe his troubled soul and, with luck, send him swiftly off to sleep.

6

Older pupils, Zena and Gregor Oakley among them, occupied
the desks towards the rear of the classroom while the infants
squatted on low benches at the front, slates and reading books
balanced on their knees.

'They can be imps when it suits them,' Zena told Susanne.
'Some of them think schooling's a waste of time and would
rather be at the fishing. You can gut as soon as you're tall
enough to reach the troughs and sail with the netters when
you're big enough to haul a bucket.'

'How big is that?' said Susanne.

'Smaller than me,' Gregor said.

'Why don't you go out with the netters then?' Susanne
asked.

'Papa won't let me,' Greg said.

'Papa wants Greg to become a preacher,' Zena said. 'But
you need a brain to be a preacher and if you have a brain then
you're not going to become a preacher, if you see what I
mean.'

Zena was close to Susanne's age but taller and more robust.
She had flame-red hair, eyes the colour of the sea, and a full
figure. She wore a strange assortment of clothing, though:
loose print dresses and patched jackets and a felt hat with a
seagull's feather in the band. Her brother, Gregor, only a year
her junior, was clad in hand-me-down breeks and a hammer
jacket. He was a well-muscled boy on the verge of manhood
and, unlike his father, had not one vain or malicious bone in

his body. There were younger Oakleys in class, too, including Freddie, who, at twelve, had graduated from the infant benches to a desk at the rear of the room.

Every morning, about half past ten, Mr Oakley strode into the classroom and Miss Primrose retreated while the minister led the children in prayer and delivered a short sermon. Most of the pupils, his own children included, drifted off into waking dreams, scribbled covertly on their slates or gouged at the wood of their desk with penknives or pen-nibs or, if all else failed, jiggled shells and pebbles in their pockets and smirked as if they were already beyond all hope of redemption. Only the youngest held the minister in awe. They became agitated when he appeared and stared up, round-eyed, as he outlined the horrors that awaited sinners in the murky world of the hereafter. The moment Mr Oakley left, however, Miss Primrose would walk along the row and touch each child on the head as if to absolve them from sin and leave them once more pure, innocent and mischievous.

Susanne rose early and breakfasted with Buckie in the parlour. More often than not Aunt Bette appeared at the last moment to inspect Susanne, tuck in a strand of hair or snip off a loose thread and administer a parting kiss before her niece set off along the track to the village. Miss Primrose would have the stove lit and a pot of tea ready to welcome Zena and Susanne, her pupil-teachers, and for a half-hour would talk to the girls as equals and outline the day's lessons.

At noon the village children scampered home, those from further afield ate 'pieces' in the yard, and Miss Primrose instructed Zena and Susanne in the rudiments of French grammar. When spring blossomed into summer and the days grew long, the affinity between Susanne and the Oakleys increased and, after school, she would often linger with Zena and Greg at the gate of Rose Cottage, blissfully unaware of the time.

'Where the devil have you been, Susanne?' Louis demanded. 'I've been waiting to take you for a walk on the beach.'

'I've been chatting to Zena,' Susanne said. 'I'll put away my books and we'll go now, if you wish.'

'Too late, far too late,' said Louis, sulkily. 'It's almost supper time.'

'After supper we can—'

'I have things to do after supper.'

'What sort of things?'

'Music to write.'

'Would you rather write music than walk on the beach?'

'Well,' Louis said, 'that's a fine sort of question. I might turn it around and ask if you'd rather gossip with Zena Oakley than come home. I think you prefer that red-haired girl to me.'

'What if I do?' said Susanne. 'Zena is very good company.'

'Ah! And I'm not, I suppose. I'm no longer interesting enough for you.'

'Louis, for goodness' sake,' Buckie put in, 'Susanne's entitled to have friends of her own.'

'What do you talk about, hour upon hour, you and your friend?'

'This and that,' said Susanne, casually.

'Do you talk about me?'

'Hah!' said Buckie, scornfully, from the depths of his armchair.

'We've better things to talk about than you, dearest,' Susanne said. 'Now, I'm going out to look at the sea. If you're too tired, or too lazy, to accompany me I'll take Ajax instead.'

'Oh, all right, all right,' Louis grumbled and, much to his father's amusement, followed the teasing little minx out of doors.

★   ★   ★

Effie held Roland over the chamber pot and urged him to do his business while Zena sat nearby with Wayland wriggling on her lap. Zena didn't subscribe to her mother's theory that Waylie would be shamed into easing his bladder by being forced to watch his younger brother on the pot. She wasn't convinced that Waylie was being stubborn. She feared that there was something wrong with him, a fear that had dogged her with each of her brothers and sisters ever since she'd been old enough to realise that her mother had drawn the short straw in the lottery of life and that motherhood was just another name for anxiety.

'Wee-wee, Roland, wee-wee,' her mama said, encouragingly. 'Look, Waylie, see what a clever boy your brother is.'

Roland kicked his bare legs and reared backward. Wayland rolled his eyes and chanted. Four-year-old Petal, who was hiding under the kitchen table, let out a shriek. Dishes were piled in the tubs, unwashed clothing on the table. Crusts of bread and an apple core lay on the floor, a puddle of milk where Petal had knocked over the jug. Fortunately Greg had led Morven and Freddie out on a foraging expedition, which meant stealing coal from the heap behind Mr McKinnon's cottage on the far side of the barley field.

'Where's Papa?' Zena asked.

'Gone into the village. Old Mrs Mazzucco is ailing again.'

'High time she gave up the ghost,' said Zena.

'What a thing to say!' said Effie. 'She suffers greatly, you know; your father gives her comfort.'

'It's not Papa's prayers give her comfort, it's the whisky. Mammy Mazzucco hasn't been sober since her husband died. She's pickled all the time, pickled like a herring in a barrel, so Prim says.'

'Prim? You're very familiar all of a sudden.'

'Papa takes her whisky, doesn't he?'

'I've no idea what he does for the poor old lady.'

'Or for her granddaughter?' Zena said.

Roland crouched over the pot and concentrated on producing a tiny trickle of pee-pee. Wayland peered down at Petal who had crawled out from under the table and had spread herself on the floor in the shape of a starfish.

Effie said, 'She's rich, you know.'

'Prim? Nonsense, Mama. She's even poorer than we are.'

'The Hollander girl, I mean.'

'Susanne? She's isn't a Hollander. Her name's Thorne.'

'Whatever she calls herself, she's rich.'

'Aye,' said Zena, 'her papa died last February.'

'And left her a tidy fortune. I wonder how much she's worth?'

'She's worth no more than I am by the look of it. If she has lots of money, why is she a pupil-teacher in Strayhorn an' not boarding in St Andrews?'

'It's Bette Hollander's way of disguising her intentions.'

'Intentions?' said Zena. 'What intentions?'

'Of marrying Susanne off to that good-for-nothing son of hers.'

'Louis?' Zena raised a fiery eyebrow. 'He's ten years older than Susanne.'

'Only five years,' said Effie. 'But what matter if he's Methuselah? If Bette Hollander has set her mind on it the English girl won't escape. Mark my words, as soon as she comes into her womanhood, she'll be married off to Louis Hollander.'

'Balderdash!' Zena said. 'Just because you can't stand Mrs Hollander doesn't mean to say she's a grasping ogre.'

Effie narrowed her eyes. 'Ask her, ask your friend.'

'Ask her what?'

'What she thinks of her cousin.'

'She likes him. She makes no bones about it. Why shouldn't she like him? He's—' Zena bit off the end of the sentence.

'A wastrel,' Effie said. 'Him an' his music. No profit in music.'

'No profit in preaching either; that didn't stop you marrying Papa.'

'Times were different then,' Effie said. 'I was young, an' knew no better.'

'Well,' Zena said, 'you've learned.'

'Aye, that I have,' said Effie Oakley and plucking Roland from the pot, wiped his bottom with her sleeve and put him down on the floor to play.

The glass was falling and the spell of fine weather was coming to an end. Susanne and Zena were seated on the wall that separated the school yard from McKinnon's barley field, sharing buttered bread and cheese.

Zena said, 'My mama thinks you're rich.'

'I am,' said Susanne, without hesitation. 'At least, I'm told I am.'

'Huh,' said Zena. 'If I were rich I think I'd know it. I mean, who looks after your money for you?'

'A Bank in London.'

'Which Bank would that be?'

Susanne shrugged. 'The Merchants and Traders, I think.'

'There's one of those in Dundee,' said Zena. 'Near the church in Nethergate. I saw it when Papa took me to hear Mr Congleton preach.'

'Who's Mr Congleton?'

'An evangelical from America. We had to go in secret in case Mr Gamrie found out. Angus doesn't approve of evangelicals.'

'Why not?'

'Angus doesn't approve of anything,' Zena said. 'Never mind Angus, tell me about all this cash you'll inherit.'

'Nothing to tell,' said Susanne. 'Papa owned a printing shop and a paper-making factory, and we had a house in Holborn.

When he died everything was sold and the profits put into a Bank by Mr Reeve. He's a lawyer. He pays my aunt for my keep.'

'An' the rest?'

'Mine, I suppose, when I come of age.'

'How soon will that be?'

'I'm not sure. Eighteen, or twenty-one, or' – Susanne giggled – 'when I decide to marry.' She nudged her friend with her elbow. 'In Scotland a girl can marry when she's thirteen. Mr Reeve told me.'

'Everyone knows that,' said Zena. 'Last year two of our girls left school to marry sailors, and they weren't hardly out of short clothes – the girls, I mean, not the sailors.'

'You could marry?' Susanne said.

'I'm never goin' to marry.'

Susanne broke off a fragment of cheese and handed it to her friend as if to reward her for her candour. 'Well,' she said, 'I think I'll marry my cousin Louis as soon as he completes his musical studies.'

'Oh!' said Zena. 'Does Louis know about your plans?'

'Of course not. I'm too young.'

'That's not what you were sayin' a minute ago.'

Susanne sighed. 'I'll wait for him.'

'Aye,' Zena said, 'but will he wait for you?'

'He will if he loves me.'

'Love!' Zena said, scornfully. 'I don't believe in love.'

'More fool you, then,' said Susanne.

Tom had declared that the cave was too dangerous and too damp. It was, Tom said, the potting shed or nothing, and, Bette's need for love being undiminished, she had surrendered to his ultimatum.

Tom was a well-built man, forceful and energetic, more so than Buckie had ever been. Coupling with him, in whatever circumstances, made her feel young again. She longed to waken beside him in a warm bed and, with stealthy fingers, rouse him to unrealistic passion. To this end, she conceived a bold and hare-brained scheme.

'Dundee?' Tom buttoned himself up. 'What possible excuse could I have for going to Dundee?'

'Make one up.'

'Bette, I'm a minister of the Gospel. I can't be seen skulking around the knocking shops of Dundee.'

'Knocking shops?'

'Inns where rooms are leased by the hour, I mean.'

'I've taken a room in Ralston's Hotel.'

'Good God, are you proposing that we spend a whole night together?'

'Wouldn't you like that?'

'Of course, of course,' Tom said, hastily. 'Nothing I'd like more. But . . .'

'It'll cost you nothing,' Bette said.

'It'll cost me my livelihood if we're spotted together,' Tom said. 'There are, in fact, times when I think that it might be better to stop meeting and—'

'Hush.' She clapped a hand to his mouth. 'Don't say it, Tom, I beg you. Don't say that you're tired of me.'

He detached her hand, finger by finger. 'Tired of you? How could I ever tire of you, dearest? Dwell on this, however: if the faintest whiff of scandal attaches itself to our friendship then it's over between us. Isn't it better to stay as we are than gamble everything on one night of love?'

'You don't love me, do you?'

Tom leaned back against the door.

It had finally begun to rain, a fine grey drizzle that matched his mood. He was irked at being put on the spot by this greedy, inconsequential little woman and regretted having given in to temptation in the first place.

He kept an arm about her to simulate affection, and said, 'My wife and your husband, not to mention Angus Gamrie, would surely put two and two together if we both happen to be in Dundee at one and the same time.'

'Then go to Kirkcaldy.'

'What?'

'Tell them – tell everyone that you are going to Kirkcaldy.'

'And come to Dundee instead, do you mean?'

'Yes.'

His anger was tempered by apprehension. He had already lost one pulpit because of a woman. There had been little enough to that friendship: a tryst, a kiss, a gesture or two, followed by repentance on the woman's part. He had resigned his charge before the storm of opprobrium broke and had pretended to Effie, the Arbuthnots and the Presbytery that he really wanted the vacancy in Strayhorn, and was willing to step down a peg to get it.

'Give me a little time to think about it, my dear,' he said. 'I'll have to consult my calendar and, of course, my better half. I take it you're going to Dundee to collect your dues from the Bank?'

'I am,' Bette said. 'I'll stay overnight.'

'Will Louis not wish to go with you?'

'If he does, I'll dissuade him.'

'And the girl?'

'Susanne will be at school.'

Tom chuckled. 'A clever move that, Bette, enrolling her in school.'

'She's happy there and has made friends, your daughter among them.'

'And it earns you a few extra pounds every year, does it not?'

'I'm sure I don't know what you mean,' Bette said.

'Oh, come now,' Tom said. 'I'm certain your lawyer friend

in London – Reeve, is it? – that Reeve isn't aware that our little orphan has become a pupil-teacher and is receiving free schooling. How much do you charge him?'

'That's none of your concern, Tom Oakley.' The minister laughed and Bette, in spite of herself, smiled. 'Well,' she said, 'a few extra shillings aren't going to be missed. I've Louis's fees to meet and lodgings in Edinburgh will not be cheap.'

'Indeed not.'

She adjusted her clothing, tidied her hair and was in all respects ready to face the world again. He kissed her, then opened the door of the potting shed and peeped out into the rain.

'We must go,' he said. 'I'm due at the schoolhouse.'

She caught his arm and lifted herself up, pressing against him.

'I'll be in Dundee on Tuesday next,' she whispered.

'And I,' Tom said, 'will be in Kirkcaldy – if I can.'

She pulled back a half-step but did not remove her hand from his arm.

'Do *not* disappoint me, Tom,' she said. 'Do *not* let me down.'

'No,' he said, evenly. 'No, Bette, I won't,' and, with a little shove, directed her out of the shed towards the slippery path that straggled down the cliff face to the beach.

Whatever the reprobates in the Dalriada might think of him Angus Gamrie was no hypocrite. The posts he filled had not been taken on for self-aggrandisement. He was, without doubt, the best man for each of the jobs and, as session clerk, he did his best to ensure that Tom Oakley's muddles were quickly straightened out. He organised the diary, dispensed Communion cards, tallied the Poor Box, recorded the minutes of meetings, informed Mr Oakley who was sick, who might soon be in need of burial and whose child deserved to be baptised. Angus was the finger on the pulse of the community, in fact, the bridge to the Presbytery, and the fellow who went, cap in hand, to Edward Arbuthnot whenever parish funds ran low.

He lived alone in a cottage west of the village, a cottage with a big dry barn behind it in which were stored the crates and packages that arrived from the warehouse in Dundee. The barn also housed a flat-bed cart with a canvas hood and Matthew, a sturdy old horse. Commissions kept Angus in beef, butter and tea, and the horse in oats.

Angus might be mocked in Strayhorn but he was respected in most of the farms across the shire where his moral certainty was regarded as a virtue and a prayer went down well with a dish of tea and a griddle scone.

Alan Redpath had a great deal of time for Angus Gamrie. When their paths crossed, as they often did, the doctor would exchange news and views with the elder and generally make himself agreeable. He was well aware that Mr Gamrie's good opinion carried weight in the hinterland where he, an incomer, was still regarded with suspicion.

They met that rainy forenoon on rising ground a mile or so from Alan Redpath's lodgings in Seameads, horse and pony drawn up, flank to flank. Alan leaned from under the dripping hood and called out, 'Not much of a day for June, Mr Gamrie.'

'Not much at all, Dr Redpath.'

'Are you going far?'

'To Caddis, then round by the river to Hask.' Rain trickled on to his hat brim. He cleared his throat and said, 'If I might be askin', Dr Redpath, an' if it would not be injudickious of you in your professional capacity to answer, how is the health o' auld Mrs Mazzucco?'

'Alas,' Alan Redpath said, 'I fear she's failing.'

'Medicines no good?'

'Not my medicines at any rate.'

'Her time has come at last, d' you think?'

'I think, Mr Gamrie, she would welcome a visit from an elder.'

'Aye, thank you for the hint. I'll nip in on my way home. She's a good God-fearin' woman, even if she is o'er fond o' the drink. A prayer will comfort her. Will you be droppin' by again tonight?'

'I've done all I can for her,' Alan said. 'Her daughter knows where to find me if a crisis occurs, but my feeling is that the old lady will slip away peacefully some time towards morning.'

'I'd better not tarry, then?'

'Not too long, Mr Gamrie, not too long.' The elder made to flick the reins but Alan stopped him. 'I've a question for you, Mr Gamrie, if you can spare one more minute.'

'By all means.'

'Bette Hollander's niece, Susanne, I hear she's teaching at the school.'

'She is that.'

'I haven't been out to High Cross in a while,' Alan explained. 'The old man's in a settled spell and my services have not been required. The girl, though, is she happy, do you think?'

Mr Gamrie nodded. 'Aye, she's a bright one, Dr Redpath, but is she not a wee thing on the young side for you?'

'Come now,' Alan said, 'my interest is purely – well, she is appealing, I'll grant you, but she's not much more than a child, Mr Gamrie.'

'Children grow up fair quick in these parts, Dr Redpath.'

'Were you present at the interview?'

'I was – an' I did not let her off easy. The teacher was all for her from the start, an' one more pupil-teacher will do the school no harm.'

'I take it,' Alan Redpath said, 'that Bette Hollander proposed the girl for the post.'

'She did, backed by the minister himself.'

'By the minister?' said Alan, surprised.

'Fortunately, the lassie was reasonably versed in Scripture.'

'But the minister, Mr Oakley, pushed her forward?'

'He brought the matter to me.'

'I see,' Alan Redpath said.

'Is there somethin' wrong wi' that?'

'On the contrary, Mr Gamrie. I'm pleased that the girl's finding her feet. She struck me, as she seems to have struck you, as personable, and intelligent.'

'An asset to our community, aye,' Mr Gamrie said. 'Now, if there's no more you'll be needin' to know about the Hollander girl, or anythin' else, I must be on my way.'

'A good-day to you then, Mr Gamrie.'

'A good-day tae you, Dr Redpath.'

With a parting nod the elder flicked the rein against Matthew's cruppers, carefully steered the cart around the doctor's gig and set off down the empty road to Caddis, leaving young Alan Redpath, somewhat puzzled, to forge on into the rain, alone.

It struck Tom Oakley as curious that in the middle of the nineteenth century, with progress a national obsession, man had to travel by such a damnably circuitous route to reach the port of Dundee on the far bank of the Tay. He put the matter of route temporarily to one side while he dropped a hint to Effie that he would be spending Tuesday night in the town of Kirkcaldy, which lay in entirely the opposite direction to Dundee.

'Kirkcaldy!' Effie exclaimed. 'What are you going there for?'

'To address the Jute Workers' Christian Association.'

'On whose invite?'

'Roger Sanderson's.'

'Who's Roger Sanderson when he's at home?'

'Secretary of the Workers' Association. I may have to stay overnight.'

'Stay overnight?' said Effie.

'With Mr Sanderson.'

'Does Mr Sanderson have a wife?'

'What a strange question to ask, my dear. I believe Mr Sanderson does have a wife – and children, too.'

'Daughters?'

'Effie, Effie! I know little or nothing of the fellow's circumstances.'

'Why has he asked you, of all people, to address this Jute thing?'

'I do have a certain reputation as a speaker, you know.'

'Is there a fee?'

Tom hesitated. If he told her that a fee was involved she would expect him to clap the cash down on the table as soon as he got home. If he told her that no fee was involved then she would bristle, become suspicious and might even put her foot down.

He said, 'Two guineas.'

Effie pursed her lips. 'Is that all?'

'Oh, it's fair payment, I think,' Tom said. 'I'll be given an extra shilling or two towards my travel and, no doubt, supper and breakfast. After all, Effie, it's incumbent upon me to spread the Word and not be too mercenary about it.'

Effie was bathing Roland and Waylie in the same wooden tub in the middle of the kitchen. She filled a rag with lukewarm water, squeezed it over Waylie's soapy head and ignored his howls of protest as the suds stung his eyes.

Tom caressed his wife's spine, reassuringly. 'Two guineas will buy us several good joints of beef, will it not?'

Effie worked the rag savagely over Wayland's chest.

'I suppose it might,' she conceded. 'One night?'

'One night.'

'Kirkcaldy?'

'Kirkcaldy.'

She lifted her hands, dripping, from the tub and scowled. 'What do they want you to talk about?'

'Genesis,' Tom said and, smirking at his little conceit, wandered off into the study to plan in a little more detail his illicit trip to Dundee.

7

Buckie's joints had been aching for the past day or two, threatening another spell of feverish illness, but he said nothing that might spoil Bette's trip. Sandy Raiker was due at half past nine to drive Bette to the coach that left the Dalriada at ten. At twenty minutes past the hour Buckie dressed and, leaning on his stick, hobbled out to bid his wife farewell.

Bette was at the table, finishing off her breakfast. She was dressed in the voluminous cape that she'd bought in London and with powdered cheeks and rouged lips, Buckie thought, looked as tasty as a sugar plum.

'You're not exactly travelling light, Mother, are you?' Louis said.

He wore a greasy dressing-gown over his nightshirt and was eating strips of fried bacon with his fingers.

Buckie stuck his nose around the living-room door.

Bette dropped the porridge bowl. 'Is that Raiker now?'

'No,' Buckie said. 'Not yet.'

'He's late. What time is it?'

'Just gone the half hour,' said Buckie.

'See if he's coming down the hill.'

Buckie was hungry. He wanted his breakfast. He wanted a big dish of coffee, and peace to drink it. He fumbled with the front door and teased it open. Ajax lay on the porch step as if even his high spirits had been dampened by the weather. He rolled his shaggy head and looked up at Buckie, balefully.

It was a miserable day for June, a miserable day for

travelling. Buckie was glad that he had decided not to accompany his wife to Dundee.

He would have enjoyed seeing the ships, smelling the tar, hearing the deep-sea sailors cry out as they raised sail, scraped hulls or loaded stores. He would have enjoyed striding along the High Street and down by Seagate to join other retired mariners on the Esplanade and jaw about the old days. But town traffic was dangerous to an old man who could hardly walk and he was too realistic to imagine that he could rediscover his youth just by crossing the Tay.

Bette appeared in the doorway. She peered into the mist. 'Where is that man?'

'He'll be, he'll be,' said Buckie.

Louis, cup in hand, leaned on the doorpost. 'Are you dining with the Coburns, Mama?' he asked.

Bette shot round. 'Why would I be dining with the Coburns?'

'I thought you said you were dining with Harry Coburn.'

'No, I said I might dine with the McLeans.'

'I don't think I remember the McLeans,' said Louis.

'Albert McLean was a Guild councillor for a year or two,' Buckie said. 'Griselda was a friend of yours at one time, wasn't she, dearest?'

'Where *is* that man?' said Bette, distractedly.

Ajax rowed himself along the planking on his belly, slipped, like a seal, from the end of the porch and padded off around the house.

'What's in the bag, Mother?' Louis asked, casually. 'Your ball gown?'

'I'm not visiting Dundee for amusement, Louis,' she snapped. 'It's business that takes me there, family business.'

'Collecting cash from the Merchants and Traders is hardly going to consume more than ten minutes of your time, Mama.' Louis sipped coffee and wiped his lip with his forefinger. '*Are* you dining with some of the old crowd?'

'I – I . . .'

'Sandy,' Buckie said. 'Here he comes at last.'

With a nervous whinny, Bette snatched her bag from the hall, threw herself down the steps and, three or four minutes later, vanished into the mist without so much as a farewell kiss for her son, or her husband.

'Nancy,' Susanne said, 'do let me help you.'

Nancy hugged the mixing bowl to her chest. 'It's not your place to help me.'

'I used to beat batter for Cook when I was small.'

'Aye, well, I'm not one o' your fancy London servants. Awa' an' keep Louis amused.'

Susanne felt no animosity towards the woman, none of the resentment that the woman seemed to harbour towards her. After all, she'd spent the afternoon teaching five-year-olds and was surely responsible enough to stir pudding batter.

'Why don't you like me? What harm have I done you? Just because I'm small doesn't mean to say I'm simple. I teach school, you know.'

'I'm well aware o' that,' said Nancy. 'The lady put you up for it. An' you've never thought to ask yourself why, have you?'

It was early evening, close to the longest day of the year but the light was like that of a winter afternoon.

Nancy put the bowl down, kicked open the gate of the stove. A blast of hot air wafted across the floor and Thimble, who'd been dozing by the grate, transferred herself to a more comfortable position.

Susanne hesitated, then asked, 'Nancy, why *did* she do it?'

The woman's big yellow teeth showed under the curl of her lip. 'Your auntie's a born cack-ulator. She knows Louis'll never be able to take care o' himself. Clever Louis, aye. So clever he'll never be fit to earn a crust for his own breakfast, let alone feed a family.'

'What does this have to do with me?'

'How does a poor woman make her way in this world?'

'I don't know,' said Susanne.

'She marries into money. Why shouldn't a man do the same?'

'Do you think Aunt Bette brought me here to marry Louis?'

'It's as plain as the nose on your face.'

'What if Louis doesn't want to marry me?'

'He'll do what his mother tells him.'

Susanne felt herself rise like a sponge pudding, growing lighter by the second.

'What are you grinnin' at, girl?' Nancy said. 'God preserve us! You're already filled wi' the lust that allowed sin to enter the Garden an' brought us all low in the sight o' the Lord.'

'Stuff and nonsense, Nancy,' Susanne said. 'What about you?'

'Me?'

'Why have *you* never married?' Susanne said. 'Is it because nobody ever asked you? I'm not surprised, given the low opinion you have of gentlemen.'

The woman opened her mouth, then closed it with a snap. She released a little 'uh' from the back of her throat as if she were choking on a fish bone.

'Gentlemen?' she said. 'I only ever met but one gentleman an' he's sittin' in the chair next door. Your uncle is my Samaritan, my shepherd. If it hadn't been for him I wouldn't be here. Nah, nah, it's not gentlemen I've a low opinion of, it's *men*. I was dropt in a lane near the Camperdown docks, sick unto death, when he went off on the boats. Hardly older than you, I was. He went off on the boats an' never looked back. I'd have died in the gutter if Captain Hollander hadn't took me in. I've served him ever since an', if God wills it, I'll serve him till one o' us dies.'

Susanne was too young to comprehend the nature of the

paradox that Nancy Bissett represented. She preferred simple narratives of love and devotion.

'La, la, la,' Susanne said, gaily. 'I have you, Nancy, do I not?'

'Have me?'

'I know your secret.'

'There's no secret to me, girl.'

'Oh, I think there is.' Susanne dipped a finger into the pudding bowl and sampled the sticky mix. 'In any case, nobody found me languishing in the gutter. If I'm destined to marry Louis, there's nothing you nor I can do about it.'

'If you believe that,' said Nancy, 'hell mend you, Susanne Thorne.' Then, taking up the bowl, she began to beat the pudding mix once more, and refused to say another word.

If Tom Oakley had been less concerned with hiding his destination he might have found time to consult the *Fifeshire Advertiser* in whose columns he would have discovered the announcement of a cattle fair in Perth.

He walked six miles from the manse to the railway halt at Caddis where, huddled on a bench on the platform, wrapped in a shabby overcoat and a floppy hat, he felt like the biggest fool in Christendom. He felt even more of a fool when the train from Burntisland arrived and he discovered that no seats were available in the covered carriages and that he would be obliged to travel in a fourth-class open truck behind the locomotive, along with three giggling lassies, two farm labourers and a sheepdog.

As if that wasn't bad enough, out in the middle of nowhere a flange on one of the engine's wheels gave way, the train slid off the rails, crunched to a jarring halt and Tom was projected into a tangle of screaming girls and agitated dog. Clutching his hat with one hand and his bag in the other, he struck his head against the side of the truck. For good measure, he was clawed across the cheek by the collie, and wound up, bleeding profusely, with his nose buried in the lap of a hysterical girl. Well aware that he was supposed to be in Kirkcaldy, not lying in a heap in an iron-sided box thirty miles in the opposite direction, he quickly disentangled himself, clambered out of the truck and, with blood running down his face and his head splitting, started out across the fields.

He walked for half an hour in pouring rain over rough pasture before he stumbled on a lane lurking between hedgerows and a hamlet by the name of Bonniebank, though there was nothing 'bonnie' about it. He wandered into a blacksmith's shop and told his tale of woe to a lanky bellows-lad who nodded stoically, as if railway disasters were a daily occurrence, and then loped off to find his father.

The blacksmith was much affected by the news that the noon train from Burntisland had slipped off the track and that Tom's grandmother was lingering on her deathbed in Dundee. He informed Tom that although Bonniebank was some miles south of the Tay and a fair way from Perth he was willing to put a horse and cart at Tom's disposal and, for the sake of expediency, drive him to the ferry at Tayport. Concussed and desperate, Tom agreed to monetary terms so usurious that in normal circumstances he might have forgotten that he was a man of the cloth and told the blacksmith where to stuff his horse and cart.

About half past three they set off for Tayport.

About eight that night Tom finally arrived in the Ralston Hotel.

Bette Hollander was lurking in the lobby.

'Where the devil have you been?' she snapped.

Soaked, starving and with an aching head, Tom did not deign to reply.

*   *   *

'This is awfy kind o' you, Mrs Oakley,' Angus Gamrie said. 'It wasn't my intention to cadge supper, only to deliver the monthly list o' marriage banns to your husband who, so you tell me, has gone out of town.'

'He has, that he has,' said Effie. 'Eat your broth, Mr Gamrie. There's a nice bit of steak to follow.'

'Steak, is it, Mrs Oakley? My, my, it's not often an old bachelor like me gets treated to steak.' With a napkin tucked into his collar, Angus Gamrie spooned up broth. He clucked in appreciation. 'I can taste the ham bone in this, ma'am, an' it fair tickles the palate.'

'We don't have much, Mr Gamrie, but what we have, we share.'

'That's the Christian way, Mrs Oakley, the Christian way.'

The frying-pan rested on the hob and a small beef steak, drenched in flour, on a tin platter. Effie had intended to eat the steak after she had fed the children and put them to bed. But the arrival of the elder on such a dreary night and his little gift of cotton drawers – infant size – had softened her heart. She had invited him in to join her for supper, something she wouldn't have dared do if Tom had been at home. When Mr Gamrie had appeared Zena and Greg had taken flight, dragging all the children, except Roland, upstairs.

Effie snuggled Roland, half asleep, in the crook of her arm and, one-handed, slipped the beef steak into the frying-pan and put it on the hottest part of the stove. 'Bloody or burned, Mr Gamrie?'

'As you wish, Mrs Oakley. I take my meat as it comes.'

Roland, thumb in mouth, glowered over his mother's shoulder.

Mr Gamrie waggled a finger at him. 'Cuckoo,' he warbled. 'Cuckoo.'

Roland sucked hard on his thumb, and scowled.

The meat hissed, sizzled and released a cloud of savoury blue smoke.

Effie flipped it over with a broad-bladed knife. She would have fried onions too, except that she had run out of onions and the crop in the manse garden wasn't yet ripe for drawing. Meagre fare: a small piece of beef steak taken with brown bread, not even a fried potato to enhance it, nor a scrap of the gingerbread pudding that the children had consumed for afters.

Mr Gamrie rose and, carrying bowl and spoon, went to the tub by the window and washed the items thoroughly. He dried them on a handy rag, put them on a shelf, and returned to his chair at the table.

Mrs Oakley stared at him.

'What?' Angus said.

'Nothing,' Effie said and, turning away from him, smiled.

The bony remains of a tough old hen and some scraps of salad lay on a plate on the floor, together with a bottle of sour red wine, now empty.

The whale-master's wife lay naked on the bed, waiting for her lover to finish chewing. He had scrawled a name in the register, as the laws of the town required, had snatched up the key and marched her off upstairs. She had trotted after him like a little poodle dog, calling out his name, 'Tom, Tom, Tom,' panting upstairs to the first-floor room. There he had torn off his overcoat and hat and tossed them on the bed, had ripped off his collar, unbuttoned his coat and shirt and, with the frayed towel that Ralston's had provided, mopped rain-water from his hair while Bette had loitered uncertainly in the doorway.

'You,' he'd said, 'go back downstairs and find me some food.'

'Food?'

'I'm starved, woman. Order food and a bottle of wine.'

'Brought up, you mean?'

'Yes, to your room, not mine.'

'But Tom, I thought . . .'

'You're not here to think,' Tom had said. 'You're here to do as I say.'

'Hot food?'

'Anything, damn it.'

She had hesitated, scared that she would be held accountable for whatever disaster had befallen him on the way to Dundee, then she had gone downstairs. Now she lay on her back on the bed and stared at the flicker of lamplight on the ceiling. She had never lain like this before, spread out like a sacrifice, her breasts flattened, the swell of her stomach displayed. She was ashamed, deeply, bitterly ashamed of the conceit that had brought her here and exposed her for what she really was – the fat, unlovely wife of a useless failure, waiting to be mounted like a mare.

She heard him smack his hands together and, lifting from the bolster, saw that he was naked too, naked and massive in the light from the lamp. Her anxiety turned to fear. She drew up her knees and tried to hide herself but he reached out and grabbed her by the ankles and pulled her round again, pulled her legs wide apart. He put his hand on her, not gently, and made her cry out. Still holding her with his fingers, he smacked himself again and straddled her, thrust himself into her face.

'Isn't this what you want?' he hissed.

She swallowed, open-mouthed, and winced.

He put his left hand to her cheeks and pinched them.

'Uh-huh! Uh-huh!' he said. 'What's wrong, woman? Have you lost your tongue? Isn't *this* what you came for?'

And Bette, almost choking, mumbled: 'Yes.'

*   *   *

Buckie was asleep in his chair by the fire. Ajax sprawled at his feet, breaking wind and sighing. Thimble snuggled against the dog, paws over her nose, the tip of her tail twitching languidly. Nancy had retired to the kitchen, Louis had spread out his musical sheets and Susanne, half asleep, browsed over a little pamphlet that Miss Primrose had given her to read. London seemed a long way off, in time as well as space. Papa would not have felt at home in Strayhorn but she wondered if he would have approved of Louis. Miss Ashworth would have taken to her cousin, she felt sure, for Miss Ashworth had always had an eye for handsome young men.

'You're nodding off, cousin,' Louis said. 'I suggest you surrender gracefully and toddle upstairs to bed.'

'It's early.' Susanne wriggled and sat up.

'No, dear heart, it's late,' Louis said. 'Shall I carry you upstairs?'

'And tuck me in?'

'If you wish.'

'No,' Susanne said. 'Thank you all the same.'

'You've become very independent of late.'

'Have I?'

'I think it's the influence of that girl, that Zena.'

'Nonsense!' Susanne closed the pamphlet, tucked it into her skirt, rose and kissed her cousin's cheek. 'With your mama away, I'm the woman of the house, remember, and must, therefore, be treated with respect.'

'Hah!' Louis put an arm about her and drew her to him. 'Just as well for us chaps, then, that Mama's due back tomorrow.'

'Oh, don't you think I manage a household just as well as your mother? Don't you think I'll make someone a good wife some day?'

Louis let his hand slide from her waist to the curve of her hip.

'Possibly,' he said, 'in time.'

His lips were stained with wine, his eyes huge. She saw the muscles of his jaw tighten, the long vein in the muscle of his neck swell. She pulled herself away but his hand lingered, sliding across the material of her dress.

'Not so hasty, young 'un,' he said, thickly. 'Ae fond kiss afore we part.'

'You've had one.'

'I want another.'

She made a game of it, teasing.

She held him at arm's length, or almost so, placed her lips on his lips and kissed him with a smacking sound just loud enough to cause Thimble to open one eye and Ajax to lift his shaggy head.

'There,' Susanne said, 'that's all you're having.'

'That's all I want. Goodnight to you, madam.'

'Goodnight to you, sir,' said Susanne, and took herself off to bed.

The hour was late, the weather foul. Mr Gamrie seemed in no hurry to leave, however. Effie, her hunger appeased, sat knee to knee with him, toasting in front of the stove, Roland fast asleep in her arms.

Mr Gamrie's capacity for tea almost matched her own.

They were well into a second pot before Zena put her head around the door, said, 'Oh!' sharply, and went off upstairs again.

'May I?' The elder gestured towards the teapot.

'Help yourself, Mr Gamrie.'

'An' yourself, ma'am?'

'Well, perhaps just a drop more, thank you.'

He held the pot carefully and poured into her cup, watching for her nod and cutting off the stream of pale brown liquid at exactly the right moment.

'Milk?'

'Please,' said Effie.

'An' I know you take sugar.'

'I do.'

There were those who might have considered the polite little exchange banal but Effie Oakley wasn't one of them. She relished every courteous word, however hackneyed. Mr Gamrie leaned across her and stirred her tea. Effie held the cup away from the baby, and sipped. Mr Gamrie sat back, legs stuck out, and sipped tea too.

'If it wouldn't be too forward, Mrs Oakley, might I remark that the minister's loss has been my gain.'

'It's not forward at all, Mr Gamrie,' Effie said, 'though I'm not sure quite what you mean by it.'

'Oh no, no, nothin' that doesn't confolate wi' modesty,' Angus Gamrie assured her. 'I meant it as a compliment.'

'Then I'll accept it as a compliment.'

'I meant only that if Mr Oakley had been at home, I wouldn't have enjoyed an evenin' in your company, an' such a grand supper.'

'Hardly grand, Mr Gamrie.'

'Grand by my standards, ma'am.'

Effie hesitated. 'How long have you known me, Mr Gamrie?'

'Since you first came here. What would that be – seven years ago?'

'Nearer ten,' said Effie.

'Is it really? My, my, how time flies.'

'After ten years, Mr Gamrie, since we – you an' I – are friends, would it be improper for you to call me Effie?'

'Well?' Mr Gamrie raised a startled eyebrow. 'Well, I'll have to think about that one, Mrs Oakley.'

'Mightn't I be permitted, at the least when we're alone, to call you Angus? Would you think about that, too, Mr Gamrie?'

'I would,' Angus said. 'I will.'

'And you'll be sure to let me know what you decide?'

'How will I be doin' that, Mrs Oakley?'

'A nod, a nod at the gate on Sunday.'

'Noddin' on a Sunday?' said Angus, dubiously. 'Aye, now that does require some serious deliberation.'

'Did our Saviour never nod on a Sunday?'

Angus chuckled. 'You have me there, Mrs Oakley. To the best o' my knowledge there's not a word in the Gospels about Him noddin' at all. It's hardly the sort o' theologic problem that's discussed in the General Assembly. If you like I could raise the question wi' the minister, or, come to think on it, you could raise it wi' the minister yourself since you're like to see him before I do.'

'I doubt,' Effie said, 'if it's the sort of question my husband would give much heed to, especially if it came from me.'

'In the absence of contrary factors, then,' said Angus, 'an' for the sake o' avoidin' debate, I think I'll jump in an' give the nod now.'

He put the teacup on the hob and got to his feet.

He stood before her, legs apart.

'Tell me, Effie,' he said, 'where is the minister, since he's not at home?'

'Kirkcaldy.'

'An' what, Effie, is he doin' in Kirkcaldy?'

'Addressin' the Jute Workers' Christian Association.'

'The Jute Workers' Christian Association!' Angus said, nodding.

'They're payin' two guineas for the lecture.'

'Are they now?' said Angus. 'Well, that'll not go amiss.'

He rocked on the balls of his feet then seemed, Effie thought, to give himself a little shake as if he had reached a decision.

He smiled down at her and her baby. 'You make a very

pretty picture, Effie,' he said. 'Now, if you'll permit me, we'll say a wee blessin' for you an' your children to keep you safe in God's hands till such times as the minister returns.' He paused. 'When will that be, by the way?'

'Tomorrow.'

'Tomorrow, aye,' Angus Gamrie said, then, laying one hand on Roland's sleepy head and the other on Effie's shoulder, thanked the Lord for His bounteous mercies and asked Him to bring peace to this house.

Susanne wakened suddenly. She had not, she felt, been asleep for long. She lay motionless for a second before she realised that the sheet had become wet. She slipped a hand between her thighs and found that her nightgown was wet too. Even as a small child she had never been a bed-wetter. Flinging back the covers, she groped for the candle, lit it, stared down at her lap, and screamed.

The bedroom door flew open.

'My God!' Louis shouted. 'What is it? What's wrong, Susanne?'

'*I'm dying. I'm dying. Look, look at the blood. Help me, help me.*'

Louis disappeared.

She sat on the edge of the mattress watching blood drain from her body. Soon there would be none left. Louis couldn't save her. She was too far gone. She dropped to her knees and flopped to the floor, expecting to be carried up to heaven at any moment.

Nancy came clumping upstairs.

Susanne heard her uncle shout, 'What is it? What's wrong with the child? I'll run for the doctor? Will I run for the doctor?'

Even in her final moments, the notion of her poor crippled uncle running anywhere struck her as ridiculous.

Louis yelled, 'There, Nancy, there, didn't I tell you?'

The woman's bulky shape blotted out the candlelight. She wore a faded flannel nightshirt, patched with bits of lace, feet and legs bare. She squatted by Susanne's side and turned her over.

'Huh!' Nancy said. 'Dyin', indeed!'

Doomed and helpless, Susanne lay in Nancy's arms.

Louis loomed over the woman's shoulder, staring.

'You,' Nancy said. 'Get out.'

'What – what is it?' Louis asked.

'She's not dyin',' Nancy said. 'It's only the curse of Eve all we women have to suffer when we reach a certain age.'

'The curse of . . .' Louis's brows shot up, his mouth popped open. He stepped back. 'Oh!' he said, in a shocked whisper. 'Oh, that's disgusting!' then lurched out of the bedroom, and slammed the door.

Nancy changed the bed, fished a clean nightgown and a pair of heavy winter drawers from the dressing-table and told Susanne what to do to make herself comfortable. She helped the girl back into bed, gave her brandy to drink then seated herself on the velvet chair.

'Laudanum's my comforter,' Nancy said, 'when the grippe takes me bad. He knew what to do, the old doctor did. He left me enough o' the mixture to see me through the worse, but it's not in Redpath's nature to be generous.'

Susanne sat up against the bolster. She was calmer now. The presence of the big woman was consoling; so too was the realisation that nature had decreed that she was a woman at last, fit to marry and bear children.

'Where's Louis?'

'Hidin' under his bed, I expect,' Nancy grunted.

'Did I scare him?'

'All women scare him.'

'He said I was disgusting.'

'He's not the first man to be scared o' what happens inside a woman's belly, nor what comes out o' it.'

'Will he – will he hate me now, Nancy?'

'Not if he's as clever as he thinks he is,' said Nancy.

Louis sat at the organ with the dog at his feet. Moonlight scuffed the window, picking out rain spots on the glass. He was afraid that if he lit the oil lamp Susanne, all soiled and stained, would creep across the passageway, scratch at his door and cajole him into letting her in. The thought made him shudder, for he could not shake off the fear that he was responsible, that touching her had caused her to bleed.

At one time, he had flirted with the notion of studying medicine. He had envisaged himself as a famous surgeon, wealthy enough to please Mama. But, having bought a collection of textbooks, he could not bear to look at them, to study depictions of writhing intestines, babies curled up like runner beans and breasts disfigured by disease. Even the language had made him queasy, and his dream of being a doctor, let alone a surgeon, passed swiftly, like so many of his other fancies. Meanwhile he needed money and assumed that Mama would find him a wife to attend to his material needs. Now that he had seen his cousin in her natural state, however, marriage seemed even less attractive than medicine, for Susanne was so small and vulnerable in her parts that the thought of joining with her filled him with dismay.

Ajax raised his head, and growled.

Footsteps in the passageway. Louis rose from the bench like a shadow and looked around the littered room in search of a suitable hiding place.

Boards creaked outside his door. Someone was searching for him. Susanne was searching for him. He sank into a squatting position, a hand cupped over Ajax's snout. He could hear Susanne breathing, sense her expectation, and closing his eyes tightly, could see in his mind's eye her squalid nakedness.

'Go away,' he hissed. 'Go away.'

And with a wry little grunt, her duty done, Nancy did.

She had put the youngest out on the drying lawn. The grass was still wet but Effie was of the opinion that a gentle soaking would do her babies no harm. Petal was old enough now to fetch her if Waylie became too adventurous or Morven toppled over. Once she'd finished the washing, she would bring them in, dry and change them before Tom arrived home from Kirkcaldy.

The kitchen was thick with steam from the boiler at the back door. She worked soap into a dirty napkin and applied the scrubbing brush. She was damp and sweating, hair straggling, her stockings, all wrinkled, hanging halfway down her shins. Even so, she was happy this morning, thinking about Angus Gamrie and how much pleasure his visit had given her.

She did not hear him enter the kitchen.

He put both hands about her waist and jerked her away from the tub.

Effie shrieked, then, swinging round, said, 'You!'

'Indeed, it is, my dear,' Tom said. 'Who did you think it would be? I caught the first train from Kirkcaldy.'

Effie said, 'Did it all go accordin' to plan?'

He released her. 'What do you mean – plan?'

'Were you cheered to the rafters?'

'The attendance was, I confess, a wee bit thin.'

'Did they pay you?'

'They did.' Tom dug into his wallet and fished out two worn sovereigns. 'See, we'll have meat for many a Sunday to come.'

'Uh-huh!' Effie said, less pleased than she should have been. 'What happened to your face?'

'Oh that!' Tom touched the scratches on his cheek. 'I had a fall, a tumble.'

'Drunk, were you?'

He laughed, mirthlessly. 'Now you know that isn't my habit. In any case Mr Sanderson is steadfastly opposed to the taking of strong waters.'

Effie peered at the livid scratches and his bruised forehead.

'They weren't throwin' things at you then?'

'Hah,' Tom said. 'No, I stumbled on the stairs of Mr Sanderson's tenement in Clarence Street, put my hand up to protect myself and my nails . . .'

'Your nails?'

'Self-laceration,' Tom said. 'Yes, and a knock on the head.'

'Before or after?'

'Before or after what?'

'You addressed the multitude?'

'After.'

Effie nodded, less convinced than uninterested.

She held out a soapy hand.

Tom dropped the sovereigns into her palm.

She closed her fingers on the coins, and her doubts shrivelled. He looked pale, almost waxy, in the sunlight, and very tired. But she had no reason to question him further and, with the fee safe in her possession, turned to the washing tub and pushed up her sleeves.

By the time she looked round again Tom had wandered off into the study, taking his overcoat and baggage with him but not the chased-silver snuff horn which – though Effie knew it not – he'd 'popped' to a dealer in Market Street to mark an end to his fling with the whale-master's wife.

8

On the butt of the old harbour wall three industrious fishermen were washing ballast stones from the *Cormorant* to freshen up the bilge water. On Monday night there had been a drove east of the Bass. By Wednesday the shore at Anstruther was strewn with herring, and prices had dropped to five shillings the barrel.

'A hunded cran, I hear,' Sandy Raiker said.

'A hundred an' eight,' said Bobby Benbow.

'Now that's a haul and a half, that is,' Louis said. 'Pappy tells me the Anstruther boats have been shooting nets three in the day. Is that so?'

'Aye, it's a fact,' said Sandy.

'There'd be more too,' said Benbow, 'if those French luggers hadn't been lyin' off Earlsferry.'

Sandy Raiker puffed on his pipe and peered from the window of the Dalriada at the fishermen labouring in the rain. 'Aye, now,' he said, 'if the season lives up to its promise there'll be some damned wealthy citizens on this coast.'

'An' a shoal o' weddings as well,' said Benbow.

'Weddings?' Louis frowned.

'Hardly a lassie on the length o' the shore won't lift her skirts for a man wi' a pocketful o' chink,' Benbow said.

'Really!' Louis exclaimed.

'Aye, an' I don't just mean the whores,' the tiger went on. 'I mean lassies who keep themselves so tight you'd think butter wouldn't melt in their mouths. Then along comes the drave to end all draves an' the skirts go up an' the drawers come down an' before you can say "knife" there's puddin' in the pot an' a ring on the finger, an' another good man gone to the bottom.'

'To the bottom, aye.' Sandy nodded.

'All lassies?' said Louis. 'All girls?'

'All but the few who don't know what it's for,' said Benbow.

'What what's for?' said Louis.

The carter and the tiger stared at him in silence for half a second.

Benbow laughed. 'Is it the missie you're thinkin' of? Well, I'm here to tell you she'll not drop for anyone. She might nibble a bit o' shortbread in your house, Louis, but she'll nibble nothin' else.'

'Oh,' Louis said. 'You mean Darsie?'

'Who else?' Benbow said. 'You could pile herrin' barrels from here to St Giles an' it would cut no ice wi' her ladyship. It'll take a better man than you, Hollander, to peel the gilt off *her* gingerbread.'

'She'll marry a duke or an earl,' Sandy said. 'Coburn will settle a huge dowry on her to lure them in, but it'll take a big fish to fill her barrel.'

'Aye, I've seen her strut,' said Benbow, with relish. 'She might tickle your fancy wi' those pantalettes but she's got a figure to tempt an anchorite.'

'An' you're no anchorite, are you?' Sandy said.

'Me? Nay, I'd as soon ride a sharp sickle as tackle that girl. She'll never love anyone but herself.'

'Benbow,' Louis interrupted, 'what are you doing here, apart from slandering Miss Coburn? Shouldn't you be grooming Harry Coburn's horses or jumping up and down like a jackanapes on the board of the curricle?'

'What's got into him?' the tiger enquired.

Sandy Raiker shrugged. 'Hey, Louis, have you a notion to be Darsie Coburn's catch?'

'Answer my question, Benbow, please,' said Louis.

'The curricle's in the yard,' Benbow said. 'Mr Coburn's off talking to Jackie Longmuir.'

'The harbour-master!' Sandy shook his head. 'What does Harry Coburn want wi' the harbour-master?'

'It's business.'

'What sort o' business?'

'Land business,' said Benbow.

'Land? Here?' said Sandy. 'There's no land here.'

'There's the sheds.'

'What, the old curing sheds?' said Louis.

'Aye.'

'Jackie Longmuir doesn't own the sheds?' said Sandy.

'No, but he'll know who does,' said Benbow.

Louis sat back and cocked one knee over the other. He had put away three pots of ale and his head was by no means clear. He had been offended by the tiger's slur on the person of Darsie Coburn, but intrigued and titillated too. Business, though! Coburn business had more merit as a topic. It struck him that he might curry favour with Mama by fetching home a tasty bit of gossip.

'I thought,' Sandy said, 'the government were puttin' up a sum o' money to repair the harbour wall an' open up the curin' sheds.'

'Nothin' will come from the government,' said Benbow. 'The only way trade'll come back to this god-blighted spot is if somebody's daft enough to build us a railway line, an' nobody in their right senses is goin' to do that.'

'Been talk for years about a railway line,' said Sandy.

'Talk, aye, all just talk,' said Benbow.

'If it's all just talk,' said Louis, 'why is Harry Coburn sounding out the harbour-master?'

'Hah!' said Benbow. 'Do you think he's goin' to tell me? I'm only the chap who feeds the horses an' polishes the tack.'

'An' keeps his ear to the ground,' said Sandy.

'True,' Benbow admitted. 'I do hear things I shouldn't.'

'Like what?' said Louis.

'Like that our Mr Coburn has it in mind to go into railway stock again.'

'After the last fiasco,' said Louis, 'nobody will give him the time of day.'

'If there's one thing I've learned in my years o' service at Macklin House,' said Benbow, slyly tapping his nose, 'it's never to underestimate the will o' the master. If Mr Coburn sets his mind on somethin' he has ways an' means undreamed of by the likes o' you an' me to get it.'

'He's a broker, for heaven's sake,' said Louis, 'not a magician.'

'Same thing in some folks' book,' said Sandy Raiker. 'Mr Coburn'll not be flyin' so high this time, though, if he's only got his eye on our old fish sheds.'

'It's a start,' said Benbow.

'A start for what?' said Louis.

'Linkin' Strayhorn to the rest o' the world,' said Bobby Benbow.

And Louis, a little too tipsy to share the tiger's optimism, or Mr Coburn's vision, brayed with laughter, stepped over Ajax and tottered to the counter to buy another round.

'Drunk, you're drunk, you lumpkin,' Bette Hollander shouted. Bouncing up on her toes, she boxed Louis's ears while he stood in the hall, head bowed, and meekly accepted his punishment. 'Where did you get the money for drink, that's what I'd like to know? Did he give it to you? Did your father – Buckie, did you give this boy money?'

Her uncle glanced at the door of the bedroom as if calculating the possibility of escape. 'I – ah – I might have done. Inadvertently.'

'Inadvertently?' Bette yelped. 'Inadvertently? How can you give away money inadvertently when you know I have to count every penny just to keep bread on the table?'

Buckie lifted his shoulders and leaned into the stick. 'Well, I just thought he deserved a bit of respite.'

'Respite? Respite from what? From me, do you mean?' Bette raged. 'Do you think he has to escape from me, his own mother, his' – she cuffed Louis once more – 'his own – loving – mother? How much did you spend?'

'I gave him a shilling,' said Buckie.

'A shilling! Where did you get a shilling?'

'I – I found it in my pocket.'

'Found it?'

Bette kicked at her husband's stick but he was a shade too quick for her. He whipped it out of her reach and braced his shoulder against the clock case.

'Here am I working my fingers to the bone to keep you nourished and you go squandering money as if it grew on trees. I'm sick of you, both of you, all of you,' Bette shouted and stalked into the living-room where Nancy, feigning deafness, continued to set out the table for supper.

Crouched at the top of the stairs, Susanne resisted an urge to rush down to console her cousin. She was, after all, a woman now, though Aunt Bette had offered few words of consolation on her changed state, and no advice at all. Her uncle had been kindness itself, though, feeding her almond toffees from a tin in his bedroom and allowing her a sip of the brandy and soda with which he warmed his bones in rainy weather. Even Nancy had been less gruff than usual and had shepherded Susanne into the kitchen when it seemed that Aunt Bette's anger was about to boil over. But Louis – Louis who until now had been her anchor, her rock, had hidden himself away, skulking in his room and hammering tunelessly on the harmonium, or slipping off to town.

Susanne watched her uncle limp forward and help his son out of his overcoat. He looked, Susanne thought, so helpless and forlorn there in the hall, hair plastered to his brow and head bowed.

'A shilling!' Louis muttered. 'One damned shilling.'

'Now, now,' said Buckie, an arm about his son's shoulder. 'Now, now.'

'As if one damned shilling mattered when we're sitting on a gold mine.'

'Louis,' Buckie murmured. 'Please.'

'Well, we are, aren't we?' Louis snapped, then, turning, charged upstairs, almost knocking Susanne over in his haste.

'Louis?'

'Out of my way, girl,' he snapped. 'Get out of my way,' and, trampling over her, blundered along the passageway and vanished into his room.

To his father's surprise, and Susanne's dismay, Louis came down for supper. He had shaved the stubble from his chin and washed his face. He wore a faded velvet smoking jacket over a frilled shirt, like a portrait of Lord Byron, but had the dazed appearance of a person still under the influence of drink and refused to answer questions except with a shake of the head or a curt nod.

Silence was not in Bette's nature, though.

'Is the soup too salty?'

'No, my dear, it's . . .'

'I see the weather's improving.'

'Yes, the wind's . . .'

'Will we have a fine spell? I wonder.'

'If the glass is anything . . .'

'Susanne, do you wish a glass of water?'

'No, thank you. I have . . .'

Bette rattled on and on, too impatient to allow a response.

Powdered cheeks, rouged lips; like Louis, she had taken care with her appearance, as if mother and son were actors in a play.

Susanne kept her eyes down and dutifully ate a few mouthfuls of the baked cod that Nancy had spent so much time preparing.

Louis ate voraciously, grabbing and stuffing with total disregard for courtesy. With each mouthful, he seemed to swell within the velvet jacket. His ashen cheeks grew flushed and little beads of sweat glistened on his brow. He cleaned the dish of the last few flakes, wiped the sauce with a heel of bread, then murdered the apple charlotte that followed by stabbing it with a fork and drowning it in cream.

He wiped his mouth on the back of his hand, stretched his arms above his head, smiled a faint, crooked smile and called out, 'Nancy, bring in the cheese, if you would be so good.' The request, though polite, seemed shocking after his long silence. 'And the oatcakes.'

He placed his forearms flat on the table, watched Nancy enter the living-room and set down a plate of cheese and oatcakes and, with it, a pat of butter floating in a little water-dish. The servant, too, had rehearsed her part. How many times, Susanne wondered, had similar scenes been played out?

She felt her stomach tighten when Louis lifted the butter knife and, wagging it between finger and thumb, finally addressed his mother.

'You're killing me, you know,' he said. 'You are, Mother, you're slowly killing me. I don't think you'll be happy until I'm dead.'

'Louis, what a thing to say,' Buckie put in.

'No,' Louis went on. 'No, it's true. If I don't get out of this house soon I will die.'

'One does not die of indulgence,' Aunt Bette said. 'One may

die of *self*-indulgence, of course; that, I believe, is the direction in which you are travelling. It has nothing to do with me.'

'Does it not?' Louis dropped the butter knife on to the plate with a clatter. 'Oh, does it not? *Nothing* has anything to do with you, Mama. You have absolved yourself of all responsibility out of a sense that you are better than we are, that we do not deserve you.'

'Huh!'

'You bring a stranger into the house without asking my permission.'

'I do not need your permission, Louis.'

'I am tolerated here, that's all. Barely tolerated.'

'Are you drunk, still?' Aunt Bette said.

'I am as sober as you are,' Louis told her.

The tenor of the argument was oddly formal; not a voice had been raised and only the clatter of the butter knife indicated that strong emotions lay behind the exchange. Susanne crimped her elbows to her sides. If she had been less grown up, she would have slithered under the table, like Thimble.

'If you are sober, as you claim,' Bette said, 'then I believe you owe your cousin an apology.'

'Do I? Why?'

'Because you insulted her.'

'No, Mama, it is I who have been insulted.'

'You have the skin of an elephant, Louis.'

'I have feelings, Mama, feelings that you cannot possibly understand.'

'You feel nothing that isn't related to your own selfish pursuits.'

'Pappy gave me a shilling. I had a jug of ale with the gentlemen . . .'

'Gentlemen?'

'. . . the gentlemen at the Dalriada. What, tell me, is the harm in that?'

'It is money wasted, money we can ill afford. You are being indulged, Louis, favoured in a manner that any young man would envy. We have paid for your schooling, now we are sending you to Edinburgh to fritter away your, *our* meagre portion learning – what d'you call it? – harmony.'

'I am to study musical form, Mama, as well you know.'

'Oh, I know, I know. Only too well do I know.'

'If you do not wish me to pursue my passion for music why did you buy me a harmonium?'

'A question,' Aunt Bette said, 'that I often ask myself.'

'Is it grudged?'

'No, son, of course it isn't grudged,' Buckie put in.

'Do you know what sacrifices we have made, your father and I, and what sacrifices we will have to make?' Bette said. 'Yes, and your cousin, too – the cousin whose presence you seem to resent.'

'She's taking my place, isn't she?' Louis said. 'That's why you fetched her from London, to take my place.'

'Nonsense! Utter nonsense,' Bette said.

'That's why you want rid of me.'

'Rid of you?' Bette's voice rose. 'I can think of less expensive ways of being rid of you, Louis, than by sending you to study silly music in Edinburgh.'

'Silly music?' Louis's voice rose too. 'Silly music, is it? What, would you have me become a preacher, like your friend Oakley, and have to depend on the charity of fat old women for a living?'

'Louis,' Buckie said, reaching out a hand, 'that's enough.'

'Oh yes,' Aunt Bette said, with a curious little smirk, 'I am indeed a fat old woman, Louis, at least in your eyes, but I am not a wastrel.'

Louis shook off his father's restraining hand. He lifted himself on his forearms, gaining eight or ten inches in height.

He seemed massive, suddenly, massive and threatening. There was no stopping him now.

'Money,' he shouted, 'that's all you ever think about. There's no soul within you, Mama, no heart. You do not understand that what drives me is not your good opinion, for your opinion of me is like a butcher's account, calculated in shillings and pence. I'm not something to be cut up and sold to make you rich so that you can swank about in the frowsy drawing-rooms of Dundee. Hah!' he bellowed. 'Oh, God Jesus, I am dying here.'

He flung himself away from the table with such force that he tripped and fell sprawling on the floor. Thimble shot from beneath the table to the kitchen door but finding it closed, ran round and round the room like a black streak, leaped on to the back of Buckie's armchair and cowered there.

And Susanne, deeply embarrassed, covered her face with her hands.

The sun had finally slipped down and stars were beginning to prick the heavens when Tom Oakley stole along the path by the schoolhouse and hid in the gorse bushes that surrounded the garden of Rose Cottage.

The light flickered like a firefly from room to room, from the table, Tom thought, to the bed, but all he could discern of Gillian Primrose was a glimpse of material, wispy as gossamer, reflected in the candlelight. He knew that she had not gone to bed, though, and, yes, he thought, this is the best time, the perfect time to make my intentions known.

That forenoon he had buried old Mrs Mazzucco, while her son and grandsons looked on, dry-eyed. There had been no wake in the Irish style, but after the committal he had repaired with the mourners to an upstairs room in the house and had consumed several glasses of whisky and flirted, albeit briefly, with Martin Mazzucco's daughter, who was by no means adverse to flirting and gave as good as she got. Indeed, there's no saying what might have transpired if Angus Gamrie had not been hovering in the vicinity, monitoring his every move.

Soon after supper Effie had taken the babies to bed with her and Zena and Greg had been chased off upstairs with the others. Tom had locked the study door and, leaving the lamp alight, had clambered out of the window and set off to make a late-night call on Miss Gillian Primrose, the least impressionable of all his parishioners, and by far the most attractive.

He watched the candle flame steady, saw the teacher's face lit from below and the shadows that her breasts made on her shift.

Blowing out his cheeks and screwing up his courage, he stepped out of the gorse bushes and rapped, not too imperiously, on the cottage door.

She was no fool, Miss Primrose.

She did not open the door.

She lifted the window three or four inches and peered out at him.

'It's you,' she said. 'What do you want at this hour?'

'A word, that's all.'

'Mr Oakley, I am preparing to go to bed.'

'Yes, I do apologise for the lateness of the hour, but this is not a matter that can be conducted in the classroom.'

'Is it not, why not?'

He insinuated himself along the path.

Candlelight shaped a halo out of her thick fair hair and shone through the puffs and tucks of her shift, showing the tint of flesh beneath.

She was still cautious, still wary; he could not blame her for that.

She held the window up with one hand, propping it with her elbow. If he had been a robber he could not have forced his way in through the window. One move towards her and she would let the sash fall, trapping his hand or his head.

He hunkered down to present less of a target.

She had unpinned her hair. It fell about her shoulders in thick curling fronds. In the half-light her freckles stood out like spots of ink. The soft fold of flesh at her bare elbow reminded him of other things. He felt himself grow stiff, closed his knees and, unbalanced, put out a hand to steady himself and, without intention, touched her forearm with his fingertips.

He spoke softly. 'I am very appreciative of your conscientiousness, Miss Primrose. During a recent visit to Dun— to Kirkcaldy I took the liberty of purchasing a gift as a small token of my gratitude for all that you do on behalf of the juvenile community.'

'What are you after?'

'After?' He adjusted his balance. 'I am after nothing, Gillian,' he said. 'It is, as I say, a token of my esteem that requires no more from you than a gracious acceptance.'

'What are you blethering about?'

He did not dare stand up for fear that she would see how her presence affected him. He squeezed his hand into his breeches' pocket, fished for the packet that he had wrapped himself, using brown paper preserved from Bette Hollander's gift, and held it up by the string.

'See,' he said. 'For you.'

'For me? Why?'

'I told you why.' He thrust the little packet out at her. 'Take it. Please.'

'What is it? A widow's mite?'

'Almost,' Tom said. 'We've little enough to give to one another, for none of us are rich in anything but love – God's love, I mean.'

'I'm sure that's what you mean,' Gillian Primrose said. 'But if I may make so bold as to enquire, why now and not tomorrow?'

'I prefer to avoid giving my children a wrong impression,'

Tom said. 'You know better than I do, my dear Gillian, how impressionable children can be and how easily they pick up the stick by the wrong end.'

Prim peered at the package. 'I've no idea what you're talking about, Mr Oakley, or why you're bringing me gifts. I'm not going to invite you in.'

'That would be most improper.'

'I imagine that the only way I'm going to get rid of you . . .'

'Is to accept my gift in the spirit in which it is given,' Tom said.

'Very well.'

Her hand appeared in the space below the sash and plucked the package from his grasp.

He stood up. 'Aren't you going to open it?'

The scent of roses filled the night air. The moon had disentangled itself from the tree branches and shed silvery light upon the cottage wall. He could hear the sea, far, far off, rocking rhythmically against the shore. The woman looked so beautiful, so desirable that he almost forgot that he disliked her.

'No,' she said. 'I'll open it later when you've gone.'

'Prim,' he said, 'Gillian . . .'

'Goodnight to you, Mr Oakley.'

'Goodnight,' he purred. 'Goodnight, my dear Miss Primrose,' and snatched his fingers from the windowsill an instant before she dropped the sash.

For almost a quarter of an hour Prim sat motionless with the parcel on the table before her; then she struck a match, relit the candle and glanced at the window to make sure that the minister wasn't still spying on her.

She was too sensible to be flattered by Tom Oakley's attentions. He was not the first fellow to fancy bedding her. In fact, she had been forced to resign her last teaching post to escape the unwelcome attentions of a libidinous rogue on the parish school board.

She was all too well aware that an unmarried woman was a natural target for unscrupulous men who held positions of power, however petty. She had been born in servants' quarters in Bluefoot House, in the shadow of the Pentland Hills, where her mother had been a servant to the elder son of Lord Fotheringham who was her natural father. She had been condemned, it seemed, to a life of drudgery until the master had taken it into his head to have her educated and had paid to send her to school. With a young wife and a family to contend with, he had been pleased enough to see the back of her and had encouraged her to strike out on her own and follow a career as a governess or teacher as far from Bluefoot as possible. She wrote to her mother now and then. Her mother could not read or write, but the butler read out the letters and, once or twice in the year, penned a brief reply on her mother's behalf. That was all the contact she had or wanted with her 'family' at Bluefoot House.

Now this man, this minister, this arrogant fool, who assumed that a woman alone must be pining for a man, had put her security at risk.

She sighed and lifted the so-called token of his esteem, unpicked the string, unwrapped the paper, removed a smooth glass bottle and examined the label: *Raven's Bouquet d'Arabie: an Elegant Essence of the Most Exquisite Fragrance, without the Evanescent Quality peculiar to many Advertised Perfumes.*

Scent, cheap penny-a-gallon scent in a fancy bottle: was Tom Oakley trying to tell her something? she wondered. She split the paper seal with her thumbnail, extracted the cork with her teeth and sniffed the sickly sweet odour, then, pulling a face, carried the bottle at arm's length to the door.

She opened the door and poured the perfume into the flowerbed.

Shaking out the last sticky drops, she tossed the bottle into the gorse bushes, bolted the door behind her and went, quite alone, to bed.

The door of Louis's room lay open. Susanne could make out the harmonium, all shiny planes and angles in the cluttered room. The pungent stench of tobacco hung in the air and the room seemed horribly empty. It was something she would have to get used to, Susanne supposed, when Louis left for Edinburgh. She threw a shawl over her nightgown and tiptoed downstairs.

It was well after eleven and the house was in darkness. Aunt Bette had taken herself to bed. Thimble had gone out to hunt for mice in the grasses and Ajax, after padding about the house in search of his master for a while, had fallen asleep in front of the fire and did no more than lift his head when Susanne quietly opened the front door.

Louis was seated on the porch steps, smoking one of his father's cigars.

Smoke drifted upward in a gentle spiral for there was no breath of wind. There were stars all over the heavens, more stars than Susanne had ever seen before, little fiery beads showering down to the horizon, close enough to catch in a shrimping net. She leaned on the rail, staring up at the sky.

'Did she send you out to fetch me?' Louis asked.

'No, she's gone to bed.'

Louis said, 'I suppose you think they're lovely?'

'The stars?' Susanne said. 'They are. I've never seen so many.'

'I hate them,' Louis said.

'Oh, Louis, how can you say such a thing?'

'They aren't just stars, you know. They're suns, suns with planets just like ours wheeling round them, thousands and thousands of them and, far away in the darkness, beyond anything we can see, millions more.'

'That doesn't make them any less lovely.'

Louis flicked away the stub of the cigar and watched the coal extinguish itself in the sand. 'There's no end to them, Susanne, no end but infinity.'

'Why do you hate them?'

'Because they're dying,' Louis said. 'Because one by one they will burn out and die, just as we burn out and die, and everyone, everything on all those thousands of planets will die too – as I'm dying now.'

'You're not dying,' Susanne said, quietly.

'I am. Oh, but I am. We all are, dearest; even you.'

'But not for a long time yet.'

'Soon,' Louis said. 'All too soon. In a spark, in a flicker it'll be gone.'

'What will?'

'Life. My life, and nothing done with it, nothing achieved.'

'What's wrong with you? Are you ill?'

He shook his head and then, to Susanne's astonishment, wiped tears from his eyes. She knelt beside him, an arm about his shaking shoulders.

'I didn't mean it, Susanne,' he said. 'I didn't mean what I said in there. She goaded me. She's always goading me. She's always so certain, so positive and she expects so much from me. I'm to be her salvation, and I don't think I'm up to it.' He sniffed and covered her hand with his. 'I'm glad you're here, glad you came. I hope – I pray – that you'll stay in Strayhorn.'

'I've nowhere else to go, Louis.'

'Stay until I come back from Edinburgh, or wherever my talent takes me. It's not just money, you see: it's time. I've no time.' He dropped his head back and, chin pointing to the stars, said. 'I'm burning up, Susanne, burning out. I need to be sure that I have a future, that there's someone steady and secure in my life who will be here for me and who will remember me after I have followed the stars into extinction.'

'I'll be here for you, Louis. I'll always be here for you.'

He gave a trembling sigh, then, disengaging himself, held her at arm's length and looked straight into her eyes.

'Do you promise that you'll look after me?'

'Yes, my dearest darling, yes,' Susanne said, and would, at that tender moment, have kissed him, if he hadn't pulled away.

PART TWO

9

Skilled labour was hard to find in Strayhorn and the diggers that Harry Coburn brought in to demolish the curing sheds soon made their presence felt. They pitched camp on the slopes just north of the harbour, three sailcloth tents and an open-sided hut housing a brazier and a cooking pot the size of the Bass Rock. Barred from the Dalriada, they purchased beer and whisky by the cask from a dealer in Caddis and, after work, drank, brawled and danced until they fell down. Within a week, petitions were raised to curb their antics and a delegation of outraged citizens were treated to a torrent of abuse and dark threats of retribution.

Enquiries unearthed the fact that the sheds had been owned by Mrs Mazzucco's husband and, on the widow's death, had become the property of Martin Mazzucco who, it seemed, had sold them to Mr Coburn, along with thirty-two acres of scrub land bordering the Fisherfield burn. Riled by the navvies' ungodly behaviour, Mr Gamrie requested a meeting with Mr Coburn and thus, on a raw February afternoon, found himself face to face with Flash Harry in the gun-room of Macklin House.

Three labradors and a young deerhound, steaming like dumplings in the heat of the fire, occupied the panelled room. The indignation that had moved Angus to request a meeting had all but evaporated before Mr Coburn strode in, carrying a decanter of French brandy and two lead-crystal glasses.

'A bumper, sir, a bumper?' Harry said, already beginning to pour.

A butler brought in a kettle of hot water, a sugar shaker and a dish of freshly cut lemons, though where Mr Coburn had managed to find lemons at that season of the year was more than Angus could imagine. He was, in any case, distracted by the attentions of the deerhound who had leaped up on him and was vigorously licking his face.

'Down, Loki, down.' Harry Coburn aimed a half-hearted kick at the dog who administered a last swipe at Angus with his tongue, then spun round and collapsed in an ungainly heap beside the labradors.

Angus mopped his cheeks with a handkerchief and accepted a glass of brandy punch to erase the taste of the deerhound's kiss.

Perched on a padded chair, Harry raised his glass.

'To progress, sir,' he said. 'To progress.'

'Umm,' said Angus, sipping the scalding liquid.

'Now, Mr Gamrie,' Harry Coburn said, 'I assume you've come to talk to me at the behest of the Reverend Oakley. Truth to tell, I'm rather surprised that the Reverend Oakley hasn't come knocking at my door in person, given that he has been instrumental in fomenting the revolt against the work I've put in hand.'

'In fact . . .'

'Of course,' Harry went smoothly on, 'I sympathise with the distress that progress must cause to the villagers of Strayhorn, but I'd hoped that gentlemen like the Reverend Oakley and yourself would be more forward-looking and would encourage the good folk of the parish to put up with a modicum of disruption for the sake of the material benefits that will accrue.'

Angus was baffled by the events to which the broker alluded. Something was missing: the chapter on 'progress' had somehow fallen out of the book.

He said, 'Material benefits?'

'The iron way, man, the iron way,' Harry Coburn told him.

'One cannot make an omelette without breaking eggs, Mr Gamrie; a homily attributed to Rousseau, I believe, or some other damned Frenchie.'

'Eh?' said Angus.

'Dismantling fish sheds is hardly the sort of job that demands the attentions of skilled workmen, but levelling and laying does. The gentlemen – well, hardly that – the labourers I've employed are thoroughly experienced in those arts and may, therefore, work unsupervised.'

'Levelling and laying what?' Angus said.

'The new railway line and, more importantly, a turntable.'

'Turntable?'

'A magnificent invention.' In his enthusiasm Harry Coburn tugged the stopper of the brandy decanter as if it were a lever. 'A great circular pit with a geared wheel sunk in it that can reverse the direction of a section of rail and, sir, the locomotive upon it.'

'Does such a thing exist?' said Angus.

'It does, Mr Gamrie, most assuredly it does,' Harry Coburn said. 'I've observed one in operation.'

'Where?'

'Whitstable.'

'Whitstable? Kent, is that?'

'Indeed, Kent. A branch line runs from Canterbury to a point almost opposite the Isle of Sheppey. Here are copperhouses where green vitriol is manufactured. The company that owns the copper-houses has installed just such a turntable – the first in England – to ensure that the locomotives that transport coal from collier vessels in Whitstable Bay and the wagons that take out the vats of green vitriol are not delayed at the terminal point of the branch line.' Harry Coburn paused for breath, and concluded, 'Time is money; that's simple commercial logic.'

'Aye,' Angus more or less admitted, 'but I fail to see what

this has to do wi' drunken labourers runnin' amok in the streets o' Strayhorn.' He drank the remains of the brandy, leaned an elbow on his knee. 'Are you tellin' me that you're layin' a railway line into the heart of Strayhorn?'

'Not,' said Mr Coburn, 'quite.'

'But he is, isn't he?' Tom Oakley said.

' 'Course he is,' Mr Gamrie said. 'But he's leery o' givin' out too much information at this stage, just in case.'

'In case what, Mr Gamrie?' Zena asked.

Personally she saw nothing wrong with the navigators' obstreperous behaviour. She had made friends with one of them, a young man with a stubble beard and a pigtail, who went by the name of Danny. He had already invited her to meet him by the well-that-gave-no-water on the banks of the Fisherfield on Sunday afternoon and she would have gone too if she hadn't been teaching Bible Class. Her father would have been furious if he'd known that she had been sneaking down to the camp accompanied by Greg and Susanne to sample the fiery stuff that the men called whisky and dance in a ring with them, chanting nonsense about the Pope, the Queen and the Earl of Aberdeen.

Danny had tickled the gull's feather in her hat and put an arm about her waist. He had kissed her and run his tongue across her lips. She might have allowed him further liberties if Susanne and Gregor hadn't been there, and Greg hadn't shouted, '*Here comes Angus*,' and they, all three, had fled.

When Mr Gamrie turned up at the manse on Tuesday night, Zena was afraid that he had come to berate her for consorting with heathens, but the clerk had other things on his mind. He, it seemed, had gone out to Macklin House to talk with Henry Coburn, and had learned some disturbing news.

She sat very still in the corner, Roland asleep on her lap, Greg crouched by her side, the rest of the children upstairs.

'In case it affects the stock market,' Papa said.

Zena thought the notion of anything that took place in Strayhorn affecting the stock market was ludicrous.

'The stock market?' Mama said.

'Coburn's a broker in stocks and shares, isn't he?' Papa said.

Mr Gamrie said, 'Aye, and it's my guess he's fishin' for investors.'

'To rook and rob again,' Mama said.

Angus Gamrie pushed out his lips. 'Well, Eff— Mrs Oakley, Coburn's a gambler, no doubt about that, an' gamblers sometimes lose their stake like everybody else. I am, however, reminded o' the parable o' the talents.'

'Matthew twenty-five, verse fourteen,' Papa muttered.

'An' Luke six, verse forty-seven,' Mr Gamrie added. 'The master berates the servant an'—'

'Yes, yes,' her father interrupted. 'We're all familiar with the text, Mr Gamrie. Get on with it, if you please.'

'Coburn tells me there's great freight potential in the east of Fife.'

'Everybody with an ounce of sense knows that,' Papa said.

'Aye, but not everybody knows that the Leven Railway Company is plannin' to run a track through to Anstruther.'

'Won't that cost a fearful lot of money?' Mama asked.

'Fifty-eight thousand pounds is the estimate,' Mr Gamrie said.

'Whooof!' Mama blew out her cheeks.

Mr Gamrie said, 'But a seven per cent return on investment is expected within a year of the openin'.'

'Anstruther isn't Strayhorn, however,' Papa reminded him.

'That's the beauty of it,' Angus Gamrie said. 'For another thirty thousand pounds the track can be run through to Hask, then, following the course o' the Fisherfield burn, to a terminal in Strayhorn.'

'A terminal?' said Papa. 'Well now, a terminal does mean money.'

'A terminal wi' a turntable.'

'Great heavens!' Papa said. 'A turntable!'

Mr Gamrie said, 'You're obviously better versed in the feats o' engineerin' than I am, Mr Oakley. There's only one such device in the land an' that's on the coast o' Kent.'

'If it can be done there, can it not be done here?'

'Harry Coburn's argument in a nutshell,' Mr Gamrie said.

'Thirty thousand pounds?' Mama snorted. 'I'll look in the flour jar then an' see if we've thirty thousand to spare this week.'

'Not this week, Eff— Mrs Oakley,' Angus Gamrie said. 'Not this year, nor next year, but some time in the not too distant future a railway line will be laid to Anstruther. If a branch line with a terminal already exists then the potential for gain to our town, let alone the investors, will be considerable.'

Papa was nodding as if his head would fall off. 'Uh-huh, uh-huh. Grain, potatoes, cattle, sheep, not to mention fish; the Edinburgh markets wide open, and the London markets, too, in time.'

'Eight and a half thousand souls in the east of Fife,' said Mr Gamrie. 'Twenty-seven registered vessels of over one thousand tons. Two hundred-odd boats engaged in herring fishin', a hundred or so in white fishin', an' the price o' fish a hundred per cent up from a decade ago.'

'Which,' Papa said, still nodding, 'is why English buyers are turnin' up in the mart at Anstruther for the winter sales.'

'An' why English buyers are sniffin' about for permanent curin' establishments,' Mr Gamrie added.

'A terminal here in Strayhorn, a line across the moor via Hask to join the main line at Anstruther.' Papa's eyes gleamed. 'By heaven, Mr Gamrie, it could be the making of us – I mean, of the town.'

'Where,' her mother asked, 'did you come by these figures, Mr Gamrie?'

'From Mr Coburn. He had them in his head.'

'Well,' Mama said, 'it might be better for all of us if they remain in Mr Coburn's head.'

'How is that so?' said Mr Gamrie, politely.

'He has sold you too, Angus, sold you a pipe dream,' said Mama.

'An opportunity,' said Mr Gamrie, 'to put our town on the map.'

'It will not, I fear, be the sort of project that will come to pass quickly,' Papa said. 'Even with Harry Coburn's – what shall we say? – his talent for squeezing blood out of stones, he'll have difficulty in recruiting investors.'

'That,' said Mr Gamrie, 'is why he's buildin' the turntable.'

'*He's* building the turntable?' said Papa.

Mr Gamrie nodded, gravely. 'At his own expense.'

'I don't believe it,' Mama said.

'There's the evidence before your eyes,' said Mr Gamrie. 'The diggers are already at work. Surely that's a signal that Harry Coburn means what he says. If he's willin' to stump up large sums o' his own money to clear the sheds an' prepare the acres, then there's more to this scheme than pipe dreams.'

'I'll believe it when I see this turn-about thing in operation,' Mama said.

'Oh, Effie, you have no vision at all.' Papa threw a hand in the air in exasperation. 'I tell you this, my dear, if I had money to spare I would give considered attention to any proposal that Mr Coburn might put to the public in the course of the next two or three years.'

'Then it's just as well that we're skint,' her mother said.

'What, what then? Do you think it's a bubble, Mrs Oakley?'

'I do, Mr Gamrie, I do.'

'Women!' Papa said, scornfully. 'What do women know of such things?'

'Your friend Bette Hollander seems to know rather a lot,' Mama said. 'If you think so little of my opinion, Tom, why don't you consult Mrs Hollander. After all, did she not get her fingers burned by Harry Coburn?'

'Rumours, just rumours.'

'If it was rumours,' Mama said, 'why did she fetch the London girl here?'

'Christian charity, Mrs Oakley?' Angus Gamrie suggested.

And, to Zena's consternation, her mother laughed out loud.

'Zena, are you sure you know what you're doing?' Greg said.

'Aye, I'm going to have a word with Danny.'

'Danny?' The fact that his sister was on familiar terms with one of the diggers increased his apprehension. 'Which one is Danny?'

'The pretty one,' said Zena.

'With the pigtail and the ring in his ear,' said Susanne.

Reluctantly Gregor acknowledged that his sister had grasped, at least in part, the significance of what had passed between his parents and Angus Gamrie. He wasn't quick enough to understand the facts and figures, though even he realised that a rail link with Edinburgh would bring huge changes to Strayhorn and improve the lot of those who lived there.

'Be careful, Zena,' Greg warned. 'Don't get too inquisitive. I don't think those men will like you asking questions. Besides, is it not a bit dangerous to give them encouragement?'

'I can take care o' myself,' Zena said.

In her patched overcoat and the hat with the frayed gull's feather, his sister was tall and robust, just the sort of girl, Greg imagined, that a navigator might like for a wife or a mistress.

'If you're so worried about my safety,' Zena said, 'come with us?'

'I think I'd rather not,' said Greg.

'Right, we're off then,' Zena said and, gripping Susanne's arm firmly, strutted down the path towards the tents.

Prim was surprised when Alan Redpath turned up at the door of the schoolhouse. She had been washing slates and dusting desks and wondered if she looked as grubby as she felt.

The doctor was his usual tidy self. He reminded Prim of a young priest who had presided over the Catholics in Bluefoot; not only Catholic hearts had fluttered when Father Finnegan had done his rounds, but that, her mother had told her, was because priests were 'forbidden fruit'. Alan Redpath was not forbidden fruit, however, and Prim had no hesitation in inviting him in.

He brought the bag with him, the shiny new bag that clicked and tinkled when he set it down. He looked around, and said, 'It's very clean for a pigsty.'

'It hasn't been a pigsty in thirty years,' said Prim. 'Besides, I give it a wipe every day and a good scrub on Saturdays.'

'Cleanliness being next to godliness?'

'If that's what you choose to believe,' Prim said. 'I prefer to subscribe to the notion that cleanliness equates with health, which is not, I think, an entirely unscientific theory these days.'

'Quite right, Miss Primrose.'

'I take it,' Prim said, 'that you haven't called to discuss hygiene.'

'In a manner of speaking, I have.' Alan picked up his bag and extracted a crudely printed leaflet. 'An outbreak of scarlatina has occurred in Hask. Five cases, so far. I've recommended that the school there be closed for three weeks to prevent the fever spreading.'

'Surely you're not asking me to close my school?' Prim said, anxiously.

'That won't be necessary at this stage.'

'Isn't scarlatina a disease of the autumn months?'

'The winter's been too mild,' said Alan. 'I've been dealing with a full load of sore throats, coughs and wheezes, far more than usual. A week or two of hard frosts would ensure a healthier community.'

'The fever, is it evident in Strayhorn?'

'Not yet,' Alan said. 'I've been in touch with the other doctors and we've printed off a pamphlet listing signs and symptoms.'

'I'm sure I'll recognise the signs,' said Prim. 'Lord knows, I've seen them often enough.'

'Have you? Where?'

'Where I come from.'

'And where might that be?'

'Near Edinburgh.'

Alan had heard from Buckie Hollander that the schoolmistress could be prickly. He closed his medical bag and tucked it under his arm.

'At the first sign, Miss Primrose, please do inform me.'

'And you'll come running to the rescue?'

'To assist recovery, as well as I am able.'

'How well is that?'

'Quite well.'

'How long have you been engaged in the practice of medicine?'

'Four years.'

'Ah!'

Her tone was scornful. Alan felt his cheeks redden. 'How long, if I may ask, have you been engaged in teaching?'

'Much longer than four years.'

'In Strayhorn?'

'No,' she said, carefully, 'not in Strayhorn. I have a question for you, Dr Redpath. Have you visited the camp on the Fisherfield acres and examined the labourers?'

'Of course not.'

'Isn't it possible,' Prim said, 'that the diggers have brought the sickness?'

'The outbreak is confined to Hask.'

'Other fevers, other disorders then?'

'I may be a greenhorn in medical matters – at least in your view – but I'm not entirely stupid. Do you suppose for one moment that I'd barge into a navigators' camp and demand that they subject themselves to examination? I'd be lucky to escape alive.'

'They're filthy, you know.'

'Of course they're filthy,' Alan said. 'Good God, they labour all day long in mud and muck. But, apart from bad teeth and an occasional rotting liver, navigators are, for the most part, healthier than most folk.'

'I meant morally,' Prim said.

'Morally?'

'Moral diseases.'

'Oh!'

'As some of my poor misguided pupils may discover to their cost.'

'Your pupils? I'm not sure I . . .'

'My girls,' said Prim. 'So far the town fathers have failed to curb their natural curiosity. What are the navigators doing here anyway?'

'The rumour is that the railway is coming to Strayhorn,' said Alan. 'But I honestly don't see what that has to do with an outbreak of fever in Hask. If you're searching for a remedy to stop the march of progress, Miss Primrose, I'm afraid you'll be disappointed. Have you something against railways?'

'Not a thing.'

'Against the men who build them, then?'

'I'm against men who make money from the sweat of another's brow.'

Jessica Stirling

'Navigators?'

She smiled then, showing a perfect set of teeth. She was, he realised, teasing him, and doing a good job of it. He tried to calculate her age by staring at her teeth, as if she were a filly or a mare. He had a sudden mad vision of himself with his fingers in her mouth, examining her gums, and, flustered, hoisted the medical bag to his chest.

'My concern is for my girls,' Prim said. 'The rest is merely a cast of mind, a personal idiosyncrasy, if you like. A couple of my girls are down there now.'

'Down where?'

'At the camp with the navigators.'

'Why didn't you stop them?'

'How could I?' Prim said. 'Half the juvenile element in the town hangs about the camp. One can hardly blame them, I suppose, but I thought Susanne and Zena would have more sense.'

'Susanne?'

'You know Susanne, of course.'

'Yes,' Alan said. 'I know Susanne. How long since the girls set off?'

'A half-hour, or so.'

'Are you sure that they've gone to the camp?'

'Certain.'

'And you want me to make sure they come to no harm?' Alan said.

Miss Primrose smiled, apologetically. 'Please.'

There were no engineers, no surveyors; the crew worked without supervision, and if Harry Coburn was indeed the paymaster he displayed no interest in how his money was being spent. The men laboured from dawn until dusk with shovels, pickaxes and long iron spikes, unearthing stones and digging ditches. Measuring was done with poles and string, levelling with an arrangement of four brass rods and a ball pendulum, and the old tar-black fishing sheds were soon demolished and the Fisherfield acres scored by shallow trenches.

The navvies might have been barred from entering the Dalriada but no one had the nerve to stop them buying fish, bread and butcher meat. Once a week, on Saturday, a gig appeared from the direction of Anstruther, two burly gentlemen in old-fashioned flounced overcoats and top hats climbed out and unloaded an iron chest and the labourers were paid, at a rate, so Danny told Zena, of nine shillings a day, which was more than a humble fisherman could earn even at the height of the season.

The thought of all that cash jingling in the pocket of handsome Danny increased his appeal and Zena wondered if there was any truth in his stories about the rich life on the road. She also wondered if having a man of her own, a man like Danny, would compensate for the hardships, and if her mama had felt once as she did now, keening for release from drudgery and ready to throw herself at the first chap who came along.

Pursing her lips, she clung to Susanne's arm as the navvies' campfire showed in the gloaming. The men were trailing in from the acres. Buckets of hot water stood on the grass and several navvies, stripped almost naked, were washing off the dirt of the day's labour. Danny was one of them. He had broad shoulders and a narrow waist and, with his pigtail unknotted, his hair hung about his shoulders like a hood.

He groped for a cloth and, rubbing his chest, looked up.

'Ladies,' he called out. 'Is this not a sight to gladden a man's heart?'

His thighs were downed with dark hair and Zena could not help but admire the shape of him under the drawers. She knew, of course, what a boy's parts looked like, for modesty in the manse was tempered by the necessity of sharing tubs, chamber pots and beds. But Susanne, less experienced in matters of anatomy, pressed her brow into Zena's shoulder and uttered a little moan.

'Is it for the dancin' you've come, lassies? It's early for that, though not so early I couldn't give you a bit of a jig, if you've a mind for it.'

The men, gathered by the brazier, sniggered as if they thought she was a tinkerish type, a whore in the making. No matter how much Danny stirred her senses and appealed to her primitive instincts, when it came to wit and intellect Zena was confident that she could dance the daylights out of any navvy man.

'Aye,' she said. 'I'll dance with you; a reel, though, not a jig.' She caught his wrists and jerked him towards her. 'Are you drunk already, Danny, or just worn out?'

'By God, I'm not wore out.' He spun her round. 'Drunk or sober, girl, I can match you any night. See.' He clutched the back of her thighs and, to cheers from the onlookers, mimicked the motion with which Adam took Eve. 'Now, me sweet darlin', what's it to be, a jig or just a reel?'

Zena twirled away from him, hips tilted and head flung back, no longer the girl who taught infants, who explained the parables to fractious children on Sabbath afternoons, no longer her mother's helper or her father's darling. 'A jig, is it?' she cried. 'Aye, Daniel, you would drag me into the lion's den with you, I'm thinking, then you'll be up and off, leaving me in tears.'

'Up an' off?' he shouted back, grinning. 'I haven't even been in yet an' you've got me up an' off.'

'When?' Zena cried.

'Tonight,' Danny told her. 'Now, right now.'

'Then you'll be gone and leave me.'

'Aye, we're up and off come Saturday.'

He wanted her and thought that he might have her by telling her that, come Saturday, her chance would gone for ever.

Zena said, 'Is it rails you'll be laying for the Anstruther line?'

'Nah!' Danny said. 'We're off to shore the canal at Smeddum. There's no more work for us here, and the Anstruther line is just dream talk.'

'You're finished then? Finished in Strayhorn?'

'Aye,' Danny said. 'If you ask me, this is a hole will never be filled.'

He grabbed her, pulled her across his back and carried her, kicking and squealing, across the grass to the nearest tent.

Susanne ran after them but an elderly man with grey locks and side whiskers snared her by the waist. 'Nay, nay, wee lass,' he growled, 'this is not somethin' for you to interfere in. Your time will come.'

And then, out of the darkness, a very polite and proper voice said, 'I think you should put her down, don't you?'

The grey-haired man glanced over his shoulder. 'Who the hell d'you think you are, givin' me orders?'

Alan Redpath was in no mood for small talk. He swung the shiny leather bag into the grey-haired man's groin. The digger uttered a choking sob, doubled over and dropped to all fours. The doctor struck him again, on the back of the neck.

'Run, Susanne,' Alan said. 'Greg's waiting for you on the hill.'

'Zena – Zena – she . . .'

'I'll take care of Zena,' said Alan.

She was draped over Danny's shoulder like a side of beef. His skin was icy-cold, his hair wet. She scratched his neck with her nails, drawing blood. He cuffed her and pinned her arms. She couldn't imagine what he would do to her when he got her into the tent. She saw the mouth of the tent, slack folds of sailcloth draped over a pole. He squatted, shook her off and dragged her inside.

Cold air poured over her belly. Her skirts rode over her thighs and Danny's hands were upon her, ripping at buttons and ribbons. She shouted at him to stop. His mouth was on her breast. He sucked at her teat and, reaching down, fingered her belly. She reared up, fighting frantically. He called her a filthy name and struck her with the flat of his hand. She thrashed under him, trying to lock her ankles one over the other. He struck her again. Her head snapped back. He pressed her down into a tangle of musty blankets, straddled her and offered himself to her mouth. She opened her mouth and bit him. He cursed and reared back, knocking all breath from her lungs. Flames danced across the skin of the tent. Danny glanced up. Zena pressed her knees to her chest, and kicked out. He shot away from her, falling backward. She kicked out, kicked and kicked, crawling towards the firelight in the mouth of the tent.

She thrust her head and shoulders out into the air, and saw the doctor.

He wore a tweed overcoat and half boots. He clutched his bag in one hand and one of the tarry flares that the navvies used for light in the other. The cook-shed was on fire, flames, fanned by the wind, eating into timbers.

Zena scrambled to her feet.

'Did he harm you?' Alan Redpath shouted.

'No.'

Danny charged out of the burning tent on all fours. The doctor handed Zena his medical bag. She hugged the bag against her chest and stepped to one side as Danny staggered to his feet. Alan Redpath lashed out at him. Danny's head seemed to fly off his shoulders, and he toppled and fell. Alan kicked him away from the flames, for the rest of the navigators were motionless, unwilling, it seemed, to tackle a gentleman wielding a torch.

'Time to beat a retreat, I believe,' Alan said and, taking Zena by the arm, led her swiftly off into the darkness.

'What time is it?' Susanne asked.

'Gone six,' Greg said.

'My aunt will be worried. She doesn't like me being out after dark.'

'I'll take you home shortly,' Alan said.

'You won't tell her what happened, will you?' Susanne said.

'No.'

'What about Zena?' Greg said. 'Is she all right?'

'I'm all right. I am, I'm fine.'

'You don't look fine,' said Greg.

'Shock,' Alan said. 'Quite mild.'

Prim said, 'What possessed you to go there in the first place?'

Wrapped in a shawl, Zena huddled by the fire. The violent tremors that had affected her soon after they'd reached Rose Cottage had abated, though Alan had administered nothing more sedative than hot, sweet tea. She was a strong girl and, apart from a little bruising, had suffered no physical injury.

Greg said, shamefaced, 'We were bored.'

'Bored?' Prim said. 'Did they ply you with drink?'

Zena answered. 'No, the pig had other things on his mind.'

She had her back to them, face hidden by the shawl. She looked, Susanne thought, like a little old woman, as if what the navigator had tried to do had aged her.

Prim said, 'Were you flirting with this fellow, Zena?'

'Aye, I suppose I was.'

'Did you have a fancy for him?'

'I thought I did.'

'Will they come after us, Mr Redpath?' Greg asked.

'I doubt it,' Alan said. 'They know they're at fault and probably expect us to summon a sheriff's officer. If Harry

Coburn gets wind of what happen he'll refuse to pay them their dues, I expect.'

'Did you really burn down their tents?' said Prim.

'Oh yes,' said Susanne, with disquieting relish. 'Sent them up in smoke. We saw it all from the hill, didn't we, Greg?'

'I just caught them off guard,' said Alan.

'What if they'd been drunk?' said Prim.

Zena swung round. 'Would you have come for me if they'd been drunk?'

The doctor raised his hands. 'I don't know.'

'Would you?' Zena insisted.

'Probably.'

And Zena, hugging the shawl about her, smiled.

Later that night the navvies went on the rampage. They stoned the Dalriada, smashed herring barrels on the quay and hurled boulders on to the decks of the fishing boats. They tried, and fortunately failed, to set the harbour-master's house alight. Crazed with whisky and fuelled by inexplicable rage, they tore up and down the narrow streets of Strayhorn breaking windows and cursing foully.

No one dared venture out to reason with them. In fear of their lives, the fisher folk of Strayhorn bolted their doors and stayed indoors.

Come morning the navigators were gone.

They left nothing behind but the wreckage of the cook-shed and a few charred scraps of sailcloth; that and the cleared ground at the head of the harbour and the long diagonal ditches on the Fisherfield acres across which, one day, the railway would ride into Strayhorn.

IO

Louis's letters home were few and far between and invariably contained requests for money. At the end of each letter he added greetings to his little cousin, but for Susanne postscripts were not enough. She was more hurt than angered by Louis's neglect and as winter drifted sluggishly into spring, did her best to put him out of her mind.

By the month's end the fishing grounds were dotted with boats and the average catch was almost the equal of a good summer haul. Curers and cadgers crowed and rubbed their hands and trade, even in Strayhorn, was brisk.

On 10th March two English fish agents arrived in the village to survey the old curing sheds with a view to purchase. They were dismayed to find that the sheds had been demolished. They met with Martin Mazzucco in a back room of the Dalriada. Martin emerged from the meeting with tears in his eyes for, so the story went, he hadn't sold the old sheds or the Fisherfield acres but had leased them to Harry Coburn in exchange for shares in a company that, it seemed, had no capital assets and no other shareholders. A better man than Martin might have contemplated murdering the broker, or at least taking him to court, but Martin was so ashamed of himself that he just lay about the house in a haze of rum, moaning so loudly that you could hear him halfway across the bay.

Mild weather kept Alan Redpath on his toes. Scarlet fever spread as far as Caddis, three small children died and three others became so ill that they were removed to the hospital in Dundee.

Scarlatina was only one of the plagues that winter visited on Fife folk. Never had there been such hacking and wheezing as there was that spring, never such a demand for coffin-makers and grave-diggers, with the dead queuing up for Tom's attention and Angus Gamrie snapping at his heels to administer Protestant unction in the form of prayer to the sick as far afield as Brogan's Farm, out on the edge of the moor.

Tom had visited Brogan's Farm several times in the past, when it seemed that old Guy was knocking on death's door, and had had 'dealings', as it were, with Guy's servant, Annabel, a dark-haired, dark-eyed girl of nineteen, who, if not quite all right in the head, was quite all right in the hay-loft. In the minister's judgement, Annabel had required the administering of something other than Protestant unction on a fairly regular basis until, to his chagrin, old farmer Guy miraculously recovered his strength and chased the girl off in one direction and Tom in the other, shouting, no doubt deliriously, that he didn't need a minister to do for him what he could perfectly well do for himself.

With so many commitments, Mr Oakley's attendance at the schoolhouse suffered greatly and Prim, to her relief, saw little of him across the span of the spring. The main victim of Tom Oakley's neglect was the whale-master's wife who, unlike Miss Primrose, wasn't in the least amused to find herself being written off. At Sunday services a nod or a half-hearted bow substituted for conversation and no notes were hidden under the stone in the potting shed to arrange a rendezvous.

Then one March morning Bette clambered up the cliff path to the church and left a note – unsigned, of course – under the big stone that secured the door of the potting shed. The following Sunday she sat under the prow of the pulpit and scanned Tom's face for a sign that he'd found her letter and would grant her request for a meeting. No signal, no response. She tried to corner him after service but somehow the minister made himself scarce and she wasn't rash enough to beard him in the vestry where beady-eyed Angus Gamrie stood guard on the collection plates. On the following morning, Monday, she scrambled up the sheep path again, peeped under the stone and found her note, wet and disintegrating, still there, unread.

That night, long after everyone had gone to bed, Bette took off her clothes and tilted the cheval glass above her dressing-table and, by the flattering light of a solitary candle, gazed at her body and realised that her time had passed, that no man, least of all a man as discerning as Tom Oakley, could possibly find her attractive. Compliance, complicity and occasional expensive gifts would not bring Tom back to the bloated old woman who stared at her from the glass.

Her affair – her last affair – was over and done with.

In time, she felt sure, Tom would find another mistress.

And when that time came, she would have her revenge.

'Susanne,' Miss Primrose said, 'are you happy?'

'In school?'

'In Strayhorn?'

'I am not unhappy.'

'Do they treat you well, your aunt and uncle?'

'Yes, they are very kind.'

It was a little after three o'clock. Prim had dismissed the class early, for the wind was picking up and a storm was clearly brewing.

Susanne was not dismayed by the prospect of foul weather. She loved the rain and the mighty gusts of wind that whipped the sea into a frenzy, for, though she'd grown a bit recently, she was still slight enough to slip beneath the wind like a field-mouse or a vole.

'And your cousin? How is your cousin?'

'Louis?' Susanne answered. 'Poof! I don't care about him.'

'I thought you did?'

'If he can't be bothered to put pen to paper, why should I care?'

'You write to him, of course?'

'I do. Well, I did,' Susanne said. 'It's like casting stones into a well.'

'Perhaps he'll regret his indifference when he sees how you've changed.'

'Have I changed? Have I really?'

They were in the classroom, not the cottage. Prim had made tea and brought it through from the kitchen. They were seated on the infant benches, nursing cups. Zena and Greg had gone home.

Prim nodded. 'You're growing up, Susanne.'

'I don't feel grown up.'

'Growing older, I mean.'

'You mean I'll soon be of an age to marry?'

Gillian Primrose hadn't meant that at all. She raised an eyebrow. 'Marriage?' she said. 'I hadn't thought of that.'

'I have,' Susanne said.

'And who would you marry?'

'Anyone who'll have me,' Susanne said. 'But no one will.'

Prim laughed. 'Why not?'

'I'm too small, too ugly.'

'You're not ugly, And' – Prim paused – 'you're rich.'

'I will be, I suppose, when I come of age,' Susanne said. 'That, I think, is the problem. How will I know if he loves me?'

'Life isn't written like a novelette, Susanne. The choices we're offered aren't conveniently arranged in black and white. I wish to heaven they were.'

'Is that why you've never married?'

Six months ago the question would have seemed impertinent; not now.

Prim sighed. 'Nobody ever asked me.'

'Perhaps somebody will, one day.'

'One day, one day,' Prim said. 'I no longer believe that all my dreams will come true – one day.'

'I do,' said Susanne.

'And so you should,' Prim told her, tapping her knee. 'So you should.'

'One day,' said Susanne, 'there will be a knock upon the door and when you open it there will be the man of your dreams.'

'Hah!' Prim said, sceptically.

Then the door of the classroom opened and a voice called out, 'Hello.'

Macklin House lay three miles inland, a bland Georgian mansion, square, upright and elegant, surrounded by eighteen acres of parkland. Nine bedrooms and five public rooms seemed an excessive amount of space for one small family, Tom thought, enviously, as he scurried up the driveway to the front door.

A servant girl relieved him of his overcoat and hat and ushered him into a drawing-room so sparse in its furnishings that there was barely a chair to sit upon. Tall windows were spotted with rain and far away Tom could just make out the scribble of the sea bowed by the weight of storm clouds. The room would have been depressing had it not been for the log fire that blazed in the grate and the fragrance of pine it released. Tom had no appointment with Coburn. He had taken a chance that the fellow would be at home, not on business in Edinburgh or, more likely, out shooting whatever it was that one shot in the breeding season. He rather hoped that the gorgeous child, Darsie, would be at home too, but, so far, there had been no sign of the girl.

Harry Coburn had not been born with a silver spoon in his

mouth – his father had been a weaver in Selkirk – but he had found a way of promoting himself into a class to which he, Tom Oakley, felt that he rightfully belonged. Coburn was a widower now but all this spacious elegance, Tom thought, looking round, had stemmed from a judicious marriage.

Claws clicked on the floor of the hall.

Pushing open the door with a massive shoulder, an enormous hound peered in at him and, a second later, Harry Coburn dashed into the drawing-room, trailed by a lanky butler and three female servants bearing an assortment of tea-things on a trolley the size of a traction engine.

'Reverend.' Harry jerked Tom's arm up and down as if he were a pump in need of priming. 'An unexpected pleasure. Most unexpected.'

'I trust I did not interrupt you?'

Servants darted about, fetching kettles and dishes, and clothing the enormous trolley in a linen shroud that, almost miraculously, became littered with cups and finger bowls, plates of seed cake and buttered brown bread.

Tom was pressed into a chair, a linen napkin spread on his lap and, within seconds, was served tea from a silver teapot, after which all the servants, save the lanky butler, trailed out again, the deerhound pattering in their wake.

'Done!' Harry Coburn extracted a watch from his fob pocket and checked it, as if he were supervising a military manoeuvre. 'Not too shabby, though I say so myself.'

'What,' Tom said, 'do you do about dinner?'

Harry Coburn laughed. 'I give them a running start.'

'Life below stairs,' Tom said, 'can never be dull.'

'No, it is, I fancy, rather less dull for them than it is for me.'

Tom sipped tea and looked around. 'You are alone here, sir?'

'I am, alas. I am.'

'Your daughter . . .'

'Boarding at school in St Andrews.'

'You must miss her.'

'What? Yes, I suppose I do.'

'My children,' Tom said, 'provide rather more distraction than companionship. There are, of course, seven of them.'

'You have a wife, do you not?'

'I do, sir, a very able helpmate.'

'You see,' said Harry, brightly but vaguely. 'There you are!'

'There I am?'

'No.' Harry leaned over the trolley. '*Here* you are, Mr Oakley, *here* you are, and . . .'

'You're wondering why.'

'Hmm, I am, rather.'

Except for the fact that his collar was askew and his necktie loosely knotted Mr Coburn might have been an advocate, or one of the more eccentric members of Tom's own profession. He was clad in a tight black morning suit and a grey waistcoat and, stripped of riding boots and kidskin breeches, looked a good deal less 'flash' than usual.

'You cannot have dropped in merely to chastise me for hiring a party of labourers,' Coburn went on. 'The admirable Mr Gamrie has already done that.'

'To good effect, I believe.'

'If you mean that the party has gone, certainly to good effect.'

'The abrupt departure had nothing to do with my session clerk's complaint, though, did it?' said Tom.

'No, the work is finished.'

'The work does not appear to be finished,' Tom said.

Harry Coburn wiped his lips with a napkin. He tossed the napkin on to the trolley and rocked back in his chair, tilting and tipping until it seemed that he was about to somersault backward into the fireplace. He crooned to himself too, an odd, pigeon-like sound, stared up at the ceiling for several long seconds, then brought the chair down with a thud.

'It's not parish business that brings you to my door, is it, Mr Oakley?'

'No, sir, it's not.'

'What do you want from me?'

The lanky servant still hovered by the door. Tom glanced round and Harry, taking the hint, motioned the man to leave.

As soon as the door closed, Tom said, 'Will there be a railway line to Strayhorn?'

'One step at a time, Mr Oakley.'

'Is such a venture in hand?'

'It is,' Harry said.

'When will the bill be presented to parliament?'

'Let me repeat, sir: one step at a time,' said Harry. 'First we have to see the line through to Anstruther and, before that, to win round the goodwill of those landowners who object to the track travelling through their grounds.'

'Edward Arbuthnot, for instance?'

'Dear God, no! We're not within twenty miles of Eddie Arbuthnot's place. Besides, Eddie's a sensible fellow. He won't stand in our way.'

'*Our* way, Mr Coburn?'

'I'm not in this alone, of course.'

'Of course.'

Harry hesitated, then, pushing the trolley to one side, rode his chair closer to the minister. 'May I depend upon your discretion, sir, your utmost and absolute discretion?'

'I'm a man of the cloth, Mr Coburn; I'm used to keeping secrets.'

'In two years, three at most, a line will link Leven to Anstruther; a single track, admittedly, a single track at first. Passing loops will be erected to serve all stations except Lundin Links and Pittenweem. A further extension will be driven through to Anstruther and if we're ready, if we're prepared, a short link will unite Strayhorn to that line.'

Tom strove to remain impassive. He said, 'How short will that link be, Mr Coburn?'

'Four miles and forty-five chains.'

'Bridges?'

'A single span over the Caddis at Farmington.'

'Your agents have surveyed this route, I take it?'

'They have, sir, they have indeed.' Harry Coburn smiled. 'I am, however, a little puzzled as to why these proposals are of material interest to a man of the cloth. After all, the spiritual welfare of the parish will not be affected – or will it? I'm not, as you may have gathered, of a religious turn of mind.'

'Are you building a line to Leven, too?' Tom said.

'*I'm* not building anything,' Harry said.

'Your company, then.'

'No, I'll leave that project to the bankers, specifically to shareholders in the East of Fife Railway Company. Rumour has it that an amalgamation has been mooted between the Leven and the East of Fife companies, that they'll be incorporated under an extension bill to—'

'And Strayhorn?' Tom interrupted.

'Will be ready and waiting,' Harry Coburn said.

'Under the banner of a private company?'

'You have it, Mr Oakley, there you have it.'

'So the line from Strayhorn harbour, with a turntable in place, will be ready for use as soon as the East of Fife Railway Company—'

'Breaches through to Anstruther, yes.'

'Two years?'

'Possibly three.'

'Then you, Mr Coburn, will reap your rewards.'

'Not I,' said Harry. 'My investors.'

'How long is the term of the lease you acquired from Mazzucco?'

'Fifty years.'

'Fifty years! The man's mad!'

'Not mad – ill-informed,' said Harry.

'You traded on his ignorance, in other words.'

'On his greed, rather.' Harry placed a hand on Tom's arm. 'Martin Mazzucco will have the last laugh, however. Four or five years from now he will be the wealthiest man in Strayhorn.'

'How much have you invested so far?' Tom blurted out.

'Come now, sir, that's stretching confidentiality a little too far.'

'Capital, though, do you not need capital to advance the scheme?'

'Why, Mr Oakley? Do you have capital you wish to invest?'

Tom shook his head. 'I'm a church mouse, sir, broke to the wide.'

They were close now, conversing in undertones, brow touching brow.

Harry said, 'We know where there is money, though, do we not?'

'Do we?' Tom said.

'At High Cross, sir, there's money.'

'Thanks to you, Mr Coburn, Buckie Hollander barely has two halfpence left to rub together – or so his wife informs me.'

'No, but the girl has.'

'The girl?'

'The niece, Susanne Thorne.'

'Ah!' Tom said. 'Ah, yes!'

'If only we could persuade *her* to invest in railway stock.'

'How would we do that, Mr Coburn? By trading on her innocence?'

'On her aunt's greed,' said Harry. 'For reasons too complicated to explain, Bette Hollander no longer trusts me. It would, therefore, be advantageous to all of us – yourself included – if Mrs Hollander could be made to see the light. Do you think, sir, that you might be able to assist me in bringing this golden opportunity to the lady's attention?'

'Do you know, sir,' Tom Oakley said, 'I do believe I might.'

'What is it this time, Dr Redpath?' Prim said. 'An outbreak of typhus?'

'Nothing so serious,' Alan said.

'What then brings you here?'

'This young lady.' Alan nodded at Susanne.

It had been weeks since Dr Redpath's last visit to High Cross. Buckie had enjoyed comparatively good health throughout the winter, the ache in his joints quite bearable, though Susanne suspected that he might be putting a brave face on it just to save on the cost of treatment. Her cousin's education had put a great drain on the family budget and, on more than one occasion, she had overheard her aunt and uncle arguing about money.

'I've come to rescue her,' Alan said.

'Is rescuing young girls becoming a habit?' said Prim.

'Perhaps it is,' Alan said.

He wore a long oilskin coat and a muffler was wound round and round his throat. He looked, Susanne thought, like a highwayman, more debonair than dangerous.

'Rescue me from what?' she asked.

'The brutal forces of nature,' Alan answered.

'Impossible, quite impossible,' said Prim.

Susanne did not understand why the doctor found this remark amusing.

He said, 'I've just been down at High Cross, Susanne, and your uncle is concerned that you will be blown away if you don't start home soon.'

'Ah, the storm,' said Prim, nodding.

'According to the whale-master we're in for a very big blow,' Alan said. 'Come along, Susanne, pop on your bonnet and we'll be on our way.'

'Are the boats coming in?' Prim asked.

'Running hard before the rain-cloud,' Alan told her. 'It'll be a race for the nearest ports, I imagine, all up and down the coast.'

Susanne glanced at Prim whose cheeks had warmed sufficiently to throw her freckles into relief. She's blushing, Susanne thought. Great heavens, Prim's blushing! And, catching the woman's mood, she turned flirtatious, too.

'You came all this way just for *me?*'

'It's hardly the road to Babylon,' Prim said.

Susanne executed her best twirl, gay and charming. She had practised it on Buckie, who had praised her for her grace. She spun on tiptoe, plucked her cape from the hook by the door and her bonnet from the shelf.

The gale battered on the unlatched door, chalk dust swirled in the draught. Rain pattered on the windowpane, the gorse bushes thrashed in the gale. Susanne felt the throb of the storm in her veins and danced around the classroom for the sheer joy of it.

'Stop that silly cavorting,' Prim said, snappishly. 'If Dr Redpath has been kind enough to go out of his way to see you safely home, Susanne, the least you can do . . .'

'It's all right.' Alan placed a hand on the schoolteacher's arm. 'It's only a spring storm. No cause for alarm.'

'I'm not in the least . . .' Prim began, then impulsively covered the doctor's hand. 'Yes, I am alarmed. I hate storms.' For no longer than it takes to blink an eye, Prim rested her head on Alan Redpath's chest. 'However, I'll shutter the windows, rope the doors, bank down the fire, and be quite safe and snug. Thank you for your concern.'

Bonnet tipped over one ear, Susanne stopped in her tracks.

She stared at Prim's parted lips and flushed cheeks, at Dr Redpath's tender little smile and, disgruntled that her performance had earned her no praise, said, curtly, 'Very well. I'm ready. Let us be on our way.'

Before they were halfway along the shore road the rain had become so dense that sea and land were linked in a lashing grey haze. The pony forged into the teeth of the gale as if he were pulling a load of pig-iron. Susanne clung to the doctor as the gig tilted and, cresting the summit of the hill, almost overturned.

'Not a moment too soon, Susanne,' Alan shouted.

He seemed to enjoy the battle against the elements almost as much as she did. Holding on to her bonnet, she peeped round the doctor's shoulder at a fishing boat struggling to round the point. How she would have loved to be on board, clinging on for dear life, while the fishermen fought with canvas, ropes and rudder. Then the boat was gone. For an instant she thought it had been sucked under and the poor fishermen drowned, then it reappeared, fleetingly, pitching on the troughs, and vanished again, blotted out by the rocky headland.

Alan steered the gig into the kitchen yard.

The hens had waddled into hiding and only the cockerel, showing his mettle, clung to the slope of the ash-heap, crowing and shaking himself, then he too put pride behind him and, neck thrust out and wings spread, chased past the pony into the coop.

Nancy stood by the kitchen door. Buckie watched from the window. Susanne hopped from the gig and ran for shelter. Alan freed the pony from the shafts and led him into an outbuilding.

'What's he doing?' Susanne shouted.

'Dryin' the beast off,' Nancy told her. 'There's straw in there, though it's none too fresh, I'm thinkin'.'

'Is Dr Redpath staying for supper?'

'He'll not dare make a dash for home tonight,' Nancy said, as the gig swayed, toppled and fell with a clatter, one wheel spinning madly, and the hood, torn from its frame, flew off over the rooftop like a kite.

Before supper Buckie invited them to bow their heads and offer a prayer for those in peril on the breast of the deep. The solemn moment passed. The parlour was cosy, the supper table, under a swaying lamp, an island of tranquillity.

Dr Redpath was given Louis's chair. A dry shirt had been found for him, dry stockings dug from a drawer in Louis's room. He was shorter than Louis, quite lean and slight, and looked very casual for a guest, Susanne thought, with his hair still damp and the baggy sleeves of her cousin's shirt rolled up to expose his hairy forearms. He had lovely hands, she realised, slender and long-fingered, the nails not bitten or broken. She watched him break bread into his broth and, with impeccable manners, eat.

Nancy had cooked a flank of mutton and with hashed potato cakes, peas and onions there was just enough to go round.

The wild ride home from the schoolhouse had sharpened Susanne's appetite. She ate hungrily, glancing up now and then at the doctor to see if the menu suited him. He murmured, nodded approval and even winked at her, as if they were sharing a secret.

Buckie poured wine; any excuse, Bette declared, being good enough for her husband to visit the cellar. They drank claret, several glasses each, and Susanne was given a glass to herself, unwatered. Her head swam a little and the fury of the storm outside seemed to recede. She caught herself just in time. Another sip of the soft red liquid and she would have turned tipsy and embarrassed herself in front of the doctor.

'These women you lodge with . . .' Bette was saying.

'The Misses Allardyce,' Alan said. 'Sisters.'

'Are they respectable?' said Bette.

'Auntie,' Susanne heard herself protest, 'of course they are.'

'You know them, do you?' Aunt Bette snapped.

'No, but Dr Redpath wouldn't lodge with – well, just anyone.'

'I know the Allardyce girls,' Buckie put in. 'Girls no more, I fear. Be in their sixties by now. Twins, are they not?'

'Identical twins,' Alan said.

'Isn't it odd,' said Bette, 'sharing a house with twins?'

Susanne was aware that her aunt was displeased about something but she couldn't imagine what it might be. Aunt Bette's moods had been up, down and round about these past months. Buckie said she was missing Louis more than she cared to admit. Dr Redpath had nothing to do with Louis, though, except that he was wearing Louis's shirt and stockings and occupied her cousin's chair.

'Most odd,' Alan said. 'Mildred and Maude are as alike as two peas in a pod. I pass one on the staircase and find the other in the dining-room a second later; very disconcerting.'

'They were good-looking girls, as I recall,' said Buckie. 'Copper-nobs?'

'They're rather snowy now,' said Alan, 'but yes, I believe they are, or were, red-haired. They have that sort of pallor.'

'Treat you well, do they?' said Bette.

'Admirably.'

'I knew them when they were lassies in Buckhaven,' Buckie said. 'The father was a factor for the old duke, a fine, well-set-up man with a loud voice. The mother had a bit of money on her side, I think. The girls were schooled in the domestic arts and crafts.'

'But they never married?' said Susanne. 'What a waste.'

'They had each other, I suppose,' said Buckie, with a shrug.

'Lord knows, they had suitors aplenty; none seemed to please them.'

'You weren't a suitor, Uncle, were you?' Susanne asked.

'Not me, sweetheart, not me. I was just a poor lad from the quays,' Buckie said, with a hint in his voice that he had been at one time an admirer, if not a suitor, of the pretty red-haired twins.

'Old women now,' Bette stated and, to Susanne's surprise, helped herself to a third glass of claret. 'We're all old women now, aren't we?'

'You're in your prime, my dear, still in your prime,' Buckie said, though Susanne had a feeling that his thoughts were elsewhere.

She wondered if he was thinking of the Allardyce girls and if he ever regretted having fallen in love with Aunt Bette. She glimpsed her own life as a maze of possibilities, shaped by unpredictability. If Papa had not died, for instance, she would never have come to Scotland, would never have met Louis.

'Have you never thought of getting married, Alan?' she asked.

It was the first time she had used his forename. The doctor did not seem to mind. The doctor did not seem to mind about anything very much. To all appearances he was an amiable chap, though he'd been audacious enough when it came to confronting the diggers.

'Oh, I've thought of it,' Alan said. 'I just haven't found the right girl yet.'

'Man in your position – much to offer – need of a wife to look after you – two old crones – not satisfactory.'

Susanne listened with half an ear to her aunt dispensing advice to a man who required no advice from anyone. Louis would have flown into a rage by now, would have shouted and stood up to his mother, resentful of her interference. Alan Redpath was more mature than her cousin, of course, and owed no more deference to Aunt Bette than courtesy demanded. How civilised, and how civilising, he seemed: Susanne propped an elbow on the table, a wee bit tipsily, and studied him admiringly.

'All true, Mrs Hollander,' Alan said. 'I confess my guilt on every count. However, I'm not in a position to offer a young lady any sort of life.'

'Balderdash!' said Buckie. 'Look at you, man: you're a doctor.'

'Given the sums we've paid you,' Bette said, 'you can hardly plead the poor lip, can you?'

'Alas, few of my patients are as prompt in making payment as you are.'

'Do you not dun them for your fee?' Bette said.

'No, not often,' Alan admitted.

'I wouldn't let them off with it.'

'Alan is a healer first and a doctor second,' Buckie said.

'That's not something you can say about all the members of the medical profession,' said Bette. 'Look at them, riding round Edinburgh in their painted coaches and silk hats as if they owned the world. There's money in sickness, and you won't convince me otherwise. Why don't you set up shop in Edinburgh?'

'I don't want to practise in Edinburgh.'

'Don't you have connections there? Your brother, for instance?'

'Mrs Hollander,' Alan said, 'I'm happy as I am, in Fife.'

'In Fife,' Buckie sang, trying to lighten the tone, 'without a wife.'

Bette went on, 'If my son had set his mind to it he could have been a doctor. He'd have made a grand doctor, my son. I've no doubt the rich would have been calling upon his services and he wouldn't have to wait for his fees.'

'It takes time,' Alan said, 'to build a reputation.'

Buckie nodded agreement. 'Guineas follow fame.'

'As they do in all professions,' Alan said. 'How is your son, by the by?'

'He's well!' Aunt Bette said cryptically, and, setting down her glass, yelled at Nancy to fetch in the pudding.

They stood by the window, Buckie and he, the curtain billowing like a loose sail. Nancy and Susanne had given him a hand to drag the gig into the lee of the outhouse and tomorrow he would examine it for damage. The hood would probably be halfway to Crieff, shredded beyond repair. He'd have to ride out without a hood for a while, for he had no funds to pay for a new one.

He might borrow from his father or his brother but had never been, and never would be, a debtor. He had two good suits of clothing and three shirts, one pair of boots in good repair and shoes for Sunday. His medicine case was stocked, his rent paid to the end of April. He doubted if the ladies would toss him out if he asked for a deferment but one never quite knew how people would react when money was involved. Surely he would earn enough to buy a new hood before next winter; if he didn't, then he would cover his head with a canvas sack and ride about like a cadger.

He placed a hand on the whale-master's shoulder and murmured, 'I've a feeling your wife isn't happy to have me here. Perhaps the wind has dropped enough to let me ride the pony home.'

'Nah, nah,' Buckie said, quietly. 'These damned north-easters never back down before dawn. It'll not be high water for another hour but, like as not, the track to the hill will already be swamped. Pay no heed to my wife, man. She's as angry as a wasp in a jam jar these days, no rhyme or reason for it.'

He held on to Alan's arm and glanced over his shoulder.

Bette was helping Nancy to clear the table and Susanne had gone into the bedroom to feed Ajax who had become over-excited and had been locked up.

'Has she complained of headaches?' Alan asked.

Buckie gave a little grunt, possibly laughter. 'She complains of flatulence now and then, nothing more.'

Alan nodded and, still supporting the old man, peered from the window into the swirling darkness. The sea boomed on the shore and with the rain came debris, strands of weed and fistfuls of sand hurled against the glass.

'Aye,' Buckie said, 'the lifeboats will be out tonight, I fear, if they can breach the surf. Even for spring tides this is a bad one. The salvage crews will be licking their chops, though, for an ill wind blows good their way.'

Lost in the roar of the storm Alan didn't hear the bedroom door opening. He glimpsed the glimmer of a candle, the wick laid almost horizontal by the draught in the hall, and, turning, saw Susanne there, watching him.

Poised in that limbo between girlhood and womanhood, she was elfin and charming, yet somehow sinister too. He experienced none of the pity for Susanne Thorne that he felt for the girls in the farm steadings or the over-worked daughters of fisher folk.

'Ajax's asleep,' Susanne said. 'I thought he'd be frightened, but he only wanted fed.' And then, to Alan's disappointment, she went off upstairs to bed.

The wind was still strong and the sea restless under a band of clear sky. Tom had taken one look at the steep cliff path and, with his coat whipping about his knees and his hat struggling to take wing, had decided that a long walk was a better option than an early grave.

On the streets of Strayhorn fishermen were checking boats and tackle and householders were surveying the damage to slates and chimneypots. One of the Macfarlane boys was combing the hillside in search of lost creels and from him Tom learned that a coal sloop had foundered at the mouth of the Eden and a trader from Leith had been smashed to pieces on the harbour wall at Pittenweem, but how the news had travelled so rapidly was a mystery.

The High Cross beach was littered with flotsam, and damp sand had scoured the wooden steps and built ramps on the window ledges.

Tom knocked on the door. Bette opened it. She wore an ornate robe in an Oriental pattern and had already titivated her hair and applied a little false colour to her lips and cheeks. Startled, Tom wondered if she had been seducing her gouty husband before breakfast; the very idea appalled him.

'You!' Bette exclaimed. 'What do you want?'

'I came to see if you had withstood the rigours of the night.'

'Did you now?' Bette said. 'Well, we did, thank you. Good-day.'

'Bette,' he hissed, 'have some pity. I fretted about you all last night as the wind raged and the waves tossed and . . .'

'Oh, come in, for heaven's sake,' Bette said, and showed him into the living-room. 'I believe you know Dr Redpath.'

'Of course,' Tom said. 'Please, do not let me interrupt your breakfast. I came to see if all was well with you in the wake of the storm?'

'Nah, Mr Oakley,' said Buckie, 'our house is built on rock and has withstood many a worse storm and will withstand many more, no doubt.'

The parlour was filled with an appetising aroma of hot bread, bacon, kippers and coffee. Saliva trickled on to Tom's tongue and his stomach growled. He watched the girl, Susanne, shovel up a forkful of kipper laced with the yolk of a runny egg.

'Still, it's a kindly gesture,' Buckie went on, 'so, since you're here now and we're all hale an' hearty, will you not sit yourself down and have a bite?'

'I'm sure Mr Oakley has better . . .' Bette began.

'I'd be honoured to break bread with you,' Tom said, quickly.

A chair was brought in from a bedroom and he was served.

He wasted no time in apology or discussion but fell to with knife and fork while the doctor and the girl eyed him, quizzically.

'Did you come in by the town?' Buckie asked.

'I did.'

'Is there much damage?'

'There is, alas,' Tom said and, between mouthfuls, told the whale-master what he'd learned from the boy. He had no rapport with the old man, no bond, save that they shared the same woman. He still found it difficult to believe that this old chap had ever had the stuffing, let alone the imagination, to couple with plump Bette Hollander other than flat on a bed with the candle snuffed out. He glanced at Bette's painted features and silk robe and wondered if she was out to impress the doctor. Surely not even Bette Hollander would have the gall to throw herself at a man half her age?

Buckie said. 'There will be more, I fear.'

'Uh?' said Tom. 'More?'

'Shipwrecks,' said Bette.

'Aye, the quays are lined with herring barrels needing transportation to Edinburgh. If the weather prevents the luggers putting out the catch will spoil.'

Tom pricked up his ears. 'Now,' he said, 'if only we had a railway link with the capital, bad weather wouldn't matter.'

'We'll never have a railway link to Edinburgh,' Bette said.

'Mr Coburn thinks otherwise.'

'Have you been speaking to Harry Coburn?' Bette said.

'No,' Tom said, 'but a sagacious investor like Henry

Coburn would hardly lease the Fisherfield acres and bring in a digging crew . . .'

'Those savages!' said Bette.

'. . . bring in a crew of labourers if there wasn't *something* in the wind.'

'Hot air,' said Bette.

'I have heard talk that the Leven and the East of Fife railway companies hope to merge, with a view to driving a line through to Anstruther,' Alan said.

Bette snorted. 'We'll all be dead before that happens.'

'Not all of us, Auntie,' Susanne piped up, 'surely not all of us.'

'You're young enough to see it happen, I suppose,' Bette conceded.

'I tell you,' Tom ventured, 'if I were wealthy and inclined to gamble I'd wager a fair stake that Henry Coburn will push this thing through.'

'What do you know of railways?' said Bette, scathingly.

'Enough,' said Tom, 'to recognise a good thing when I see it.'

'I thought the railway bubble had burst,' Alan said.

'Far from it,' Tom said. 'New lines opening up every day. Like it or not, sir, the railway is destined to become the backbone of trade in this land of ours.'

'Do I detect an element of missionary zeal, Reverend?' said Buckie.

'The more cash that flows into the parish,' said Tom, 'the more cash flows into the church. I'm only interested in my parish and my church.'

'Well!' Alan Redpath tapped the table gently. 'Well, Mrs Hollander, I regret that I must abandon this fascinating discussion but I'll have to be on my way, particularly if Susanne wants dropped off at the schoolhouse.'

'Yes, please,' said Susanne, and leaped to her feet.

'First, though, we'll have to right my gig and see if it's damaged.'

Buckie heaved himself up and reached for his stick.

Tom remained seated, staring across the breakfast plates at Bette.

She did not meet his eye but dabbled her spoon in the spillings in her saucer until her husband hobbled out through the kitchen into the back yard on the heels of Redpath and the girl.

'Why did you come, Tom?' Bette whispered.

'Because, my darling, I've missed you.'

'Liar!'

'For both our sakes, I have tried to give you up – but I cannot.'

Bette blinked rapidly several times, her chest heaving under the robe. She was, he realised, in a highly agitated state. He glanced at the kitchen door, saw only empty daylight slanting in from the yard.

He caught her hand, lacing his fingers into hers.

'I tried, the Lord God knows how I tried,' he said, 'but it's impossible.'

'Can't what?'

'Give you up,' he said, through his teeth.

'I thought you'd grown tired of me?'

'Tired of you? My dearest girl,' Tom said, swallowing hard, 'I love you.'

'Tom, is that true?'

'Upon my word, it's true,' he said, and, as Susanne pranced back into the living-room, snatched his hand away just in the nick of time.

Susanne knelt on the box by the window and stared out at the sea, restless, dark and mysterious now as dusk swept over the headlands. It was a year, almost to the day, since she had come to High Cross. She could barely remember what life had been like in London, the rhythm of it, the tempo, the little joys and pleasures that it had doled out. She remembered the bleak afternoon in the lawyer's chambers in the Staple Inn well enough, though, how Mr Reeve had patronised her and what he had told her concerning marriage.

Kneeling on a dusty chest at the salt-stained window in her cousin's room, she did not feel at all like a wealthy young heiress, but more like a waif who had strayed into lives that had no connection with her own.

She slipped from the window seat and crossed to the harmonium. A cotton sheet was draped over the instrument and dust had accumulated in the creases. In any other room in the house she would have folded the sheet neatly but here it hardly seemed to matter and she tossed it into the air and let it spill across the bed.

It was almost, but not quite, dark.

Candles, stiff as mortar, stood in holders and the lamp had lost most of its oil, but she needed no light.

She seated herself on the stool and placed her toes on the pedals.

In Miss Millar's Academy, Mr Rayburn had instructed a class in music every Wednesday afternoon and, on Fridays, Susanne had had a half-hour with the feathery old gentleman all to herself. The Academy's piano was a deal less complicated than Louis's precious harmonium, however.

She placed her fingers on the keys, fished for a pedal, depressed her left foot slightly, and heard the instrument sigh. She pressed a little harder and heard the voice of the organ throb within its casing. She lifted her arms, spread her fingers and, without touching the keys, wrung from the harmonium a great cascade of silent notes that matched the Voluntary that rang in her head.

Extravagant, flamboyant, Louis to a tee, she threw her head

back and mouthed the melody, her elbows working like pistons.

When, a moment later, Ajax padded into the room and stared up at her, she laughed and continued her soundless performance while the dog, unsure of what she was up to, cocked his shaggy head and whined.

II

Roland had a head cold and Waylie's bowels were bound. Morven's nightmares had not abated and Freddie had fallen, or been thrown, into a gorse bush and had a rash all over his face.

'I'm sick of it,' Zena said. 'I'm sick of being a nursemaid. They're not *my* children. Why should I have to look after them?'

'Hmm.' Susanne had heard her friend's complaints before.

They were seated on the wall of the school yard, eating bread and cheese. Prim had gone to the village to buy fish and a general air of anarchy pervaded the school yard.

'I don't even have Sunday off,' Zena went on. 'Fact, Sunday's worse than a school day. I wash them, dress them an' wipe their blessed noses, then I have to sit in church for hours listening to Papa tell everyone what sinners we are and how undeserving of God's grace.' She leaned forward, knees spread, and spat a crumb of hard rind on to the grass. 'For two pins, Susanne, I'd be up and off.'

'You've been telling me that for weeks now.'

'This time I mean it,' Zena said. 'I tell you, if those diggers ever return to Strayhorn, I'll not be begging to be rescued. He wasn't so bad, my Danny.'

'He was horrid,' Susanne said. 'You've forgotten how horrid.'

'If I'd gone off with Danny at least I'd be sharing a bed with a man.'

'I won't share a bed with anyone,' said Susanne.

'You would, though, if he asked you.'

'If who asked me?'

'Louis.'

'No, I would not,' said Susanne, indignantly. 'I won't share a bed with Louis, or anyone, until I'm properly married.' She popped a crust into her mouth and, in a muffled voice, asked, 'Who would you *like* to share a bed with?'

'Dr Redpath; he's a gentleman,' Zena said. 'I wouldn't turn up my nose at your cousin either, now you mention it.'

'Louis can't marry you,' Susanne blurted out. 'Louis is going to marry me when he comes home.'

'*If* he comes home.'

'Of course Louis will come home.'

'If I had a billet in Edinburgh, you wouldn't catch me rushing back.'

'Dr Redpath doesn't want to live in Edinburgh. He told me so.'

'I'm sure,' said Zena, with a crooked grin, 'I could change his mind. You like him, don't you; the doctor, I mean?'

'I like him very much.'

'So does our Prim.'

'Really!' said Susanne, feigning surprise.

'She's awfully keen on fresh air these days, in case you hadn't noticed,' Zena said. 'Off to the village at the dinner time almost every day.'

'Do you think she has an assignation with Dr Redpath?'

'I don't know what she has with Dr Redpath,' Zena said, 'but I can guess what she'd like to have.'

'But she's *old*,' said Susanne.

'Not so old as all that.'

'She's too set in her ways.'

'She'd *unset* herself quickly enough if the right man came along.'

Zena had been very annoying of late, teasing her with talk of matters that she, Susanne, did not quite understand. It was all very well for Zena; she knew a great deal about love and marriage and other sordid facts of life.

'Prim has no money,' Susanne said.

'What's that got to do with it?'

'Dr Redpath has no money either.'

'Balderdash!' Zena said.

'It's true; he told me so. He told me he can't marry because he has nothing to offer a wife.'

'He told *you*? Why did he tell *you*?'

'Oh, very well; he told my aunt and I overheard.'

'Quite the little eavesdropper, aren't you, Susanne?'

'I wasn't eavesdropping. The conversation took place at the supper table and everyone heard him.'

'Everyone isn't there to hear what my papa says to your aunt, though, when they meet in secret,' said Zena.

'In secret?'

'Don't pretend you don't know,' said Zena.

'I don't know. I don't know what you're talking about.'

'She sneaks up to the manse garden, behind the church, to see him.'

'Yes, she brings things for—'

'They meet in the cave on the shore, too, in the summer.'

Susanne hadn't forgotten that morning on the beach when she'd found the drawers, and Louis had been so upset. She shook her head, frantically.

'No, that can't be right.'

The chit-chat had become serious all of a sudden. Susanne wondered if Zena was making it up, and, if so, why.

'We all know what's going on,' said Zena. 'Well, some of us do.'

'Your mama, too?'

'I'm not sure about Mama,' said Zena. 'I'm not going to tell her.'

'But – but what – I mean what do they do? Kiss?'

Zena said, 'We were better off in the last place. I liked the last place. We had lots of rooms in the last place. Then we were up and packing to come here. I was too young to realise what was going on but it's my guess my papa misbehaved.'

'Misbehaved?'

'Kissed someone he shouldn't have,' said Zena.

'This is just a story, isn't it?'

'Yes, it's just a story,' said Zena. 'Anyway, what's wrong with stealin' a kiss when nobody's lookin'?'

'Nothing, I suppose,' said Susanne.

'Nancy,' Susanne said, 'where did Mr Oakley come from?'

The woman bent over a scrubbing brush, back bowed, hair wisping across her face. She lifted her head and glanced at Susanne. 'What sort o' question is that?'

'Just a question. Where did he preach before he came to Strayhorn?'

Nancy went back to scrubbing, pushing a tide of suds before the brush. 'Somewhere in the Lothians,' she growled. 'Your chum Zena will be only too pleased t' tell you all about it.'

'Perhaps,' Susanne said, 'Aunt Bette will tell me all about it.'

Nancy sat back on her heels.

'I mean,' Susanne went on, 'Aunt Bette *is* Mr Oakley's friend, is she not?'

'He's the minister. It's his burden in life to be friends wi' everybody.'

'His special friend.'

Nancy slapped the cloth into the pail and hoisted herself upright, mouth slack, eyes hooded. Susanne leaned on the chopping block and calmly observed the servant's pantomime of indecision.

'Aye,' Nancy said, at length, 'the devil will find out your lies an' tease you wi' them, given time an' rope enough.' She touched Susanne's cheek, one thick forefinger pressing against the girl's lips, the broken nail hard as horn. 'Leave it. Not a word about Mr Oakley's murky past in this house.'

'I only asked where—'

'Wheesh now, wheesh,' the servant said. 'Not another word about this business, lassie, if you know what's good for you.'

'Is it true?'

'God's word is the only truth, though Satan devises a thousand ways o' hidin' it from us. We sleep perpetual on a bed o' lies, Susanne Thorne, but it's better to sleep sound than not sleep at all.'

'Nancy . . .'

But Nancy had stalked out into the yard to pour away the dirty water and wash out the pail at the pump.

It came as a considerable surprise to everyone when, on a Saturday morning early in the month of April, Harry Coburn's curricle clipped down the track from Strayhorn with Benbow, in full livery, at the helm and young Miss Darsie Coburn, all alone, reclining in the passenger seat.

Buckie, on the porch, was surveying the state of the weather and Susanne was on the beach throwing sticks for Ajax when the carriage slithered to a halt at the steps. Benbow curled his whip, hopped down and opened the door for Darsie.

The girl, grown taller, stepped on to the sandy strip and paused to allow Buckie to admire her. There was certainly much to admire: a slender waist, narrow shoulders, a bosom thrust up pertly by a basquin bodice, a pale fine-boned face peeping out of a mass of ringlets in whose midst lurked a tiny lace-fringed bonnet.

'I have come to visit,' Darsie said. 'Am I welcome?'

'Of course you are, dearest,' Buckie said. 'Come in, come in.'

Darsie spun round and, lifting herself on a slippered toe, batted her green eyes in the direction of the beach.

'Is that my friend Susanne?'

'It is,' said Buckie.

'What's she doing?'

'Playing with the dog,' said Buckie.

'Oh, the dog,' said Darsie and, with Buckie limping after her, sailed blithely into the hall.

Benbow was in the yard attending the thoroughbreds by the time Susanne screwed up enough courage to return to the house. She knew perfectly well who the visitor was; even from the edge of the ocean, several hundred yards away, Darsie Coburn was unmistakable. With the hem of her skirts wet, her shoes caked with sand and her hair tangled, Susanne trailed up from the beach and, calling Ajax to heel, slipped around the house into the kitchen yard.

She had no desire to square up to Darsie Coburn, no wish to share whatever gossip the girl had brought from Macklin House. She hadn't forgotten the first and only time she had encountered Darsie and how inferior the girl had made her feel.

Even so, Susanne nursed a little worm of curiosity. Over the past fortnight several letters addressed to Aunt Bette had arrived from Harry Coburn and Aunt Bette had spent hours closeted in her room with pen, ink and paper answering them. There had also been arguments, hissing little spats between Buckie and Aunt Bette and, salted away in the back of Susanne's mind was a suspicion that Zena's tale of infidelity might very well be true.

Benbow was brushing one of the thoroughbreds with a handful of old straw while the other animal, tethered to the pump, drank from the well cup. The curricle, mud-splattered and not so elegant as Susanne remembered, was drawn up by the chicken coop, the rooster flapping arrogantly on the driving seat as if the vehicle had been wheeled in merely to provide him with a perch.

'Damned bird.' Benbow flung an arm in the rooster's direction, making the horse shy and whinny. 'Freck off, you clout, freck off.' Then he spotted Ajax and, being hardly much bigger than the dog, sought shelter behind the horse's crupper. 'Call him off, missy, afore he frightens my cuddies.'

'He won't harm you.' Susanne grabbed Ajax by the ruff and hung on to him with all her might. 'What are you doing here?'

'My job,' said Benbow. 'More's the pity.'

'I mean,' said Susanne, 'what's *she* doing here?'

'Came on a whim, she says,' Benbow answered. 'But she never does nothin' on a whim, that one. I reckon she was packed off to visit. He's shootin' today an' has a party on the grounds.'

'Shooting what?'

'Rooks,' Benbow said.

He crept from behind the horse but kept a hand on the animal's crupper, stroking and soothing it. The thoroughbred's big wet eye flared, warily.

'Do you mean,' Susanne said, 'that he wants rid of her?'

Benbow had just enough discretion to hesitate. 'Think what you like.'

'I thought your mistress was at boarding school in St Andrews.'

'Holiday. Easter.'

'Oh!' Susanne said and, thus primed, headed for the kitchen door.

'Oh, my dearest, my darling friend.' Darsie smothered her with kisses. 'Where have you been? Why didn't you write? I've missed you so much.'

'Really?' said Susanne, sourly.

'Were you playing with the dog?'

'What? Yes.'

'We have dogs. They are not very friendly and I don't like them. They are hunting dogs, of course, not pets.' She clasped Susanne's arm, dragged her across the living-room and forced her into a chair. 'Where's Bette? I'm so eager to see my dear friend again.'

'Bette's gone out for a while,' Buckie said. 'She won't be long.'

'Gone out? Gone out?' Darsie trilled. 'Where has she gone?'

'To call on the minister's family. She has a basket for them.'

'A basket, what sort of basket?'

'Comestibles,' Susanne said.

'What's that?'

'Food.'

'Ah! Because they are hungry?'

'Yes.'

'But why are they hungry?'

'Because they're poor.'

'Why are they poor?'

'Because they haven't any money.'

Buckie cleared his throat loudly and waved his stick as if to herd a pair of skittish lambs back into the fold. 'It's a charitable act, Miss Coburn.'

'Well, I shall wait,' Darsie said. 'Is there refreshment?'

She seated herself and stretched out her legs. She had exchanged the pantalettes for stockings, Susanne noticed, which was something at least to be thankful for.

'Tea?' Buckie offered.

'A glass of sherry wine, perhaps?' said Darsie.

Buckie glanced in the direction of the kitchen but decided not to convey the request to Nancy for fear, perhaps, that the servant would say something rude. He shuffled into the hall to fetch a bottle and glasses from the cupboard that he called 'his cellar'.

Susanne and Darsie eyed each other in silence.

At length, Darsie said, 'Your cousin asks to be reminded to you.'

'Louis?' Susanne said. 'Have you seen Louis?'

'Yes, in Edinburgh. He took us to dinner in the Café Royal. Have you ever been in the Café Royal? No, of course you haven't. We dined behind a partition.'

Susanne squeezed her knees together and clung to the sides of the chair. As evenly as possible, she said, 'Is my cousin well?'

'Bursting with rude health,' Darsie said. 'He's very sweet, really.'

'Did he play the organ for you?'

'The organ?'

'Louis is studying music; didn't you know?'

'Ah yes, of course, yes, the organ.'

'If he didn't talk about music,' said Susanne, 'what did he talk about?'

'Me,' said Darsie, and smiled.

A voice inside Susanne's head shrieked, *Lies, Lies*, but she kept her composure, and said, 'It must have been a very brief dinner.'

'I'm sure I don't know what you mean.'

'If the conversation was so limited.'

'Oh no, it lasted for hours. Hours. It was long after eleven before Benbow took us home to our hotel.'

'Benbow dined with you?'

Darsie's smile was effortless. 'Silly puss,' she said. 'Benbow waited in the mews. Do you know what a mews is, dearest: a mews is—'

'I know what a mews is,' said Susanne.

Buckie was huffing and puffing in the confines of the

cupboard; Susanne wished that he would hurry. Her chest was so tight that she felt as if she might stop breathing altogether. She fixed her gaze on Darsie Coburn's painted face, on those pale green, flickering eyes. Darsie was a fool, a simpering fool, and she, Susanne Thorne, was a fool for being sucked in by her lies; yet the thought of Louis and this doll-like creature supping together reduced her caution.

'Did he ask about me?' she heard herself say.

'Did he? Did he?' Darsie rolled her eyes. 'No, I don't believe he did. He asked after his mama. He asked after his papa, but . . .' Her sympathy was cloying. 'I'm sorry, dear friend, he just did not seem to care about you.'

'But you said he asked to be reminded . . .'

Pursed lips, a beautiful little moue: 'I made that up.'

'Made it up?'

'To make you feel better,' Darsie said, and pretended to be surprised when Susanne flung herself from the chair and fled from the living-room in tears.

Spring! Aye, Effie thought, it must be spring since Bette Hollander has found her way up from the beach again. Outlined against a streaky morning sky, she could make out the fat little woman conversing with Tom on the bench by the graveyard. There would be a basket of food, no doubt, and Tom would tell her a pack of lies about what the woman wanted when it was all too obvious what the woman wanted. With a disgruntled sigh, Effie returned to hanging out washing.

She had stripped the beds and trampled the blankets through two tubs of hot water and, without Zena's help, had wrung them out and spread them on the beech hedge to dry. She had pinned the sheets to the rope and was just finishing that task when a voice behind her, a voice both soft and rough, like a cat's tongue, said, 'Could I be givin' you a hand with that, Effie?'

She turned, startled, slapped away a sheet, and found herself face to face with Angus Gamrie.

'It's done now, Angus, thank you all the same.'

She could smell soap from the sheets, so clean, and feel the breeze, gentle as a kiss, drifting over the hem of the cliff. She wiped her brow with the back of her hand. 'If it's Tom you're looking for he's down by the church with the Hollander woman.'

'They'll be praying, I expect,' said Angus.

'That,' said Effie, 'I doubt.'

Waylie, Roland and Petal were penned in the grass yard, a strip of ground by the drying green. Effie could see Petal's bonnet bobbing up and down and hear the shrieks and giggles of the game they had invented; her children were safe and, for the time being, happy.

She tidied her straggling locks, and waited for Angus to speak.

'Aren't you going down there?' she said, at length.

'I'll wait here with you – if it suits.'

'It suits fine,' said Effie. 'Is it kirk business you want him for?'

'It is,' said Angus. 'To pin him down to a date for the baptisms.'

Effie chuckled. 'The usual winter crop, I suppose?'

'Aye, three registered so far. Three more to come.'

'When the nights grow long . . .'

Angus chuckled too. 'Well, Effie, if you do your arithmetic, you'll see it's not long nights that foster new generations: it's mid-summer madness.'

'Sure,' said Effie, 'I should've known that.'

They walked together and peeped over the hedge at the children.

Angus placed a hand on her waist, very lightly, to steady her. She waited for Angus to say more about Bette Hollander but he was too mannerly to pursue that topic. Out of the corner of her eye she watched her husband stoop over Mrs Hollander in earnest conversation. She wondered what he was saying to the woman and if all his fancy words contained as much meaning as the light touch of Angus Gamrie's hand upon her back.

'He went to see Harry Coburn, Effie: did he tell you?'

'No.'

'Benbow let it slip to Sandy Raiker. Raiker told me.'

'What could Tom possibly want from Harry Coburn?'

'I was hopin' you might be able to enlighten me,' said Angus.

Effie shook her head. Whenever nice things happened to her, Tom was always there to spoil it; Tom and Tom's affairs were inescapable even on a fine spring morning on the drying green.

'It might be the railway,' she said. 'He's been chattering on about railways a lot of late.'

'There is no railway,' Angus said.

'But there will be – there might be.'

'It's another of Coburn's tricks,' Angus stated.

Effie leaned against the sagging hedge. The elder did not move away but, to Effie's disappointment, there was no warmth in his eyes now.

She said, 'Coburn's building a turn-thing, isn't he?'

It had been weeks since she had been in Strayhorn. Zena and Greg brought in provisions, sugar and bread, butcher meat and fish. Milk, butter and eggs were delivered in Mr Latimer's cart every other day. She had heard from Greg, however, that work on the Fisherfield diggings had stopped and that the labourers had not been seen since the night of the riot.

'What evidence is there of that?' Angus said. 'The sheds have been knocked down, some pits and trenches have been dug in the acres; that's the only sign of railways that we have so far.'

'Tom says it'll take time.'

'Does Tom also say it'll take money?' Angus asked.

Effie was aware that she was being interrogated and that any answer she might give would be a betrayal of her husband's confidence.

'Tom talks of little else but money,' she said.

'Any man who gives his money to Henry Coburn is a fool.'

'Well, whatever he might be,' Effie said, 'Tom's no fool when it comes to money. Besides – hah – we've none of it, not a spare penny.'

'Effie' – Angus moved closer – 'are you sure?'

She gestured at her patched dress and wrinkled stockings. 'Look at me,' she said, ruefully. 'Do I look like a rich man's wife?'

'No, Effie,' Angus said. 'But . . .' He inclined his head and stared in the direction of the graveyard and the figures outlined against the sky.

'He – he wouldn't borrow, would he, Angus?' Effie asked.

'I know not what he'd do,' the elder answered.

She gave herself a shake and, pushing herself from the clutches of the beech hedge, tapped his sleeve. 'Well,' she said, crisply, 'it's a good thing for the parish that it's you, not Tom, who holds the purse-strings.'

Too modest to acknowledge the truth of Effie's statement, Angus nodded and, under cover of the beech hedge, gently squeezed her hand.

Bette had enjoyed Tom's 'company' both in and out of the potting shed and had felt wonderfully restored in spirit, if somewhat weakened in the knees, by the encounter. She had been slightly less than overjoyed by the turn of conversation afterwards, however, when, instead of expressing undying love, Tom had fallen to talking about the railway, that mythic mile or two of track that would bestow wealth and happiness on the citizens of Strayhorn.

In spite of the drabness of life at High Cross, Bette had retained a spark of optimism and Tom's persuasive argument had swung her round into the wind again, raising her hopes and blinding her to the sad lessons of experience. Was it then, she wondered, mere coincidence that Harry Coburn's daughter happened to be sipping sherry in the living-room when she returned home from her tryst, or was there a conspiracy, some twisted plot to part her from the few savings she had left?

'Aunt, Aunt, Aunt,' Darsie chanted, bussing her cheek and wrapping slender arms about her. 'How good it is to be here with you again after so many months of misery.'

'Ah! Oh! Yes,' Bette managed to get out. 'Is your papa . . .'

'Shooting.' Darsie linked arms with Bette and steered her to a chair. 'He sends you his warmest regards and hopes to call upon you very, very soon.'

'I'll look forward to . . .'

'She saw Louis,' Buckie put in.

'Louis? In Edinburgh?' Bette cried.

'They dined,' Buckie said, 'at the Café Royal.'

'Behind the partition,' Darsie added and, pulling a chair up close, fondled Bette's arm while she recounted the tale of her visit to Edinburgh and supper with the prodigal son.

Susanne's first impulse was to throw herself upon Louis's bed and weep into the bolster. *She*, not Darsie Coburn, should have been in the Café Royal. *She*, not Darsie Coburn, was Louis's loyal friend. *She*, not Darsie Coburn, would nurture his talent and protect him from the corruption of the world.

She stamped into Louis's room and stood, quivering like one of Benbow's thoroughbreds, with her hands over her face, then, wiping away her tears, gave herself over to a spasm of pure, unholy rage. She jumped up on the bed and ground her heel into the bolster. She tore off the patchwork quilt and threw it to the floor. She jerked open the drawers of the dressing-table and scattered clothing about the room. She ran to the stacks of books intending to topple and scatter them too – but at that moment something stayed her. She clenched her teeth, stepped up to the harmonium, peeled off the dust sheet, seated herself on the bench, glared at the keys and rested her foot on the blowing pedal.

It had to be done right, had to be done properly. If she extracted from the instrument nothing but a pitiful wail then she would be exposed as a silly little girl filled with pique and envy.

She closed her eyes and strove to recall what Louis had told her about the instrument's range: five octaves, F to F, the same basic pitch as a piano, only one row of keys to contend with, plus three pedals. Cautiously, she pressed her toe upon the bellows.

The organ groaned. She touched the bellows pedal again, depressed a key with her forefinger and jumped when a note emerged from within the casing.

From the living-room below came laughter.

Susanne hardly heard it.

She lowered her head, concentrated on the keyboard and experimented with the pedals, swelling and lowering the tone of that single soft note.

Holding her breath, biting her lip, she coaxed out a simple little melody that Mr Rayburn had taught her. The touch was different; the notes once depressed went on sounding and ceased the instant they were released. Precision was required, precision, and practice.

She began, very softly and just a little squeakily, to play.

*   *   *

Ajax, dozing on the porch, lifted his head and peered up at the window. Buckie, in the living-room, held a second glass of sherry wine an inch from his lips and stared at the ceiling.

'Good God!' he said. 'What's that?'

Darsie stopped chattering and, leaping to her feet, said, 'Oh, it's music, it's music. Is Louis here? Has Louis come home?'

Bette and Buckie exchanged glances.

'Nah, nah,' Buckie said. 'It can't be Louis.'

'Who can it be then? Who *can* it be?'

The music faltered, then began again, the same melody rendered with more assurance, fewer squeaks and squeals.

'Hoh!' Buckie said, grinning. 'It must be Susanne.'

'Susanne can't play the organ, can she?' Darsie said.

'The minx,' said Buckie, 'has kept her talent to herself.'

'Tell her to stop,' Bette snapped.

'I'll do no such thing,' said Buckie.

'Tell her, tell her to stop this instant.'

'Why?' Buckie said. 'She's not doin' so badly.'

'We – we – we have guests.'

Believing that his master had returned, Ajax clawed at the front door as the tune was repeated in changed key, in quicker tempo.

'Well, well, well,' said Buckie. 'Two musicians in the family. What do you make of that, Darsie, my dear?'

'I think it's awful,' Darsie said, and for reasons that no one – least of all Darsie – could possibly explain, suddenly began to cry.

Susanne played the little melody again, then she washed her face in the basin in her room, brushed her hair and went downstairs to square up to Darsie Coburn.

The girl was at the table, Bette by her side. Darsie's cheeks were streaked with tears. Bette patted her and fed her little sips of sherry. Guilt and a sense of power mingled in Susanne as she lingered in the doorway. Her first impulse was to apologise, but she resisted it. She had done nothing wrong. She was not the trespasser in High Cross; she belonged here.

'You – you did this,' Bette said, furiously. 'You – you *deceiver*.'

'Louis gave me permission to use his room,' Susanne said.

'He did, of course he did,' said Buckie. 'I heard him.'

'You touched – you played . . .' Bette could hardly get the words out.

Darsie covered her face with a crumpled handkerchief, and sobbed.

'You surprised us, that's all, sweetheart,' Buckie said. 'We had no idea you were musically gifted.'

'I'm not,' said Susanne. 'I can only play one tune.'

Darsie cried, 'Oh, no, dearest, you have all the gifts, all the talents, and I have none.'

Susanne pulled out a chair, seated herself, leaned an elbow on the table and rested her chin on her hand. The simple little tune that Mr Rayburn had taught her had had a surprising effect on Harry Coburn's daughter.

Darsie wailed, 'I don't understand what music is about, or arithmetic, or half the books I'm given to read. I've no talent for anything. Nobody admires me, not even Papa. He thinks I'm dull and cannot stand to have me near him. That's why he sent me away to school.'

Susanne listened, cynically, chin on hand.

'I am a shallow thing and Papa will not allow me to be otherwise.' Darsie reared up and flung her arms around the woman. 'I wish I could stay here with you, Bette, stay here for ever and ever, with you and my dear friends.'

'Your papa would never stand for it,' Bette said, without conviction. 'Besides, we have an insufficiency of beds.'

'Well,' Buckie said, dubiously, 'if Harry will allow it, let the girl stay for a day or two. If there's even a grain of truth in what's she's saying, then . . .'

'For the holiday, just for the holiday,' said Darsie. 'I will be company for Susanne, will I not? I'll be as quiet as a little mouse. You will hardly know I am here.' She smiled through her tears. 'Benbow can fetch my dresses and you can write a letter to Papa telling him where I am.'

Buckie frowned as if he had a faint glimmering of what was to come, a vague sense that all was not as it seemed and that the vulnerable girl was not quite so vulnerable as all that.

Darsie gave Bette a little dig with her elbow. 'Please,' she begged. 'Please write to Papa and tell him I have been invited to stay. Papa will not refuse you. He has always respected you as a dear, dear friend.' Then the smile again, the rainbow smile, as she looked directly at Susanne. 'And we will be friends, such friends, will we not, Susanne? Please say that we will.'

'I'm sure we will, Darsie dear.' Susanne leaned across the table and squeezed her rival's hand. 'You may have my bed, if you like.'

'And where will you sleep?' Aunt Bette asked.

'In Louis's room, of course,' said Susanne.

Benbow returned about half past four. Harry Coburn had sent a little note thanking Bette for her gracious offer and granting permission for Darsie to stay at High Cross for the rest of the spring holiday.

Cursing under his breath, Benbow hoisted the girl's trunk from the curricle, carried it across the kitchen yard and, with Darsie leading the way, staggered through the living-room and upstairs to the little bedroom at the back of the house. He dumped the trunk on the floor and, on the girl's instruction, loosened the straps and lifted up the lid.

Bette, puffing, came into the room and looked down into the trunk. Susanne took herself off into Louis's room. She heard Darsie give Benbow permission to leave and the tiger go clumping downstairs; then Aunt Bette saying, 'My, but you do have a lot of pretty dresses, Darsie. Does your maid look after them?'

'Papa won't let me have a maid; when I'm older, he says. With Papa, it is always when I'm older. I had a nursery-maid when I was small, after Mama passed away, but she has gone now. When I marry I will insist on having a maid of my own. Did you have a maid, Aunt Bette, when you lived in Dundee?'

'I – we – yes, we had several maids.'

'Why did you leave Dundee?'

'Buckie fell sick.'

'Why have you no maid now, only that woman?'

Seated at the organ in Louis's room, Susanne listened attentively. The Hollanders could not afford to employ a maid, but her aunt would never admit it. 'Nancy is the only servant we need,' Aunt Bette said.

Susanne gazed from the window at the blue sky. Even with the door open she felt detached from the household, yet, at one and the same time, part of the family at last. She might have chosen to share a bed with Darsie Coburn and no one, least of all Darsie, would have thought it strange. She would share a bed with nobody, though, not girl or boy, woman or man until her bridal night. Nancy had changed the sheets but the blankets had a musty smell, a Louis smell. Dr Redpath had also slept here, of course. She wondered if he had left his imprint, too, a faint leathery odour, perhaps, like the smell of his medicine bag.

'I'll help you unpack, shall I?' Aunt Bette said from across the passage.

'I thought that Susanne might like to look at my clothes,' said Darsie.

Susanne rose from the bench and hastily closed the door.

*   *   *

'The really distressing thing about it,' Susanne said, 'is that she imagines I'm her friend and, for the sake of good manners, I have to pretend that I am.'

'What's she up to?' Zena said. 'I mean why is she so eager to spend the holiday with you when she lives in that fine big house in Macklin?'

'Perhaps she wants her feet under the table,' said Prim.

Susanne nodded. 'That's the conclusion I've reached.'

'Under the table?' said Zena. 'Don't they feed her at home?'

'A foot in the door, if you prefer it,' said Susanne.

'But why?' said Zena, still puzzled.

'Because of Louis,' Susanne said.

'Oh,' said Zena. 'Do you think she's setting her cap at your man?'

'I'm sure of it,' said Susanne.

'Louis?' Prim raised an eyebrow. 'Is he your man, Susanne?'

'Not – no, not exactly.'

'She's sweet on him, though,' said Zena. 'Aren't you?'

'What if I am?' said Susanne, pleased.

'He's certainly very prepossessing,' Prim said.

'Not as nice as Dr Redpath, though?' Zena said, slyly.

Prim had no dignity to stand upon and was not stuffy enough to resent the girl's familiarity. It had been many years since she had engaged in talk of this sort, not since she had left the servants' hall in Bluefoot, in fact. She was flattered that Susanne and Zena had included her in their conversation.

'Dr Redpath,' she said, cautiously, 'is certainly a repository of many manly virtues.'

Zena and Susanne laughed.

'What's so amusing about that?' said Prim.

'Manly virtues,' said Zena.

'Repository?' said Susanne. 'You make him sound like a strong box.'

'Oh, very well,' Prim said. 'I do like Dr Redpath. There, are you satisfied?'

'If you like him,' said Susanne, 'why are you always so rude to him?'

'Rude? Am I rude to him?'

'Horrid,' said Susanne.

'Dr Redpath is a young man,' said Prim. 'He has to be kept in his place.'

'He's not old, not ancient,' said Susanne, 'but he's not young either.'

Prim sighed. For a moment she had shared confidences with her pupils, had been at one with them. Mention of age, however, brought her swiftly back to earth. At thirty-two, she was only three or four years older than Alan Redpath, but she was a female, and being a female made all the difference.

'All men have to be kept in their place,' said Zena. 'If you show the least wee bit of interest in them – well, look what happened to me.'

'That,' Susanne said, 'was your own fault.'

'No, it was not.' Zena turned to Miss Primrose. 'It wasn't, was it?'

'Perhaps you were just a little bit too – too trusting,' Prim said.

Zena nodded. 'I thought he liked me, just liked me.'

'For some men,' Prim said, 'liking means only one thing.'

'What?' said Susanne.

Surprised at Susanne's naïvety, Prim and Zena exchanged a glance that indicated to the schoolmistress that at least the minister's daughter was versed in the basic facts of life.

'Well,' Susanne persisted, 'what?'

'Kisses,' Zena said, flatly. 'Cuddles.'

'That's not it at all, is it?' Susanne said.

'No, that's not it at all,' said Prim as Freddie Oakley and the youngest of the Macfarlane boys sidled into the classroom, indicating, to her vast relief, that the dinner hour was over.

At church on Sunday, Darsie Coburn had been the centre of attention. She had worn a fine white hooded cashmere cloak lined with pink silk, trimmed with fringed corded white and pink silk ribbon and pink and white tassels, and a bonnet of plaited white horsehair, white silk ribbon and petite blue flowers.

In the midst of soberly dressed fishermen and women she had stood out like a gorgeous flower. However much envious muttering had gone on about the unsuitability of Darsie's Sabbath garb, the eyes of males and females alike had hardly left her throughout the service – and afterward it had seemed that Mr Oakley would never let go her dainty hand and release her back into the Hollanders' care.

They had all gone to church for the Holy Communion, Bette, Buckie and Darsie riding on the board of Sandy's trap, Nancy and Susanne walking behind. In the afternoon, after a cold lunch, they had strolled on the beach again, all save Buckie who had fallen asleep in his chair. Susanne had been bored by Darsie's ceaseless chatter and the manner in which she had clung, fearfully, to Aunt Bette's arm when a tiny crab appeared on her path or a seagull skimmed too close to her horsehair bonnet. She had even been afraid of the wavelets that had rippled up the beach and threatened to wet her kidskin shoes.

In the evening, at Buckie's insistence, they had played cards, when all Susanne really wanted to do was rummage among the books in Louis's room in search of knowledge and instruction.

On Monday afternoon she raced eagerly home from school. Her uncle was on the porch, enjoying the thin spring sunshine. Ajax was down on the beach chasing seagulls watched, from a safe distance, by Thimble. There was no sign of Darsie or of Aunt Bette.

Buckie explained. 'They've gone into Strayhorn to buy fish.'

Susanne could not imagine Darsie haggling with the fishermen on the quay. In fact, she could not imagine Darsie ever doing anything practical.

'Did Sandy take them in the trap?'

'No, they walked.' Buckie coughed; it may have been laughter. 'At least she wasn't wearing yon pantaloons.'

'I thought you liked her pantalettes?'

'Very pretty,' Buckie said, staring out to sea. 'Aye, very pretty.'

'I think she's grown out of them,' Susanne said, tentatively.

'If she has,' said Buckie, 'it's all she's grown out of.' He shifted his weight carefully on to his stick and rested his hip against the upright. 'You're not jealous, sweetheart, are you?'

'Why would I be jealous of Darsie Coburn?'

'I thought you might feel – well, left out.'

'She's making up to Aunt Bette, isn't she?'

'Aye, she is,' Buckie said, 'but she'll only be here for a week, then we'll have the place to ourselves again. I think she's a lonely soul, so be as nice to her as you can. Bear in mind that you've nothing to fear from Darsie. You're my wee angel, Susanne, and nobody will ever take your place.'

'Oh!' said Susanne, embarrassed. 'Thank you.'

'Now,' Buckie said, 'if you've nothing better to do, why don't you go upstairs and play me a jolly tune on Louis's harmonium?'

'Really?' said Susanne, pleased. 'I'm not very proficient, you know.'

'Practice,' Buckie said, 'makes perfect.'

Medicine, midwifery and music; Louis's room was no longer a midden of discarded toys and boyhood trash but an Aladdin's cave of knowledge that, while not forbidden, was certainly arcane.

Susanne had already unearthed an instructional manual that detailed the workings of the harmonium. She had also discovered a number of primers on musical theory, and several medical textbooks. Unlike her cousin, Susanne was not in the least squeamish. She had pored intently over the diagrams of male and female reproductive parts before moving on to a massive tome on the conditions and complaints of women. She had become so fascinated that she had lost all track of time and had knelt by the cot, reading, until the oil in the lamp had run out. She had known vaguely what was involved in creating babies but the cloudy nature of the event and its aftermath had been beyond the limit of her imagination. She was more intrigued than shocked by what she discovered. She was not so immodest as to examine herself in the light of the diagrams but the illustrated embryos seemed so out of scale that she had placed a hand upon her parts through her nightgown with a sense of wonderment, and apprehension.

She had said nothing to Prim or to Zena about her discoveries but, to appease her uncle, pulled out a tattered musical primer and, seated at the harmonium, picked out notes and, in fairly short order, managed to play a little scherzo that had been adapted especially for the reed organ.

Below in the hall Buckie cheered and tapped his stick in time to the music. Susanne's fingering became less awkward. When she played through the piece for a third time, she experienced a sense of maturity so exhilarating that when Aunt Bette, back with the fish, shouted, 'Stop that infernal racket, Susanne, and come downstairs at once,' she cried out, 'No, not until I'm finished,' and attacked the simple little scherzo once again.

It was just after nine o'clock, too early for bed. Buckie, in pain, had retired soon after supper and Aunt Bette had gone into her room to write letters. Nancy, yawning, had cleared away the teacups and with a grunt in lieu of 'goodnight', had vanished into her cubby behind the larder, leaving the girls alone in the living-room with only Ajax drowsing before the fire, and Thimble asleep on Buckie's chair. Darsie had flitted restlessly about the room, touching this object, staring at that, flicking up the curtain and letting it fall again. Susanne had put her hands over her ears and had concentrated furiously on the book that she had brought down from Louis's room, but Darsie would not be denied.

'Are you angry with me?' Darsie asked.

'Of course I'm not angry with you,' Susanne answered.

'Are you sulking?'

'I never sulk.'

'I think that you are sulking now.'

'I'm busy, Darsie, that's all.'

'Reading, you're always reading. Why won't you talk to me?'

Susanne recalled how Louis had answered his mother on that stormy night over a year ago: 'I'm here, am I not?' he'd said. 'My concentration is absolute and talking does not put me off.' She could almost hear him say it, like a whisper in her ear.

'You may speak, if you wish,' she told Darsie. 'My concentration is absolute and talking does not put me off.'

Nevertheless, she laid the book aside.

'I don't know why you don't like me,' Darsie said. 'We have so much in common, we might even be sisters.'

'Oh,' Susanne said, patiently. 'Tell me, what do we have in common?'

'We are both orphans.'

'You're not an orphan.'

'I can hardly recall what my mama looked like.'

'Nor can I,' Susanne admitted. 'She died soon after I was born.'

'I was three, I think,' Darsie said. 'Yes, three years of age. I have a portrait in a locket, a tiny painting, but she looks so thin and pale that I cannot believe that it is my mama. I have a strand of her hair, too, in a little box. What do you have, Susanne?'

'Nothing,' Susanne said.

'You have something, surely, from your papa?'

'A few small mementoes,' Susanne said. 'Two or three books.'

'Books? Is that one you're reading now?'

'No.'

'If my papa does not marry again,' said Darsie, 'I will have everything.'

'Will you, indeed?'

'Macklin House will not be mine, of course, for it's leased, but I will have the horses and the curricle, and – and all sorts of other things.'

'Do you think that your father will marry again?'

'He is looked upon very favourably by certain ladies.'

'In Edinburgh?'

Darsie was puzzled by the question. 'Edinburgh?'

'I thought perhaps that your father was visiting a lady there.'

'Oh no. Papa has *business* in Edinburgh.' Darsie sank down on to a chair. 'I do so hate it when he has business. It's all he thinks about, all he talks about. Business, horses and shooting. He has no time for me. If I were a boy he would have time for me. He tells me I'm my mother born over again but when I look at the little picture I see no resemblance.'

'Perhaps he means that you have your mother's character.'

'Perhaps that's it.' Darsie hesitated. 'I told you a fib, Susanne. We didn't go to Edinburgh just to visit Louis. We went to call upon my mother's sister and her husband. He took me with him to show them what a fine lady I had become. I think Papa wanted to borrow money but they gave us short shrift. They did not even offer us tea. My grandfather has a great house in the Borders near Jedburgh. I met with him once, years and years ago and I would like to see him again, but he will not reply to my letters.'

'Why are you telling me this now?' said Susanne.

'I'll have to marry well,' said Darsie.

'Hmm, you will, won't you?' Susanne said.

'Papa will find me a beau, a husband, when I'm ready.'

'Can you not marry now?'

'In two years, or three, Papa says I will be – ripe.'

'Like a peach?' said Susanne.

'Or a plum,' said Darsie.

Susanne recalled the diagrams in the books upstairs, babies tucked in the womb like stones in fruit. She had a fleeting image of Darsie too fat and heavy to fit her pretty dresses, the childish pantalettes, like her own dented silver mug, put away for ever. She felt an unwarranted stab of pity for the girl.

'Papa says he will find someone for me,' Darsie said.

'Someone who will love and cherish you.'

'Yes,' Darsie said, wistfully. 'Someone who will love me for myself alone.'

They were not in the least alike, Darsie and she. She had more affinity with Zena Oakley than she had with Mr Coburn's daughter. With Zena she shared a sense of expectation but Darsie already thought of herself only as an object of trade.

'You have Louis, of course,' Darsie said.

Susanne sat up. 'Who told you that? Did Louis tell you that?'

'I wish I could have Louis, a husband like Louis.'

'Did Louis say . . .'

'Ah well,' said Darsie. 'Ah well,' and, kissing her friend Susanne on the cheek, went off upstairs to bed.

*   *   *

All had not gone according to plan. Louis had been plucked at the April examinations. Professor Bertini had taken him to one side and read him what amounted to the riot act, had said, in effect, that he, Louis Hollander, had no natural talent and that if he did not apply himself more rigorously to his studies then he would be fit for nothing but to grind a barrel organ in the cattle mart.

After the interview, Louis returned to his lodgings and took to his bed in a paroxysm of despair. He wept and wept all afternoon, wept himself so dry in fact that at around nine in the evening he was forced to venture out in search of something to eat and, more importantly, to drink.

In the lingering afterglow of a perfect spring day, whores paraded in the streets of the Old Town and students from Bertini's Academy gathered, as usual, in the cellars of Mother Malone's tavern where they tickled and teased the girls and feasted on oysters and salt herring, washed down with quantities of beer.

If Louis could not match his peers in musical ability, at least he could top them in profligacy. He tipped the dregs of his purse upon the table and ordered three quarts of ale for all to share. He laughed, roared, joined in the choruses of rousing songs and even let one of the pretty young whores fondle him under the table until a sudden fit of conscience, or revulsion, overwhelmed him and he thrust her away in disgust.

The girl, who reminded him a little of Darsie Coburn, shrilled and shrieked, claiming that he had cheated her.

He gave her a shilling out of his diminishing funds and recoiled in horror when she tugged down the collar of her blouse and thrust her breasts into his face. The young men, packed under the arches, like beasts in a cave, jeered and egged her on and Louis flung himself away and, clambering over the table and scattering oyster shells, wine glasses and ale pots in all directions, fled from Mother Malone's.

12

After Darsie's departure the little house at High Cross slipped into monotonous quietude, each day more or less like the day that preceded it, the evenings all very much the same. There were occasional visits from Dr Redpath, chats with Zena, lessons from Prim and the not unpleasant task of teaching small children to sound their vowels and count without using their fingers. Mr Oakley continued to instruct on matters spiritual and now and then, especially in church, Susanne would fix her gaze on the minister and try to imagine him locked in her aunt's arms, for she had finally put behind her the notion that kisses and cuddles were all that went on between women and men, or that love came signed and sealed only in the marriage bed.

Buckie and Aunt Bette bickered more than usual. Nancy was instructed to practise rigid economy, which meant more fish and less meat.

As for Louis, Bette kept his letters to herself, saying only that he was 'doing very well', and sent his cousin affectionate greetings.

Susanne told herself that she did not care but care she did. She cared very much. If it hadn't been for music she might have fallen into a state of melancholy and, like Prince Hamlet's rejected sweetheart, have done away with herself. She was far too wrapped up in her own delicious obsessions, however, to contemplate bringing her life to an end just to teach Louis a lesson.

Play was no longer a romp on the beach with Ajax: play was scales and arpeggios, pedals and keys, and she spent hours in the room upstairs, struggling to improve her technique. Her favourite primer was Ainsworth's *Hymns and Tunes Printed Again from the Originals in Arrangements for Instruction upon the Cottage Organ*, a tubby volume containing tunes both solemn and simple. On tranquil summer evenings, she would play two or three of Ainsworth's tunes with hardly a fault and sometimes, all too rarely, felt so much in control that the music seemed to be playing her.

Below in the living-room, or resting in bed, her uncle would sing to himself or wag his swollen hands as if he were conducting a celestial choir. Even Nancy, who professed to detest organ music, would stand stock still in the gloomy kitchen and listen with a far-away look in her hooded eyes.

Only Bette remained opposed to Susanne's affinity with things musical, for she continued to believe that her son's talent was being challenged, if not mocked, by this weak wisp of a girl.

Susanne was no longer weak and wispy, however. Her features had sharpened, she had grown an inch or two in height and had acquired, almost by stealth, hips, a waist, and a bosom of sorts. Her spurt of growth was nothing compared to Gregor Oakley's, though. He had shot up like a bean-sprout and was taller now than his father. With height he had gained confidence and a degree of independence. He worked long hours on the quays and sometimes stayed overnight with the Macfarlanes, in their crowded little cottage above the harbour and, after one spectacular row with his father, announced that he was leaving for Dundee next day, with Peter Macfarlane, to sign on as a green hand on a whaling vessel.

Effie wept, Zena wept, Freddie wept; even Susanne shed a tear.

Only Thomas Oakley remained dry-eyed.

One week after Gregor's departure, Louis returned home.

Supper was over. Susanne was upstairs in Louis's room, too wrapped up in her music to realise how dark it had become. She wore one of her old grey dresses that Aunt Bette had let out but it was tight across the bust and crimped under the arms and she wriggled and tugged impatiently at the bodice. She heard Ajax bark, a yelp from Buckie, thumps and bumps and muffled voices, but, bowed over the keyboard, muttering to herself, she was unaware that someone had climbed the stairs and entered the room.

'What's all *this*?' Louis said.

Susanne lifted her hands from the keys, turned and peered at the figure in the doorway. 'Louis?'

'Yes,' he said. 'Susanne, what are you doing?'

Her first impulse was to throw herself into his arms and smother him with kisses but she had no reason to suppose that Louis had spared her more than a passing thought while he was in Edinburgh, or that he was pleased to see her now. 'Playing the – you said it would be all right.'

'What's the piece?' He remained in the doorway, arms folded. 'Is it the Allegro from Arne's *Toccata in C*?'

'Yes.'

'Difficult?'

'Yes.'

Breathless and uncertain, Susanne remained seated as Louis crossed the room. For an instant she thought that he intended to take her into his arms and kiss her. She stretched her neck and closed her eyes, expectantly.

Louis leaned on the top of the harmonium, closed the music folder and tossed it on to the pile on the floor. 'You shouldn't be playing this stuff.'

'Why not?'

'It's unsuitable for beginners.'

'I'm not – I mean, I can . . .'

'Mama wants you downstairs.'

Susanne said, 'I haven't finished practising.'

'Yes, you have,' Louis said. 'Come.'

He gripped her arm and pulled her from the stool. The fact that she had followed him down a musical path did not please him after all.

She shook herself free before he could hurt her.

And followed him out of the room.

Buckie clung to a chair back and filled Susanne's glass with champagne. Foam slithered down the side of the glass. Susanne licked it, and studied Louis from the tops of her eyes. He was much too thin, hadn't shaved, his hair was shaggy and unwashed and his clothing stained. He looked, Susanne thought, seedy and disreputable, not confident but halting, as if he were unsure what was expected of him.

'So,' Buckie said, 'lift your glasses, please, and join me in a toast to the Hollanders, all together after far too many months apart.'

Louis drank the contents of the flute in a single swallow and held out his glass for more. 'I'm thirsty,' he said. 'I've been on the road since daybreak.'

'How did you travel?' Buckie asked. 'By the railway?'

'By boat from Leith to Burntisland, then I cadged a ride on a farm wagon to Whitfield, from whence I walked.'

'So you've no money,' Bette said. 'You had to travel cheap.'

'True,' Louis said. 'Absolutely true.'

'And whose fault is that?' said Bette.

'Mine,' Louis declared. 'There! I confess. I've wasted my portion in riotous living. Isn't that what you need to hear, Mama? The truth of it is that I travelled cheap not because I'm broke but because I'm economical. If there is one thing

Edinburgh has taught me it's thrift.' He reached into his pocket, brought out a leather purse, opened the draw-string and poured a stream of silver coins into his mother's lap. 'Is this enough to pay for my bread and meat?'

'Where did you get it?' Bette said. 'Did you steal it?'

'If I had turned to theft – which I have not, of course – do you suppose I would tell you?' Louis dropped the purse into his mother's lap. 'Besides, I would have stolen a good deal more than a few florins. Count it, Mama.'

'I don't want to count it. Take it away.'

'Turning down money?' Louis said. 'Well, that is a novelty!'

'How much is here?' Bette enquired, reluctantly.

'Four pounds and eleven shillings.'

'Is that all? It's less than it looks,' Bette said.

'Isn't that the way with everything?' Louis said.

'I'm sure I don't know what you mean,' said Bette.

'He's teasing you, dear,' said Buckie.

'That's it,' Louis said, with a chilly smile, 'just teasing.' Then, turning to Susanne, 'And you, little cousin, what do you have to say for yourself?'

Susanne raised her glass. 'Welcome home, Louis,' she said.

No stars were visible, no moon either; a wet wind drifted across the bay, pushing a tide of dense pearly rain that reflected the candlelight in the darkness beyond the window-pane. Louis sat on the stool, his back to the harmonium, legs thrust out. Poor Ajax had been pushed out to sleep on the porch but Thimble had slyly insinuated herself into the room and crouched tensely behind Susanne's skirts.

'Why didn't you tell me you could read music?' Louis said.

'I do not read it very well.'

'Well enough, it seems, to tackle the Arne?'

'I've been practising over the winter.'

'Who gave you permission to touch my harmonium?'

'You did,' Susanne retorted. 'You said I had the run of your room.'

'Did I?' Louis said. 'Well, if I *was* foolish enough to say that, I certainly didn't anticipate that you would tamper with my harmonium.'

'Tamper?' Susanne said. 'I am as respectful of the instrument as you are. Why? Is it out of tune?'

Louis shrugged. 'How would I know?'

'Try it.'

'No,' he said, firmly. 'I've had enough of music for a while.' He gestured towards the bed. 'Have you been sleeping here, too?'

'Only when Darsie Coburn comes to stay,' Susanne said. 'Why didn't you write to me? I wrote to you but you didn't reply, not once.'

'My life in Edinburgh is very, very dull.'

'Except when you're dining at the Café Royal.'

'So that's it.' He laughed. 'By God, you're jealous.'

'I'm not jealous. I'm annoyed, Louis. Disappointed is a better word.'

'Ah yes, I am, you might say, a paragon of disappointment.' He lifted himself from the stool and, before Susanne could back away, put both hands about her waist and hoisted her on to the bed. He seated himself beside her and slipped an arm about her shoulder. 'What is it, old soldier? Tell Uncle Louis what ails you.'

'For heaven's sake, Louis, stop pretending that everything is as it was between us,' Susanne said. 'I'm not a child now.'

He locked his fists between his knees and stared down at the floorboards.

'I didn't steal that money, Susanne. I borrowed it.'

'Borrowed it? From whom?'

'Harry Coburn.'

'You asked Mr Coburn for money?'

'I didn't ask; he offered.'

'Why did you have to borrow money at all?'

'That's not your concern, Susanne.'

'It *is* my concern,' Susanne said. 'I'll lend you money if you need it.'

'One does not borrow from friends.'

She leaned against him. His body gave off a faint rank smell that Susanne found more manly than offensive. She liked him more now that he had lost his unctuousness, now that he needed her.

'You may suppose that studying music is a joyful experience,' Louis went on, 'but under Professor Bertini it isn't joyful at all. He asks so much of me, expects so much. And it's so damned expensive. I pay extra for the use of an organ on which to practise. I pay an exorbitant rent for rooms. If only I'd known how difficult it would be, Susanne, I wouldn't have gone to Edinburgh in the first place. There are times when I think I'd be better off as a whaler.'

'Music is your life,' said Susanne. 'You mustn't give up now.'

He covered his face with his hand. 'Now I'm in debt to Harry Coburn. How can I tell Mama *that*? She has a horror of debt, you know.'

'How much did you borrow from Mr Coburn?'

'Ten pounds.'

'I'll withdraw ten pounds from my account with Mr Reeve.'

'How will you do that?'

'I'll write to him.'

'He'll demand a full accounting from Mama, you know.'

'Then she must give it to him,' Susanne said. 'There's nothing to hide.'

'No, of course there's nothing to hide,' Louis said, 'but I would prefer – indeed, insist – that Mama knows nothing of our transaction.'

Susanne rubbed her brow with her fingertips, frowning. 'I don't see how it can be avoided. I mean, Louis, your mother is my guardian, appointed by the court. She is responsible for all I do until I come of age.'

'Or,' Louis reminded her, 'until you marry.'

'Yes,' Susanne said. 'Until I marry.'

'In the meantime,' Louis went on, 'it does seem a trifle unfair that you can't use your money as you wish. This Reeve fellow, he can't refuse to give you that which is legally yours, can he?'

Susanne shook her head. 'I'm not sure.'

Louis drew away from her and got to his feet. He took a turn about the room, his shadow moving across the candlelight. Crouched on top of the harmonium, Thimble watched, unblinking.

'No,' Louis said, at length, 'leave it with me, dearest. I'll find out how the land lies in respect of your trust fund and precisely what governance Reeve has over your affairs.'

'It's only ten pounds,' said Susanne.

'Yes,' Louis said, quietly, 'only ten pounds.'

If the weaning of Waylie had been difficult the weaning of Roland was next to impossible. Gregor had been able to coax his smallest brother into taking a few spoonfuls of bread and milk or a little chopped egg from a cup but with Greg gone no one in the Oakley household had, it seemed, the patience necessary to lure Roland off the breast once and for all.

'Eat, damn you,' Zena said.

'I hardly think it fitting for you to address your brother in such fiery terms, Zena,' Tom Oakley said. 'You are not with your school friends now. This is a manse, an adjunct to the house of God.'

'Like the garden?'

'The garden is also part of God's dwelling.'

'The potting shed, too?' said Zena.

Even with Petal crawling about the floor and tugging at his trouser leg, her father maintained an air of aloof distraction. He was eating a bannock and drinking tea, for he had been out on a parish visit and with Effie busy upstairs and Zena busy down, would have to wait for someone to cook his supper.

He dusted oat crumbs from his lips and watched Roland spit out a mouthful of mashed green peas.

'Perhaps,' her father said, 'he isn't hungry.'

'He can't stay on the teat for ever,' said Zena. 'If he doesn't eat, he won't grow. You haven't answered my question.'

'What question is that, dear?'

'About the potting shed.'

Petal clambered up her father's leg and struggled to hoist herself on to his lap. He pushed her down, then said, 'By its close proximity to the church, the potting shed must be deemed holy ground, though I doubt if one would actually consider it consecrated.'

'Perhaps that's just as well,' said Zena.

She longed for him to express bewilderment but he, for once, was lost for words. He dabbed a wetted thumb into the oat crumbs and sucked it, his Adam's apple bobbing against his collar. Green mash dripped from the spoon to the floor where Petal lapped at it like a little dog. Roland shrieked at the sight of his sister stealing the supper he had rejected, and Tom, chastened by Zena's remark, retreated to the study across the hall.

Susanne lay on her back beneath the bedclothes, a hand tucked between her thighs. Now that she understood the mechanics of love, she was no longer quite so sure that she wanted Louis for a husband, or any husband at all.

Fragments of melody bobbed in her brain. She thought of the reed organ across the passageway and felt a twinge of resentment at Louis's refusal to play for her, or to ask her to play for him. She wondered if Thimble was sleeping on Louis's bed, and why Ajax had been shut out, wondered if she could cope with Louis's whims, wondered what it would be like to have his hands stroking her belly, wondered if this was desire, and if desire itself was a sin.

She quivered and, twisting, stuffed her face into the pillow.

'Louis,' she murmured. 'Louis, Louis, where are you?'

But from the room across the passageway, no answer came.

The first hot spell of summer weather arrived in the wake of the rain. By Saturday noon the sky was blue and cloudless as far as the eye could see and the beach sizzled under a blinding sun. Susanne lay on the porch with her back against a pillow, languorous and deliciously fatigued, pretending to read a novel.

Nancy had lugged Buckie's chair from the living-room and her uncle was out on the porch too, settled in a patch of shade, Ajax at his feet.

The novel, translated from the French, was tedious in the extreme and, after a page or two, Susanne put it aside, closed her eyes and listened to the lazy plash of the waves and the faint hiss of seaweed drying in the sun.

From within the house came a drone of voices. Louis and Aunt Bette had stayed in the living-room but Susanne had no notion what they were talking about; she had too many concerns of her own – if only she could be bothered to think of them. She had just leaned her head against the pillow and stretched her arms above her head when, to her astonishment, Louis appeared in the doorway clad in a striped bathing costume as tight as the skin on an onion.

He peered towards the sea, scowling.

'We are, it seems, to bathe,' he announced, sourly. 'Mama has found you a suitable dress. Go and put it on. I'll wait for you.'

Susanne sat up, wide-eyed. 'Bathe?'

'Don't dare laugh,' Louis said. 'I haven't worn this hideous thing since I was fifteen years old. I'm surprised it still fits, if one can call this a fit.'

'Bathe?' Susanne scrambled to her feet. 'In the sea, do you mean?'

'No, in the copper tub in the yard,' said Louis. 'Of course in the sea. It isn't my idea, I hasten to add.'

'Perfect day for it,' Buckie said. 'Tide's right, too.'

'In the sea, in the sea.' Susanne clapped her hands, then, with hardly a glance at her cousin, rushed indoors to change into the bathing dress that Aunt Bette had found for her.

The waves licked her body like fronds of weed and the cold crimped her flesh. She spread her arms and breasted the breakers, then it was all green water, bright bubbles and an airiness the like of which she had never known. She bent her knees, squatted in the shallows and shot up again into the sunlight.

Louis caught her by the waist and whirled her about.

She screamed with delight, but Louis was not being playful.

'You fool, Susanne. I thought you'd drowned. Stop it, stop it.'

She spread her knees and righted herself, astonished that they were only a few yards from shore, for she had supposed that they were already far out on the deep, like gulls or fishing boats.

She waded around her cousin, trailing her arms in the water. The salt on her lips was like the kiss of the sea, the swell against her back like the rocking of a cradle. She surged round Louis as if he were a sea god, and he rolled with the motion of the waves, raising himself up and puffing out his cheeks when the waves slapped against him.

Barking, Ajax raced in and out of the waves. Demure in a

large sun bonnet and protected by a parasol, Aunt Bette trotted down the beach to watch the fun. Susanne scooped up armfuls of the ocean and flung them at her cousin. He covered his face with his forearm and begged her to stop. She flopped like a seal in the shallows and kicked her heels, showering him with spray.

'Can't you swim, Louis?'

'Of course I can swim.'

'Swim, then. Go on, dearest, let me see you swim.'

'I – I choose not to,' Louis said. 'I have to look out for you.'

She waded out a little way then swung behind him and, with a sudden swoop, leaped on to his back and laced her arms about his chest.

Aunt Bette waved her parasol encouragingly.

'Take me out,' Susanne implored. 'Take me out on your back, Louis, out to the rocks. Go on. Carry me, carry me.'

'I can't. You're too – too . . .'

The tips of her breast were as hard as pebbles and when she wrapped her legs about him she felt the curve of his buttocks between her thighs.

'Swim,' she chanted. 'Swim, swim, swim.'

He threw himself backward, shaking her off.

The sea closed over her.

She swallowed water, choking.

Clouds of sand stung her eyes. Louis fell on top of her. She flailed, kicked her legs, pawed at the straps of his bathing costume. He bore down on her, crushing her, like a bubble in the bladder wrack. She saw Ajax's paws, the hair on his belly, then the weight was gone. She drifted to the surface and found the sand with her feet. She rose, spluttering, wiped her eyes and, as if the whole incident was just a game, boisterously attacked her cousin once more. Fending Ajax off with both hands, Louis floundered, slipped and vanished beneath the surface. Susanne pounced upon him.

She had never felt so gloriously alive, splashing in the sea with the big Newfoundland and her big, muscular cousin. She fell upon Louis, arms and legs spread, oblivious to her aunt's cries of alarm and the sight of Buckie hobbling over the shingle as fast as his bent old legs would carry him.

She was one with the sea, her element, wrestling with Louis as if they were lovers in a great, cold bed, legs and arms entwined. Only when his cries became too urgent to ignore did she roll away and, seated on the sand with the water up to her chest, watch him flail as if he were drowning and, on all fours, crawl, howling, back to his mama on the beach.

'May I bathe again tomorrow?' Susanne asked.

'Not without Louis.'

'Is he all right?'

'He does not care much for bathing,' Bette said. 'Aren't you cold?'

'Not at all.'

'Even so, you had better get out of that wet dress. Here, let me help you.'

'I didn't mean to frighten him.' She was too exhilarated to be embarrassed. Surely, she would find someone to teach her to swim, then she would swim out to the rocks, swim past the rocks into the deep blue-black water, and come to no harm. 'I thought he could swim.'

'He . . .' Bette thought better of it and shook her head. 'Would you prefer it if I left you to yourself?'

'No, no,' said Susanne.

She stripped the damp bathing dress from her shoulders and, turning, stooped over to allow her aunt to towel her bare back.

Salt pinched her flesh and the tips of her breasts were still hard. Aunt Bette worked the towel. The chafing roused a tingling warm in Susanne. She took the towel, dried her arms and legs, then worked the costume down to her stomach and rubbed herself there. She was thinking of the sea and of Louis across the passageway, towelling his back and buttocks and humming as he dried that part of himself that had been too obvious to ignore.

Louis was not across the passageway, however. Louis was downstairs in the living-room, shivering in front of the fire, a blanket over his shoulders, a glass of hot toddy clasped in both hands.

Susanne tugged down her bathing dress and stepped out of it.

It lay in a ring in a puddle of sea water.

She draped the towel about her hips and seated herself on the bed.

Aunt Bette hovered by the door.

'You're quite grown up, Susanne. I hadn't realised.'

'I suppose I am,' Susanne said. 'I'll grow a bit yet, though, won't I?'

'I imagine you will,' said Bette, and, with a little nod of satisfaction, left Susanne to get on with it, undisturbed.

13

Until Alan Redpath entered her life, it hadn't occurred to Prim that the qualities that attracted the unwelcome attentions of scallywags might also stir the interests of a man of virtue. The fact that Alan Redpath did not come calling did not deter her. She felt sure that it would only be a matter of time before their paths crossed again.

Meanwhile, on the other side of the barley field, Thomas Oakley was undergoing torment. Only strength of will prevented him pressing his suit more frequently or, on those mornings when he imagined that Prim was wearing 'his' perfume, from dragging her out of the classroom into the gorse bushes.

It was late evening but still warm when the minister turned up at Rose Cottage. Prim was kneeling on the grass, planting bulbs.

Motionless and silent, Tom watched her shift her weight, and stretch. She had large feet and her calves were smooth and shapely. Her hands were soiled and fragments of autumn leaf clung to her hair which, unloosed, fell thick as oat straw across her freckled cheek. Tom's mouth went dry as he watched her plunge her fingers into the moist, warm earth.

'Miss Primrose?' he said, hoarsely. 'Gillian?'

She reared up as if an arrow had struck her. 'You!' she said. 'What do you want?'

Tom said, 'It's a beautiful evening and, as I was passing, I thought I would call in to pay my respects.' She slumped back on her heels and scowled at him. He saw the curve of her throat, the swell of her breasts and, like water trickling through a hole in a dam, desire threatened to overcome prudence. 'I mean you no harm,' he said. 'Why are you afraid of me?'

'I'm not afraid of you, Mr Oakley. I may not care for the nature of your preaching or the effect it has on my pupils, but I'm not afraid of you. I do not respect you enough to be afraid of you.'

'You wear my perfume.'

'I poured your perfume away.'

'No, that can't be right.'

'There.' She nodded. 'I poured it into the flowerbed.'

'But why?'

'Even if you were not married, Mr Oakley, and your children were not under my charge, I would not accept a gift from you. I have no interest in you and no wish to get to know you more intimately.'

'That's plain enough.'

'I hope it is, sir,' Prim said. 'I would be obliged if you would go now.'

He blinked several times then tossed back his head and, in a haughty, pulpit tone, said, 'I would not be too hasty in dismissing me, Miss Primrose. I have a great deal of influence in this parish.'

'You are not on the school board.'

'Perhaps not, but I have the ear of Angus Gamrie who has the ear of Edward Arbuthnot. I suggest you bear that in mind before you reject me.'

'Am I being threatened?'

'No, Gillian, you are being warned.'

'And what if I do not heed your warning?'

'It would pay you to be more accommodating, that's all.'

'By wearing cheap scent?' Prim said. 'No, Mr Oakley, I can't be bought, and I will not be intimidated.'

'As you wish,' Tom said. 'May I remind you, however, that a woman in your position may yet have need of a friend.'

'What makes you suppose that I do not have a friend?'

'Does this friend have a name?'

'He does, Mr Oakley, but it is none of your concern.'

'There is no friend,' said Tom. 'I do not believe you.'

'Then don't,' Prim said and, turning her back on him, dropped to her knees and went back to planting her bulbs.

Louis knew that he had made a complete ass of himself. He was no longer sure that he could fulfil his promise to Harry Coburn. He had been dismayed to discover that Susanne had musical talent, particularly as he had all but reconciled himself to emerging from the Academy fit for no other occupation than that of piano-tuner or a teacher of scales to small children.

Susanne knocked on the bedroom door.

'Louis?'

'What is it, Susanne?'

'Are you sulking?'

'I'm resting.'

'Nancy says she won't cook for you unless . . .'

'I'll cook for myself then.' He sat up. 'Have you no school today?'

'Louis, it's half past four in the afternoon.'

He heaved himself from the cot and sought to find the floor with his feet.

He had drunk more than was good for him last night and his head ached, and he needed to make water. He cupped his hands over his parts, and said, 'I sat up late, studying. Now, pop downstairs and tell Nancy I'll be down soon and anything she has on the hob will do me for breakfast. Will you do that for me, dearest?'

'I will,' Susanne said. 'Then will we go bathing again?'

'No, Susanne, not today.'

He heard her laugh and scamper off downstairs, and, hoisting up his nightshirt, he yanked the big china chamber pot from beneath the bed and, not a moment too soon, noisily relieved himself.

'I think I know what you're up to, Bette,' Buckie said.

Bette looked up from her sewing. 'What on earth do you mean?'

'You're trying to marry him off, aren't you?'

Bette let out her breath and went back to stitching a waist panel into one of Susanne's dresses. The girl was growing so fast that she would need new clothes soon and Mr Reeve would have to release enough money to pay for them.

She snipped off an end of thread with her teeth.

'What if I am?' she said.

'Louis isn't right for her,' said Buckie.

Nancy had cleared away the supper things and had served tea early. Susanne and Louis were outside on the porch, laughing together. Susanne might have grown in stature but she still giggled like a little girl.

'They seem to be enjoying themselves,' said Bette.

The ache in Buckie's legs had spread to his back. Only the fine spell of weather prevented him from taking to his bed. He cursed the distracting pain and leaned forward in the armchair. The cat, stretched along the chair, dabbed at him softly with one black paw, as if to draw him back.

'You're not thinking of announcing a betrothal, are you?'

'Don't be ridiculous!' Bette said. 'The girl's too young.'

'No,' Buckie said. 'That's the trouble: she's not.'

'She's in love with him, you know.'

Buckie said, 'It would be surprising if she wasn't in love with him, given that she's had no opportunity to meet any other young men. She doesn't seem to mind, though. She never complains.'

'She's too clever to complain.'

'Clever?' said Buckie, frowning.

Bette said, 'She cares nothing for us. As soon as it suits her she'll be up and off, and we'll be left high, dry and penniless.'

'Hardly penniless,' said Buckie. 'Still, I wouldn't blame Susanne if she spread her wings. Wouldn't you do the same in her position?'

'If I were rich, you mean?' Bette said. 'Oh, I'm quite reconciled, Buckhaven, *quite* reconciled to going to my grave as a pauper. I've no concern for myself. I've made my bed and I will lie on it. But I am concerned about Louis. If she's in love with him – well, why shouldn't they marry?'

'Because Louis is not in love with her.'

'He likes her.'

'Louis is in love with no one but himself.'

'How can you say such a thing?'

'Because it's the truth.'

'Nothing of the sort,' said Bette. 'Listen to them out there. Does that sound like selfishness to you, Buckie? No, it sounds like two young people falling in love.'

Buckie sank back in the armchair and stared at the ceiling for half a minute before he spoke again. 'What will your friend in London, the lawyer, what will he have to say if Susanne decides to marry before she comes of age?'

'I'm sure Mr Reeve will have no objection.'

'He'll lose the trade, will he not?'

'The trade?' Bette laughed. 'Mr Reeve is a Chancery officer, Buckie, not a fishmonger. If Susanne elects to marry her cousin—'

'Louis isn't her cousin.'

'Oh dear, you are in an argumentative mood tonight.'

She put the piece of sewing to one side, glanced at the

window, then, to Buckie's surprise, came to him and plumped
the brocade cushion. 'Stop fretting about Susanne,' she said.
'Isn't it better to keep Joshua's money in the family than hand
it over to a stranger?'

'Well,' Buckie admitted, 'I suppose it is.'

'Of course it is,' said Bette, smugly.

And returned to her needle and thread.

Dusk had stolen over the sea and the seabirds had ceased their
mewing. The tip of the tower of the church was silhouetted
against the afterglow and far off to the west faint stars showed
cool and steady in the summer night sky. The young couple
sat together against the wall, legs stretched out like net-
menders.

Susanne said, 'It's just a matter of writing to Mr Reeve, then
you shall have what you want, Louis. I do not like Mr Coburn
and would prefer you not to be in his debt.'

'I think,' Louis said, 'it's Darsie Coburn you do not like.'

'If you're implying that I'm jealous – yes, I confess it: I am.'

'You've no reason to be,' Louis whispered. 'She's nothing to
me.'

'She would like to be something to you.'

'Perhaps, perhaps,' Louis said. 'But she's so – so shallow.'

'She's very pretty.'

'Beauty is in the eye of the beholder, dearest.'

'Come now, you're not going to turn my head with clichés.'

'It would take a better man than me to turn *your* head,
Susanne.'

'I don't think I could find a better man than you in a day's
march.'

'Obviously you know nothing of the world.'

'I'm happy with the world as it is.' She squeezed his hand.
'At this very moment, my darling, I am as happy as I ever hope
to be.'

Louis let his head rest against the wall, and sighed. 'I feel so guilty about taking your money,' he said.

'I do not care about "my" money,' Susanne said, 'You can have every last farthing for all I care.'

'Mama must know nothing of our arrangement,' Louis said. 'She would be furious if she thought that I was sponging off you.'

'You're *not* sponging.'

'Nonetheless, it must be our secret.'

'Yes,' Susanne whispered. 'Our secret.'

'Shall we go inside?'

'Soon, dearest,' Susanne said. 'Soon, but not just yet.'

Louis had promised to come for her as soon as the household was asleep and she had kept the little candle burning in the water-dish. She tiptoed to the window and stared out at the stars, then returned to the dressing-table to study her image in the mirror and ensure that her floral robe covered her night-dress and that the dab of Aunt Bette's rouge she had applied to her lips was not too daring.

By candlelight she looked more like a ghoul than a girl, though, and she stuck out her tongue and pulled at her cheeks to pass the time while Louis, across the passageway, made ready to receive her.

At length, a creak of floorboards, a muffled knock upon the door: 'Susanne,' he murmured. 'Come.'

She snuffed out the candle, opened the door, glanced towards the stairs, then whisked across the passage into Louis's room.

To her disappointment he was still dressed. He wore not only shirt and trousers but a waistcoat and collar, long stock-ings and boots, as if he were ready for the road, not bed.

An oil lamp had been placed on the table and a candle in a brass holder was perched on the top of the harmonium.

The room was too bright for Susanne's liking. Only the bed and the columns of books against the gable wall were in shadow. Louis took her by the arm. She waited for him to pull her to him, to kiss her, to run his hands over her hips and up to her breasts. Instead, he led her to the table which had been cleared of books, papers and pipes and held only a single sheet of lined foolscap, a long, brown paper envelope, an inkwell and a wooden pen-holder.

He pulled out a chair. She seated herself upon it.

He pulled out the organ bench and seated himself by her side.

As if he were an inquisitor intent upon obtaining a confession, he put an arm about her shoulder and pressed her down so that she was staring at the blank foolscap.

'What shall I write?' Susanne asked.

Louis dipped the pen into the inkwell and placed it in her hand.

'This,' he said, and solemnly began to dictate.

The heat in the downstairs room was stifling. Bette sprawled on top of the blankets dewed with unladylike sweat.

If, like Nancy, she had been superstitious, she might have supposed that her ward was sucking the energy out of her, for her encounters with Tom Oakley no longer soothed her and brought no more than temporary relief from the fear that she was heading for an early grave.

Louis was still up, pacing about his tousled room.

She fancied she could hear him muttering to himself or – she sat up – to someone else. She rolled from the bed and placed both feet cautiously on the floor. She peered up at the beams and imagined that she could make out the rhythmic squeak of bed-springs. She went to the door, opened it, slipped out into the corridor and padded to the foot of the stairs.

The house was uncannily quiet, so quiet that she could hear Ajax snoring on the porch outside. The window was etched by starlight, the furniture in the living-room magnified in the gloom. She moved into the living-room. The sounds were directly overhead now, Louis droning like an old preacher reciting the Catechism, but no squeak of bed-springs, no squeals of fear, or delight.

She was just about to return to bed when she heard Susanne say, distinctly, 'Is that all there is to it?'

Louis answered.

Susanne said, 'Now what do you want me to do?'

Louis answered again, his voice pitched too low to be intelligible.

Bette waited for laughter, or tears, or questions – but there was only silence, a curious silence that seemed to last for minutes. She closed her eyes tightly, striving to make out what was going on, something, anything that would erase the misty pictures in her mind's eye. She imagined them kissing, the girl's nightgown pooled about her feet, Louis touching her breasts, Louis fumbling with buttons, clumsy and inexperienced, her baby, her son . . .

'What's going on?' Buckie said. 'Are you walking in your sleep again?'

'No,' Bette told him. 'Hush.'

He had limped from his room with the aid of the stick and leaned against the wall by the grandfather clock.

'Are you sick? Are your bowels—'

'Buckie, be quiet.'

Footsteps pattered on the floor, doors opened and closed.

Silence once more, a silence so dense that the ceiling beams seemed to sag beneath its weight.

Bette sidled back into the hall.

Buckie said, 'Bad dream, dearest?'

'Yes,' Bette told him. 'Bad dream,' and, taking him by the arm, helped him hobble back to bed.

*   *   *

As soon as lessons were over and the children released, Susanne flung her books into her satchel and, with a wave to Prim and Zena, hurried out of the schoolhouse and headed off home, eager to take advantage of the warm weather and persuade Louis to go bathing again.

Buckie was seated on the porch, a newspaper over his face, Ajax dozing at his feet. He drew the paper down, and sat up.

'Susanne?' he said. 'You're prompt home today.'

'Yes, I ran all the way. Where's Louis?'

'Oh!' Buckie said. 'Did he not tell you? He's gone.'

'Gone?' Susanne said. 'Gone where?'

'Back to Edinburgh. I thought you knew he was leaving this morning.'

'He – yes, I believe he did mention it. I'd forgotten.'

She glanced towards the open door as if she expected Louis to leap out and to hear her uncle laugh at the ease with which she'd been fooled.

Buckie touched her arm. 'He didn't tell you, did he?'

Dazed by disappointment, Susanne looked at the sea curling and slithering over the sand, at the black rocks and the rock pools and flocks of gulls white against blue-green water. She dropped her satchel and, leaning on the arm of Buckie's chair, kissed his feathery white pate.

'No,' she said. 'He didn't tell me.'

'The conceited devil, probably thought you'd burst into tears.'

'I'm not the weepy sort, Uncle, am I?'

'I don't know what you are, sweetheart,' Buckie said. 'He tells me he'll come back in August for a week or two, but whether he does or not remains to be seen. Did he ask you for money?'

'No,' Susanne said, hiding her alarm. 'How could I give him money? I have none to give.'

'Aye, but you have,' Buckie reminded her.

'Oh that!' said Susanne, shrugging.

'Don't fret over Louis. I think your auntie slipped him a guinea or two to tide him over.' Buckie patted her hand gently. 'Will you miss him, lass?'

'Yes,' Susanne said. 'I'll miss him,' but even as she spoke, she realised that she would not miss him quite as much as all that.

She bussed her uncle's brow once more then went indoors.

Sunlight streamed through the window of the upstairs room. The bed was unmade, the table bare save for the inkwell and pen-holder. The letter she had written to Louis's dictation and the envelope she had addressed to Neville Spencer Reeve were gone.

She sighed and peeled the dust cover from the harmonium in the faint, fond hope that her cousin might have left a tender billet-doux on the keys, which, of course, he had not. She tossed the dust cover to the floor, seated herself on the bench and began to play the simple nursery tune that she had learned so long ago, while Ajax, cast off and bewildered, whimpered on the porch below.

In the heat of a summer afternoon Macklin House seemed peaceful and prosperous. Cattle grazed in the pasture, sheep on the hill and the labourers had just begun to bring in the hay. Through the open window of the drawing-room Louis could make out the crooning of wood pigeons and, now and then, the plaintive bellow of a bullock bothered by black flies.

Beer and a dish of cold meats had refreshed him after his hike from High Cross. As far as Mama and Pappy were concerned he was halfway to Edinburgh, and as far as Susanne was concerned – well, it hardly mattered what Susanne thought now that he had what he wanted.

Mr Coburn breezed into the drawing-room, trailed by three large dogs and a female servant. He wore a loose lace-frilled shirt and looked brisk and lively in spite of the heat. The dogs slumped before the empty hearth while the servant removed the plates and refilled the empty beer jug. As soon as the servant had gone, Harry seated himself at the table and poured beer. He took a long swallow, wiped his lips, and said, 'Well, Louis, did the young lady deliver?'

'Yes, sir, she did.'

Louis fished the brown paper envelope from his pocket and handed it to Harry who slit the sealing with his thumb and spread Susanne's letter carefully upon the table.

'It is,' said Louis, 'exactly as you requested. I dictated it to her myself.'

'So I see.'

'If I may make so bold as to ask, sir, what do you intend to do with it?'

'That's really no concern of yours.'

'But – I mean, you will pay me?'

'Oh yes,' Harry said. 'I am, if nothing else, a man of my word.'

'Forty pounds . . .'

'Thirty-five,' said Harry. 'You've already received five.'

Louis nodded. 'Thirty-five pounds does seem to be a lot to pay for a letter that guarantees me no more than ten.'

'It doesn't guarantee you anything,' Harry said.

'Susanne requests the lawyer fellow to pay the money to me.'

Harry glanced at the letter. 'Why so she does. How remiss of her.'

'To be sent in the form of a draft to my lodging in Edinburgh.'

'So that you may waste it on wine and women, eh?' Harry laughed. 'No, young man, there are better things to do with money. Did your mama teach you nothing?'

'Mama? What does my mama have—'

'Not a thing. The less Bette knows of our arrangement the better.'

'Will I endorse this draft and forward it to you?' Louis said.

'Certainly not,' Harry said. 'You will deposit it in the account of the Strayhorn Railway Company at the Union Caledonian Bank in Gordon Street. Do you know where it is?'

'Yes, off the High Street, near St Giles.'

'You will deposit the draft and all subsequent . . .'

'Subsequent?'

'. . . all subsequent drafts from the same source. You will draw five pounds in cash on each occasion. The balance will be credited to your account in the form of shares.'

'Shares? What sort of shares?'

'Shares in the Strayhorn Railway Company, of course.'

'Do I want – do I need to buy shares in this company?'

'I thought you wanted to be rich, Louis?'

'I do. I want to be – well, successful.'

'And so you shall be, my boy, so you shall be.'

'But Susanne – I mean, will we not be cheating . . .'

'Cheating?' Harry's eyes flared. 'We're not cheating anyone. We are merely conducting business.'

'With Susanne's money, without Susanne's knowledge,' Louis said. 'With due respect, sir, if that isn't theft, what is it?'

'The girl will not lose by it.'

'Who owns this railway? Is it a public company?'

'Not yet,' said Harry. 'Shares will be floated in due course.'

'What does that mean?' said Louis. 'In due course?'

'You're a very curious young man, aren't you?'

Louis pursed his lips and did his best to appear intelligent. 'I believe, sir, that I am entitled to be told what's going on.'

'In two years, three at most, when we have tangible assets to show for our endeavours, the shares will soar in value and be snapped up like hot cakes. You and I, and Susanne Thorne will draw substantial returns on our investment.'

'If that's the case,' said Louis, 'why don't you put the proposal to Susanne and let her assign more of her capital to the venture?'

'Ah!' Harry tapped his nose. 'Do you suppose that the trustee, this Reeve fellow, will agree to release capital for such a scheme? Of course he won't. Fife is as foreign a place to a London lawyer as Fiji or Fujiyama. He might permit a portion of Miss Thorne's capital to be invested in a railway line between Brighton and Hove, say, but Fife – oh, dear me, no.'

'When she comes of age . . .'

'We can't wait another five years. We must stake our claim before others awaken to the value of a railway link into the heart of Fife, and claim the rewards.' Harry reached across the table and patted the young man's shoulder. 'Rewards in which you will share, Louis.'

'But why?' said Louis. 'I mean, I have done so little.'

'You have done more than enough,' Harry assured him. 'All that is required of you now is to receive a banker's draft from Neville Spencer Reeve, and transfer it to a company account in the Union Caledonian.'

'Five pounds won't buy many shares.'

Harry Coburn rose so abruptly from the table that the dogs drowsing by the fireplace looked up. 'Oh, you Hollanders are all the same,' he snapped. 'You say you want to be wealthy yet you've no stomach for the cut and thrust of business.' He stepped around the table and taking Louis's head between his hands turned the young man's face towards the window. 'Look out there, Louis, and tell me what you see.'

'Sheep?'

'Land,' Harry told him. 'An estate that stretches from the Macklin road as far west as the Caddis. How do you suppose one comes into possession of all that land? By being hesitant? By being impatient? By refusing to seize a golden opportunity when it presents itself? No, Louis, if you wish to advance your

position in life you must co-operate with opportunity, before it
flies off in another direction. Now, tell me, wouldn't your
mother like to live in a grand house like this, with servants at
her beck and call?'

'Well, yes, I'm sure she would.'

'Do you love your mother, Louis?'

'I love her with all my heart.'

'And yet you continue to hesitate?'

Perhaps it was the cold beer or the heat of the day but Louis's
brain was clouded. He had more questions and several doubts
but, charmed by Harry Coburn's promises, saw only the green
pastures under the stately oaks, the flocks and herds that ensured
that Mr Coburn would never find himself in want, and that
Darsie would arrive at the altar worth her weight in gold.

He blinked, rubbed his eyes like a sleepy child and looked
up, trustingly, at Darsie's father.

'No,' he said. 'No, sir, I'll do whatever you ask of me.'

'Without argument or quibble?'

'Without argument or quibble,' Louis promised and rising,
just a little unsteadily, to his feet, offered Flash Harry his hand.

Fife was bathed in afternoon sunlight but brooding blue-black
thunderheads filled the far horizon. Buckie and the girl had
walked a long way to reach the sea, for the tide was at its lowest
ebb. They looked, Bette thought, not like people at all but like
two tiny birds pecking about on the sand.

She was apprehensive about allowing the girl to bathe and
had forbidden her to do so unsupervised, though neither
Buckie nor she would be of much use if Susanne got into
difficulties; Ajax, bounding joyfully in the waves, would be a
more likely rescuer. As a rule she stationed herself on the
porch to watch over her ward but on that Thursday afternoon
late in June someone more interesting came to claim her
attention.

Thomas Oakley had deigned to descend from the heights. Intrigued by the sight of the girl splashing about in the ocean, he had succumbed to curiosity and picked his way down the crumbling cliff path to see what was going on – that, at least, was his excuse.

Bette stood behind him, as close as decency allowed.

Tom asked, 'Where's Nancy?'

Bette answered, 'Gone to buy fish.'

'Gone long?'

'A quarter-hour.'

Tom peeped over his shoulder. 'Aren't you going to offer me tea?'

'If you feel a need of refreshment . . .'

He swung round and, to her astonishment, opened the buttons and showed himself to her. She glanced towards the track then at the beach and finally, distractedly, looked down at him. He grabbed her hand and brought it to him and she closed her fingers over him, so clumsily and so tightly that he winced.

'Are you sure Nancy has gone?'

'Yes,' Bette told him, shrilly. 'Yes, yes.'

'And the girl? How long will the girl . . .'

She stroked him while looking past his ear at the tiny figures outlined against the waves. 'Half an hour, or more.'

'If we step inside, Bette, no one will think it strange.'

'No,' she agreed. 'No, they won't,' and steered him hastily indoors.

The proximity of a pretty young girl in a bathing dress was better medicine than anything a doctor could prescribe. Those hours on the beach watching Susanne splashing about in the sea were the high points of Buckie Hollander's days. He would have reeled from the suggestion that there was anything remotely sexual in his love for Susanne Thorne. He loved her as he would have loved a daughter and took from her the assurance that although he had grown old, the world was still young. He wished that he had still been able to wade out by her side and experience the thrust of the ocean upon his belly and the gorgeous cold kiss of the waves. Susanne seemed to understand his longing and when she stumbled, dripping and laughing, out of the shallows she let him drape the towel about her and, no matter how keen the breeze, did not dart off but walked with him, at his dreary pace, across the sand and up the seaweed slope to the house.

'Ah,' said Buckie, sinking into his armchair. 'I see that you are being royally treated; the best china, no less.'

'The best tea, too, by the taste of it,' Tom Oakley said.

The minister was seated at the table, upright and flushed. Buckie was too exhausted to notice. Bette, he assumed, had gone upstairs with a jug of warm water for the girl to wash the salt from her hair and the sand from her feet. He heard the creaking of floorboards and Ajax scratching at the kitchen door, though the dog would be kept out of the house until the air had dried his coat.

Buckie had no inclination to converse with the minister and wished that the fellow would drink up and take his leave. He wanted a dish of tea, a scone or a ginger biscuit, then peace to nap.

Tom Oakley said, 'I could not help but remark that your niece, like my daughter, has burgeoned into a fine young woman.'

'She has, that she has,' said Buckie.

'She is, as the French say, *très petite*, but she has her figure now.'

'What?' said Buckie, gruffly. 'Aye.'

'She'll be looking for a husband soon.'

'It's a while before she'll be thinking of such things,' said Buckie.

'I would not be so sure,' Tom Oakley said. 'From my observations as a father, let alone my experience with brides, I'd say that young girls are all too eager to taste the pleasures of matrimony.'

Buckie frowned and, because he could think of nothing to say that would not be embarrassing, asked, 'Where's Bette?'

'I believe she's upstairs.' Tom Oakley helped himself to a ginger biscuit. 'I assume that you'll announce the betrothal some time in the autumn.'

'Betrothal? What betrothal?'

Tom dabbed a finger to his lips. 'Heavens! Have I spoken out of turn?'

'I've heard nothing of a betrothal,' Buckie said. 'If you're meaning our Susanne, Mr Oakley, I think you've grasped the wrong end of the stick.'

'Of course, of course. My apologies.'

Buckie cranked himself forward in the armchair. Ajax was no longer scratching at the door and the floorboards had stopped creaking. He wished that Bette would appear to relieve him of the burden of this bewildering conversation. 'What's my wife been saying?'

'I jumped to the wrong conclusion, I fear.'

'Susanne an' our Louis, is it? Are they betrothed?'

'I'm sure,' the minister said, 'that you will be among the first to be told when such a happy event is announced.'

'My son has his heart set on a musical career.'

'Marriage to a wealthy young woman would hardly put a damper on his ambitions. Indeed, it would be the making of him – musically, I mean. I take it you would not object if your son and Miss Thorne were to become engaged.'

'Susanne may do as she likes,' Buckie said, 'as soon as she comes of age.'

'And what sort of age is that?'

'Eighteen,' said Buckie. 'Or is it twenty-one? Ask Bette. She has it all written down in black and white.'

'Do you not care for the girl?'

'Aye, I care for her. She is as dear to me as a daughter.'

'Would you not like to keep her?' Tom Oakley said. 'By all accounts, she has a very kind heart. She'll not desert you when you grow old. I count myself fortunate to have daughters who will take care of me when I reach your – when old age overtakes me.'

'No,' Buckie said, 'I'll not be putting a mooring rope on Susanne just to suit my selfish ends.'

'If Susanne were to marry your son, though . . .'

'Since when did you become a matchmaker, Mr Oakley?'

The minister laughed. 'I'm teasing you, Buckie, just teasing.'

'It doesn't sound like teasing to me.'

Bette stepped into the living-room. 'What doesn't, dear?'

'Mr Oakley thinks it's time Susanne found herself a husband.'

'Oh, she's far too young for that,' Bette said and, to Buckie's consternation, patted Tom Oakley's shoulder. 'I think, Tom, you've been carried away by all those wedding services you've conducted recently.'

Oakley, looking up at her, laughed.

'Perhaps I have,' he said. 'Perhaps I have at that.'

It had been so hot in London in the August month that Neville Spencer Reeve had been sorely tempted to close shop and, like most officers of the courts, head for the coast. Only the arrival of a letter from Scotland had deterred him, that and the fact that he had recently lost a great deal of money on speculative investments. If not quite on his uppers he was not in the best of financial health and, mainly for that reason, had agreed to meet with Henry Coburn who, it seemed, had travelled to London with a proposal that promised profit.

Mr Reeve and Mr Coburn had met at a grand dinner of the Congleton and Limehouse Railway and Canal Company, a dinner hosted by no less a person than Sir Charles Everard. By chance, Mr Reeve and Mr Coburn had been seated together at table and had soon fallen into conversation in the easy way that men of like mind do. Between them they had decided that Sir Charles Everard's deceitfulness was too obvious to ignore and had, in consequence, saved face by not purchasing shares in a company that had gone bust within the year. When Sir Charles Everard's arrest on charges of fraud had been announced, Mr Coburn had sent Mr Reeve a letter of congratulation couched in terms more frivolous than sombre. Mr Reeve had replied in kind. Beyond that, however, the Scottish gentleman and the Officer of Chancery were strangers to each other and had not, so far, done business together.

It was an hour past noon, and far too hot to think of lunch.

The roof of the Staple Inn sizzled in unblinking sunlight and the cobbles of the courtyard were almost too hot to walk upon. The gulls had gone, pigeons too, and lawyers, advocates and clerks had followed them. Mr Reeve's chambers were as quiet as the grave in Gray's Inn Road churchyard where Joshua Thorne lay at rest.

'I was not aware,' said Neville Reeve, 'that you were acquainted with the Hollanders. Is Fife such a small place that everyone knows everyone else?'

'Fife is not small at all,' Harry Coburn informed him.

'I would not have supposed that you were the sort of fellow to court the friendship of mere whale-oil dealers.'

'Mrs Hollander and I are related.'

'Are you, indeed?'

'Vaguely,' Harry Coburn added, 'through maternal cousins, I think.'

'Is this connection relevant to the matter on hand?'

'Not in the least,' said Harry.

He had asked permission to remove his coat and unbutton his waistcoat and, seated before the wide-open window, picked up just enough of a breeze to restore activity to his wits. Neville Reeve, however, remained wrapped in sober gabardine, little milky droplets of sweat beading his brow. He pushed the letter about on his desk with a forefinger, as if it held no more interest for him than a scrap of blotting paper.

He said, 'So it is not because of your family connection that you've been entrusted to deliver this letter from Mrs Hollander's ward?'

'No,' Harry said. 'It's not.'

'Let me understand you, Mr Coburn . . .'

'Harry, if you please.'

'Let me understand you, Mr Coburn,' Neville Reeve went on. 'You were given this letter to deliver into my hand by . . .'

'By young Miss Thorne, of course.'

'Who trusts you?'

'She has no reason not to trust me.'

'As the letter came in a sealed envelope, I take it that you have no knowledge of its contents,' said Neville Reeve.

'She – and the young man – discussed it with me,' said Harry. 'Asked my advice as a person experienced in financial matters.'

'Did Miss Thorne compose the letter according to your directive?'

'Certainly not.'

'So,' Neville Reeve said, 'you've co-opted the young man, have you?'

'I beg your pardon.'

'Susanne Thorne did not write this letter.' Neville Reeve flicked the foolscap across the desk and watched it float to the floor. 'This letter is a forgery.'

'Good God!' said Harry. 'A forgery!'

'A forgery, sir, yes – and not a particularly good forgery at that.'

'Does it have to be?' said Harry. 'A good forgery, I mean.'

'It has to be better done than this, Mr Coburn. The courts have call upon experts in the science of handwriting, any one of whom would swear that this letter does not represent the authentic hand of Susanne Thorne.'

'But you, sir, are no expert, are you?'

'That,' Neville Reeve said, 'is true.'

'I take it that it's not unusual for you to receive requests for money from those of your clients who are fortunate enough to have trust funds?'

'The girl,' Neville Reeve said, 'is still, under law, an infant.'

'She's sixteen, fast approaching seventeen.'

'Yes, Mr Coburn, I do know how old she is,' Neville Reeve said. 'Even so, I question if she had the slightest notion what she was doing when she wrote this letter. Is the aunt behind it?'

'The aunt is not behind it. The aunt knows nothing of this matter.'

'Is there a letter, a genuine letter?'

'Yes.'

'Which you, or one of your cohorts, have copied and altered?'

'Yes.'

'This is blatant fraud,' Reeve said. 'I will have nothing to do with it. In fact, Mr Coburn, you may consider yourself fortunate that I do not have you arrested for attempting to deceive a servant of the court.'

'But you haven't, have you?' Harry said. 'And, unless I miss my guess, you won't.'

'Won't I?' said Neville Reeve. 'What, sir, is to prevent me?'

Harry swung his leg from the arm of the chair and said, 'Where's the money? I mean, Mr Reeve, where's the bulk of the Thorne fortune? Oh, I know about the piece invested with the Merchants and Traders to provide the girl with board and lodging. But the rest – where have you placed the rest?'

'In securities,' said Neville Reeve.

'Gilded securities?'

'Safe from the vagaries of the market, yes.'

'At a yield of one or two per cent per annum?'

The lawyer hesitated. 'Slightly less.'

Harry threw up his hands. 'I thought as much.'

Neville Reeve stroked his nose with his forefinger, then, stooping, scooped the letter from the floorboards. He studied it carefully for half a minute before he spoke again. 'I assume, Mr Coburn, that you have somehow managed to persuade Louis Hollander that you and he between you can leach away a portion of Susanne Thorne's inheritance and put it to better use than I can? Is that the meat of the matter?'

'The meat, Mr Reeve, but not the gravy.'

'Perhaps, sir,' said Neville Reeve, 'you should tell me about the gravy.'

Harry leaned closer. 'Each other month, thereabouts, you will receive a letter requesting you to send the sum of one thousand pounds to Louis Hollander at his lodging in Edinburgh. The letter will be identical to the one you have in hand, and only the date will alter. I assume that you have received no recent communication from Susanne?'

'None at all; only one letter from the aunt.'

'Good.' Harry nodded. 'As you have already informed me, you are no expert in handwriting and have no reason not to accept the letters at face value. Any suspicion you may harbour as to their purpose can be put to one side, in view of the fact that the draft is being sent to Louis Hollander.'

'I fail to see . . .'

'In a moment, in a moment,' Harry said. 'You, sir, will put the letters into your file and, as requested, sell a small block of securities to cover payments which, in your judgement, are justified expenditure on behalf of your client. On receipt of the drafts, Louis Hollander will present them at the Union Caledonian Bank in Edinburgh and transfer payment into the account of the Strayhorn Railway Company in exchange for shares.'

'Ah-hah!' Neville Reeve exclaimed. 'Railway shares. Of course.'

'Louis will be paid five pounds in cash for each transaction. In due course, the company will accumulate the capital necessary to build a link line into the town of Strayhorn.'

'Do you have the land?'

'I have some of it.'

'How much?' said Neville Reeve.

'Enough to lay rails and build a turntable.'

'Yes,' said Neville Reeve. 'Yes, a turntable will be a great attraction for investors. When will you take the company to the public?'

'As soon as I possibly can.'

'On the strength of a turntable and a few miles of iron rail,' said Neville Reeve, 'you will reap a very tidy profit, indeed. In the meanwhile, you'll have used a piece of the Thorne fortune to capitalise the scheme and, if it all goes wrong, you will not be out of pocket.'

'It will not go wrong.'

'But if it does . . .'

'You, and I, will not lose.'

'Why is that?'

'Because you and I will have sold our shares in advance. The Hollander boy will carry the blame for plundering Miss Thorne's inheritance. He's young, greedy, ambitious, and inexperienced in financial matters. He'll be excused for his errors of judgement.'

'The law will not excuse him,' Neville Reeve said.

'No, but Susanne Thorne will.'

'Will she, indeed? Why?'

'Because she will have what she most desires.'

'And what is that?'

'A husband,' Harry said.

'Louis Hollander, you mean?'

'Of course,' said Harry. 'Louis Hollander, her one true love.'

'All bought and paid for,' said Neville Reeve.

'And hers for ever more,' Harry Coburn said. 'Now, Mr Reeve, what do you have to say to it? Is the gravy thick enough for you?'

The lawyer did not answer at once. He squared the foolscap on his desk, smoothed it with the palm of his hand, then, still without a word, rose, unlocked his safe and salted the letter away in the parcel of documents marked with the name of Joshua Thorne. Then, smiling thinly, he offered Mr Coburn his hand.

'Come, Harry,' he said. 'Now the air has cooled a little, shall we partake of lunch – washed down with a drop of champagne, perhaps?'

'And what shall we drink to, Neville?' Harry enquired.

'True love, of course,' the lawyer answered, and, taking Harry's arm, led him out into the searing heat of the city.

PART THREE

14

The winter of Susanne's seventeenth year was the harshest in living memory. Snow came early to the north and bitter, bone-biting frosts affected the whole of Scotland. Days were leaden, nights numbing and, for weeks on end, the coast was shrouded in icy fog. Huddled in the Dalriada, local weather experts predicted that the cold snap would not last, but the year drew to a close without a sign of thaw and January rattled in with hail on its breath. Blizzards obliterated the coastal towns and brought turnpike traffic to a standstill. Snow lay thick on the beaches, and the sea froze. Wrapped in furs and woollens, Buckie peered into the ivory gloom and declared that it had been warmer in Greenland in his whaling days.

Susanne's fingers swelled and her lips cracked. She was not alone in suffering and Dr Redpath supplied Prim with a huge tub of zinc ointment to soothe the ugly red blisters that affected little fingers and toes. Then, just before the snow started in earnest, Mr Gamrie appeared with a barrel stove roped to the back of his cart. He manhandled it into the classroom and erected it by a window to accommodate the pipes by which air was let in and smoke out. Next morning, Arbuthnot's factor arrived with a load of logs and a basket of small coals, and the classroom was soon warm and comfortable.

Susanne was no longer a pupil-teacher. She had been taken on as Miss Primrose's assistant, at fourteen pounds per annum. Mr Gamrie had endeavoured to negotiate a post for Zena too but Thomas Oakley had vetoed the application by pointing out how unseemly it would be for a minister's daughter to be employed as a servant of the parish.

There was a queer timelessness to the days and the weeks sped by without mark or moment. London seemed like a dream, faded and almost forgotten. Seasonal pastimes shaped Susanne's life now. In summer she bathed in the sea. In autumn and winter she read a great deal, played interminable games of cribbage with Buckie and Aunt Bette and, if it wasn't too cold in Louis's room, continued to practise on the harmonium.

Louis had been gone for twenty months, his promises to return unfulfilled. He still wrote regularly to his mama, asking for money. Money was always found. He wrote to Susanne too, though not often. She, in turn, wrote to Mr Reeve requesting that five or ten pounds be released from her fund. In due course, without quibble, a draft would be posted to Louis in Edinburgh and Susanne would receive a letter of thanks and some word on how he was reshaping his life now that he had left Bertini's.

He had, it seemed, apprenticed himself to a cabinet-maker in the Old Town to learn how to work wood and metal and hoped eventually to travel to France and Germany to study the great masters of instrument-making and direct whatever talent he had to building, not playing, pipe organs. His enthusiasm was apparent, his objective less so, but Bette seemed reconciled, if not content, to let her one and only have his head.

Alan Redpath called upon Buckie regularly and had taken to fishing from the rocks that hemmed the bay and to swimming in the deep water when the weather was warm, but so far he had firmly refused to give Susanne swimming lessons, in spite of all her pleading. Now and then he spent a night in Louis's room and took a hand at the whist table or, with a certain glee, showed Buckie how cribbage should be played.

Darsie Coburn was a frequent visitor and Susanne became resigned to the young woman's weepy ways. Harry, it seemed, was seldom at home in Macklin House. He was here, there and everywhere, Darsie said, drumming up business, though precisely what sort of business Darsie did not know. Now that she had finished with school she seemed vaguer, lazier and more flighty than ever. She was happy to sit in the Hollanders' living-room, sipping little glasses of sherry wine, talking, talking, talking to Susanne or Aunt Bette about her own lack of purpose, and her father's cruel neglect.

Much to Buckie's delight, Gregor Oakley and his chum Macfarlane, fresh from their adventures on the *Merrilyn*, came out to High Cross to swap stories and, when Bette was looking the other way, share a bottle of rum that Peter had hidden in his pocket. Peter was as lean as a whippet and sported an impudent grin and a daft little tuft of a beard that wagged when he talked. Gregor Oakley, however, had grown tall, with broad shoulders and a deep chest that, Buckie said, came from hauling on the oars of a sealing boat for hours on end. The boys would sail again in early March, and Freddie would accompany them as an apprentice, for Tom Oakley had, it seemed, finally given up on his sons.

Seated on the porch on a warm September night listening to the men talk, Susanne rather wished that she had been born a man and could go roving with Peter, Greg and Freddie and see great whales rising out of the deep, icebergs like floating mountains and ice curving away up to the crown of the world. As if reading her thoughts, Greg glanced at her out of the corner of his eye and gave her a wink, for they shared the bond that all old school-fellows have, male and female alike. Then, by way of farewell, he had kissed her on the cheek, and called her 'Teacher', and promised that he would drop in again before he set off for Greenland in the spring.

For the best part of a week Fife lay buried under snow. Miss Primrose closed the school, and Tom, without consulting his elders, postponed Communion.

He instructed Zena to build up the fire in the study, and, armed with a bottle of brandy and a jug of hot coffee, shut himself away shortly after lunch to pore over his ledger and calculate the amount he had saved from his stipend and the sums that Bette Hollander had given him by way of loans. He had no idea where Bette had found the money, or why she made no complaint when he asked for more. Heaven knows, she complained enough about how much it was costing her to maintain Louis in Edinburgh where, it appeared, the young man was pursuing a proper trade at last.

Tom had no interest in the Hollanders' affairs, except in as much as they affected his dealings with Harry Coburn. Money and its acquisition had replaced sexual desire and his pursuit of Gillian Primrose had eased in the face of her constant rejections. He still longed to taste her breasts and dip into the treasure that lay beneath her petticoats, but, with so many other things to occupy him, he had postponed his wooing of the schoolmistress.

Snow mounded on the window ledge, ice smeared the glass.

Tom sprawled in an armchair with his feet on the fender, sipped coffee spiced with brandy, and mulled over the figures in the ledger. He could recite the sums in his sleep, of course, but found them so comforting that he mouthed the numbers silently, like a prayer, as he ran his pencil down the page. But then an insistent tapping disrupted his concentration and, glancing up, he saw Angus Gamrie's pug-dog face peering at him through the window.

Startled, Tom stuffed the ledger into a drawer and, rising

hurriedly, went into the hall and pulled open the door. Powdery snow drifted past on a blast of air so cold that it made his toes curl.

Angus flapped his arms and stamped his feet.

'Might I be comin' in, Mr Oakley, please?'

'I think you'd better, before you freeze to death.' Tom ushered the session clerk into the hall. 'What is it, Mr Gamrie? What brings you out here on this foul afternoon?'

'A matter of some gravitation.'

'I have already cancelled Sunday's Communion services, you know.'

'Nah, nah, it's not that.' Angus glanced in the direction of the kitchen. 'Is Effie – is Mrs Oakley at home?'

'Of course she's at home. Where else would she be on a day like this?'

'In that case,' said Angus, 'perhaps we should look for a bit o' privacy.'

Hearing voices, Effie yanked open the kitchen door.

Mr Gamrie promptly removed his hat and twisted his frozen cheeks into the likeness of a smile. Behind Effie the youngsters gathered, round-eyed. She held them back with her hand. 'Oh, Angus!' she said. 'What a state you're in. Come into the kitchen and warm yourself by the stove.'

'Thank you most kindly, Mrs Oakley,' Angus said. 'But I have business to discuss with the minister an' I can't tarry long.'

'Where's your horse and cart?'

'At the Dalriada,' Angus said. 'I came across the barley field on foot.'

'It's not our Gregor, is it?' said Effie, alarmed. 'Has something happened to our Gregor? Are you the bearer of bad news?'

'No, Effie, nothin' of that sort,' Angus assured her.

'Communion,' Tom stated.

And hurried Gamrie into the study and promptly closed the door.

Angus unbuttoned his greatcoat, loosened his muffler and teased the wet woollen mittens from his hands. He accepted the cup of lukewarm coffee that the minister offered.

He gulped it down, then solemnly announced, 'Old Guy Brogan's dead.'

'Is he, indeed?' Tom said. 'Who told you: Redpath?'

'No, I found the body myself,' said Angus. 'Dead for a day or two, by the look of him, sat in a chair by the fire, starin' into space, stiff as a board, with slitter all down his beard. It seems the boy had been feedin' him gruel, not realisin' he had passed away.'

'Boy?' said Tom. 'What boy?'

'Her boy,' said Angus. 'Annabel's boy.'

'Annabel?'

'Brogan's servant.'

'Didn't she have enough sense to tell the boy that the old man was dead?'

'Annabel is somewhat wantin' in sense, Mr Oakley, as well you know.'

Tom threw his hands in the air. 'If burial is required we'll have to wait for a thaw. Meanwhile, the sheriff must be informed, and the body kept' – he shrugged – 'somewhere.'

'We haven't seen old Guy at church for long enough.'

'No,' Tom agreed. 'Come to think of it, we haven't. Odd that neither the girl nor Brogan said a word about there being a child.'

'Aye,' Angus agreed. 'Very odd.'

'Are there no relatives?'

'None known.'

'Neighbours, servants?'

'Just daft Annabel,' said Angus, adding, 'and her bairn.'

'This boy – how old is he?'

'Three years, or thereabouts.'

'One must assume that Brogan is the father.'

'That's not what Annabel says.'

Tom cleared his throat. 'What *does* Annabel say?'

'She says the bairn's yours, Mr Oakley.'

'What utter nonsense! The woman's obviously lost her wits entirely. How could the child possibly be mine?'

'She says you an' she were – well, that there were acts of intimacy between you the first time you visited the farm, four years since. She says you're the only man she's ever lain with.'

'Now *that*,' Tom cried, '*is* a damned lie. Brogan had her before . . .'

'Before what, Mr Oakley?' said Angus, gently.

'Before I – before she . . .'

Blood drained from Tom's face. He staggered and sat down again. Angus took the empty cup, poured a dash of brandy and held the cup up as if he were feeding an invalid. A trickle of brown liquid escaped the corner of Tom's lips.

Angus wiped it away with his sleeve.

'Well, Mr Oakley,' he said. 'I'm sure it's all a mistake. Annabel McQueen must have you confused wi' some other gentleman.'

'McQueen, is that her name?'

'Aye,' said Angus. 'Didn't you even think to ask?'

'The boy hasn't been christened, has he?'

'Not yet,' said Angus. 'Old Guy wouldn't let her bring him to the kirk.'

'See. You see.'

'See what, Mr Oakley?'

'It's obvious Guy Brogan was the father; *that's* why he stopped coming to church, why he refused to let his bastard be baptised and why he was too embarrassed to tell me that there was a baby in the house.'

'Aye,' said Angus, soothingly. 'I expect that's the way of it. Nonetheless, given that Brogan kept Annabel an' the bairn hid away for the best part o' four years, I think questions might be asked.'

'Questions?'

'If the Church authorities get wind o' the girl's claim.'

'Oh, come now, Gamrie! Do you suppose the word of a half-witted farm girl will stand against the word of a man of God?'

'If any hint o' the girl's accusation leaks out then an enquiry's inevitable.'

'An enquiry by the sheriff's officer, you mean?'

'No, Mr Oakley, by the Presbytery.'

'Oh, God!'

'A trial, Mr Oakley,' Angus said, 'a trial to test the libel.'

'God! Oh, God!'

'However, there is a way for us to avoid a' that sort o' unpleasantness.'

'Is there?'

Angus nodded. 'After he fell ill, Brogan let the farm run to ruin. The girl did what she could, but the pastures are sore overgrown an' the byres stink. It seems Brogan sold most o' his cattle and kept just two or three o' the best milkers to hold body an' soul together. Only the generosity of Mr Arbuthnot's factor allowed him to retain the tenancy. There's nothin' left to provide for the girl and her bairn.'

'Are you telling me the girl can be bought off?'

'Annabel would hardly know what to do with your money,' Angus said. 'It's not cash she needs: it's a place to lay her head – and raise her son.'

'Is she capable of caring for a child?'

'She seems to have managed well enough so far.'

'If the girl's not right in the head,' Tom said, 'would it not be best for the child if he were put out to foster, and a place found for her in the workhouse in Anstruther or Pittenweem?'

'We've no jurisdiction in those parishes.'

'You have influence, Mr Gamrie, do you not?'

'Annabel McQueen was born in Whitfield. Her mother worked on the old Fisherfield estates. Nobody knows who the father was. When the mother died the Fisherfield factor was for throwin' Annabel on to the parish. Brogan took her in. She'd be eight or nine years old then. She was his only servant. He worked her hard, but looked after her well enough.'

'And fathered a bastard on her,' Tom said.

Angus was silent for a moment, then he said, 'She's lived in Strayhorn parish all her days, Mr Oakley. It wouldn't be right for us to toss her out.'

'Pay her then. Pay her from the Poor Fund.'

'Sixteen shillings the quarter, at the present rate?'

'She can survive on that, can she not?'

'Survive where, Mr Oakley? She needs a home,' Angus said. 'Annabel McQueen may lack some of her wits but she has a strong tongue in her head.'

'You mean, she'll prattle.'

'Oh aye, Mr Oakley, she'll prattle. And if she does the Presbytery will be obligated to examine the libel,' Angus said, 'to gather evidence not just from Annabel but from any person who might have a grudge against you.'

'I do not need a lecture in Church procedure, Mr Gamrie.'

'No,' said Angus, 'I don't suppose you do, Mr Oakley.'

'What are we going to do with her?' Tom said.

Angus went to the window and stared out into the gloom.

There was no fleck of colour to be seen, no shoot or green sprig to herald spring. Tonight there would be more snow and by morning the cleared pathways through the town would be blocked again. He had been unable to breach the drifts that cut off the inland farms and had a cart full of undelivered orders. Having learned from Dr Redpath that Guy was sick, he had reached Brogan's place that morning only by the skin of his teeth.

He would never forget the sight of the old farmer propped in a chair by the fire, the boy, a lively, brown-eyed three-year-old, seated on a little stool by the old man's feet, supping porridge from a bowl as if he had no care in the world. Wrapped in a shawl, her boots sticking out from her sturdy bare legs, Annabel was setting milk pans up on the cool shelf before she went out into the icy yard to fork hay for the cows and feed the two skinny wee grey calves that she had driven in from the frozen fields.

'I'll take her in,' Angus said. The minister ran a hand over his hair and stared at the wee man's back. 'I've a loft above the stable that'll do for her an' the bairn. There'll be talk, no doubt, but what do I care about tittle-tattle?'

'Where is she now?' Tom said.

'I left her at the farm. I put Guy's corpse in the bedroom an' bolted the door,' said Angus. 'When the weather eases, I'll summon Dr Redpath to examine the body an' inform the sheriff's officer, then we'll bring Guy here to the church to lie until the ground softens.'

'Is it wise,' said Tom, 'to bring him to my church?'

'He was a good, God-fearin' Christian man, even if his manners were a bit rough,' said Angus, turning at last. 'If I take in the girl an' the child, the least you can do is give Guy Brogan a decent burial.'

'Are those your terms, Mr Gamrie?'

'Terms?' said Angus. 'I'm not bargainin', Mr Oakley.'

'Of course not,' Tom said. 'But Mr Gamrie – Angus – I do appreciate what you're doing for me.'

'I'm not doin' it for you. I'm doin' it for Annabel McQueen.' He paused, then added, 'An' for Effie.'

'My wife? What does my wife have to do with it?'

'Only you can answer that question,' Angus said, and, buttoning up his greatcoat, stalked out of the manse without another word.

*   *   *

On Tuesday the barometer soared and on Wednesday morning great grey-purple clouds brought rain. It rained, torrentially, all day long. High tides gobbled up the snow and the tiny frozen streams that streaked the cliff face swelled into water spouts that, blown back by the wind, drenched old 'Muckle Tam', Strayhorn's grave-digger, at his labours in the churchyard.

There were four new graves to be dug: a baby and a child had died during the cold spell, together with an elderly tacklemaker. The occupant of the fourth grave remained something of a mystery until the minister announced Guy Brogan's death at Sunday service, by which time Guy's body was safely coffined and stored, upright, in the broom closet in the church vestibule, a fact that Tom Oakley elected not to make public.

Out at the farm, Mr Gamrie and Dr Redpath proceeded to settle the farmer's affairs and, aided by Arbuthnot's factor, saw to it that the cows would be milked and the calves fed until such time as a new tenant could be found to take on the property. Nobody, not even the sheriff, made any objection to Angus Gamrie's offer to provide temporary shelter for Annabel McQueen and her son, and, as soon as the back road became passable, the girl, her child and her few scant possessions were removed.

Angus drove the cart, Annabel, with the wee boy on her lap, huddled beneath the canvas awning behind him. She was a fine, big girl, fresh-complexioned, with a wide mouth and slate-grey eyes. She spoke rarely but when she did skeins of words came spooling out of her mouth and she would babble for many minutes before, like cloth sheared by scissors, her voice cut off and she would fall silent and watchful once more.

As far as Alan Redpath could tell the boy was healthy in mind as well as body; a sharp-eyed little imp full of curious questions, who, disconcertingly, bore no physical resemblance to his mother.

He had a round head topped by a mat of reddish-brown hair and, even at three, a gruff voice that demanded not so much attention as obedience. He was not at all intimidated by what was taking place and endured Alan Redpath's examination of his teeth, hair and ears stoically enough. He seemed to sense that his mother was not as bright as he was and while he clung to her and allowed her to pet him, he was also prepared to defend her.

It was still pouring when the cart drew up in the yard behind Angus's house. Rain had washed away the fog but the straggling streets of Strayhorn, the quay and harbour wall were watery and indistinct, and the sea, pitching against the shore, vanished into a netherworld of impenetrable cloud. It hadn't dawned on Angus until that moment that the boy's existence had been proscribed by the rolling hills around Brogan's farm, by a byre, a barn, a milking shed and the slithery muck of the yard, that the boy had never seen the sea before. He turned, frowning, and looked at his mother, then out past the corner of the house at the oblong of heaving black water, and uttered a strange whimpering cry that went straight to Angus's heart. He plucked the frightened child from the girl's lap and, cupping the boy's head, climbed to the ground.

The girl leaped from the cart and grabbed at her child. Angus fended her off, then, with the boy clinging to his chest like a monkey, laid an arm about Annabel's shoulders and led her not to the dank loft above the stables but into the shelter of the house where a good fire burned in the grate, a stew pot bubbled on the stove and she and the minister's child would be safe until he, Angus Gamrie, decided how best to make use of them.

Alan Redpath's brother, Stephen, had been promoted to the lesser chair of surgery in the Royal Infirmary in Edinburgh and had taken it upon himself to post a variety of interesting papers on medical developments to the wilds of Fife in the hope of persuading Alan to join him in the capital. He also sent a crate of glass dishes and a number of chemical substances to enable Alan to pursue an examination of the etiology of podagra, by which he meant gout.

Bored by long winter nights in Seameads with only the spinster sisters for company, Alan opened a journal in which to record his observations of that scourge of middle-aged gentlemen and, with several cases to hand, discovered that he had much to write about.

Buckie was flattered when Alan Redpath asked for a sample of blood.

Susanne held the measuring cup and watched Alan make a neat incision into a vein on her uncle's forearm and tap off a drachm. She bathed the little incision with a weak solution of salt, and bandaged it while Dr Redpath transferred the sample from the cup to a thin glass vial which he sealed with a rubber stopper. That done, they all sat down to supper.

'Now what will you do with it?' Susanne asked.

'Add it to a stew, I'm thinkin',' said Nancy.

'A tasteless sort of sauce my blood would make,' Buckie said.

'I'll place the sample in a covered dish for two or three days, drain off the serum, add two minims of acetic acid and' – Alan paused for effect – 'a small piece of unbleached thread.'

'An' a stag horn button?' Nancy suggested, scornfully.

'No, Nancy, no button,' Alan told her. 'I'm testing Mr Hollander's blood for uric acid, not reading his fortune.'

'Satan's work,' said Nancy. 'It's more o' Satan's work,' then backed into the kitchen and slammed the door with her heel.

'Pay no attention to that stupid girl,' Buckie said. 'Tell us more about this work you're engaged upon, Redpath? Will it result in a cure for my affliction?'

'In time, perhaps,' Alan said. 'Not, alas, immediately. My contribution—'

'Our contribution,' Buckie put in.

'Our contribution will be to measure fluctuations in the formation of uric acid crystals in the bloodstream before, during and after an attack.'

'So you'll need more, will you?'

'If you're willing, Buckie?'

'In for a penny,' Buckie said, 'in for a pound.'

Susanne said, 'Do crystals form around the thread?'

Allan glanced up, surprised. 'Why yes, they do.'

'Like salt from sea water?'

'Very similar,' Alan said.

'How do you take a measure of such minute quantities?'

'By using a milligram scale,' Alan said. 'You seem well versed in scientific procedure, Susanne.'

She shrugged. 'I've read about it in books.'

'Nose in a book, always her nose in a book,' Bette Hollander said. 'It's not right for a girl of her age.'

It had not escaped Alan's attention that Susanne had grown into a pretty young woman. Maturity added considerably to her appeal and he was wary of her in the way that men are with women who might upset their natural equilibrium. He knew, however, because Bette Hollander was never done telling him, that Susanne was entranced by her cousin and that it would only be a matter of time before they married.

'This study you're engaged upon,' Susanne said, 'will it require you to visit Edinburgh?'

'I doubt it. Why do you ask?'

'Doesn't your brother wish you to work in his hospital?'

'It's hardly Stephen's hospital, Susanne, though he does have some sway there, I suppose. I'm a simple physician, however, and lack the necessary skills to practise surgery.'

'You could learn, could you not?'

'Now, now, Susanne,' Buckie said, 'don't put ideas into Alan's head. Anyone would think you were trying to be rid of him. We don't want him running off to Edinburgh and leaving us, do we?'

'No fear of that,' Alan said. 'I've too much to do here.'

'Measuring my crystals?' Buckie said.

'Among other things,' said Alan.

The cottage had no attic, as such, but a square, wooden-framed box, like a large dovecot, had been grafted on to a corner of the roof. It had two square windows and a tiny square fireplace and, in windy weather, shook like a dicebox. Angus used it to store a few spare sticks of furniture and a chest of old clothes, and he had never attempted to light a fire in the grate before.

He did so now with a deal of trepidation, fearing that the whole house might suddenly fill with smoke or even become engulfed in flames. He had brought up a basket of dry kindling and small coals together with a lighted candle. When the fire was set, he touched a flame to it and, sitting back on his heels, observed it, nervously. If he could not warm the room sufficiently then he would be obliged to lodge the woman and child outside in the hayloft, for, he told himself, it would be unseemly to have them sleep in the kitchen when he was in bed next door.

Smoke curled up in a lazy spiral, kindling caught, crackled, glowed. Angus expected smoke to belch into his face but none did and, within a minute or two, the coals ignited and the fire began to burn quite merrily.

'Fire lighted?'

The boy stood behind Angus, blinking at the flames.

'Aye,' Angus said. 'What's your name, son?'

'Brogan.'

'Brogan? Oh!'

The boy steadied himself with a hand on Angus's shoulder. 'Mr Brogan gone to set the table wi' Jesus,' he said, gruffly. 'We're stayin' here now.'

Angus smiled. 'That's right, Brogan. You're stayin' with me now.'

'Where's the coos?'

'I don't keep cows,' said Angus. 'I'm not a farmer, like Mr Brogan.'

'You've a horse.'

'That's true. I do have a horse. His name's Matthew.'

'You left him outside.'

Angus sat up straight. 'By Gum, son, you're right,' he said. 'I'd forgotten about poor old Matt out there in the rain.'

'Bring him in now.'

'I will, I will,' Angus said, and, rising, helped the little boy down the steep stairs to the kitchen, and left the fire to take care of itself.

On Monday morning farmer Brogan was lowered into the ground. The service was short, almost perfunctory. Odd, Angus thought, for Guy to be buried by the sea when he had lived his life enclosed by fields and hills.

Mr Arbuthnot's factor said a few words in praise of the deceased, Tom intoned the committal, and Muckle Tam, on hand with his spade, had the first clods thumping down on the coffin lid before Angus reached the gate. He had considered bringing the girl but that would have meant bringing the boy too and as women and small children were not permitted to attend a burial they would have had to stand behind the wall, like outcasts.

Farmers and cattle dealers who had ridden out of the hinterland to bid farewell to Guy Brogan trudged off to their carts. Tom headed for the vestry to fill in the funeral register. Angus wondered if the minister would have the gall, or the gumption, to record the name of the child – if he even knew the name of the child – or if he would simply leave a blank under the heading of kin.

He accompanied Alan Redpath as far as the church and would have turned and gone in if he hadn't caught sight of Effie standing by the hedge of the drying green, apron off and bonnet on, arms folded across her chest, as if she were about to break into a hornpipe. She gave no sign that she required his attention but Angus sensed that she was there for a reason and, parting from the doctor, picked his way down the path towards her.

Winter had not been kind to the minister's wife. The fact that her children were growing more independent and that she had Zena at home to help her had not brought her relief. Angus experienced once more the trembling sense of pity that represented itself as love. Politely, he removed his hat, and held it across his chest.

'What's this I hear?' Effie began.

'About what?' said Angus.

'About you takin' on a woman?'

'Oh, that!'

'Yes, that!' Her lips were pursed, not sweetly, her brow so furrowed that he could barely see the temper in her eyes. 'You've taken in Brogan's woman, have you not, her and her bastard? Is it yours?'

'Pardon?'

'If it's not Brogan's bairn, is it yours?'

'I never said it wasn't Brogan's bairn.'

'Aye, but you never said it was.'

Angus had no idea what question he was supposed to answer or how he was supposed to answer it. He had known, of course, that he would not be able to keep Annabel's presence in his house secret, that his age and good reputation would not protect him from gossip, but he hadn't expected to be placed on the spot by Effie; nor had it crossed his mind that anyone, least of all the minister's wife, would suppose that he had fathered the boy.

'Tom told you, didn't he?'

Scowling, she nodded. 'He did.'

'Well,' Angus said, 'he had no right to do that.'

'She's a fine tasty piece, I hear,' said Effie.

'Hardly that,' Angus said, tightly. 'She's a poor soul, not quite right in the head.' He thrust his shoulders back and kept his voice even. If he had to tell a lie, he must make it as convincing as possible. 'The bairn, the boy is Guy Brogan's. I've only taken them in because it was that or the workhouse.'

'Nothing wrong with the workhouse,' Effie said. 'They have an easy time in the workhouse, so I hear, with nothing to do all the day but fritter away the hours until somebody serves their dinner.'

'It's not like that, Effie, not like that at all.'

'I thought you were a good man.'

'Does hirin' a servant make me bad?'

'Have you brought her to your bed yet?'

''Course I haven't brought her to my bed.'

He might have reached for her hand if they'd been alone, but he had no inclination to touch her now. Their friendship had been pure and affectionate, not sexual. He had known from the first that however much he admired and pitied Effie Oakley, he and she would never be joined like Eve and Adam, and, in consequence, he was shocked by her accusation that he had taken in the girl merely to satisfy his lust. For a fleeting moment he was tempted to tell her who had really fathered Annabel McQueen's child, but he was not so callous as all that. He stepped back and put on his hat.

'She will cook an' keep my house clean,' he said, stiffly, 'but if you think so little of me, Effie, as to imagine I'd take advantage of a poor, soft-headed girl, then your opinion of

me is not what I had thought it was. So, Mrs Oakley, if you've
no more to say, I'll be biddin' you a good-day.'

'Mr Gamrie – Angus . . .'

Too late: Angus had already turned on his heel and was
heading away from her, heading back home, with nothing but
sorrow, and a certain growing hardness, in his heart.

15

The lady's maid that her father had promised hadn't materialised. Darsie was obliged to make do with a girl from the kitchens to help her dress and pin her hair. She had exercised all her wiles on Papa, had sulked, raged, wept, and had even thrown herself at his feet and begged him to give her what she wanted: all to no avail. It wasn't that Papa was unsympathetic, just that he did not regard the employment of a lady's maid as essential.

How often had Darsie heard that excuse? As a child she had been willing to accept all Papa's excuses, but she was no longer a child. If she was ever to become mistress of Macklin House, or any other house for that matter, she deserved the privileges that went with responsibility, privileges that, in Darsie's opinion, began and ended with the employment of a lady's maid.

Darsie had no ear for music, no patience for embroidery, no stomach for shooting, and had never learned to ride. She could not bring herself to go down to the kitchens to arrange the weekly menus or chide the servants for laziness. She had no power, no authority. Even the girl who was called upon to help her dress pulled faces behind her back. Small wonder that she preferred the company in High Cross and spent as much time there as politeness would allow. She was always assured of a warm welcome from the Hollanders, and a few hours of intelligent conversation, albeit with folk who were not her social equal.

She had another reason for visiting the Hollanders' house,

however. She lived in hope that one day she would find Louis lounging on the porch or sprawled in the cramped parlour and that she, by some miracle, might wrest him away from the clutches of his cousin, to whom, in Darsie's opinion, he was entirely unsuited. The silly girl was addicted to sea-bathing, practising on the harmonium, teaching ignorant children their letters, walking miles along the shore with only that great smelly dog for company; skipping and laughing for no reason that Darsie could fathom, fawning over the old man and rubbing his swollen feet as if she were a slave and not heir to a fortune which she could use to hire a dozen lady's maids if she wanted to, which, apparently, she did not.

Papa had been absent for a week when the blizzards swept over Macklin and trapped Darsie indoors with the dogs and the servants.

She whiled away her mornings by changing from one dress into another and, pirouetting before the mirror, in deciding which one Louis would find most appealing. After a solitary lunch, she drank more sherry than was good for her, dozed in the chair before the fire, wakened with a sour stomach and a sore head and wept tears of self-pity at the prospect of the long, lonely night ahead. Then, after almost a week as a prisoner, she wakened one morning to the sound of rain drumming on the window and snow sliding from the roof.

She dressed and hurried downstairs to enquire of Samson, the butler, what state the roads were in and just how soon Benbow would be able to roll out the curricle. Samson relayed the message to the stables and, as Darsie was finishing her tea, Benbow stuck his head around the door and told her, 'To-morrow, if we're lucky.'

'Tomorrow, not today?'

'You wouldn't be wantin' one o' your father's horses break-in' a leg on the ice, now would you, miss?'

'Tomorrow it will have to be then,' Darsie said. 'Tomorrow

we'll drive to High Cross where I'll stay until Papa elects to come home again.'

With the aid of the sniggering kitchen girl, she chose what she would wear for her visit to the Hollanders and, in early afternoon, carefully packed her dresses into her trunk. She was seated on the bed, about half past three, wondering what to do next when there came a thunderous knocking on the front door. Alarmed and curious, Darsie ran down to the hall just as Samson appeared from his cubby, buttoning his waistcoat and pulling on his coat, and opened the enormous front door.

The caller wore a loose, oil-proofed greatcoat and a floppy-brimmed hat, both black with rain. He looked so menacing that Darsie experienced a queer glow of excitement at the sight of him.

'Louis!' she shrieked in delight. 'What are *you* doing here?'

'Is your father at home?'

'No.'

'When will he be back?'

'I haven't the faintest idea.'

'Damn!' Louis shook water from his hat. 'Damn and blast! I assumed he would be stuck here because of the snow.'

'My father hasn't been home for ages,' Darsie said. 'We've no reason to expect him to return tonight. Samson, do not stand there like a fool. Relieve Mr Hollander of his coat and hat and see to it that they are hung in the drying-room. When you have done that' – she sounded imperious, not at all like herself – 'fetch brandy to the drawing-room and a kettle of hot water, then be good enough to inform Cook that we will be one more for dinner, after which you may instruct Morag to make up the bed in the second-floor bedroom, and to be sure to put in a warming-pan.'

Samson's eyes bulged.

'Do it now,' said Darsie.

The butler, stone-faced, bowed, and said, 'Aye, Miss

Darsie,' then, with unusual alacrity, leaped to help the young gentleman out of his overcoat.

When the first of the blizzards arrived, Prim closed the school at once and packed all the children off home. Next morning she dug paths through the drifts to the cesspit and the school-house and settled down to wait out the weather.

For days she saw no signs of life except a few gaunt rooks and an optimistic robin that she fed with crumbs and bacon scraps from a saucer on the window ledge. She went to bed early and rose late, stumbled out into the whitewashed dark-ness only to carry the chamber pot to the cesspit or scuttle to the schoolhouse to make sure that the roof hadn't collapsed or that the mice hadn't eaten the chalk.

Huddled by the fire, or snuggled in her narrow bed, Prim found herself thinking more and more of Alan Redpath. She was, she told herself, educated, intelligent and not unsophis-ticated. She could be modest and unassuming when it suited her, and could cook, sew and clean a house more efficiently than any servant. She was sound in wind and limb, would bear healthy children, and remain unswerving in her devotion to any man who could be persuaded to take her for a wife.

By any man, of course, she meant Alan Redpath.

And when the thaw finally set in, off she went to seek him out.

'Ah, Miss Primrose?' Alan said. 'Released from bondage, I see.'

'I am, indeed, free at last, Dr Redpath.'

'Has the school reopened?'

'Indeed, it has.'

'Do you require me to visit?'

'You are welcome to visit at any time, Dr Redpath.'

'To call at the school, I mean?'

'If you can spare the time,' Prim said. 'We've used up almost all the white application that you were kind enough to leave.'

'Application?'

'The zinc ointment.'

'Oh yes, the zinc.'

'Had you forgotten?'

'Of course not.'

'It was very beneficial.'

'A remedy tried and true,' said the doctor, lamely.

He had driven into Strayhorn to check on a patient and the Allardyce sisters had suggested that he might also make a few purchases at the Saturday market to save them sending a servant into town.

The boats had ventured out on Friday. The remains of the catch were spread out on the quay and the fishwives were doing fair business amid the guts and gulls, masts, nets and creels. On the cobbled hill six or eight little wooden stalls had been erected where farmers' wives peddled eggs, butter, cheese and fresh butcher meat. The bakehouse lad had been sent out with a tray of hot cakes and gingerbread, the miller's daughters with small sacks of meal and barley, and a yarn dealer from Whitfield had laid out a drawer of ribbons, threads and buttons to gather in the young girls. After the long spell of bitter weather, the good citizens of Strayhorn felt compelled to spend money they did not have, and, hidden inside a canvas booth, two solemn young men in tight black suits doled out loans in exchange for notes and vouchers.

No horse dealers, peep shows, sword dancers or wailing pipers graced Strayhorn's crooked little square but trade was brisk, nonetheless, and there was a bustle to the sullen town that Alan found stimulating. He'd promised himself that once he'd purchased provisions for the Allardyce twins, he would repair to the Dalriada for a plate of stew and a glass or two of ale.

Then Gillian Primrose had put in an appearance. He had forgotten how distinctive she was, not pretty like Coburn's daughter, not as buxom as Zena Oakley or as neat as Susanne, but very much an individual, with her thick fair hair and her bonnet askew. She seemed remarkably radiant and healthy, he thought, for someone who had been shut up in Rose Cottage all week long.

'Are you restocking your larder?' he asked.

'I should, I suppose,' Prim said, 'but that must wait.'

He did not press the point. Village schoolteachers were not well paid. He would have loaned her a florin or two, if she had been less independent. He said, 'I have a few provisions to purchase, but first I plan to take a plate of stew at the inn. Will you join me?'

'Are ladies welcome at the Dalriada?'

'There's a snug at the back,' Alan said, 'where, I believe, ladies are served refreshment.'

'What sort of ladies?' said Prim. 'Respectable ladies?'

'I – I can't honestly say,' Alan admitted.

'I do have a position to uphold, you know.'

The trouble with talking to Gillian Primrose was that he could never be sure when she was being serious and when she was teasing.

He said, 'Perhaps you'd rather not.'

'Yes,' she said. 'I would.'

'What, rather not?'

'Rather.'

'Oh!' Alan said. 'Well, I mean, shall we eat now?'

'By all means,' Prim said and, to his amazement, took his arm.

'If I'm not mistaken,' Zena said, 'that's our Prim and Dr Redpath walking out together.'

'Where?' said Susanne, on tiptoe. 'Oh yes, so it is.'

She was on the point of calling out when Zena tugged her sleeve.

'Wait.'

'Why?'

'Use your eyes, Susanne. What does it look like to you?'

'An assignation?'

'My, my! I didn't think our Prim had it in her.'

The girls slipped behind the banker's booth and watched the teacher and the doctor descend the hill towards the harbour.

'I wonder where he's taking her,' Zena whispered. 'Come on, Susanne, let's see if they're heading for Rose Cottage.'

'What about the children?'

'Damn the chi— All right, all right. Petal,' she called out, 'Morven, come here this instant – and find Waylie, wherever he is.'

Petal hugged a whole cod fish against her chest like a rag doll, its slippery tail smearing scales across her skirts. Morven had a loaf of bread tucked under each arm, and no free hand to drag her brother from under the butcher's table where he, like a little mongrel, was searching for scraps. She fished him out with her foot while Zena shouted, excitedly, 'This way, this way,' and pranced off down the hill with Susanne hard on her heels.

The snuggery at the rear of the Dalriada was tiny. Females who came to the inn for refreshment were few and far between and those women who did partake of a bowl of broth or a dish of stew were, as a rule, too hungry to care about their surroundings. The Saturday market had brought farmers and servants into town, however, and both parlour and snug were crowded. Only one small table, hard by the window and far from the fire, was vacant. Alan settled Miss Primrose there and fought his way to the serving counter to place his order.

'Aye, Dr Redpath,' Sandy Raiker said, 'is that no' the teacher lady you're hidin' over there?'

'It is, Sandy,' Alan admitted.

'She's a fine bit handsome woman for a teacher, I'm thinkin'.'

Benbow craned his neck and peered past Sandy's shoulder. 'Is she for givin' you an edu-kay-shun, then, sir?'

'Now, now,' Sandy said. 'The doctor's no' requirin' an education. He's got one o' them already.'

'The doctor,' Alan said, 'requires food.'

'Plump for the stew,' said Sandy.

'Don't touch the skink,' said Benbow.

'What's wrong with the skink?'

'Reekin' o' onion it is,' said Sandy. 'Sits ill in the bowels.'

'An' breakin' wind is no way tae win fair lady,' said Benbow.

'I had no idea you were so knowledgeable about intestinal disorders,' Alan said, 'or so well versed in matters of the heart.'

'Oh, so the heart's involved, is it?' said Sandy.

Alan laughed, a little uneasily. 'Only the stomach.'

He looked round at Prim who was observing the exchange through the arch that separated the parlour from the snug. She grinned, waved a hand and gestured to her mouth. For no reason that Alan cared to dwell upon, Benbow and Sandy Raiker chuckled, and went back to supping their ale.

Susanne said, 'What are they doing now, Petal?'

'Eating their dinners.'

'What're they eating?' said Morven.

'Bones,' said Waylie.

'Nah, they're not,' said Morven. 'Big people don't eat bones.'

'Dogs eat bones.'

'Stop it,' Zena said. 'Go closer, Petal, and tell us what you see.'

Still clasping the cod to her chest, the little girl pressed her nose to the glass and peered into the snuggery. The window had not been washed in months and she could make out very little of what was going on within.

'Nothing,' she said. 'I see nothing.'

'You must see something,' Zena said.

'Bones,' said Waylie.

'Wayland, if you don't stop ranting on about bones . . .' Zena began.

'She's got his hand,' said Petal, suddenly.

'In her mouth?' said Waylie.

'Holding his hand,' said Petal, her voice muffled. 'Miss Primrose's holding the man's hand.'

'Alan's hand?' said Susanne.

'The man's hand, aye,' said Petal.

'I told you they were lovers,' said Zena.

'Here, let me see for myself,' said Susanne.

Pushing Petal and the cod fish to one side, she peered through the window. If Prim had indeed been holding Alan's hand she had released it again. A serving girl was in the process of sliding two plates of beef stew on to the table and Alan and Prim were looking up at her.

'Is she kissing him?' said Zena.

'No,' Susanne said. 'She's breaking bread for him.'

'That's a start,' said Zena.

'What *do* you mean?' said Susanne.

'She's not feeding him up for nothing,' Zena said. 'Next thing you know she'll be dragging him back to Rose Cottage to sample her pudding.'

'Alan's not like that.'

'They're all like that,' said Zena. 'Mark my words, Susanne, now she's sunk her hooks in him, she'll find a way to keep him.'

'Zena!' Susanne said, shocked, and, just as Miss Primrose

raised her fork to her mouth and turned her gaze to the window, stepped hastily to one side.

'I do believe,' Prim said, through a mouthful of hot beef, 'that we are being observed. I assume you recognise them?'

'Of course. It's the Oakleys, and Susanne.'

'Are you embarrassed?'

'Why would I be embarrassed?' said Alan.

'Unless I miss my guess they'll forget all they've learned of arithmetic and make two and two add up to five,' Prim said. 'Girls are all too ready to matchmake. They've probably concluded that I'm in pursuit of a husband.'

Fork poised, Alan said, 'Are you?'

'I've managed very well without one so far,' Prim said, adding, 'of course, I'm not getting any younger.'

Alan speared a piece of carrot and examined it as if it were an anatomical specimen. 'I thought you were committed to teaching,' he said. 'I mean, that you'd decided to devote your life to . . .' Waylie thumped his fist upon the glass. 'What *is* that child doing?'

'Making a thorough nuisance of himself,' Prim said. 'It's unfortunate that I don't have a father to arrange suitors for me. If I do wish to marry then I'll be forced to make the arrangements myself.'

'Where are your parents?'

'Bluefoot House, in the Lothians.'

'Is your father a landowner?'

Prim laughed. 'No,' she said. 'My mother's a servant. I was born on the wrong side of the sheets and spent my childhood in the scullery, until the master of the house put me to school.'

'Ah, he was one of the enlightened ones?'

'You might say that,' Prim answered, 'but I think he just wanted rid of me. That is my history, such as it is.'

'Too scant to be accurate,' Alan said.

'I beg your pardon!'

'There must be more to it, to you.'

'Must there? Why?'

'Because of what you are, what you have made of yourself.'

'A spinster teacher in a village school?' said Prim.

'I wish that lad would go away.' Alan waved his arm in the direction of the window. 'What are they waiting for now? What do they expect from us?'

'I think they're rather hoping that you'll kiss me.'

'Kiss you? For heaven's sake, why would I want to do that?'

'I have no idea,' said Prim.

'If I kissed you, do you suppose it would make them go away?'

'It might,' Prim said.

Alan put down his fork, pushed the plate to one side and wiped his mouth on a napkin. 'On the cheek, will that do it?'

'On the lips might be more convincing,' Prim said.

She drew her forefinger across her lips and leaned a little towards him.

'I'm not sure this is wise,' Alan said.

'Chalk it up as an experiment,' said Prim.

He sucked in a deep breath and with a quick, darting motion, brushed her lips with his. He would have pulled away at once but Prim's fingers were on his cheek, steadying him. Before he could retreat, she pressed her mouth, warm and firm, against his lips.

'My God!' Sandy Raiker said. 'Will you be lookin' at that?'

'Aye,' said Benbow. 'I don't know what this town is comin' to.'

While outside in the cobbled street, Susanne and Zena cheered.

Darsie was hiding under the crib in the old nursery when her father arrived home. Collarless and dishevelled, Louis was tiptoeing from room to room on the darkened upper floor, crooning, 'Where are you, darling? Where are you hiding, my sweetheart? I'll find you, you know. I'll find you, and when I do . . .' When the master of Macklin appeared at the foot of the staircase, however, he stopped dead in his tracks, like a locomotive running out of steam.

'Ah!' Louis stammered, holding the candle aloft. 'Ah! Harry?'

'What, may I ask, are you doing in my house?' Harry Coburn enquired.

Harry wore a voluminous brown wool cape, riding breeches and brown leather half boots. He had travelled by the railway as far as Leven and by coach to the gates of the estate. His hair was long and tousled and he held his hat down by his side, one fist planted on his hip and one leg thrust out as if he were about to charge up the staircase and, like a French musketeer, run Louis through.

'I came to talk with you, sir,' Louis, rooted to the landing, said.

'Where, pray tell, is my daughter?' said Harry.

'I'm looking for her,' said Louis.

'And why, pray tell, are you looking for her?'

'Because she's – she's hiding.'

'And why is she hiding? Is she hiding from you?'

'Yes – but it's a game, sir, only a game.'

'How long have you been here?'

'Three – no, four days.'

'I see,' Harry said. 'Find my daughter, wherever she is, and fetch her down to the drawing-room.'

'Yes, sir,' Louis said.

'And while you're about it,' Harry Coburn said, 'might I suggest that you button your breeches.'

'Oh!' said Louis, looking down. 'Oh, dear me! Yes, of course.'

* * *

Persuading her babies to eat was no longer a problem. It was all that Effie could do to keep her voracious brood fed. She did not dare leave a ham bone or a scrap of beef unattended or Waylie would carry it off to his 'den' behind the coal heap or fight over it with Roland while Morven, a nervous child, would weep and beg them to stop. The outing that afternoon had subdued them, however. Morven was asleep upstairs. Roland, Waylie and Petal were happy in the hallway, playing with wooden clothes pegs, and Freddie had gone into town, for, like Gregor before him, he had already acquired a taste for independence.

Zena was laying the table when Tom entered the room. He had a hazy look in his eye that suggested he had been oiling his intellect with a little too much brandy and that his sermon tomorrow might be even less coherent than usual. At least, Effie consoled herself, he hadn't been prowling about the parish, doing she knew not what. He seated himself at the table, and sniffed.

'Something smells good.'

'Pie. Mutton,' Zena informed him.

'Not fish?'

'No, not fish,' said Zena. 'Tomorrow, fish.'

'How was the market?'

'Not without interest,' said Zena.

Tom propped an elbow on the table and rubbed his hand over his hair. There was grey in it now, great streaks of grey that no amount of trimming and plucking could eliminate. He was curiously haggard, his face, in repose, sagging. In a year or two, Effie thought, maliciously, his charm will have turned to cheese and women won't give him a second glance. She poured water from a jug and washed the smell of mutton from her hands. She was still upset about Angus and the farm girl who could give him so much more than she ever could. She had never thought of herself as Angus Gamrie's wife, or his lover; touch, tenderness, murmured words of affection had been enough for her, but not, apparently, for Angus who had proved himself to be nothing but a false, fair-weather friend.

Zena said, 'Dr Redpath's walking out with Prim.'

The silence, not the statement, caused Effie to turn from the tub.

The haze vanished from Tom's eyes. He lifted his chin a little, tilting it forward so that his features seemed to sit back, as if they had been squashed by impact with a wall or a door.

'Balderdash!' he said.

'It's not balderdash,' Zena said. 'We saw them together.'

'Doing what?'

'Kissing,' said Zena, matter-of-factly. 'They were eating dinner in the snug in the Dalriada. She kissed him first, then he kissed her back.'

'In the Dalriada,' said Tom. 'What were you doing in the Dalriada?'

'We were outside, by the window,' said Zena.

'He kissed her, do you say?'

'After she kissed him,' Zena said. 'If you don't believe me, ask Petal.'

'Tom,' Effie said, 'are you ailing?'

Zena seated herself at the table, folded her arms and leaned back, making the chair creak. She had that twist to her mouth, that cock of the head that indicated that something deep and sinister was going on.

'I think,' she said, 'they'll announce their betrothal before long. If Prim goes off with the doctor, Susanne could be appointed as the new teacher, and I could be her assistant, could I not?'

'You're talking nonsense,' Tom said. 'Redpath is perfectly entitled to buy Gillian a dinner. What did they do next?'

'Purchased a few provisions,' Zena said, 'and rode off.'

'Together?'

'Aye, together.'

'In Redpath's gig?'

'Aye.'

Effie watched the sagging lines about her husband's mouth tighten and his upper lip curl. He looked, she thought, as he sometimes did in the pulpit, filled not with the Holy Spirit but with painful self-righteousness. She had an inkling then of what the news meant to him, how it roused a jealous rage much more fierce and fiery than her watery envy of Angus's young servant girl.

'And,' Tom said, 'where did they go in the doctor's gig?'

'Back,' said Zena, with studied care, 'to Rose Cottage.'

'How do you know? How can you be sure?'

'Because, when we passed an hour ago, his gig was still there.'

Darsie stood before him in the drawing-room, pale as a ghost but too frightened to weep. Hollander, though, had assumed an unrepentant air, a clumsy sort of confidence that Harry found unsettling. He poured sherry and handed a glass to his daughter who accepted it with trembling fingers. He invited the couple to sit side by side on the sofa which, reluctantly, they did.

'How long,' he said, 'has the snow been gone?'

'Since Tuesday,' Louis answered.

'So it wasn't the weather that kept you here?'

'Darsie invited me to stay.'

It had been the best part of a year since he had seen Louis Hollander and the young man had changed considerably, had thickened and coarsened, had become more artisan than artist.

'Did she, indeed? I take it you've been to High Cross?'

Darsie was seated on the edge of the sofa, knees pressed together. She twirled the sherry glass round and round in her fingers as if she were mixing a philtre. Soon, very soon, he would have to find a husband for Darsie, if only to keep her from making a fool of herself.

'No,' Louis said. 'I haven't been to High Cross, nor do I have any intention of going to High Cross. There is nothing for me there.'

'Darsie,' Harry said, 'please go to your room. Louis and I have something to discuss. You may join us for dinner in, say, an hour.'

'Is – is Louis staying tonight?'

'Are you?' Harry asked.

'If it is not too much of an imposition,' Louis said.

'Stay as long as you wish,' said Harry.

'Thank you, Papa,' Darsie said and, with a sigh of relief, trailed meekly out of the drawing-room.

Annabel McQueen settled so swiftly into Angus Gamrie's life that he wondered how he had ever managed without her. She had the stove cleaned and lighted, water boiling and breakfast ready before he emerged from his bedroom and, when he returned from his rounds in the dark of the evening, had supper warming on the hob.

The little boy, too, was eager to make himself useful and would tackle any task that seemed to need doing, even those that were far beyond his capability. He would have fed Matthew, for instance, if he could have reached the meal bin, and would dart, dangerously, under the horse's belly to keep up with Angus in the stable. Fascinated by the crates that arrived from Dundee, he sat cross-legged and watched Angus unpack the goods and transfer them to the cart, and when Angus rode out on the cart of a morning, he would run to the end of the yard and stand there, waving, so small and easily broken that Angus felt guilty at leaving him behind.

He purchased a warm woollen shirt for Brogan and a new apron for Annabel. When he unwrapped the presents, spanking new and smelling sweet, the girl thanked him by hopping on one foot which, Angus deduced, was her version of a curtsey. He promised himself that when his next payment came from Dundee he would buy stockings for Annabel and shoes for the boy. He wished he could afford to give them more, for he knew that Annabel McQueen and her son were only his on loan and that when he'd made use of them there would be no place for them in Strayhorn and he would be obliged to pass them on to another master.

Meanwhile, very soon, he must take them to church.

'Church?' the girl said.

'Aye,' Angus told her, 'where people say their prayers an' give thanks to God the Father.'

'Churrr-ch.' Annabel nodded.

She was seated on a wooden armchair by the fire, the child asleep in her lap. The floor had been scrubbed, supper dishes washed and put away, the lamp trimmed. Busy at his accounts, Angus heard her crooning to the boy, a low, tuneless lullaby that he found more soothing than distracting.

'Have you never been to church, Annabel?'

She thought about it for fully a minute: 'Nup.'

Nods, frowns and grins, shakes of the head; her emotions were swift-changing, like clouds skimming over the sea. She could hold an idea for no more than a few seconds yet, in repose, she looked as normal as any of the young women who strolled the Strayhorn quays.

She continued to nod and grin until Angus spoke once more.

'I'll take you to church on Sunday,' Angus said, 'to hear psalms being sung and what the minister has to say about our Saviour, Jesus Christ.'

'Jesus!' Annabel said.

'Have you heard of Jesus? Do you know who He is?'

'Our Saviour?'

Angus turned from the table. 'Do you know what a minister is, Annabel?'

'He's our Saviour, too.'

'Do you remember Mr Oakley? He visited you when Mr Brogan was sick, a long time ago?'

First a frown, then a smile. 'He wored a black coat.'

Angus waited for her to trawl more painful impressions of Tom Oakley from her memory, but her expression remained blank.

If he'd been conversing with Effie or the Primrose woman he might have suspected evasion, but Annabel did not have the guile to be evasive. He knew that she remembered Mr Oakley for, when he had questioned her on that bitter cold morning out at the farm, with Guy dead in the armchair, she'd told him about the man in the black coat and what he had done to her. But now the question seemed to slither off her, like sleet off glass.

Angus rubbed his brow, clicked his tongue, and said, 'It's time the wee chap was put to his bed, Annabel.'

She nodded agreement, handed the boy to Angus, and got to her feet. Brogan wore his brand-new shirt. His limbs were smooth, his bare feet small as cockle shells, his body warm and weighty in Angus's arms.

Angus watched Annabel clamber upstairs. He followed her on to the stairs and held up the sleeping child, like Abraham offering Isaac to the Lord. The girl wrapped her arms about her son and took him into the boxroom. Angus watched from the stairs until there was nothing left to see but shadows in the lamplight. Then he went down into the kitchen to find his New Testament, to pore over Paul's first letter to the Corinthians, and pray.

Samson had dragged in two huge pine logs, still somewhat damp, and had placed them on top of the coals in the fireplace.

The logs hissed and spat and stubbornly refused to ignite. Harry and Louis drew their chairs closer to the fire for, with the coming of night, the drawing-room had become chilly.

Sherry had been put aside and they were drinking brandy now, but cautiously, for neither Darsie's father nor Darsie's lover wished to lose control of his mental faculties and yield advantage to the other.

'Now, young man,' Harry said, affably, 'what is the matter with you?'

'Matter? Nothing is the matter with me,' Louis retorted.

'I was under the impression that you were employed.'

'I am employed. I am apprenticed to George Rennie.'

'And who is George Rennie?'

'A cabinet-maker. He's exceedingly well known in Edinburgh.'

'I will take your word on that,' said Harry. 'However, Mr Rennie must be an unusually generous employer if he allows you to trip off to Fife in the middle of the month of January.'

'I told him I was sick.'

'Ah!'

'I am sick,' said Louis, boldly. 'Frankly, Harry, I'm sick of your prevarications and wish to sell my shares in your railway company.'

'*Your* shares?'

'Do I not hold a sheaf of shares in the Strayhorn railway?'

'I suppose you do,' Harry conceded.

'I wish to sell them. Now.'

'May I ask why?'

'Because,' Louis said, 'not one yard of track has been laid, not one wagon purchased. There is no Strayhorn Railway Company, is there? It's a bubble, a house of cards.'

'Now, now, Louis, calm yourself. Do you have a price in mind?'

'You won't trick me as easily as that,' Louis said. 'I know exactly how much money has been placed into your account.'

'I would hope so,' said Harry, 'considering that you put it there.'

'I am also aware that you have embroiled me in a high crime.'

Harry raised his hands in horror. 'A crime! A high crime!'

'Don't mock me, sir,' Louis said. 'You're using me to gain access to Susanne Thorne's fortune. You've made me your agent in fraud.'

'Of course I have,' Harry said. 'The purchase of shares in the Strayhorn railway has been done in your name, under your signature. *You* hold the shares: *I* do not. In the unlikely event of the purchase being examined by a court of law you will be exposed as the beneficiary, and if the Strayhorn Railway Company *is* a house of cards, then the charge against you will surely include forgery.'

'Forgery!'

'Did you not provide a letter from Susanne Thorne?'

'Yes, but I gave it to you.'

'Did you?' Harry said. 'Or did you present it to Mr Neville Reeve, a respected member of the Chancery Division of the Inns of Court? I suspect that Mr Reeve, acting in innocence, has done no more than obey your letters of instruction, letters of instruction purporting to be from Miss Thorne; an unfortunate young lady who fell under your malign and conniving influence and upon whose affections you have shamelessly traded. It will be my word against yours, Louis, and who do you suppose a jury will believe?'

'Dear God! What have you done to me?'

'Nothing,' said Harry. 'True, I am trying to raise the wind to build a railway into the heart of Fife, but that's hardly a crime. It appears that you seized the opportunity to cheat your cousin—'

'She is not my cousin.'

'Whatever she is – that you have used me in the execution of a scheme to stick your paws into the poor girl's fortune.'

'But there *is* no railway?'

'There, my dear chap, you're much mistaken,' Harry said. 'At this very moment Mr Gordon Bagshott, a reputable engineer, is assembling a crew to begin work on building a terminal in Strayhorn. In a matter of weeks the bills for land use will be passed by the parliament, we will drive track across the Fisherfield acres, and the value of your shares will soar. So, my dear chap, I'll be delighted to relieve your conscience by buying them from you here and now.'

'I – I don't know how much they're worth.'

'Of course you don't. You simply want rid of them,' said Harry. 'And, while we're on the subject, may I enquire *why* you want rid of them?'

'I want to travel to Germany.'

'To Germany?'

'To Frankfurt,' Louis stammered, 'to study the science of organ-building under Herr Valkler who will teach me how to construct these instruments so that I may go into business for myself.'

'I see,' said Harry. 'Do speak German?'

'I will learn. I have a great aptitude for languages.'

'This apprenticeship, how long will it last?'

'A year or two, probably.'

'I assume that Herr Valkler has actually agreed to train you?'

'We are in correspondence, yes.'

The pine logs had caught at last. Flames licked over the bark and bit into the sap wood. Harry sat back and crossed one leg over the other.

'Does Susanne know of your plan?' he asked.

'Susanne? No, she does not.'

'Would it not be prudent to discuss it with her?'

'Why?' said Louis.

'Are you and she not trembling on the brink of matrimony?'

'I've made no promises to Susanne. None that are binding.'

'Your mother seems to think otherwise.'

'Mama! Oh, Mama would have us wed tomorrow.'

'Your mama's no fool. Marriage to your cousin will secure your future.'

Louis hesitated, then, squirming a little, said, 'I do not love Susanne.'

'Oh!' said Harry. 'Do you love another?'

Again Louis paused. 'No.'

Harry placed his empty glass on the floor and, reaching out, clasped Louis Hollander's knee. He had not forgotten the sight that had greeted him less than an hour ago. He could not be sure what the couple had been up to, though, being a man of the world, he feared the worst – which was just one more reason for keeping Louis well away from Darsie. Besides, Hollander was too asinine to realise that one might use a sprat to catch a whale, that when construction work on the turntable commenced shares would be snapped up by greedy investors, and that he, Mr Henry Coburn, would quietly leave Fife to search for bigger and better opportunities elsewhere.

'Louis,' Harry said, 'do you happen to know what the Bank of England is currently declaring as a borrowing rate?'

'What? No.'

'Three per cent,' said Harry, 'a usurious three per cent. Now, even an enterprising man can't hope to advance any sort of scheme by borrowing money at that rate. I have used you, it's true, and I've tapped Susanne Thorne's fortune to finance a venture that will bring prosperity to every man, woman and child in this pocket of Scotland. Is that such an unworthy objective? Do the ends not justify the means? I can, of course, buy back the shares that have been issued in your name, but I'm not as unscrupulous as you suppose me to be.' He squeezed Louis's knee. 'If you're really set on this organ-building thing, and if you truly believe that Herr Whackler—'

'Valkler.'

'Yes, Valkler – if you really believe that he is the man to steer you on a proper course to financial independence, then I will lend you two hundred and fifty pounds for a single year's study in Frankfurt: one year, Louis, not two or three, and two hundred and fifty pounds, not a penny more.'

Louis glowered, suspiciously. 'And my shares?'

'Keep the shares,' Harry told him. 'You will thank me for it in years to come. All I ask is that when the shares are sold and you have reaped a profit on them, you restore in full the sums that you've borrowed from Susanne Thorne, and make good your promise.'

'My promise?'

'To marry her.'

'I don't want to marry Susanne.'

'Louis, Louis, what *do* you want?' Harry said. 'To stagnate in this woeful part of the world for the rest of your life? No, of course you don't. Why do you think I chose you to share in the wealth that my railway will generate?'

'Because you needed Susanne's letter.'

'Because,' Harry said, 'I marked you from the first as a man with foresight and ambition. Organ-building: what a grand partnership between art and industry that is, what an ideal profession for an ambitious young man with taste and tenacity. But it cannot be achieved without sacrifice.'

'You mean without money?'

'Without money, and the influence that money can buy. London is the place for you, and London is expensive.' He had the boy on the run now. 'Make your arrangements with Herr Valkler and have your year abroad, but do not cast Susanne out of your life, I beg you. She loves you, does she not?'

'I believe that to be the case,' said Louis, haughtily.

'Tell her what you plan to do. If she offers you additional financial assistance, accept it graciously. Marriage is more than the fulfilment of fleeting passion, Louis; marriage is, or should be, a partnership.'

'What if there's someone else, someone I like better than Susanne?'

'You will have had your year in Frankfurt and have made some money on your own account, after which . . .' Harry shrugged.

'A year abroad?' Louis brushed a lock of hair from his brow. 'And you will pay for it?'

Harry smiled, modestly. 'It's the least I can do.'

A twelve-month in Germany would be sufficient for the wayward genius to discover that he had no more talent for building pipe organs than he had for composing symphonies. One year with Louis safely out of the way would be enough for the railway scheme to bear fruit, after which Darsie and he would disappear, and Louis would have no alternative but to marry Susanne Thorne, if only to keep himself out of jail.

Harry laid a hand on Louis's shoulder. 'Sleep on it. Let me have your decision tomorrow. But,' he added, 'I suggest you weigh the pros and cons very carefully, for this is no time to act impetuously.'

'And – and Darsie?' Louis said, looking up.

'No,' Harry said, gently, 'I'm sorry, old chap. Whatever happens, whatever you decide to do, Darsie is not for you.'

It was late in the afternoon when Louis returned to High Cross. He told Benbow to drop him short of the hill and walked the last half-mile, his bag slung over his shoulder, his coat flapping in the strong wind off the sea.

Parting from Darsie had been more difficult than he'd imagined it would be. He was beginning to suspect that what she had coaxed him into doing in the flowery bedroom in Macklin House had meant a great deal more to her than it had to him. At first he had been scared and awkward. Even at the eleventh hour he would have torn himself away if she hadn't wept, begged and clung to him like a limpet.

Escape had been impossible, escape not so much from Darsie as from the creature that lurked in her loins, a demon that had snatched at his reason and devoured him like a monster. Sharp little talons had raked his belly, sharp little teeth had pricked his parts, a slippery entity had sucked out not only his essence but his will. She had cried out, reared up, had bled. He had been startled by his brutal lack of conscience, by Darsie's delight in pain, by the fact that she had refused to allow him to suffer remorse but had crawled all over him, toying, tinkering and demanding until his revulsion, and his fear, had faded away, and she, still stained, had lain back and lifted her skirts once more.

Pushing downhill to High Cross that wintry afternoon, Louis felt like two separate individuals, neither one of whom was familiar to him.

He heard Ajax barking, saw a corner of the curtain lift, caught the strains of the harmonium from upstairs, a melancholy little tune that he did not recognise but whose mood so closely matched his own.

Light spilled across the porch. His mother was framed in the doorway, the wind billowing her skirts. Pappy was close behind her, leaning on his stick, a lamp held high.

Louis stepped on to the porch, and dropped his bag.

'Mama,' he said, close to tears. 'Oh, Mama.'

And fell, exhausted, into the woman's waiting arms.

16

On the stroke of the hour, Angus lifted the Bible and walked out to place it in the pulpit. Effie, Zena and the little Oakleys occupied a pew to the right. Bette, Susanne and Buckie Hollander were just behind them, and, in the box reserved for the landowner, were Edward Arbuthnot's wife and daughter.

Angus lowered himself on to the stool, covered his face with his hand, and attempted to pray. The minister's shadow passed over him and, a moment later, Thomas Oakley's baritone voice intoned, 'Oh God, Father, Son and Holy Spirit, open Thou my heart and lips that I may worthily call upon Thy holy name, and . . .'

The prayer trailed off. Angus opened his eyes.

Tom Oakley was staring at the gallery, at a young woman who was waving her arms like a windmill, and who, when she had his attention, called out, cheerily, '*Tommy, Tommy. See, it's me. I come to see the Saviour.*'

Heads turned, shoulders tilted, murmurs of protest and enquiry rippled through the congregation. Annabel shook off the hands that tried to restrain her.

Collecting his wits, Tom hissed at Angus, 'In the name of God, man, do something.'

Angus rose from the stool, dignified as always, and in a loud but not too imperious voice cried, 'Annabel, please sit down.'

Which, to everyone's astonishment, Annabel did.

*   *   *

Drenched in sweat and shaking slightly, Tom stumbled through the service. He stammered, stuttered, dropped his notes, his attention wandering every few seconds to the little boy who peeped over the gallery rail and the girl who, Tom imagined, was on the brink of blurting out shocking accusations.

As soon as he pronounced the Benediction he retreated to the vestry, followed by his loyal clerk.

Gamrie wore a face of stone, neither pugnacious nor triumphant. He said nothing and Tom said nothing. They performed a mute little gavotte in the narrow room while the minister disrobed and Angus counted the collections.

At length, Angus put on his coat, plucked his hat from the hook and planted himself in front of the minister. 'I'll require to have him christened.'

'Christened?' Tom said. 'Who?'

'The boy, her boy.'

'Take him to Ellis at Hask. He'll do it.'

'No,' Angus Gamrie said. 'You'll do it. The boy must have a name.'

'My name, I suppose,' said Tom.

The clerk's lip curled. 'Yours is the last name in the world I'd want for him. She calls him Brogan McQueen.'

'Does she?' Tom said. 'That's all to the good. With that name everyone will assume he's Guy Brogan's bastard.'

'I don't care what they assume,' said Angus.

'Who will stand for him?'

'I will.'

Tom said, 'Do you really believe that by having the child baptised you'll gain free access to his mother's bed? She has no knowledge of sin, no morals at all. You might do as you wish with her without all this tomfoolery.'

'Sunday,' Angus said, 'two weeks from today. Baptism.'

'What if I refuse?' said Tom.

'Then,' said Angus, 'I'll resign my post as session clerk.'

'Do you think that matters to me?'

'I think it should,' said Angus.

'Ah yes, your letter to the Presbytery . . .'

'Setting out my reasons, aye.'

'So it's baptise the child, or be humiliated in public, is that it?'

'That's about the sum of it,' said Angus.

Tom moved a half-step closer to his clerk. 'What do you hope to gain by this? Do you think I can be blackmailed into doing anything you wish me to do? I'm a licensed minister and you are – well, nothing but a linen draper's hack.'

'That's true,' Angus said. 'I'll never be invited to preach to the Jute Workers' Christian Association in Kirkcaldy.'

'I don't know what you're blathering about.'

'I'm not surprised,' Angus said, 'since there is no Jute Workers' Christian Association in Kirkcaldy.'

'What *do* you want from me, Gamrie?' Tom said. 'I can't acknowledge the child and see no reason why I should.'

'Baptise him, that's all I ask,' said Angus.

'If I do, will that satisfy you?'

'Aye,' Angus Gamrie said. 'It will.'

'Was that her?' Effie asked. 'Was that Mr Gamrie's woman?'

Tom was too worn out to prevaricate. 'Yes.'

'Why was she waving at you?'

'She remembered me from my visits to Brogan's farm.'

'Remembered you well enough to call you Tommy,' Zena put in. 'Nobody ever calls you Tommy.'

'I expect,' Tom said, 'that Guy Brogan may have referred to me as Tommy behind my back.'

'How disrespectful of him,' said Zena.

'It's Guy Brogan's bairn, I take it?' Effie said.

'Of course it is,' said Tom.

Freddie had gone into town again and the children had been fed and chased out into the thin winter sunshine to play until it was time for Bible Class. Zena, Effie and he were alone in the kitchen, finishing lunch. He had known that it would only be a matter of time before Effie's patience reached its limit and the questions came thick and fast. He was heartily sick of her whining, her tantrums, and of Zena's underhand remarks.

Soon they would be forced to revise their opinion. Soon he wouldn't be a poor parish minister, but a well-to-do man of business. He had saved and borrowed enough to buy a stake in the Strayhorn railway and, after construction began in earnest, he would sell at a hefty profit; that, at least, had been his intention. Now, without warning, everything was going to pigs and whistles. Gillian had taken up with Redpath, fat Bette Hollander would lend him no more money and, as if that wasn't enough, Gamrie was threatening to expose his little indiscretion with the farm girl.

'The boy doesn't look much like Mr Brogan,' Zena said.

'How do you know what Mr Brogan looked like?' said Tom. 'It's years since he last turned up in church.'

'I remember him well enough,' said Effie. 'Zena's right.'

'About what?' said Tom.

'The boy – he doesn't look at all like Guy Brogan.'

'Well,' Tom said, 'he'll be given Brogan's name.'

'Are you baptising him?' said Effie.

'I am. Two weeks from today.'

'Baptising a bastard?' said Effie. 'My, my! That's a change of tune.'

'Gamrie insisted on it. It's my belief he's sucking up to her.'

'Sucking up?' said Zena. 'By having her son baptised? Surely you don't have to curry favour with servants? Are you saying he's using her like a wife?'

'I'm not saying he is,' said Tom, 'and I'm not saying he isn't.'

'She's a half-wit,' said Effie. 'You said so yourself.'

'Whatever she is,' Tom said, 'Gamrie and I have reached a compromise. I will baptise the child prior to morning service.'

'In private, in other words?' said Zena.

'Put it that way if you wish,' Tom said.

'What name has she picked for the wee chap?' Effie said.

'Brogan McQueen,' Tom told her.

'Not Tommy, then?' Zena murmured.

At which point Tom rose and left the room.

The excavator had been built in Belgium to an American design and purchased, along with other items of bankrupt stock, by a consortium of contracting engineers, of whom Mr Gordon Bagshott was one. It had been employed in the construction of a line between Brocklehurst and Hallam, near Newcastle, until the navvies, outraged by the machine's ability to perform the work of a hundred men in half the time at half the cost, had attacked it with pickaxes and crowbars. When Harry got wind of the riot, he had hastened to Newcastle to invite Mr Bagshott to ship the monster north.

Two weeks later, hauled by four massive stallions and accompanied by a crew of three operatives, including a horse-boy, the excavator lumbered over the hill with Mr Bagshott bestriding the platform like a colossus. A bull of a man with beefy red cheeks and effulgent side whiskers, he sported a canary-yellow vest, a silk-lined cape and a hat almost as tall as the digger's chimney. He cracked an ox-hide whip over the heads of the stallions and bellowed, '*Hay-hay-hay-yah-hah*,' in a rasping voice that made him sound more like a huckster than a civil engineer.

It was Mr Bagshott's flair for showmanship that convinced Harry that he was the right man for the job. He also had at his disposal a small but disciplined army of bricklayers, carpenters, pickmen and shovellers that would march into Strayhorn before the week was out. By that time Mr Bagshott would have conducted his survey, and Harry Coburn's railway project would be well on the way to attracting more attention than it deserved.

The excavator bobbed and swayed like the skeleton of a prehistoric reptile as it descended the hill to the quay.

Fishermen and boys, seated on the cobbles mending nets or cutting bait, gaped as the beast ground into view, smoke issuing from its wooden brakes and iron wheels. Dangling from diagonal struts and chains, the shovel seemed to be sniffing the air, as if in search of someone to snatch into its jaws.

'*Hay-yah-hay*,' Mr Bagshott shouted. '*Yoh-hoh-hup*,' and brought the platform to a shuddering halt in front of the Dalriada.

Pint pot in hand, Sandy Raiker rushed out on to the cobbles. 'What in God's name is that?' he asked, voicing the question that hung on everyone's lips.

The fishermen were on their feet. Women popped out of cottage doorways and piled into the windows of the houses that flanked the quay and, from the higher parts of the town, small children and anxious shopkeepers poured down to the harbour. From the decks of the creel boats moored along the wall more fishermen scrambled, and before the colourful stranger chose to answer Sandy Raiker's question a fair crowd had gathered.

'This,' Mr Bagshott announced, loud enough to be heard in Hask, 'is Bagshott's Patent Excavator, as used for to construct a railroad betwixt Utica and Syracuse in the mighty land of America, where gold lies under every stone and deserts and mountains are tamed and ways forged through the trackless wastes by men from every clime.'

'Aye, aye,' said Sandy, determined to remain unimpressed. 'But what does the blessed thing do?'

'Excavates,' said Mr Bagshott.

'What's it goin' to excavate then?' Martin Mazzucco had tottered out of his house in a less than sober state. 'No gold in these parts.'

'No gold?' Mr Bagshott yelled. 'Ah, but there is, young feller. There's gold in them fish you catch, gold in the coal you dig, gold in every sack of corn you shake from the fields.' He waved an arm expansively.

The crowd followed the sweep, looking this way and that, as if it expected to see nuggets appear on the beach and the bare winter acres of the Fisherfield.

'Make it work then,' one of the Macfarlane boys demanded.

'Can't,' said Mr Bagshott.

'Why not?'

'Needs steam.'

'Give it steam.'

The horse-boy, a lad of tender years, glanced up at his employer, raised his brows and smirked at the ignorance of the fisher folk for he, being English, had no high opinion of the Scots.

'Steam will be made as soon as I've taken the measure of your countryside,' Mr Bagshott explained. 'In the meanwhile, my hosses need watered and I'm nursing a thirst like an Arabian camel, so will somebody kindly lead me to the tap.'

'This way, sir,' said Sandy Raiker, with uncharacteristic obsequiousness, and steered the colourful stranger to the bar.

She was no longer sure that she loved him. She knew that she *had* loved him and that she might come to love him again, but in that handful of days at the end of January, Susanne suffered all the misery of uncertainty.

He was not the Louis that she had known. He was swollen with a kind of arrogance that she found distasteful and he would have taken all sorts of liberties if she had allowed it. He seemed to be under the impression that she required him to caress her and that fondling was a suitable substitute for conversation. As soon as Buckie's back was turned or Bette left the room, Louis would attempt to smother her in kisses, kisses that seemed to Susanne to be cold and insincere. He squeezed her waist, stroked her thigh, rubbed her knee while studying her reactions with a strange, twisted little smile, as if he knew something that she did not, and felt himself superior because of it.

Susanne had learned to identify male vanity in boys as young as five or six and had reached the conclusion that pride and vanity were present in all men. But when Louis had stumbled through the door, as weak and exhausted as if he'd been existing on husks and not on the money she'd sent him, pity and the heartache that went with it had almost overwhelmed her.

By the time supper was over, however, and Louis had downed the best part of two bottles of wine, he expanded almost visibly, and bragged about his achievements in Edinburgh and his plans for a grand tour of Europe to round out his education, once and for all.

'Once and for all,' he said. 'Truly, Mother, once and for all.'

The promise, like his kisses, seemed insincere.

He had, he said, a little money saved on his own account, some but not enough. He needed more, a borrowing. He confessed his gratitude to Mama and Pappy for all that they had done for him. He even admitted that he had been head-strong and had made mistakes. He said that he deeply re-gretted that he had to ask them to do this one thing more, but now that he had found the way forward he would not miss his footing but would make them proud of him, if only they would grant him permission to fulfil his destiny by going, first, to Frankfurt to study with some German carpenter whose name neither Bette nor Buckie could pronounce, then to examine the design of other great pipe organs in France, the Low Countries, and possibly even Spain.

Money: it always came down to money. Love, it seemed, was measured by money, and exchanged for money. Louis's attempts at courtship did not deceive Susanne. He had never been the most sensitive of men, but his lack of understanding of her true needs galled her more than ever. When she asked him to play the harmonium for her, he refused. When she suggested that they might play together, he declined. When she hinted that she might attempt a difficult piece under his guidance, he smiled indulgently, and shook his head. When, at length, he invited her into the big, untidy room upstairs it was not to make music but to lure her on to the bed beside him.

'Do you not like me, Susanne?'

'Yes, of course I like you. You are my friend.'

'I wish to be more than a friend to you.'

'Do you?' Susanne said, grimly.

She disentangled herself from his arms and seated herself on the organ bench, elbows tucked tightly into her lap. His fumbling had aroused her and she was almost as angry at herself as she was with Louis.

The Sunday afternoon light had already begun to fade. Buckie was snoring gently in his chair before the fire and Aunt Bette had taken herself off to lie on the bed in the front room. The commotion in church that morning, some mad girl yelling at Mr Oakley, had upset her and brought on a headache. Now the only sounds in the house were Ajax scratching pitifully at the door, begging for Louis's attention, and Nancy, in the kitchen, rattling pans.

Louis reclined against the bolster. He looked huge in that boyish bed now, one thigh cocked over the other, hips raised as if he were holding in his water. He stretched and readjusted his position, hands behind his head.

'Will you not come and sit by me, dearest?'

'Lie with you, you mean?'

'As you will,' Louis said.

'There isn't room for both of us.'

'You used to like lying beside me; don't you remember?'

'No,' Susanne said. 'I don't ever recall lying down with you.'

He patted the dusty mattress. 'Come, be friendly.'

Susanne shook her head.

He patted the mattress again, smiling. He was still handsome, more handsome now that he had lost weight. In the fall of light from the window, his face was grey but not sickly, his lips dark as damsons. He said, 'I trust you won't be so reluctant to lie with me when we are man and wife.'

'Man and wife?' Susanne said. 'When will that day come?'

'When I return from Germany.'

'In what – a year, two years? Ten?'

He watched her closely. 'If we were betrothed . . .'

'Would I lie with you?' Susanne said. 'No.'

'Is there another?'

'Another what?'

'Man – suitor, I mean.'

'Of course not.'

'I thought,' Louis said, 'that we were meant for each other. According to Mama, we are. I am, in effect, asking if you will consent to marry me.'

Susanne moistened her lips and paused before she answered.

'It's not the sort of proposal I'd hoped for, Louis,' she said. 'You're being dreadfully casual about it.'

He lifted himself on an elbow. 'I would not, I assure you, be a casual husband. Now, what do you say?'

'How will you keep me?'

'Pardon?'

'What will we live on?'

'I – I thought . . .'

'Where will we live?'

'In Edinburgh, possibly London.'

'Not in Strayhorn,' Susanne said, 'not here?'

'Certainly not here.' Louis pulled a face. 'We will live wherever my vocation takes me.'

'And what vocation would that be?'

'I told you. I intend to introduce the art of organ-building to Scotland.'

'Even if Scotland doesn't want it?'

'Music lies close to the heart of our nation.'

'Don't talk rot, Louis. The Scots have barely learned to sing hymns, let alone give themselves up to anthems and voluntaries,' Susanne said. 'How much do you need this time?'

'You haven't answered my question.'

'I've no intention of answering your question,' Susanne said. 'I told you once, long ago, that I'll wait for you and I *will* wait for you – but not standing on the back of a meaningless promise.'

'Meaningless? Do you not love me?'

'How much, Louis, just tell me how much?'

'Two hundred pounds.'

'I'll write to Mr Reeve tomorrow.'

'Oh, Susanne, how can I ever thank you? Tell you what,' Louis said, reaching out a hand, 'come here and let me thank you properly.'

'No.'

'Why, are you afraid of me?'

'Of you?' Susanne said. 'Of course not.'

He swung himself from the bed. 'Tell you what,' he said again, 'why don't we blight our troth—'

'Plight, Louis, plight.'

'Ah yes, plight our troth together, just you and me, here and now.'

'What would be the point of that?' said Susanne.

'It would give me – ah – hope,' he said. 'I mean, we wouldn't have to exchange rings or love tokens or anything, or even tell anyone.'

'Not even your mama?'

'Especially not my mama,' Louis said.

'Do you need to hear me say it?'

'Say what?'

'That I love you.'

'Yes, and that you'll marry me and no other.'

'One day,' said Susanne, with just a little edge, 'when you have seen the world and done all the things that you want to do, then you'll come home and marry me and take me away from all this?'

He smiled, broadly. 'In a nutshell, darling; that's it in a nutshell.'

'I'll write to Reeve tomorrow,' Susanne said.

'Oh, that's cruel.'

'Perhaps so, Louis, but isn't it better than a promise that in a year or two, or ten, neither of us may wish to keep.'

'God!' he said. 'You're so sensible, Susanne, so sensible and practical and generous. Please, say it. Please give me something to carry away, some word of love.'

She sighed and allowed him to kiss her.

'Oh, Susanne,' he said. 'I love you. I love you with all my heart.'

She did not believe him, but answered him, nonetheless: 'Yes, Louis, and I love you.'

The workers arrived on foot, trailing three horse-drawn wagons piled high with timber and tarpaulins, and set up camp on the river bank. No leaky tents for Mr Bagshott's crew but proper huts, each with its own stove and an old woman to wash the clothes and do the cooking. Meanwhile, Mr Bagshott and several other gentlemen of the engineering persuasion

installed themselves in the Dalriada and, when not out with
their measuring sticks, gathered in the snuggery to talk shop.
You didn't have to be an eavesdropper to become familiar with
the figures that were tossed about. Hard-headed fishermen,
pitching in creel boats, were soon discussing railway investment with all the nous of stock jobbers.

'The main problem in this country,' Benbow informed
Sandy Raiker, 'is the irrecoverable cost o' construction.
Now, that mechanical machine operatin' at full pelt can lay
track at three thousand, six hundred pounds per mile –
including the odd embankment an' a wooden bridge or two
– set against thirty thousand pounds per mile, average, by the
English method.'

'Aye,' Sandy told Donald Macfarlane, 'the way I see it, it's a
moral imperative, not to say the bounden duty, o' the mer-
cantile class to put up the money for development.'

In turn, the abstemious Donald Macfarlane relayed the
latest word on progress to his friends who duly augmented
it with facts and figures drawn from their imaginations, until
every man, woman and child in Strayhorn believed that as
soon as the English mannie in the fancy vest fired the boiler of
his excavator, a shower of gold would tumble down upon the
cobbled streets and, like April rain, wash all their troubles
away.

Intellect and education were no bar to optimism, it seemed.
Every two or three days, in the quiet part of the afternoon, Mr
Thomas Oakley and his wife, Effie, could be detected on the
hilltop, admiring the scenes of industry.

Effie had no notion why her husband required her company
on his daily promenade, or why he expected her to match his
enthusiasm for every shovelful of dirt that the noisy, steam-
belching machine howked out of the hole at the root of the old
harbour wall. It was almost as if Tom thought he owned the
site, and, keen to win his wife's admiration, had chosen to

reveal a secret, more practical side of his nature. He rocked on his heels and hugged her, while pointing out each new development as if he had personally brought it about. Even the sight of a cartload of shale being delivered to the pen at the side of the diggings filled him with delight and he was piqued when Effie, cold, miserable and bored, stubbornly refused to acknowledge the wonder of it all.

'I thought,' Effie said, 'they were building a railway line.'

'They are, they are, they are.' Tom inadvertently mimicked the rhythm of the steam engine. 'They are pushing on with the turntable until the track bed and its gradients are defined. It is a very subtle business, Effie, one that a mere woman cannot be expected to understand at first glance.'

'Well, this isn't first glance,' Effie told him, shivering inside her shawl, 'and since I'm not one step nearer understanding why don't you take your mere woman home so she can get on with the subtle business of cookin' supper.'

'All in good time, all in good time.'

Effie peered down at the figures that crawled like dung-beetles over the mounds of rubble, and watched the machine jerk and twitch, dip and rise, stiffening, and drop its dollop of soil by the side of the hole.

She smelled burned odours from the encampment across the Fisherfield, and watched, with a heavy, clay-like feeling about her heart, as the navvies filled the donkey-drawn cart that Sandy Raiker had provided and took the soil away, mouthful by mouthful, to tip into the sea off the end of the old harbour wall. It seemed wasteful to pollute the sea with the earthy garbage and the sight of the brown waves smearing the shore depressed her.

'It's making a fair mess of the beach,' she said.

'Oh, don't be a fool.' Tom tutted. 'One high tide and it will all be gone. One can do what one likes to the ocean without damaging it. Besides, the Fisherfield burn brings down more debris in a day than Mr Bagshott will excavate in a month.'

'Mr Bagshott?'

'Our contractor.'

'*Our* contractor?'

'Mr Coburn's contractor, I mean,' said Tom.

'Dear God in heaven, Tom, don't tell me you've staked money with Harry Coburn?'

'Money?' he answered, lightly. 'Where would I get money?'

'You – you might borrow it.'

'Who would lend money to an impoverished incumbent with no assets to call his own and far too many liabilities, namely children?'

Effie paused, listening to the faint, wild wail of the wind quartering the hillside and the harsh, ear-splitting shriek of the excavator's chains, all jumbled up with the rush and roar of the sea. She felt alien and exposed so far from her kitchen and snug hearth, felt threatened by her husband's preening, cock-sure obsession with what was going on below.

She tugged the shawl about her. 'It has nothing to do with us.'

'There, my dearest, you're wrong,' Tom said. 'If the railway comes to Strayhorn, trade will swiftly follow. With trade will come people and with people, profit. The parish will expand, the church will flourish. My stipend—'

'You've put us into debt, haven't you?'

'I've invested a small amount, yes.'

'In what? This – this mess?'

'In the future, Effie, our future, our children's future.'

'Our children? Pah! What do you care about our children?'

'Come now, Effie, do not be harsh.'

'How much?' Effie demanded. 'How much have you borrowed?'

'Oh, not much.'

'From Angus, from Mr Gamrie?'

'Good Lord, no. Gamrie would not give me the time of day.'

'From Bette Hollander then?'

'Unlike you, my love, Bette Hollander is a woman of the world,' Tom said. 'She may not have benefited from her investments in the past but she has enough sense to recognise a golden opportunity when it presents itself.'

'And where did *she* get the money?'

'Oh, she has her sources,' Tom said.

'The girl, that girl of course.'

'That girl,' Tom said, 'is fortunate to have someone like Bette Hollander to look out for her.' He fastened his arm about her waist. 'What is wrong with you, Effie? Don't you want to be rich?'

She tore herself away and, whirling, thrust herself uphill, pushing with her hands on her thighs. How could she tell him that she did not want to be rich, only to raise her children, see them settled, then to grow old and die, be free of him at last, leaving him to his schemes and his women, secure in the knowledge that one day, when his time came, he would rot in hell for ever?

'Effie,' he shouted, 'come back here. I'm not finished with you yet.' But she had already reached the crest of the ridge and, without a backward glance, scuttled off across the barley field, heading for home.

It took Mr Gamrie no more than a couple of minutes to satisfy the kirk session that the child was under Christian care and guardianship and that he, as a member of Strayhorn Old Parish, was fully entitled to offer said child for baptism even if the father was deceased and the mother a penny or two short of a shilling. It would have taken a bold man, indeed, to challenge Angus when he was riding his high horse and the elders, being men of spirit, quietly applauded his charity and turned out in force, all four of them, to see the boy christened.

Ignoring Tom's less than polite suggestion that she absent herself from the proceedings, Effie put on her best bonnet and, accompanied by all the little acorns, including Zena, traipsed into the church to join the Hollanders, the doctor and the schoolteacher for the early morning baptism.

Dr Redpath had been persuaded to serve as godfather, Miss Gillian Primrose as godmother; a pretty picture they made standing before the font, flanking Angus and the girl who, in turn, flanked Brogan who was tricked out in a tunic of chequered wool that made him look like a little Highlander. Annabel was dressed in a silk-fringed mantel, new shoes and a new bonnet with trimming inside the brim. The items had cost Angus a pretty penny, but this was his show and he would not stint on it. Besides, the girl's finery endowed her with a sense of occasion and, even if she was unaware of the ceremony's significance, she nodded, smiled and did all that Angus asked of her without a word of enquiry or complaint.

Tom Oakley was more used to christening babies than sturdy three-year-olds who glowered up at him and didn't flinch when the water was dashed over his brow in a quantity rather more copious than doctrine demanded. In the name of the Father, the Son and the Holy Ghost, little Brogan was given his name and welcomed into the community of the Church, at which point, rather touchingly, the boy reached out and took Angus Gamrie's hand while his mama hopped on one leg and bowed as if to thank her friend Tommy for his courtesy.

It required no little negotiation on Zena's part to detach Prim from the doctor. In fact, if Alan hadn't been lured away to play chasing games with Brogan and several small Oakleys it's doubtful if she would have succeeded at all.

Gillian Primrose and Alan Redpath had become, it seemed, inseparable these past few weeks. Susanne, to Zena's chagrin, had been far too reticent to press for information on the progress of what was obviously a courtship and to ask, more or less outright, when the handsome bachelor might be expected to pop the question.

'Pop the question?' Prim said. 'What question would that be, Zena?'

'Oh, don't be so coy,' Zena said. 'The marriage question, of course.'

'Dr Redpath is an acquaintance, not a suitor.'

'Hoh!' Zena said, sceptically. 'He's been seen at Rose Cottage too often to be anything other than a suitor, in my opinion.'

'Seen?' said Prim. 'By whom?'

'Us,' said Zena. 'We saw you after the market.'

'Did you, indeed?' Prim said, not displeased. 'Who constitutes "we"?'

'Susanne an' me. Ask her, if you don't believe me,' Zena said, waving to attract Susanne's attention. 'She's too shy to say anything, but I'm not.'

'I imagine,' Prim said, cautiously, 'that there might be a hint of self-interest on your part in discussing my matrimonial prospects?'

'Self-interest?' said Susanne, who had just arrived. 'What do you mean?'

'If you were to marry, surely you wouldn't continue teaching?' Zena said.

'Probably not, no,' Prim agreed.

'And there would be a vacancy for a teacher in the school.'

Miss Primrose laughed. 'Zena Oakley, what a schemer you are. Do you have your eye on my cottage, too?'

'Aye,' Zena admitted. 'I do.'

'When I do leave Strayhorn – which is not, I assure you,

likely – if I were to leave, however, what makes you suppose that you have the experience or educational attainment necessary to fill the post?'

'You taught me, didn't you? You know I can do it.'

'Yes, but your father . . .'

'My father won't stand in my way now,' said Zena. 'As things are, he'll be glad to have me off his hands.'

'What about Susanne?' Prim said.

'Susanne?' Zena glanced at her friend. 'What about Susanne?'

'She's my assistant, so, if she applies for the post . . .'

'She won't, will she?' Zena said; then, to Susanne, 'Will you?'

'I might.'

'But you're engaged to marry your cousin?'

'He isn't my—' Susanne began.

Zena bit her off. 'Whatever he is, you're promised to him. Besides, you don't need the salary, or the cottage.'

Prim intervened. 'I'm in no position to promise you anything, Zena. More to the point, whatever conclusion you pair may have arrived at, I'm not betrothed to Alan Redpath.' She folded her arms. 'Now, Susanne, tell me, how is Louis? Has he returned to Edinburgh?'

A little ripple of guilt went through Susanne at the realisation that she, not Prim, might be the obstacle to Zena's happiness. She was tempted to reach for Zena's hand, to assure her friend that, in due course, she *would* marry Louis and leave Strayhorn, but something stopped the words in her mouth, a shrinking refusal to admit that her future was already mapped out and her fate sealed.

'Louis has returned to Edinburgh,' she heard herself say, 'until April, after which time he is setting off for Germany to learn how to build pipe organs.'

'How long,' Zena said, 'will he be gone?'

'A year,' Susanne said, shrugging. 'Two, perhaps.'

'Oh, God!' said Zena, with a quivering sigh. 'Oh, God!'

'Will you miss him, Susanne?' Prim asked.

And Susanne, a little too quickly, answered, 'Yes.'

17

Shortly after two o'clock on a short February afternoon Effie turned up at Bette Hollander's door. Before Bette could invite her in, Effie said, 'Have you been giving my husband money?'

Afraid of what might come next, Bette stepped on to the porch and closed the door behind her. 'What if I have? It's no business of yours.'

'I happen to think it is,' Effie said. 'How much have you given him?'

'May I suggest, Mrs Oakley, that if you wish to learn more of your husband's affairs, you had better ask *him*, not me. I have no doubt that whatever small sums I have given Tom will be returned with interest.'

'If you think you'll ever see a penny of your money again, let alone interest,' Effie said, 'then you're a bigger fool than I took you for. It's railways, isn't it?'

'Yes,' Bette admitted. 'It is railways or, to be more specific, the branch line that will link Strayhorn to Edinburgh. For reasons I do not care to explain, I cannot do business with Mr Coburn, who is promoting this scheme. Your husband is acting as my agent and is, I believe, investing in the venture too.'

'A lot of steam and snorting,' Effie said, 'that's all it is. What tale did he tell you when he had his hands up your skirts?'

'If you're implying that my relationship with your husband is in any way improper—'

'Blessed if I care what he does with you,' Effie interrupted, 'but I won't stand by while Tom drags us into penury. Where did *you* get the money? Have you been robbing that English girl?'

'That is more than enough, Mrs Oakley,' said Bette indignantly.

'Oh yes, I see it all now, clear as daylight,' Effie said. 'Tom's talked you into using that girl's money for—'

'Out,' Bette snapped. 'Leave my house this instant.'

Effie stepped from the porch. 'Buckie knows nothing of this arrangement, does he? You *are* tapping into your niece's fortune and my Tom's helping you. When you're both in the jail, who's going to feed my children, that's what I want to know?' Then, without waiting for an answer, she headed off towards the cliff path, leaving Bette, weak and panting, to ponder not only the question but the threat that it implied.

Buckie opened one eye. 'What ails you, Bette? Is it the megrim?'

'I thought you were asleep.'

'I was,' he said, 'but now I'm awake. Shall I call Nancy to fetch you a blistering plaster or a cup of valerian?'

'No,' she said, curtly.

Buckie hesitated. 'Did she say something to offend you?'

'Did who say something to offend me?'

'Effie Oakley; that was her voice I heard, wasn't it?'

Bette massaged her brow with the heel of her hand. 'Yes.'

'What did Mrs Oakley want?'

'Nothing that concerns you.'

He guessed that Bette would retreat to the kitchen or her bedroom at any moment. He steeled himself, and said, 'I thought perhaps she didn't care for you giving cash to her husband.'

'It's charity, Buckhaven, simple charity. Go back to sleep.'

He might close his eyes and pretend to be both deaf and

blind, but some imp of conscience impelled him to continue. 'I approve of your generosity to the Oakleys,' he said. 'But this isn't charity, is it?'

'Tom and I are in partnership.'

'With Harry Coburn?'

'In fact, yes.'

'Why did you have to go to Oakley? Why didn't you ask my advice?'

'Your advice! Hah!' Bette exploded. 'Look at you! What a miserable wreck of a man, you are, Buckhaven. I wouldn't ask your advice on how to boil an egg. Tom Oakley is twice the man you are. Seals and whale oil that's all you ever cared about.' She came around the table and confronted him. 'Answer me this: who's going to look after Louis when you and I are gone? I'm trying to take care of our son's future, that's all.'

'By investing in another of Coburn's crooked schemes?' Buckie shook his head. 'You talk as if I'm already dead, Bette.'

'Oh, you are,' she said. 'You've been dead and buried for years. And I've been buried with you. I have needs and desires, Buckhaven, needs and desires that you have never understood.'

'And Tom Oakley does?'

'Yes, he does,' Bette said, then, with a curt little nod, sailed into the kitchen and slammed the door behind her.

It was Nancy who heard him calling out. She hurried from her cubby with a greasy old topcoat thrown over her shift and a candle in a tin holder in her hand. He was perched on the side of the bed, drenched in sweat.

'I – I can't breathe, Nancy,' he gasped.

'Is there any laudanum left?'

'In – in the drawer.'

The pill lay on a square of notepaper, like a rabbit dropping.

She brought it to him, placed it carefully on his tongue, poured water from the wash jug into a glass and placed the rim of the glass against his lips.

Buckie sipped and gulped. 'Aye,' he said. 'Aye. It's – it's gone down.'

Nancy brushed his brow with the back of her wrist. He was burning up. She threw off her coat, spread her arms and eased him back into the pillow.

'What in heaven's name are you doing, Nancy?' Bette asked.

'He's sick, lady. He's very sick.'

'Nonsense.' Bette advanced reluctantly into the room, not well pleased at being roused at that hour of the night.

'He needs more help than I can gi'e him.'

Bette peered over the servant's shoulder. 'What's wrong with you, Buckhaven? You've wakened the household with your nonsense.'

'Fetch the girl, fetch Susanne,' said Nancy. 'If he doesn't get proper doctorin' he might not last the night.'

Awakened by the noise, Susanne appeared in the doorway. She ran to the bed and knelt upon it. 'Uncle, what is it? Are you in pain? Shall I run to Seameads and fetch Dr Redpath?'

Buckie stared at the girl as if she were an angel come to lead him to heavenly pastures. 'No, dearest,' he gasped. 'Tomorrow will do, tomorrow.'

'Yes,' Bette put in. 'You can't expect Susanne to go all the way to Seameads in the dark. Brandy will fix him, then we can all get back to bed. Nancy, where are you? What are you doing out there?'

But Nancy had already left.

Benbow had brought the horse to the front of the house. Harry was preparing to mount when Tom appeared in the driveway.

He wore a cut-away coat, kerseymere breeches and cloth boots and carried a topper under his arm, like an extra head.

'Ah, Oakley?' he said. 'As you see, I'm just about to ride out. What brings you? Will it take long? I'd ask you to join me, but I'm meeting friends along the way and we will be going at it fast and furious.'

'I do not ride,' Tom said, 'not well enough for your pace at any rate.'

'Well, I can spare you a moment, I suppose. What brings you here?'

Tom unbuttoned his overcoat and dug into an inner pocket. 'If it's inconvenient, perhaps I should return another time?'

'No, no. What's that you have there?'

'Money, sir,' Tom said. 'Cash.'

'Cash?' Harry said. 'For me?'

'Certainly for you, Mr Coburn. Cash to purchase stock in the Strayhorn Railway Company, if such a thing is possible?'

'Whoah,' Harry said. 'It's not so simple as all that. The parliamentary bill has been suspended until next session.' He stuck the topper on to his head, laid an arm about Tom's shoulder and guided him along the gravel. 'The papers have been presented and approved, of course, but, meanwhile, I'm only entitled to build on land that's already under lease. How much do you wish to invest?'

'Four hundred pounds,' Tom said. 'Every penny I possess.'

'I trust,' said Harry, 'that you haven't put yourself in debt? How did you come by the money?'

'By scraping and saving.' Tom shook the package, sealed with string and sealing-wax, as if he were delivering a curse. 'Am I mistaken in thinking that you are seeking investors and, if that is the case, why is my money not good enough for you?'

'Given that completion of the branch will cost in excess of eighty thousand pounds and that I am exceedingly reluctant to borrow one farthing more than necessary at the current usurious rate, I am not averse to sharing the profits that will accrue when the company goes public.'

'When will that be?'

'Soon after the end of the next parliamentary session.'

'Let me in on it,' Tom said. 'Please, Mr Coburn, do let me in.'

Harry stroked his chin and seemed to be giving the matter so much consideration that Tom hardly dared draw breath.

At length he said, 'Well, Tom Oakley, your faith deserves reward. I'll take your money and invest it for you in the hope of a speedy return.' He tucked the packet into the top pocket of his cut-away. 'I'll see to it that you are sent certificates of stock to the value of payment. And Benbow will drive you home.'

'Really?' Tom said. 'Really, I'm in?'

'You are, Tom, indeed you are,' said Harry and, a few minutes later, went galloping off across the parkland with coat-tails flying and Tom's four hundred pounds buttoned safely into his jacket pocket.

Susanne was late for school. She had a valid excuse, of course. Buckie had been taken ill in the night and Nancy had walked all the way to Seameads to fetch Dr Redpath who had driven back to High Cross to administer strong sedatives and draw a quantity of blood. After Buckie had fallen asleep, she said, Nancy had made breakfast for everyone, and Alan had driven her to school. Gillian had already been treated to several lectures by Dr Redpath on the presence of uric acid in the circulating fluids and had begun to find the subject tedious. In spite of her admiration for Dr Redpath, therefore, she did not share Susanne's enthusiasm for matters medical and quickly set the young woman to work with the infants.

As soon as lessons ended for the day, Susanne gathered her books, said goodbye to Prim and set off home. As she came whizzing round the corner into the Old Kirk road, Gregor

Oakley stepped out on to the narrow pavement, and held up a hand to greet her. In the months since she had last seen him he had grown in height and had gained a great deal of muscle.

'I thought you were in the Baltic,' she said.

'No,' he said. 'We're back in Dundee to fit out for the season. Freddie will be sailing with us. Mr Jackson, the agent, has signed us all on to the *Merrilyn*. As a green hand, Freddie will have but a shilling a month and a shilling in oil and bone money but he's as keen as mustard, and was sick not once on the Baltic trip.'

'The *Merrilyn*,' Susanne said, 'was my uncle's ship.'

Gregor nodded. 'A fine ship she is too, as stout as any vessel in the Dundee fleet, though not as large as some. Since I'll be off tomorrow morning it crossed my mind I might walk down to High Cross with you an' have a gab with the old chap.'

'Oh, Gregor, no. My uncle's unwell. He'd be delighted to hear your news and tell you all about the ship, but he just isn't up to it today.'

'Never mind,' Gregor said. 'I'll walk you as far as the top of the hill, if you like.' He offered his arm and, as if it were the most natural thing in the world, Susanne attached herself to it. 'Now, tell me, has Zena been behavin' herself while I've been gone?'

'I'm not telling tales on your sister.'

'I thought not,' Greg said. 'She wouldn't tell tales on you either.'

'Tell tales on me? What is there to tell?'

'About your cousin, for one thing,' Greg said.

'Louis has decided that he wishes to be an instrument-maker and will be spending at least a year in Germany before he – before we . . .'

'Are you not engaged to marry him yet?'

'No, I am not.'

'Good,' Greg said.

She wondered if Buckie and Aunt Bette had promenaded

the quays of old Dundee, arm-in-arm, shy and uncertain as they approached the point where friendship tumbles into affection. She had no idea what Gregor Oakley thought of her, or what his intentions towards her were.

They walked until they could no longer hear the sounds of the town, only the unfading heartbeat of the sea, soft and unhurried in the calm, grey February afternoon.

'When do you sail from Dundee?' she asked.

'In eight or ten days' time, after we fit out.'

'And when will you return?'

'In September.'

'So long a time away,' said Susanne, with a sigh.

'Will you miss me?' Gregor Oakley asked, not too seriously.

'Do you know,' Susanne said, 'I do believe I will.'

Soon after lunch Alan drove out to High Cross to make sure that his patient had survived the night and to draw another small quantity of blood.

Buckie was propped up in bed, listlessly scanning a week-old issue of the Dundee *Courier*, and sipping from a mug of tea. Bette, it seemed, had gone out to visit her friend Tom Oakley. The simple surgery was soon completed and Buckie lay back against the bolster, a pad of wool pressed to the incision. He was still drowsy but pain, and panic, had receded and he was full of apology for having dragged the doctor out of bed in the wee small hours.

'I was afraid, you see,' Buckie said. 'I thought my heart was giving out.'

'Your heart's fine.' Alan wrapped the little vial of blood in a cloth and tucked it carefully into his valise. 'You'll outlast the lot of us.'

'If only that were true,' Buckie said. 'I'm not afraid of dying, but I am concerned about what'll become of Bette when I'm gone, and Susanne too.'

'I think,' said Alan, 'that Susanne can well take care of herself.'

'Maybe so,' Buckie said. 'If I'm called soon, will you look out for her?'

Alan hesitated. 'I may not be here. I've been invited to apply for a post in the Royal Infirmary in Edinburgh as a physician in the medical ward. My brother recommended me to the managers.'

'I thought you were happy in Fife?'

'I am,' Alan said, 'but there are – circumstances.'

'Is it Susanne? Is it because she prefers my son to you?'

'No, I mean, Susanne and I . . . no, no.'

'Then it's the schoolteacher.'

'What do you know of the schoolteacher?' Alan said.

'I hear talk,' said Buckie.

'Gossip,' Alan said, with a trace of ire. 'Did Susanne tell you? Why can't young women be content to prattle about their own affairs?'

'So you have set your cap at the schoolteacher.' Buckie grinned. 'She's a fine-looking woman, well educated, and not so old as all that. She can still bear children, can't she?'

'Of course she can still bear children,' Alan said, testily. 'Good God, Buckie, she's only thirty years of age. Why must everyone assume that the breeding cycle ceases when a woman passes out of her twenties.'

'It sounds to me as if you love her.'

'No,' Alan said. 'I'm not sure whether I love her or whether I do not. She has come at me too strongly. Oh, God! If only she hadn't crowded in upon me and had allowed me to arrive at my own conclusions in my own good time. I will not be bullied in matrimony.'

'Well, Edinburgh's full of clever, well-to-do matrons with clever, well-to-do daughters just dying for a fine young physician to pop into their drawing-rooms.' Buckie shifted on to his side. 'But you don't have to go to Edinburgh to find a lass of wit and beauty who can bring a bit of money to the altar rail. This offer to apply for a post in the Edinburgh Infirmary, have you given your answer yet?'

'Not yet.'

'How long will the appointment be held?'

'I have no idea,' Alan said, still frowning. 'A month, probably, or more.'

'So there's time,' Buckie said.

'Time? Time for what?'

'To tap off another pint or two of Hollander blood before you go.'

'I could cut your throat, Buckie, and be done with it once and for all.'

'Aye, be done with me, but not with your predicament.'

'That,' said Alan, rising, 'is sadly true.'

'Are you leaving?'

'I do have other patients to attend to, you know.'

'Have I offended you?'

'Only a little,' Alan said and, plucking up his bag, let himself out of the house before Susanne arrived home from school.

Effie enjoyed having company for supper, particularly such effervescent company as her son and his shipmate, Peter Macfarlane. She prepared a rich brown soup and baked two crusty fish pies to serve with roast potatoes and peas. It was a rowdy evening, to say the least, for the lads had tasted ale before their arrival and Freddie, who considered himself a man, was half seas over and much more talkative than usual. The kitchen was hot, crowded, noisy and gay; everyone was having a grand time, everyone except Tom who sat at the head of the table, picking at his fish, all stiff-shirted and disapproving.

Cheeks flushed, eyes sparkling, Zena threw back her head

and laughed along with the boys and, Effie noted, seldom took her eyes from Peter Macfarlane for long. Flirting, Effie thought: Lord above, my daughter's flirting with a sailor under her father's nose, and watched, a little enviously, as Zena and Peter nudged and shoved each other like playful pups. How young they were, Effie thought, how young and unafraid.

'Old Buckie's ailing again,' Gregor said. 'Did I tell you that?'

'You did,' Peter said. 'Twice, in fact.'

'He used to own the *Merrilyn*,' Gregor said.

'Three times,' Zena and Peter cried in unison and, having shared the thought, shared the laughter; then Zena said, 'Who told you about old Buckie?'

'I heard it down in the town.'

'Oh-hoh!' said Zena. 'A likely story.'

'The teacher told him,' Freddie said. 'He told me the teacher told him.'

'Prim?'

'The other teacher – Miss Thorne,' said Freddie.

Gregor tried to cuff Freddie's ear but the boy was too nimble for him.

'You clipe, you rotten clipe,' Greg said. 'I asked you not to say a word about Susanne.'

Zena glanced at Peter. 'Did you know he was sweet on Susanne Thorne?'

'I'm not sweet on anyone,' Greg protested.

'He is, he is, he is,' Morven chanted. 'He's gone all red again. He's got a sweetheart. Our Gregor's got a sweetheart.'

'If I did have a sweetheart, I wouldn't tell any of you,' Gregor said.

Tom put down his fork and dabbed his lips with a napkin.

'If he did have a sweetheart,' Morven continued, 'it would be Miss Thorne. She likes you, Gregor; Miss Thorne likes you.'

'How do you know, monkey-face?'

'She told me.'

'She did not.'

'Did, too.'

'Well,' Gregor confessed, 'as it so happens, I did bump into Susanne this afternoon on the Old Kirk road.'

'Isn't she promised to her cousin?' said Peter.

'No,' Greg answered. 'She isn't, not yet.'

'Better be quick then,' said Zena.

'Quick?' said Tom. 'What do you mean by quick?'

He had said not a word throughout the meal and the children had almost forgotten that he was present at all.

'She didn't mean anything by it, Tom,' said Effie, mildly.

'I'm sure she did. I'm sure she means that Gregor has designs on the Thorne girl,' Tom said. 'Let me tell you now, boy, Susanne Thorne is not for the likes of you.'

'The likes of me?' said Gregor.

'A common tar,' Tom told him.

'What's Mr Hollander then?' Zena spoke up. 'Is he not a sailor?'

'That,' Tom said, 'is beside the point. If you do have designs on Susanne Thorne, and an eye on her legacy, I suggest you put them out of mind. Susanne Thorne will marry her cousin, who is much more suited to her than you are.'

'How *dare* you say such a thing,' Zena exploded. 'Our Gregor's as good as any man alive.'

Tom ignored her. He turned his attention to Peter. 'And you, young man, if you have designs upon my daughter, I advise you to forget them. I will not permit Zena to marry a whaler.'

Mute with embarrassment, Peter stared down at his plate.

At that moment, before anyone could say anything, a loud knocking sounded upon the front door and Tom left the kitchen to answer it.

Zena sank down, fighting tears. Peter put a hand on her arm

and said, quietly, 'Never mind, Zena, never mind. I won't be a whaler for ever.'

Beside herself with rage, Effie went out into the hallway but the visitor had already been shown into the study. She rapped on the door and asked, 'Who is it?'

'Mr Gamrie,' her husband answered. 'Now go away.'

There being nothing else for it, Effie returned to the kitchen to dish out apple dumplings in the wan hope that sweet puddings would restore a little of the jollity that her husband's brutal honesty had dispersed.

'I trust,' Tom said, 'that it's parish business brings you here, Gamrie, and not some cock-and-bull request that will cause me further embarrassment?'

'It is parish business,' Angus said. 'I've convened an extraordinary meetin' of the kirk session for Friday week, at half past six.'

'For what purpose?

'To appoint my replacement.'

'Your replacement?'

'I'm resigning my eldership an' will transfer my lines to Hask,' Angus said. 'I no longer wish to worship in this parish.'

'I see,' Tom said. 'Do you intend to provide information to the Presbytery to explain the reason for your resignation?'

Angus shook his head. 'I'll not issue a libel against you, if that's what you mean. I've more respect for Mrs Oakley than to involve her in a scandal, for, if you were summoned to answer to a Presbytery court, Mrs Hollander would be required to give evidence. We're past the stage o' dissemblin', Mr Oakley. Let's just say I prefer to take myself out of your parish than bring misery on others.'

'And, presumably, to avoid your half-witted harlot being called to give evidence too,' said Tom. 'Am I supposed to applaud your sensitivity?'

'Thanks to you,' Angus said, 'this town has lost its spirit. What you've started, I fear Henry Coburn will finish with his wild promise of a railway link to Edinburgh. The only progress that'll be made in Strayhorn is when Harry Coburn leaves it, luggin' a bag o' other folks' money.'

'Now that,' Tom said, 'is a libel difficult to prove, given that Mr Coburn is investing so much of his own capital in the project.'

'Mr Coburn has no capital,' Angus said. 'He doesn't own Macklin House or its parks or the stock that grazes there. His lease is due to expire in August and we'll see what happens then. As for his precious railway, he's peddling stock to anyone who'll purchase it and issuing share certificates without parliamentary authorisation, which, under law, makes them worthless.'

Tom said, 'How did you come by this information?'

'From Sandy Raiker; he got it from Benbow.'

'Benbow? What does a stable-hand know about stocks and shares?'

'I've also made a few enquiries on my own account,' Angus Gamrie said. 'You'd be surprised how shrewd farmers can be when money's involved. The cattle dealers are laughin' up their sleeves at the gullibility o' the fisher folk. What remains a mystery is how Coburn found the capital, since he was bankrupt a few years ago.'

'Bankrupt? His wife left him a fortune, did she not?'

'His wife?' said Angus. 'There never was a wife.'

'Are you implying that the girl, Darsie, is . . .'

'I've said enough,' Angus put in. 'It's no longer my concern what happens in this sad parish. I've resigned all my offices, so you'll not be troubled by me, or the girl, or her boy in future. Goodbye, Mr Oakley.'

Angus pulled open the study door. Laughter burst from the kitchen, youthful voices, children giggling. He paused for a second in the hope that Effie might come out to bid him farewell, but the door to the kitchen remained closed, and as he rode away into the darkness, the laughter was soon lost in the whisper of the wind and the sound of the waves on the shore.

Tom slammed the front door, darted back into the study and slammed that door too. He leaned against the door and stared into the halo of lamplight, at books open on the table, a litter of sermon notes and meaningless prayers; then, fumbling a key from his vest pocket, he unlocked a drawer beneath the desk and drew out the sheaf of stock certificates that had been delivered that morning.

Beautifully printed on fresh, crisp paper, great swirling letters in italic script atop a dozen tight paragraphs: his name was written in ink under the florid banner but there was only a printed signature as footnote, no witnesses, no stamp. He might be capable of interpreting the Book of Genesis but when it came to the transfer of marketable securities he was, he realised, as ignorant as a fishwife and had been played for a fool once more.

He knelt before the table, opened the cabinet, dug out a decanter of brandy and a glass, and, seating himself in the armchair, poured three fingers of fiery spirit and began, quite systematically, to drink himself into oblivion.

The lamp, newly trimmed, warmed the sick-room and with Ajax drowsing on the floor, Thimble curled up on the quilt and Susanne on the chair by the bed, Buckie felt more at ease than he had done in weeks.

'Are you comfortable now?' Susanne said.

'Aye, much easier.'

'Will I leave you to sleep?'

'No, not yet awhile, lass,' Buckie said, 'unless you're bored with an old man's company and would rather be at your music.'

'I would rather be here.' Susanne gently took his hand. 'It's too cold to practise upstairs.'

'Have Nancy light a fire.'

'I don't think there's been a fire in that grate in years,' said Susanne. 'Louis doesn't seem to mind the cold. Though, come to think of it, he doesn't much like cold water. He'd never make a sailor, would he?'

'Alas, no,' said Buckie. 'Well, what matter! He's happy enough to study in Germany, though what will come of it, Lord knows.'

'I'd like to be a sailor,' Susanne said, 'setting off on the *Merrilyn* to see the strange creatures you've told me about, the seals and snow bears, and giant whales.'

'Aye,' Buckie said, 'but you would not enjoy the killing.'

'No,' Susanne agreed, 'I would not enjoy the killing.'

'It's more fitting, I think, for young ladies to pursue sweethearts than to go chasing whales.'

'Are you teasing me, Uncle?'

'Nah, nah,' Buckie said. 'It's just my clumsy way of asking if it's the voyage or the company that you hanker after?'

'The company? Gregor, do you mean?'

'Aye, Gregor.'

'I'm fond of him, of course. I've known him since I first came to Strayhorn. He's Zena's brother, after all.'

'And Thomas Oakley's son,' Buckie reminded her.

'Gregor's nothing like his father, not in looks, or in temperament.'

'You haven't answered my question.'

'I don't hanker after anyone,' Susanne said.

'What about Louis?'

She shifted back a little from the bed. 'Are you set on my marrying Louis, Uncle Buckie?'

'Your aunt is.' He clasped his hands behind his head and stared up at the pool of light that the funnel of the lamp cast upon the ceiling. 'You'll come of age soon, Susanne,' he said, at length. 'In a year or two you'll be free to do anything you wish to do. I think it's time you had some advice from a lawyer a bit nearer to home than London. I've taken the liberty of writing to an old friend of mine who practises law in Dundee. Greenbaum's his name.'

'A Hebrew gentleman?'

'None the worse for that,' said Buckie. 'There are precious few Hebrews admitted into the legal profession, but my friend Greenbaum has earned himself a reputation as a shrewd and honest negotiator.'

'Does Aunt Bette know Mr Greenbaum?'

'She met him once or twice some years back, but she didn't take to him.'

'Because he's a Hebrew?'

'No,' said Buckie, 'because he warned her about Mr Coburn and was proved right. She's a headstrong woman, your aunt. She doesn't like to be told what to do.'

'I don't think I like being told what to do either,' said Susanne.

'Aye, that's the point,' said Buckie. 'So far you've relied on your aunt for guidance and have fallen in with her wishes but soon, dearest, you'll be worth more than all of us put together and will have to take responsibility for yourself.'

'When I marry Louis . . .'

'Do you want to marry Louis?'

'I don't know. It just seems the right thing to do.'

'It may be the right thing for Louis,' Buckie said, 'but is it the right thing for you, Susanne? If you ask me, it's a bit of a blessing that Louis is setting off for Germany, to give you – to give us all – a breathing space. Now, pass me my laudanum pill, dearest, for I think it's time I took refuge in sleep.'

She went to the dressing-table, poured water from the jug into a glass and carried the glass and the tab of paper that held the pill to the bedside. She held out the paper and watched her uncle's tongue scoop up the sticky pill. She offered him the glass and, with his hand covering hers, he sipped water to help the pill down. She wiped his lips with a handkerchief, kissed him on the brow.

'Goodnight, Uncle Buckie,' she said. 'Sleep well.' Then, lifting Thimble and nudging Ajax before her, she went out into the living-room, to mull over this latest development and wonder just where it would lead.

Zena threw open the door of the study and stalked into the room. Tom opened his eyes. He had not been asleep. He had been brooding, brooding and dreaming. The stock certificates strewn across the desktop wafted to the floor in the draught from the door.

'*How dare you!*' Zena shouted. '*How dare you insult me in that way.*'

'Insult you?' Tom said. 'I'll do more than insult you, girl, if you continue to shriek at me like a harridan. Where's your sailor boy?'

'Gone, and Gregor with him.'

'Without a word of farewell? Ah me! Ah me!'

'Are you drunk?'

'Gone,' Tom said, 'gone but not forgotten. Sharper than a serpent's tooth is the ingratitude of – of something. Come here, child. Come, give your papa a kiss and beg his forgiveness.'

'Beg your forgiveness. I'll be damned in hell if I do.'

Tom hurled the decanter at her head.

Zena ducked.

He shot from the chair and caught her by the scruff of the neck. He closed the door with his foot, dragged Zena to the desk and pushed her across it. He brought her arm up across her back and leaned into her, roused now.

Lips against her ear, he whispered, 'If you ever – *ever* address me like that again, Zena, I'll flay the hide off your backside. As for that bearded little freak of a boy from the town – no, no, no, my dearest, he'll never have the pleasure of laying you out on the bridal bed.'

'You can't stop me marrying . . .'

'What do you know of matrimony? You think only of the pleasure of the marriage bed, not beyond it. You'll have my permission to marry only when the right man comes along, if, that is, any decent man will have a trollop like you.'

He released her. She leaped up, swung round and spat into his face. Sticky saliva drenched his cheek. He stabbed out his fist, a short, vicious blow that struck her on the breast. He punched her once more and heard her cry out. Whatever imagined grievances had driven his daughter to confront him had been dealt with, and there was no breath, or fight, left in her.

He watched her sink to her knees, coughing, her fingers spread over her breast. She looked so meek, subservient and anonymous in that position that he felt he could have done anything to her without fear of reprisal.

'Get out, Zena,' he said. 'Get out, and don't ever sauce me again.'

He jerked her to her feet, opened the study door and threw her out into the hallway, then, with a little '*hah*' of satisfaction, stepped back into the study and quickly locked the door.

As a rule Prim slept soundly in the winter months, snug in her narrow bed. The sounds that the wind made, or driving rain or the crackle of frost or even the muffled silence that comes with falling snow were all so natural and familiar that she was comforted by them and had no fear of noises in the night. She was fast asleep and did not hear him enter. Instinct rather than sensation moved her to open her eyes a split second before he peeled the sheet from her body.

She reared up and called out, 'Alan, Alan, is it you?'

Then he was on top of her, a hand clamped over her mouth, pawing at her breasts and groping her belly. He seemed huge and monstrous in the pitch-black room. He wore a broad-brimmed hat and a stiff, damp topcoat of rough material, and she could taste the sweat on the palm of his hand when he thrust his fingers into her mouth. Barbed and bloody pain pushed through her like a red-hot wire. She screamed and bit into his hand, thrashing beneath his weight. But, grunting, he was already inside her, driving her deep into the mattress. Pain swelled within her as he thrust in and out and her cries were choked by his fingers, shoved far down her throat. *Oh, God, no*, she thought, *not me, not me, not now*, before, fighting for breath, she finally lost consciousness.

18

On arriving at the schoolhouse Susanne found the children gathered outside for, it seemed, Miss Primrose was still in bed. She herded the children into class then hurried to the cottage to find out what was wrong. A cup half filled with stale tea sat upon the table but the fire had not been lighted, there was no sign that Prim had breakfasted that morning and the door of the little back bedroom was closed. 'It's me, Prim. Susanne. Are you sick?'

'Yes.'

'Shall I send for Dr Redpath?'

'No.'

'Prim, do let me in.'

After a moment the bolt was drawn and Susanne entered. Prim was huddled in a corner with a sheet draped over her shoulders. One eye was swollen and the left side of her face so inflamed that she could hardly open her mouth.

'Oh, my dear,' Susanne said. 'You've hurt yourself.'

'I fuh-fell,' Prim said, thickly. 'Attend to the chu-children.'

'No,' Susanne said, firmly. 'First we must get you into bed and I'll send Jenny to fetch the doctor.'

'I don't want Alan here. I don't want him to see me like this.'

But Susanne had already gone to instruct Jenny McNeill to find Dr Redpath, wherever he might be, and bring him back to the cottage.

'I fell,' Prim told him. 'I wakened in the night and tripped over the . . .'

'Damn it, Gillian,' said Alan, 'do you think I'm so poor a doctor that I can't see that you were attacked? Some man beat you. Isn't that what happened?' He carried a bowl of warm water to the bedside and bathed her torn lips and bruised cheek with a cotton swab.

'No,' Prim said, stubbornly.

'Why are you protecting him?'

'There was no man,' she said. 'I fell.'

'Take off your shift.'

'No.'

'Lift it up and allow me to examine you.'

'No.'

'Can you stand?' Alan asked.

'Of course I can stand.'

'Then do so.'

'No.'

'Gillian, if you were – were taken, you must let me help you.'

'You'll report me to the sheriff's officer, won't you? Then everyone will be convinced I'm the lightskirts they've always supposed me to be.'

Her mouth was torn inside and out, her lips bruised and a heavy swelling on the side of her face might cause a temporary neuralgia. She was impatient with his examination, though, as if the attack had been nothing more than a minor inconvenience.

'If a crime has been committed then it's my responsibility to notify—'

'I thought at first it was you,' Prim said.

'Me!'

'He came to me in the darkness,' Prim said, 'and I thought it was you.'

'What did he say?'

'Nothing. He did not utter a word.'

'You know who it was, don't you?'

She shrugged. She seemed to care more about protecting her reputation than bringing the devil to justice; or, Alan thought, had she discovered some strange, twisted pleasure in being taken against her will?

'Some tinker, I expect, or a navigator from Bagshott's camp who found my door open and seized his chance,' Prim said.

'Someone you know, Gillian, a friend.'

'I have no friends.'

'You let him in, didn't you?' Alan said. 'You invited him in. Is that why you won't say his name, because you think it's your fault?'

She dabbed at the corner of her lips with her forefinger. 'Yes,' she said. 'I lured him here, I tempted him, and when he came, I submitted. How could I do otherwise, a woman of my bad character?'

'Will you let me examine you?'

'No.'

'Are you bleeding?'

'Not now. It's stopped,' Prim said. 'I've no need of your medicines, Alan, or your sympathy. I'll rest today, and tomorrow I'll be as right as rain.'

'What if he comes back again?'

'He's had what he wants from me,' Gillian said. 'I've no more to fear from him. So as far as the world's concerned I tripped over a stool and struck my ugly face on the table. If you call yourself my friend, that's what you'll tell anyone who's curious enough to enquire.'

'How can you be so damnably phlegmatic? Do you place so little value on your person that you'll let the devil escape scot-free?'

'If I point a finger at him, he'll simply deny my accusations. And what sort of proof do I have to offer that I'm telling the truth? Everyone will assume that I led him on. That thought has already occurred to you, has it not?'

'I spoke in haste, in anger.'

'Why are *you* angry? Is it because I've been tainted?'

If she revealed the man's identity at least he could seek vengeance on her behalf but for some reason she would not do so. She had been taken not by some casual passer-by, some tinker or traveller. She had been taken by someone who knew that she would be alone in the cottage at night.

'My God, it's Oakley!' Alan said.

'Now do you see,' said Prim.

The north wind had risen and the sea was licking up, causing the boats moored against the quay to buck and curtsey in the gloom of the late afternoon. With a fire blazing in the grate and the lamps lighted, Angus Gamrie's cottage seemed as safe a haven as one could find in Strayhorn.

Seated by the fire, warming his hands, Alan explained the nature of his predicament. Angus listened solemnly and the little boy, just as solemnly, took himself into a corner to play with the chalks and slate that Angus had brought for him, while Annabel went on cooking supper.

'Aye,' Angus said, 'it's too serious a charge to push forward on scant evidence. Oakley could swing for it, you know, for rape's a Crown case, one of four pleas always tried by the justiciary. The case would have to be presented to a justice to obtain a prosecution order.'

'That's it, though,' Alan said, 'there is no case.'

'Can the teacher not be persuaded to accuse him?'

'She refuses to do so.'

'Are you certain, Dr Redpath, that Oakley is the man?'

'Who else could it be?'

'You?' Angus Gamrie suggested.

'I wouldn't bring a prosecution order against myself, would I?'

'Oakley might claim it was you. After all, you've been

courting the young woman, an' impeachment would be a valid defence?'

'I never thought of that.'

'Like as not, though,' Angus went on, 'Oakley would claim consent, then it would be the woman's word against his, since there are no witnesses and her injuries are consistent with a fall. Did you examine her very closely?'

'She wouldn't allow it.'

'So you can't swear that Miss Primrose wasn't a willin' party?'

'No,' Alan admitted, 'I can't.'

'Unless she brings charges soon,' Angus said, 'Tom Oakley can't be brought before a court of law. However, if she presents her case to the Church authorities an examination of all the complaints against Tom Oakley will follow as sure as night follows day. Witnesses will be called, evidence recorded an' he'll be brought to book.'

'Tell me, Mr Gamrie, have there been other women?'

Angus Gamrie's gaze shifted to the girl at the stove. She held a lid in her hand like a tambourine and peered through the steam into a pan that simmered on the iron plate. 'Aye,' he said. 'There have been other women, that's the pity of it. If you press on with charges against Oakley in a civil or Church court then a lot o' other folk are going to be hurt, too.'

'What do you think I should do?' Alan said.

'What does the woman want you to do?'

'Nothing.'

'Then that's what you must do, Dr Redpath,' Angus Gamrie said.

At first he was possessed by a terrible fear that the constables would arrive and carry him off to the prison in Kirkcaldy. But as morning drifted into afternoon and nobody turned up to question him, Tom began to relax.

He had been drunk, of course, though not too drunk to perform. Drink would not stand as an excuse, however – or would it? He might claim that he'd been drinking to his son's departure for the whaling grounds and, somewhat the worse for wear, had had to be carried up to bed. Effie would back him in the lie; Zena too if she knew what was good for her. In fact, he could easily concoct a string of lies that would cast so much doubt on the woman's reliability that no judge, let alone a jury, would believe that he had been within a half-mile of Rose Cottage. And as soon as his innocence had been established, he would drop a quiet word into a judicial ear and shift suspicion on to the brash young doctor from Seameads who had been pursuing the schoolteacher for weeks and who, perhaps, at last had lost patience with her flighty ways.

It was after noon before he came downstairs for a late breakfast. He chatted to Effie about the change in the weather and, ignoring her petulant scowls, reminded Zena that he would not entertain a fisherman as a son-in-law. What occupied his thoughts, though, was not his family's welfare or even Coburn's dud stock certificates, but Gillian Primrose, and how soon he might have her again.

'I do not see,' Bette Hollander said, 'that it's any business of yours what that woman chooses to do. Indeed, Dr Redpath, you are leapin' to conclusions with a haste that does you no credit. Did you not tell Susanne that Miss Primrose had fallen over a stool and bashed her face on the furniture?'

'Prim asked me to say that.'

'So it's only your opinion that it might be Mr Oakley?' Bette said. 'Don't tell me you've joined the conspiracy to have Tom ousted from Strayhorn?'

'I'm part of no conspiracy, Mrs Hollander,' Alan said. 'However, certain facts do suggest that Mr Oakley is not a man to be trusted, particularly where women and money are concerned.'

'Money?' said Bette, sitting up. 'What's this about money?'

'There are, so I'm told, certain financial matters in which Mr Oakley has acted irregularly,' Alan said.

'What financial matters?'

'For heaven's sake, an innocent woman has been taken by force, and all you can think of—'

'Angus Gamrie told you this, didn't he?'

'I have spoken with Mr Gamrie, it's true.'

'Angus Gamrie is a malicious wee man who, now he's been sacked as session clerk, is hell-bent on getting his own back on Tom.'

'Whatever low opinion you may hold of him, it's at Mr Gamrie's urging that I'm here at all.'

'What do Angus Gamrie's lies have to do with me?'

They were closeted in the living-room of the house at High Cross. Buckie had been sent to bed, Susanne despatched upstairs and the kitchen door closed to keep Nancy from eavesdropping.

'Mr Gamrie is concerned that even if Gillian – Miss Primrose – will not speak out against Oakley, the Presbytery . . .'

'The Presbytery?' Bette said.

'. . . the Presbytery may elect to investigate the libel without formal charge, and that you may be called to give evidence in Church court.'

'Me?' Bette shrieked. 'Me?'

'According to Mr Gamrie, you've been intimate with Mr Oakley . . .'

'Intimate?' Bette shrieked again. 'Intimate? Me?'

'. . . an intimate friend of the minister and his family, that is, and that a public examination of Tom Oakley's character may cause you embarrassment.'

'Oh, God! Oh, God in heaven!'

Bette slumped back in the armchair, fat legs thrust out, her hands clasped to her bosom. Alan reached into his bag, slipped out the spirits of ammonia, drew the cork and wafted the bottle under Bette Hollander's nose.

'Breathe,' he said. 'Breathe deeply.'

Bette coughed, sat up, and flung his arm from her.

'Take your filthy hands off me,' she cried, flapping her fingers before her face as if swatting flies. For a moment or two, she did not seem to know where she was or who he was, then, abruptly, awareness returned. 'Oh, it's you, is it?'

'Who did you think it was, Mrs Hollander?' Alan corked the bottle. 'We were discussing Tom Oakley, as I recall; Thomas Oakley and the prospect of a Presbytery investigation. According to Mr Gamrie witnesses can't refuse to appear before a Church court if the commissioners summon them.'

'All because of that slut, that harlot schoolteacher,' Bette said, viciously. 'She lured him on. I'll stake my life that she lured him on.'

Alan could take no more. If he had ever been in love with Gillian Primrose then he was in love with her no longer, but he could not stand by and hear her slandered by this self-centred woman. He dropped the smelling salts into his bag and closed it.

'I've delivered Mr Gamrie's message,' he said. 'What you make of it is a matter between you and your husband – between you and Tom Oakley, too, I imagine. Give my regards to Susanne and make my apologies to Buckie.'

'What shall I tell Susanne?'

'Whatever you see fit,' said Alan, and hurried out into the darkness before conscience got the better of him again.

It took all Bette's strength of will to wade through supper without snarling at Nancy or snapping at Susanne. To add to her distress, Buckie was curious about the doctor's abrupt departure and put one question after another to her until, in desperation, she explained that Dr Redpath had called in to advise her on a minor problem concerning her health. Surely she was entitled to some privacy in her own home? And, yes, she was perfectly all right; no cause for alarm.

In and out of the living-room Nancy came and went, dumping down broth, stew and the great blue dish filled with boiled potatoes. Nancy said nothing but squinted at Bette with an evil glint in her eye, as if she had heard every word of Dr Redpath's conversation or by supernatural means had divined the nature of the predicament in which the lady found herself.

After supper Bette buried her nose in her sewing, Susanne read, and Buckie, with Thimble on his knee and Ajax at his feet, pretended to doze.

On the surface, the household was just as it had always been, sickly, sleepy and fraught by turns, each shift in mood scored only by the ticking of the clock in the hall and the moan of the wind in the chimney. How tediously peaceful it was and that night, as never before, Bette yearned for it to be always so, for she had at last realised that happiness was an illusion and contentment the most she could hope for in this dark life.

She was close to tears when she kissed her niece, bussed her husband on the brow and took herself to her room.

Seated on the bed, she stared at her reflection in the mirror, thinking how she had betrayed the loyal lad from Buckhaven and how she had used his illness as an excuse to throw herself into Tom Oakley's arms. Consumed by self-pity, she covered her face with her hands and promised God that if He swept her sins under the carpet, she would make it up to Buckie, make good the sums she had pilfered from poor Susanne and, like the decent woman she was at heart, see her son well married.

Before all that came to pass, however, she must tackle Tom
Oakley.

And make sure she got her blessed money back.

More to escape Zena's poisonous silence than anything else,
Tom put on his galoshes, tied up his trouser legs and trudged
out to labour in the scruffy patch of ground by the churchyard
wall.

According to horticultural experts, of whom there were
rather too many in the parish, trenching was noble work
for winter, pruning could be done in all weathers but planting
required it to be mild and wet. It was wet enough underfoot
that morning, but hardly mild. The sky was black down to the
horizon and the north wind had an edge that would cut off a
man's parts if he were foolish enough to expose them. He had
scraped a few shallow furrows in the brittle soil and scattered a
bucket of two of bladder wrack that Freddie and Morven had
lugged up from the beach and boiled into sludge over a fire in
the potting shed, tarring the walls horribly in the process. But
it was not to ponder matters horticultural that Tom seated
himself on a sack of seed and, lighting a cheroot, stared out at
the charcoal-grey sky.

Now that he had dealt satisfactorily with the Primrose
woman, he must turn his attention to Harry Coburn who,
if Gamrie was to be believed, was a fraud whose promises were
as false as the Prophets of Israel. He spared no thought for
Bette Hollander, from whom he had borrowed the bulk of the
money that he had given to Coburn, and was, therefore,
surprised to see the lady in question struggle up from the
top of the sheep path and, crouched low to keep the wind from
bowling her over, canter towards him, screeching like a gull,
'Tom, Tom, Thomas Oakley. I want a word with you.'

He ground out the cheroot, dredged up a smile and offered
a welcoming one-armed hug. 'Bette, my dear! *Bonne chance,*

bonne chance, indeed! Another few minutes I would have been gone.'

'Gone to ravish your whore again?' Bette cried.

The welcoming hug became a snatch. He dragged her into the shed and pushed her against the wall. 'What did you say?'

'It was you. I know it was you,' Bette shouted. 'I want my money back.'

'Your money?'

'Everyone knows you ravished the schoolteacher.'

'Did Primrose say as much?'

'Of course not. She's your harlot. She's not going to blurt out your name. Everyone knows it was you, though. You've gone too far this time, Tom Oakley,' Bette said. 'I've given you everything and you repay me by taking up with this freckled whore. Dear God! What harm have I done you?'

'Bette, calm yourself,' Tom said. 'Sit down.'

'I want my money back.'

He put an arm around her and pressed her down on to the sack. She leaned forward, squeezing breath from her lungs. He knelt before her and endeavoured to take her hand. She shook him off.

'Tell me,' he said, 'of what I stand accused.'

'Rape.' Bette spat out the word like an orange pip. 'Rape – and worse.'

'Worse?'

'You've cheated me out of what's mine.'

'Bette, I don't understand.'

'You've cheated me out of my peace of mind.'

'Oh!' Tom said, bewildered.

'Even if your whore won't, someone else will.'

'Will what?'

'Denounce you, then you'll be summoned before the Presbytery and it'll all come out. Susanne will leave High Cross, Louis will disown me and . . .'

'Who's been putting these daft ideas into your head?' Tom said.

'Alan Redpath came to see me. He said—'

'Redpath? Hah! He's a fine one to talk. He's more likely to be the guilty party than I am. By which, my dear Bette, I mean that I've done nothing to be ashamed of and if you've sense enough to hold your tongue, the Church court will have not one shred of evidence to support anyone's accusation.'

'What about Angus Gamrie's servant?'

Tom punched the air. 'God in heaven, I might have known Gamrie would be behind this calumny.'

'He sent Dr Redpath to warn me.'

'No, damn it, Bette; he sent Redpath to stir up trouble between us.'

'I want my money back, Tom, now, in my hand.'

'Is that all you want in your hand, my love?'

She shoved him away and flew to her feet. 'My life savings, all the cash I have in the world, I've given to you.'

'In addition to the sums you've filched from Susanne Thorne, of course.'

'I've taken nothing from Susanne except my due.'

'Oh, but you have, you have, Bette. I know what you've been up to.'

'You're a devil, Tom Oakley,' Bette said. 'It wouldn't surprise me if you *had* forced yourself on that poor school-teacher. Whether you did, or whether you did not, I want no more to do with you once every penny you owe to me has been repaid.'

'I no longer have the money,' Tom said. 'What I have, my dearest, is stock in the Strayhorn Railway Company.'

'You gave my money to Harry Coburn?'

'Come now, I made no secret of what I intended to do with it. You were party to my intention from the beginning. In fact, you encouraged me,' Tom said. 'Tell you what I'll do, Bette,

I'll give you the stock certificates, all the stock certificates, and let you reap the benefits.'

'What use are stock certificates to me? Harry Coburn prints them by the handful. It's my belief that you and Harry Coburn are in this together. No, Tom, I'll have my money back, in cash, or I'll go to the sheriff and tell him what you've done.'

'What I've done? What have I done? When it comes to issuing threats, my dear, you have no leg to stand on,' Tom said. 'Precisely what will you report to the sheriff's officer? That you and I have dallied together many a time and that you've been tapping the fortune that belongs to your little English ward? Will you tell them that I bought railway stock at your behest and have the certificates to prove it? No, my love. What *you* will do is keep your mouth shut, just like the admirable Miss Primrose, and realise that if I go down you and a number of other pretty folk in Strayhorn go down with me.'

'I'm not afraid of you, Tom Oakley, nor do I care about myself.'

'Hoh! That you do, my honey, that you do,' Tom told her. 'And if you no longer care about yourself, at least you still care about Louis.'

'Louis?'

'Do you suppose your lovely little English ward will marry the son of a cheat and an adulterer, a fat, foolish woman who has robbed and deceived her? Oh no, no, Bette, there's nothing you can do to harm me that won't harm your precious son even more.'

'My money's gone, isn't it?'

Tom nodded. 'Yes, your money's gone.'

'Then I'm ruined.'

'Not if you make sure that Louis marries Susanne Thorne. When that happy event occurs, you will be secure in every sense of the word, and all this unpleasantness will be behind us.'

'You never did love me, Tom, did you?'

'Of course I did. I still do.'

For a fleeting moment he thought that she was daft enough to believe him and, reaching out, made as if to stroke her cheek. But she rose up like a banshee and butted the crown of her head into the pit of his stomach, winding him so badly that he staggered and almost fell. She kicked out at him, her tiny feet in their neat black boots sharp as hoofs, and he hopped away, hopping round and round, forearm pressed into his stomach. She gave him a shove, and barged past him into the mean daylight, heading for the top of the sheep path.

'Bette,' he croaked. 'Bette, what are you going to do?'

'You'll see, you'll see,' she shrieked over her shoulder and, like a shag or a cormorant, took wing on the breast of the wind.

19

After an hour of prayer and readings and the droning of unaccompanied psalms, Tom led the men folk out of the church to follow the coffin to the graveside.

Muckle Tam was stationed by a pile of sods and raw red earth, his bonnet held down by his side. The women – and there were few – took up position by the gate and, heads bowed, listened to the minister's voice as he hastened towards committal. 'O Lord, whom have we in heaven but Thee? And there is none upon the earth that we desire beside Thee. Our heart and our flesh faileth but Thou art our strength and our portion for ever.' Gulls squawked overhead and, far out to sea, the sails of the Strayhorn fleet were visible, pursuing the rumour of a mackerel shoal. 'Under the shadow of Thy judgements we come to Thee, seeking Thy grace to support us in our time of trial. O God, who art able to supply every loss, to heal every wound and dry up every tear, grant that as our sorrows have abounded, our consolations may much more abound. Ashes to ashes . . .'

Tom hesitated, then, with a nod, instructed the pallbearers to lower Bette Hollander's heavy coffin into the ground.

Some coffin it was, too: Buckie had had it built in the Dundee shipyard that had built the *Merrilyn*. Carpenters had cut and planed the oak timbers and varnished and polished the casket until it gleamed like old gold. What it cost, or where the money came from, nobody dared ask, for Buckie was as mute and sullen in his grief as his son was shrill and garrulous.

The procurator fiscal's enquiry had concluded that Mrs Hollander had died by accident while on her way to call upon the minister's wife. Just what had prompted her to tackle the sheep path that storm-tossed morning would never be known, for the poor woman had never reached her destination. Mr Oakley, digging in the manse garden, had heard no cry for help. On the basis of such scant evidence, it was decided that Mrs Hollander had simply lost her footing and plunged to the beach below where, to judge from the state of the body, she had died on impact, her legs, arms and pelvic bones shattered, her skull crushed like an apple in a press.

On Buckie's instruction the remains had been sewn into a lined canvas shroud and laid out upon the bed in the lady's room, only the contours of her body visible to those who came to bid her farewell.

Buckie, himself, firm-limbed, upright and resolute in grief, had greeted every visitor, had personally escorted them into the lamplit room and had seen to it that Nancy served them tea or a glass of spirits afterwards. Susanne was ever by his side, waiting for a sign of collapse, but there was no weakness in the old whale-master who, cloaked in mourning, seemed to have shed all his infirmities as he went about the sober business of burying his beloved wife.

Now, at the graveside, watching earth spray down upon the coffin, he stood as tall as he had ever done, an arm about his son's shoulders, to steady not himself but the boy. And Susanne turned her face into Nancy's breast and wept, not just for her aunt but for her uncle, and for her cousin too.

'Come now, Oakley,' Harry Coburn said, 'this is hardly the time or place to discuss matters of business. Have you no sense of the occasion, man, or have you buried too many female acolytes to be moved by the demise of another?'

'Bring your glass outside,' Tom said. 'What I have to say to you won't wait another day.'

The pair moved away from the little crowd that had spilled out of the living-room into the hall. The front door had been wedged open, as the dog, aware that something was wrong, was in and out, whining and pawing, for Louis had ignored his father's order to chain the beast up in the yard. Louis, of course, was in a waking trance. Stupefied by what had occurred, he clung not to Susanne but to Nancy as if she, and only she, had it in her gift to ease his pain.

'I'm surprised,' Tom said, sipping whisky, 'that your daughter did not attend the burial service. I understood that she was fond of Mrs Hollander.'

'Darsie has been so shaken by the news that she has taken to her bed,' Harry Coburn said. 'She will call upon Louis and Buckie when she is stronger and more able to deal with it. But you didn't draw me out here to enquire after my daughter, did you, Mr Oakley?'

'No,' Tom said. 'The stock certificates are unsigned.'

'So that you may more easily trade with them.'

'I may be a man of the cloth, sir,' said Tom, 'but I am not a head-in-the-clouds. I know that they are unsigned because they are worthless.'

'How much did you borrow from Mrs Hollander?'

Tom glanced over his shoulder before he answered. 'All but fifty pounds.'

'Well, there you are,' said Harry. 'Assuming that Mrs Hollander did not leave a record of her loans, you are free and clear of the necessity of repaying Mrs Hollander, or her heir.'

'It's not my debt to the Hollanders that concerns me,' Tom said, 'so much as your debt to me. When I return the dud certificates, I expect—'

'Keep them,' Harry said, sharply. 'Sell them, trade on them, raise money for a new roof, or an organ, or a memorial stone to your benefactress, if that's your inclination.' He drew so close that Tom could taste his breath. 'I'll print more if I require them.'

'Do you admit that you have deceived me?'

'In a matter of weeks, Mr Oakley, I'll negotiate the sale of the Strayhorn company to the directors of the North Fife Railway who have already expressed considerable interest in what's going on at the Fisherfield and are within an ace – an ace, Mr Oakley – of making an offer to take over my holdings. Once the North Fife pay me, I will pay you.'

Tom scowled. 'Is this true?'

'More than one way to skin a cat, Tom, and more than one way to make a profit,' Harry said. 'Will she marry him?'

'Who? Oh, the Thorne girl. Yes, I expect she will. He's such a feeble creature that she'll surrender to pity and traipse to the altar as soon as the mourning period is over.'

'When will that be?'

'In these modern times,' said Tom, 'six months. Will the North Fife Railway Company wait that long?'

'They'll just have to, won't they?' said Harry and, with an odd little grimace, slipped past the minister to join the other mourners in the hall.

Alan left the gig on the Old Kirk road and walked along the path by the schoolhouse which, out of respect, had been closed for the day. In the gloom of a misty March afternoon Rose Cottage seemed anything but picturesque and, in his present mood, struck Alan as no better than the bothies of the farm servants far out on the hill or the cramped dens of the fisher folk down by the harbour. As he approached, though, a light bloomed within and he was overtaken by sadness at the speed with which things had changed. He was tempted to turn on his heel and walk away, then the little door of the cottage opened and Prim, carrying a pail, stepped out on to the path.

'It's me,' Alan said. 'Don't be afraid.'

She started, and swung the empty pail up to her breast with both hands.

He said, 'I'd hoped to speak with you after the burial.'

'I'd no desire to linger there.'

'Because of him, because of Oakley?'

'I hardly knew the Hollander woman,' Gillian Primrose said, 'but Susanne is my friend and it hurts me to see her grieve.'

'I see,' Alan said. 'May I come inside for a moment or two?'

'I think it better if you do not.'

'Oh! May I ask why?'

'I have my good name to think of.'

'Ah!' Alan said. 'Yes, of course. I wouldn't wish to do anything to injure your good name. Are you well?'

'Well enough.'

'Has he called again? I mean, has he bothered you?'

'No, it appears that religious instruction has been suspended,' Prim said, 'at least in the meanwhile.'

'Have you decided what to do yet?'

'About what?'

'Your position here?'

She seemed surprised. 'My position here is not under threat.'

'I thought it was. I thought . . .'

'I know what you thought,' she told him. 'You thought that because I refused to cry out against Thomas Oakley I didn't deplore what he did to me and that I was, in part way, responsible?'

She looked so vulnerable in the gloaming, in the damp, winter-stripped garden, holding the empty pail to her breast, that Alan experienced a pang of guilt, quite inexplicable in its intensity, and wished that she would weep so that he might have an excuse to comfort her.

'I take it you went back to High Cross with the mourners?' Prim said.

'I did. It was the least I could do.'

'Was the Reverend Oakley there in all his glory?'

'I did my best to avoid him,' Alan assured her.

'And did you,' said Prim, 'avoid him, I mean?'

'Yes.'

She lowered the pail to the ground, ran a hand through her thick fair hair, and said, 'Poor Susanne. She'll marry that handsome lumpkin, you know, and be trapped in Strayhorn for ever.'

'Is that such a dreadful fate?' Alan said.

'For Susanne it is,' Prim said. 'Why don't you marry her and take her away from here? You'd be very comfortable living on her income in Edinburgh with a panel of wealthy patients to keep you from wearying.'

'I've no wish to marry Susanne Thorne.'

'Or anyone?' Prim asked.

'Gillian,' Alan said, 'I'm leaving Strayhorn.'

The teasing tone changed at once. 'When?'

'As soon as my application to practise as a physician in the Royal Infirmary in Edinburgh is confirmed. I've applied for an interview, you see.'

'Clever chap,' said Prim.

'Clever? What do you mean?'

'Moving up in the world, advancing your prospects,' Prim said. 'Strayhorn's no fit place for a man of parts. I wish you very well, Dr Redpath.'

'I'm sorry,' Alan said.

'Sorry? What reason have you to be sorry?'

'That, between us, things did not go better.'

'You made me no promises,' Prim said. 'Besides, what would you want with a woman like me, without family or connections or a penny to her name; a woman who is no longer pure?'

'Prim,' he said, helplessly. 'Gillian, I . . .'

'If you take anyone with you from this benighted part of the world, it should be Susanne Thorne,' Prim said. 'Or do you, in your wisdom, prefer to travel unencumbered?'

'Prim, what happened, what did happen?'

'Thomas Oakley happened,' Prim told him, 'which, my dear, dear man, may have been the best thing for you, if not for me.' Then, before he could protest, she stepped forward, kissed him on the cheek, picked up the pail and headed down the slope of the garden to fill the pail at the stream and, once Alan had safely gone, kneel on the bank and weep.

They forced themselves to eat the meat that Nancy put before them and drink what remained of the wine that Buckie had uncorked to refresh the mourners. It was a queer feeling, knowing that her aunt would not come bustling in from the kitchen, or from the bedroom where she had lain – sleeping, Buckie had said, just sleeping – in the lined canvas shroud.

Between mouthfuls, Louis broke down and sobbed. Now that he had done everything that a man could do for a wife, Buckie gave in to the pain in his joints that had been over-whelmed by the gnawing ache in his heart.

Redpath had been kind enough to leave four sticky brown pills in a little cone of white paper. At Susanne's insistence, Buckie took one of them, washed down with tea and, leaning on Nancy, allowed himself to be helped through the empty hallway, past the empty bedroom, and put to bed. He looked very clean, and very old, lying on his back under the covers, eyes wide open. Susanne knelt on the floor, held his hand and said nothing, for she could think of nothing to say that had not been said already.

After a time, her uncle sighed, turned his head and smiled at her.

'My angel,' he said, 'go to bed.'

'No, let me stay.'

'Nancy will be on hand if I need her,' Buckie said. 'Go now, please.'

He stroked her hair with the palm of his hand and, closing his eyes, pretended that sleep was upon him.

Susanne got to her feet. 'Will I leave you the light?'

'No, dearest,' her uncle said, 'take the light away.'

And, holding the lamp before her, Susanne went upstairs to find Louis.

He was seated on the organ bench, head bowed, hands between his knees, his feet, none too clean, planted on the bare boards. His clothes were scattered about the room and he had put on his nightshirt. He shivered, sighed and shook his head and when he saw Susanne loitering in the doorway, clapped a hand to his brow and groaned, 'Oh, Mama, Mama, whatever will I do without you?'

Susanne placed the lamp on the table, seated herself by him and let him rest his heavy head upon her breast. The position was, to say the least of it, awkward. After a moment, he straightened, wiped his eyes with the sleeve of the nightshirt, and said, 'You must not see me like this.'

Susanne told him, 'It's natural for a man to weep at a time like this.' The words sounded stilted. She patted his broad back, the material of the shirt sliding against his flesh. 'You don't have to hide your tears from me.'

'Is Pappy asleep?'

'I doubt it,' Susanne said.

'Did he take his pill?'

'Yes.'

'I wish I had a pill that would bring me ease,' Louis said. 'I wish I had a pill that would take me across to the other side to be with Mama.'

'You mustn't talk like that, my darling.'

'Am I really your darling, Susanne?'

'My one true love,' said Susanne, with only the faintest touch of irony. 'You're cold. Will I fetch you a hot pig?'

'It'll take more than a stone pig to warm me. I'm cold, Susanne, so cold within.' But when she snuggled against him, she was surprised to discover that he wasn't cold at all but radiated a strange animal heat even in the unfired room. She rubbed his back once more, as if raising wind from a baby.

Louis looped an arm about her waist. 'I've resigned my post with the cabinet-maker in Edinburgh,' he said. 'It seemed only fair to do so since my presence is needed here.'

'Is it?' Susanne said. 'I mean, of course it is.'

'Pappy will require me to help with the arrangements.'

'Arrangements?'

'Financial arrangements.' He pulled her closer and brushed her hair with his fingertips. 'She always liked you, my mama,' he said. 'It was her fondest wish that you and I be joined in matrimony.'

'Germany,' said Susanne, 'Frankfurt: I mean . . .'

'My duty is to look after you – and Pappy, of course.'

'Louis, we're in mourning.'

'In September, say, when mourning's over and not an eyebrow will be raised, nor a word of opprobrium uttered . . .'

'Are you asking me to be your wife again?'

'I am, my darling. I am,' Louis said. 'If you say that you will, you'll turn the unhappiest day of my life into the happiest.'

'What will your father have to say to it?'

'He loves you, too, and would be sorry to see you lost to a stranger. Please, Susanne, please say that you'll be mine.'

She hesitated. 'This is not an appropriate time, Louis.'

He kissed her brow and cheek, not quite tenderly.

'Now,' he said. 'I want your answer now, Susanne. Will you marry me?'

And Susanne, without quite knowing why, answered, 'Yes.'

*   *   *

Soon after cock crow, Nancy helped Buckie dress. He insisted on hobbling through to the living-room, though the fire had not been lighted and Thimble was still fast asleep, curled up in a ball on the armchair.

Nancy knew that her master wanted the day to begin, that first long empty day without the lady in the house, knew too that before the clock struck nine, he would be wishing it was bedtime. When, in a mock hearty voice, he instructed her to 'clash the pan', she merely nodded and retired to the kitchen to cook a mighty breakfast, most of which, she was sure, would be wasted.

The house was soon filled with appetising aromas and, around half past seven o'clock, Susanne came downstairs with Louis hot on her heels. The young woman wore a dove-grey day-dress with pagoda sleeves and a wide skirt that Nancy had never seen her wear before and that wasn't quite suitable for full mourning, even in a young person. She looked, Nancy thought, not only thinner and more severe, but much more grown up.

Louis was his usual ramshackle self, though he had shaved, she noticed, and had knotted the black silk cravat tidily for once. Slumped in his armchair, the cat in his lap, Buckie opened one eye and balefully contemplated his son. Through the half-open door of the kitchen, Nancy heard Louis say, 'Pappy, Susanne and I have something to tell you and, though the hour and the circumstances may seem inappropriate to you, it is not so to us. Do I have your permission to speak?'

'What?' Buckie said. 'What is this nonsense, Louis?'

'Mama . . .' Louis swallowed the lump in his throat. 'Mama was legally appointed Susanne's guardian but she, Mama, is no longer with us. Susanne's standing is, therefore, presently unclear, though I've no doubt Mr Spencer Reeve will clarify it for us upon application?'

'Application?' said Buckie. 'What application?'

Susanne intervened. 'Louis has asked me to marry him. The wedding cannot take place until the autumn, of course, but we – Louis felt that it might cheer you a little to learn of our intentions.'

'Application?' Buckie said again. 'Are you applying to me?'

'It is, I think, a courtesy,' said Susanne.

The girl had no duties at school today, which, Nancy thought, was probably just as well. The breakfast would have to do in place of a celebration, for the engagement would remain secret until mid-summer.

'Marry?' said Buckie. 'You want to marry Susanne, do you?'

'I do,' said Louis, with great gravity.

Laudanum, or grief, had blunted the master's powers of reasoning. He closed his eyes and stroked the fur on Thimble's neck, which caused the cat to stiffen and, twisting, glare up at the old man before she dropped languidly from his knee and padded off into the hall.

'As a mark of respect,' Louis said, 'we are asking your blessing.'

'Respect, aye,' Buckie said. 'She was a very respectful woman in her day, your mother. She would have approved of what you're doing. She had her heart set on it right from the first. Susanne?' He sat up a little. 'Susanne?'

'I'm here,' Susanne said.

'He wants to marry you?'

'Yes,' the girl said. 'I know he does.'

'He's doing what his mama tells him. He's being a good boy at last.'

'Uncle, are you unwell?'

'Nah, nah, lass,' Buckie said, stridently. 'I'm all hale and hearty, sound in wind and limb and singing like a linnet. Is that not so, Nancy?' he called out. 'I know you're there, Nancy, so show yourself and tell this pair how I've ordered up a feast to feed the famished, eh?'

'That you have,' Nancy called out, hoarsely. 'Aye, that you have.'

'Marry him then, my angel, if that's your wish,' Buckie said, 'or his wish, or Bette's wish, or anybody's wish, for it's no skin off my elbow, and it's your money to squander how you will.'

'You'll be taken care of, Pappy, never fear,' said Louis.

'Fear?' Buckie exclaimed. 'What have I to fear? The worst has already happened. Go on then, marry her, son, since she doesn't seem to mind.'

'With your blessing, Pappy?'

'With my blessing,' Buckie said and, as if he had suddenly been possessed by the domineering spirit of his wife, called out, 'Nancy, Nancy, where are my kippers? Fetch my kippers, and break out a bottle of our best champagne for, in the midst of death, we have, it seems, much to celebrate.' Then, sinking back in the chair, he let the tears trickle down his cheeks, and Susanne went forward to comfort him.

The letter said:

> *Pending approval of the Parliamentary sub-committee on the presented bill, the Directors of the North Fife Railway Company wish to express an interest in the extension line from Leven to Strayhorn, via Hask and Caddis, and to assure you that we are confident that further capital will be found to assist in the completion of the work which is in hand.*

In other words, the directors of the North Fife had become alarmed by the progress that the Strayhorn Company appeared to be making and would snap up whatever Harry Coburn had to offer in exchange for a lump sum and a place on the board.

Harry cared not a jot about the place on the board. He

would be gone by that time, to Florence or Rome, or to America where, according to Mr Bagshott, pickings were rich for enterprising gentlemen with capital to invest. He was proud of having brought about a negotiation that had little or no substance, for, in effect, having made bricks without straw. He had sunk seven hundred pounds of his own money into the venture and had taken several thousand more, by one means or another, from the Thorne account, and by midsummer would be riding high again.

Harry was still gloating over the letter when Darsie appeared in the drawing-room. 'Ah, there you are,' he said. 'Decided to get out of bed at last, have you?'

She had put on a robe and stockings and, he thought, might even have brushed her hair, but her eyes were swollen, her nose red, and her complexion more terracotta than alabaster. She crept across the drawing-room, slumped into a chair and stared at the eggs, swimming in oil, in the chafing dish that Samson had brought up from the kitchen a half-hour before.

'They're still warm, my dear,' Harry said, 'if you feel like partaking of a morsel or two.'

Darsie shook her head, scattering a few auburn hairs on to the cloth. 'Will Benbow drive me to High Cross this afternoon?'

'High Cross is no place for you right now, Darsie.'

'I want to see Louis.'

'Louis is in mourning,' Harry said. 'Besides, he has Susanne to comfort him. Your presence would not be welcome at this time.'

'Did you speak with him yesterday?'

'I offered my condolences, of course.'

'Did he ask after me?'

Infatuation, not melancholy, was at the root of the mysterious illness that had confined his daughter to bed for the best part of a month. The silly child was love-sick, that was all that was wrong with her. He put a hand to the silver dish and shook the eggs about. 'Why don't you eat something, dearest?'

'He didn't even mention my name, did he?'

'Ah, no, he did not,' said Harry.

Tears oozed like sea water from her jade-green eyes.

'Darsie, Darsie,' Harry said, 'the Hollander boy was barely able to converse intelligently with me, let alone enquire after you.'

Now that the charcoal in the chafing dish had disintegrated, the eggs were beginning to congeal. Harry put the lid on the dish, picked up the letter and, carrying it around the table, placed it on the cloth before her in the hope that some good news might take her mind off her misery.

'What we need, young lady,' he said, 'is a change of scene and a sojourn in a warmer clime to put you on the road to recovery. It's been a long winter, and a damp one. The chill in your bones is making you dismal. Soon we'll be in Italy, just you and Papa, picnicking in the olive groves on the hills of Tuscany, drinking lovely dark wines and eating veal lasagne, dumplings dipped in goat's cheese, and those delicious pale, smoked hams from—'

With a little rasping croak – no other warning – Darsie projected a stream of vomit across the railway company's letter, then, to her father's dismay, slid from the gilded chair and fell, whimpering, on to the drawing-room floor.

'Now, now.' Alan Redpath placed a newly washed hand on Harry's shoulder. 'You must not alarm yourself. Women do tend to breed in sorrow and are frequently indisposed, but pregnancy is not a disease.'

'Pregnancy!' said Harry. 'Are you saying my daughter's expecting?'

'That would appear to be the case, yes.'

'Nonsense! Utter nonsense! She can't possibly be expecting.'

'Every sign and symptom indicates it,' Alan said. 'You may take it from me that the young lady is in the tenth or twelfth week of her term.'

'She's never had a – I mean, she's still a maid.'

'Maids,' said Alan, 'do not, as a general rule, conceive.'

They were standing in the corridor a few paces from the door of Darsie's room. Samson had prudently retreated to the head of the staircase. The kitchen girl who had been co-opted to attend Dr Redpath during his examination of the patient was still in the bedroom, trying to console the mother-to-be. There was nothing much wrong with Darsie except that she was pregnant, and unmarried.

Harry grabbed the doctor by the lapels. 'Is it too late?'

'Too late?' said Alan. 'Too late for what?'

'To be rid of it.'

Alan squared his shoulders and said, indignantly, 'If you are suggesting, sir, that I induce an abortion . . .'

'I'll pay you. I'll pay you well.'

'The foetus and the mother are healthy. I will not abort a healthy baby just to suit your convenience,' Alan said. 'Might I suggest, sir, that you find your daughter a husband to father the child, rather than badgering me to be rid of it.'

'Father?'

'Yes,' said Alan, through this teeth. 'There has to be a father, you know, has to be a man involved.'

'Who, who?' Harry hooted. 'Did she tell you who?'

'Louis Hollander, apparently,' Alan said.

And Harry, raising his fists to heaven, rocked on his heels, and howled.

PART FOUR

20

On the day of Darsie Coburn's wedding work stopped on the Fisherfield acres; not to honour the happy couple, though, but simply because Flash Harry Coburn had not paid Mr Bagshott for the best part of a month.

Mr Bagshott had dealt with gentlemen of Mr Coburn's ilk before and no matter how persuasively Mr Coburn pleaded for breathing space, felt obliged to deliver the usual ultimatum – 'Stump up or I shut up shop' – and to prove that he meant what he said, bought his crew a side of beef and four barrels of beer and declared the day a holiday.

Mr Bagshott and other worldly wise men in Strayhorn could not understand why Flash Harry Coburn was marrying his daughter to a dolt without prospects and why, if the girl was knocked up, he didn't pack her off to stay with relatives to drop the kiddie in secret. Mr Bagshott hadn't had to suffer the torments that sweet little Darsie visited upon her father, though, or put up with the whining of that ne'er-do-well, Louis Hollander who, it was rumoured, was daft enough to imagine that Darsie would come to the altar with more than a wardrobe full of fancy clothes and a bun in the oven.

It seemed that the young fellow still believed that under the law of *jus mariti* the fruits of his wife's heritable estate would fall under his control. How surprised the gossips would have been to learn that poor old oily Harry had slithered into a *jus mariti* trap of his own devising and that by permitting his daughter to marry Louis Hollander he was flirting with not just ruin but with imprisonment for fraud.

No fiddlers serenaded the wedding party and there were no rose petals or ribbons to strew the road to the altar. Harry would have preferred no ceremony at all but Darsie had demanded proper vows and an exchange of rings. In this she was supported by the groom's father, who, to honour the wishes of his late-lamented wife, insisted that everything be done by the book.

As for the groom, he was neither in nor out of the argument. He dithered about like a pole-axed bullock, lumbering after Darsie, mumbling, tugging his forelock, and leaping to satisfy her every whim.

On a damp Wednesday afternoon, three days after the final reading of banns, Louis and Darsie stood before the altar and declared themselves agreeable to take on the other as a lawful spouse, with, or without, the endowment of worldly goods. Buckie wept, Louis wept, Darsie wept, the two co-opted witnesses, Nancy and the butler Samson, wept and even Flash Harry sniffed lugubriously once or twice. Susanne's was the only dry eye in church, for she had sense enough to realise that the play was not over and that Louis would need her more than ever now that he had Darsie Coburn for a wife.

It was more of a tea than a wedding breakfast. Harry had failed to offer Macklin House and Buckie had arranged a modest celebration at High Cross, and a very modest celebration it turned out to be. Mr Oakley claimed to have parish business to attend to, Alan Redpath was in Edinburgh and when Nancy spirited Samson and Billy Benbow into the kitchen, the wedding party was reduced to five sad souls that, within minutes, became four as Darsie, pleading fatigue, took herself upstairs to lie down and did not, pointedly did *not*, invite the groom to join her.

If the church service had been intended to appease Aunt

Bette's ghost, Susanne thought, the dismal little party afterward would surely have reduced her to tears. Louis, Buckie and Harry Coburn dolefully toasted the bride in French brandy while Susanne nibbled gingerbread, sipped tea and listened with mounting annoyance to the men's laboured conversation.

At length, unable to contain her irritation, she said, 'I assume that Louis and Darsie will move into Macklin House as soon as the honeymoon is over.'

'Honeymoon?' said Louis.

'Macklin House?' said Buckie.

'There's no room here for a baby and a nursemaid,' Susanne said, 'whereas I'm led to believe that Macklin House has many apartments.'

Harry said. 'Well – yes, I suppose that's true.'

From the corner of her eye she saw Buckie shake his head but, for once, she ignored him. 'How soon?'

'How soon?' Louis repeated.

'How soon will you move out of High Cross, my dear?' said Susanne.

'Macklin House is hardly suitable for an infant,' Harry said.

'Fine for horses, but not for children, hmm?' Susanne said.

'I'm seldom at home, you know,' Harry said.

'All the more freedom for Louis and Darsie,' said Susanne. 'Their presence will prevent the servants from slacking.'

'What do you know of servants, young lady?'

'I know that a nursemaid and a lady's maid will be required to help Darsie through her ordeal.'

'Ordeal?' said Louis, stupidly.

He had been at the brandy before the wedding service and was, Susanne thought, half seas over. She watched him pour himself another glass before she continued. 'I haven't quite forgotten what a well-managed household requires by way of servants, Mr Coburn.'

'London? Yes, well – that's London,' said Harry.

'We have four bedrooms, and a cubby for Nancy; surely not enough to ensure your daughter's comfort, let alone accommodate children.'

'Children!' Louis said, and raised his glass. 'Oh, God!'

Buckie said, 'She has a point, Coburn.'

'No, no,' said Harry. 'No.'

'Why not?' Susanne persisted.

Louis wiped his mouth. 'None of your business, Susanne.'

'I think it is very much my business, Louis. I'm the stranger here. Perhaps I should make plans to leave High Cross.'

'Heavens, no!' said Buckie, in alarm.

'You have a daughter-in-law to look after you now,' Susanne told him.

'Ah, she's jealous!' said Harry. 'That's it! Jealousy!'

'Are you, dearest?' said Louis. 'Are you jealous of Darsie?'

'On the contrary. I'm delighted that you've discovered true love,' Susanne said. 'But I've no intention of staying here if my presence will create inconvenience. Why not Macklin House, Mr Coburn?'

Harry Coburn had surrendered to Darsie's tantrums but would not, Susanne thought, yield an inch to any other female.

'I haven't been a good father to Darsie,' Harry said. 'I'll be the first to admit to the fault. Now she's found a family, a close and loving family who will keep her safe and sound. Whereas in Macklin House, when I'm away . . .' He waved airily as if the question needed no further attention.

'Uncle,' Susanne said, 'I believe it's time I spoke with Mr Greenbaum.'

'Greenbaum? Who's this Greenbaum person?' said Harry.

'My friend,' said Buckie, 'a lawyer.'

'A lawyer?' said Harry. 'What does she want with a lawyer?'

'I was promised to Louis,' Susanne said. 'I assumed that Louis would take care of me, but he has found happiness with another and I am, therefore, in need of advice concerning my future. I will ask Mr Greenbaum to draft a document appointing my uncle as my guardian until I am twenty-one – if you are willing, Uncle Buckie?'

'Of course I'm willing,' Buckie said. 'I'm flattered and delighted. But what use can a halting old man be to you, Susanne?'

'Why do you need Greenbaum,' Louis spoke up, 'when Mr Reeve looks after your interests so well?'

'My bank is in Dundee, not London,' Susanne said. 'I wish to ensure that there is no impediment to having my funds transferred into my uncle's name, now that my aunt is dead. To that end I will communicate with Mr Reeve through Mr Greenbaum, which is, I believe, the most practical manner in which to proceed.'

Harry Coburn said, 'What a sensible girl you have here, Buckie.'

'And ask Reeve for a full accounting?' said Louis.

To which Susanne replied, 'Of course.'

The brand-new husband walked the brand-new father-in-law out into the gloom. Benbow had lighted the carriage lamps and Samson was seated in the curricle with a woollen rug tucked around his knees, for the night air was keen and the butler was no longer young.

'What shall we do?' Louis asked.

'Nothing for the time being,' Harry answered.

'According to Pappy, Greenbaum has a reputation for being a stern negotiator.'

'Reputations acquired in Dundee carry no weight in London. Reeve will be more than a match for him, believe me.'

'But the money I've deposited in the Union Caledonian and all those shares of railway stock purchased in my name?'

'Look, the Thorne girl is smarting because you chose my

daughter – well, chose is hardly the word for it – however' –
Harry sighed – 'that boat has sailed. You must care for Darsie
as best you can. She's a fragile child, you know, and the next
few months . . .'

'Yes, yes,' said Louis, 'but what will I do for money?'

'You've food on the table and clothes on your back,' Harry
said. 'Count your blessings, Louis, and be patient. Placate the
Thorne girl, assure her that you are still her friend and
admirer. Convince her that you still need her and cannot live
without her.'

'If she demands an accounting . . .'

'Reeve will take care of it.'

'Are you sure, Harry?' Louis said. 'Are you absolutely sure?'

'Quite sure,' said Harry Coburn and, without a word of
farewell, climbed into the curricle and ordered Benbow to
drive him away.

A fine new double-sized bed, a wedding present from Buckie,
had been crammed into the corner of Louis's room and the old
sagging truckle lugged out and burned in the yard. Trunks
and baskets filled with Darsie's clothes were stacked between
the piles of books and bric-à-brac and the organ, draped in a
sheet, served the new bride as a dressing-table. The couple
would have been more comfortable in Bette's room but Louis
would not hear of it.

It didn't seem to matter to Darsie where she slept now that
she had escaped from Macklin. She mooched about upstairs
for much of the day and had Nancy wait upon her which, with
surprisingly little complaint, Nancy did.

The new Mrs Hollander sprawled in the big bed and stared
at the ceiling beams or, if Louis strayed too far from her side,
called out in a whimpering voice for him to come to her and if
he did not, drummed her heels on the floor in a petulant little
tattoo that drove Ajax into a frenzy. The dog, of course, was

no longer allowed upstairs and a fair portion of Louis's day was spent chasing after him to prevent the poor beast from 'annoying' his irritable wife.

In the evening Darsie did condescend to join the family in the living-room. Clad in a flowing silk robe and boudoir bonnet, she slouched in a chair at the dinner table and allowed Louis to tempt her with a little bit of this, a little bit of that, as if she were an overgrown child and, as the days trickled by, grew more robust and demanding until, at length, Buckie was moved to draw Louis aside and enquire, 'How long is she going to stay in bed?'

To which Louis replied, 'How do I know? She's isn't strong, Pappy, and she is carrying a child, after all.'

'Your mama carried you for nine months without all this palaver.'

'Palaver?' said Louis. 'What do you mean?'

'Nothing,' Buckie said, and retreated to his room to lie down.

Susanne appeared to accept Darsie's presence with a remarkable degree of equanimity. When she lay in bed just across the corridor from the happy couple, though, the thought rang through her that she was being far too loyal and accommodating for her own good and that even Aunt Bette would no longer expect her to keep faith with Louis now. And when she heard Darsie groaning, Darsie weeping, Darsie scolding poor Louis, she wondered if she would find someone who wouldn't cause her to doubt her worth, and who would keep his promises intact. Until that day came, she must go on teaching, and would remain loyal to the Hollanders who, after all, had once given her a place in their hearts.

'Are you mad?' said Zena. 'Dear heaven, Susanne, how can you say you still love him after all he's done to you?'

'It wasn't his fault.'

'No? Then whose fault was it?'

'It was a mistake, an accident.'

'No,' Zena said. 'Louis has behaved like a scoundrel, and you'd do well to pack your bags and leave High Cross just as soon as you can.'

'You just want my teaching post, don't you?'

'Yes, I do,' said Zena. 'I'd sell my soul to get out of the manse.'

They were seated on the wall outside the schoolhouse. It was a windy day but, for the season, not cold. Zena had brought a thick slice of rye bread which she ate without cheese or butter, while Susanne nibbled the last stale slice of the gingerbread that had graced the table at Louis's wedding feast. It was quite like old times, except that the gaiety had gone, the sense of anticipation and optimism that had once seemed as natural as drawing breath.

'No point in wishing, I suppose,' Zena said. 'Even if you were to leave, Prim never will. It'll take more than my father to shake her out of Rose Cottage, especially now that Dr Redpath's had enough of our rough ways and has decided that the sick folk of Edinburgh are less sick than we are.'

'Alan hasn't gone yet.'

'So you still have a chance, do you, you an' your fortune?'

'Dr Redpath has no interest in me.'

'Aye, well, he has no interest in Prim either, so it seems.' Zena cupped her hands under her thighs and rocked back and forth on the stones of the wall. 'By the way, I had a letter from Peter yesterday. He posted it in Shetland three weeks ago.'

'Oh!' said Susanne. 'How is he?'

'He's fine. Freddie's fine.'

'And Gregor, how's Gregor?'

'He's fine too.'

'What were they doing in Shetland?'

'Picking up crew,' said Zena. 'Have you heard from my brother?'

'Why would I?' Susanne said.

'I think he likes you.'

'Well, I like him,' said Susanne, which, she realised, was perfectly true.

'It's just a pity,' said Zena, 'that they're so young.'

'They're not children, Zena. If you like Peter you'll just have to be patient and wait for him.'

Zena sighed and kicked out her legs again. 'I'm not sure I do like him. I'm not sure of anything any more. I'm afraid I'll wake up one morning and find myself all alone in the world, like poor Prim.'

'Not you,' said Susanne.

'Why not me?'

'You've too much to offer.'

'Yes, and nobody to offer it to,' said Zena. 'At least you had Louis.'

'I still have,' said Susanne, softly, just as Miss Primrose rang the hand-bell to summon her back to class.

Mr Gordon Bagshott was not surprised when Flash Harry Coburn requested a meeting in the snuggery of the Dalriada. He was, however, rather more surprised when the gentleman extracted a roll of banknotes from his pocket and planted it upon the table.

'Payment,' said Harry, 'in full.'

'What's owing to date, you mean,' said Mr Bagshott.

'No,' said Harry. 'There will be no more. Our contract is at an end.'

'You employed me for to do a job of work and that job of work ain't but a quarter done.' Mr Bagshott covered the notes with his fist, as a walnut shell might cover a pea. 'I didn't ship my excavator to Fife for nine weeks' work.'

'Parliamentary approval—'

'Pish!' said Mr Bagshott. 'You've run out of capital?'

'My investors let me down.'

'Investors,' said Mr Bagshott. 'There never was investors, was there?'

'Oh yes,' said Harry, 'there were investors but they – well, what matter. You're paid until Saturday but you can leave any time that's convenient.'

'A contract's a contract,' said Mr Bagshott, his voice rising. 'If you welch on it, you'll have to pay severance. That's the law.'

'That isn't the law,' said Harry. 'Besides, there is no contract.'

'We shook hands on a verbal agreement . . .'

'Not worth the paper it's written on,' said Harry, trying to make light of the matter which, as it happened, was a grave mistake.

The roll of banknotes disappeared into Mr Bagshott's pocket a split second before Mr Bagshott grabbed Mr Coburn by the throat, hoisted him to his feet and dragged him across the table top. Benbow was out in the yard with the horses and there was no one in the bar but a scared pot-boy.

'I been let down, ha'n't I?' Mr Bagshott shouted. 'In a word, I been cheated. Know what I could do to you? I could break your sorry neck without a qualm, or run you out to the Fisherfield to tell my crew they're on the march to bleak prospects.'

Harry managed, just, to nod.

'We dug your hole,' Mr Bagshott went on, 'and we faced it nicely. We levelled your ground and trenched it. We'd have it banked in a month or less, all the way to the end o' the stretch, then we'd have bridged the river, and made the running to Caddis. That was our agreement, our handshake. Neither me nor my men are happy that it won't come to pass.'

Harry dipped his chin and lowered his eyelids, contritely.

'I'm the engineer, I'm the contractor. They'll do as I tell

them, Mr 'Arry Coburn. If I tell them to pack up and move on quiet, then they'll pack up and move on quiet. For them it concerns hard cash, but for me it's pride. Progress is my middle name, Mr 'Arry Coburn, an' you've pished on it. You've wasted my valuable time and that, in my book, sir, is a crime that needs to be punished.'

Hit me, Harry thought, please stop sermonising and just hit me.

'Fifty pounds should do it.' Mr Bagshott paused. 'Make that guineas.' He released his grip on Harry's throat. 'What do you say to that, Mr Coburn?'

Harry sucked in air. He could see nothing but Bagshott's massive stomach straining against the embroidered waistcoat. 'Say – say to what?'

'Pouring oil on troubled waters,' Mr Bagshott told him. 'Fifty guineas, cash in hand, will go a long ways to salving the hurt to my pride. Fifty guineas and we all goes off peaceful as lambs.'

'I ha'n't – haven't got fifty guineas.'

'That's a sorry story, that is,' said Mr Bagshott.

'Really, no. Honestly, no. I do not have fifty guineas. I do not have fifty pence.' Harry waited for the blow that would maim or kill him. 'It's the truth, Bagshott. I've been let down, skinned, in fact. Had to sell the last of my dear departed wife's jewellery, my last memories of her, to raise enough wind to pay you what I owe. More – no, no; there isn't any. It isn't there.'

'You've got hosses.'

'Pardon?'

'You've a nice matched pair out there in the yard.'

'They're thoroughbreds, man.'

'I've no objection to thoroughbreds.'

'They're worth hundreds, hundreds and hundreds of—'

'Then they're worth fifty guineas, I reckon.'

'One?' said Harry, optimistically.

'Both,' said Mr Bagshott, grinning.

'But not the curricle, surely not the curricle?'

'Now what would I want with a curricle?' Mr Bagshott said. 'You keep the curricle, Mr Coburn. I'll take my hosses home by railway train.'

On the journey back from Edinburgh Alan mulled over his choices. He might stay in Strayhorn, living from hand to mouth, or take up a post in Edinburgh Royal Infirmary and lodge, at least temporarily, with his brother Stephen. There was plenty of room in Stephen's house and, so he was informed, a plethora of wealthy ladies and gentlemen crying out for the services of a personable young doctor. He had a great deal to learn, of course, not only about medical practice but about Edinburgh society and the manners and mores that governed it.

If he hoped to advance his station then a well-to-do wife would certainly be an asset. Susanne would fit easily into an Edinburgh drawing-room and would not embarrass him; although he found Susanne attractive, he could not pretend to be in love with her. There was Prim, of course, but he feared Gillian's moods, her scathing tongue, and her devotion; feared even more the fact that he could not put her out of mind for more than five consecutive minutes.

Dressed in a fine bottle-green coat with a velvet collar, a shawl vest and grey trousers, all given him by his brother, Alan had put the village schoolteacher out of mind just long enough to satisfy a committee of managers that he was proficient in clinical procedure and had more than a working knowledge of the medicine chest. Seated below the table in the Senate Room answering their questions, he felt as if he were being dissected like one of the corpses in the anatomy class. At the conclusion of the examination he was offered the post of assistant physician, which he promptly accepted. Letters would be exchanged, details formalised, but to all intents and purposes he was now a member of the staff of the Royal Infirmary of Edinburgh and, within a day or two, would shake the dust of Strayhorn from his feet.

The roses were not yet in bud but gorse had sprung out early and the yellow flowers glowed like fireflies in the gathering dusk. She leaned on the little wicket that separated the schoolhouse from the cottage. It was twilight, the school closed and dark, the cottage lit by a lamp in the narrow window and the flicker of firelight on the walls. It was as if she had known that he was bound to call on her last of all his friends and acquaintances.

'That's a very pretty coat,' she said. 'Is that what the fashionable gentlemen of Edinburgh are wearing this season?'

'What would I know of fashion?' Alan said.

She stood on one side of the wicket gate and he on the other. She made no move to admit him to the garden, let alone the house. She wore a pinafore apron over a print cotton dress, and no bonnet.

'You'll learn soon enough, I expect,' Prim said. 'Susanne informs me that you've accepted a post in Edinburgh Infirmary and will be leaving us soon.'

'First thing tomorrow morning.'

'Is James Young Simpson to be your instructor?'

'Yes, I'll work under his tutelage for half a year. How did you know that Simpson would be my professor?'

'I do read a newspaper from time to time.'

'My name's not in the newspaper, is it?'

'No, but Mr Simpson's is. You'll have to bide your time, Dr Redpath.'

He longed for her to invite him into the cottage, into the light, so that he might gauge her feelings more accurately. What *did* he want from her? he wondered. Sentimental tears would have been out of character for Prim. He preferred her as she was, honest, aloof and teasing.

'Have you seen Oakley again?' he said. 'Has he been back?'

She didn't blush, didn't prevaricate. 'No.'

'When I'm gone . . .'

'It'll make not one whit of difference,' Prim said.

'To him, it might.'

'If he comes again,' Prim said, 'I'll be ready for him.'

'Ready for him?'

'I keep a sharp knife beneath my pillow.'

'Gillian . . .'

'Where's the best place to strike?' she asked, matter-of-factly. 'Is it better to aim for the belly or the chest, or to go for the throat perhaps? Come, Dr Redpath, you're an anatomist. Your advice, please.'

Prim's threat of a bloody revenge on Thomas Oakley filled Alan with pity, not alarm. He did not believe her capable of stabbing a man but with a knife under the pillow there would be no suitors now, no lovers allowed into her bed. She would scare them away, shut them out from now on.

'The heart,' he said. 'The heart is the place to strike.'

'Aye, of course it is,' Prim said. 'Have you sold the pony?'

'Yes, to Sandy Raiker.'

'And the gig?'

'The gig without a hood – that's gone too, or will be gone tomorrow.'

'Soon,' she said, 'you'll have a fine painted chaise to transport you about the streets of Edinburgh.'

'I doubt it,' Alan told her. 'I fear I'll never be rich.'

'Unless you marry well.'

'Gillian, I must go.'

'I wish you well then, Dr Redpath.'

'May I – may I kiss you?'

'I would prefer it if you did not.'

'As you wish,' Alan said. 'Well – goodbye, Gillian.'

He put his hand on her hand on the wicket gate and

squeezed her fingers before she could draw them away. There was no more to it than a touch, but he would carry the memory of that touch with him, like a leaf pressed into a book, long after he had established a new life in the capital and left the sad little schoolhouse, and its teacher, far, far behind.

'Goodbye, Alan,' Prim said curtly and, turning, went indoors.

21

The railway had brought a new prosperity to Dundee. Harbour works and docks on the Tay were crowded with big ships, a mass of sails and rigging penned by towers, churches and high stone edifices. The streets were lighted, shops, stores and banking institutions numerous, and even the servants who followed the ladies up and down wore gloves and carried umbrellas. Mr Greenbaum's chambers stood at the mouth of the Overgate, fronting the High Street. The building had a flat-capped turret at one end and had been at one time, so Buckie told her, council rooms. At three o'clock precisely they entered the narrow doorway and, at five minutes past, were seated in leather armchairs, sipping tea, while Buckie and his old friend exchanged news on the state of trade.

Mr Greenbaum had rosy cheeks, an unruly mass of salt-white hair and a sharp little beard. He was as spry as her uncle was lame and pranced about with the teapot that his clerk had brought in and did fussy things with a hot-water jug while Buckie and he roared at each other, as if affection could be measured by volume. At length Mr Greenbaum put down the teapot and, hopping up on to the table that served as a desk, slapped his thighs, drummed his heels on the panel, and said, 'Well now, young lady, what can I do for you?' as if he were a cloth salesman in one of the new emporiums.

Susanne explained her situation. As soon as she was done, Mr Greenbaum said, 'Am I to understand that you wish Buckie Hollander to become your guardian and receive, in your late aunt's stead, the quarterly payment from interest on your father's estate?'

'That is so,' Susanne said.

'Your aunt left no will?'

Buckie answered, 'No will and no instructions.'

'Tumbling off a cliff was probably not the sort of end that Bette had envisaged,' Mr Greenbaum said. 'However, as there's no will to put to the test and as Mrs Hollander had no goods, chattels or property of her own outside marriage that matter is simply disposed of. As to Buckie becoming your guardian, young lady, my feeling is that you have no need of a guardian now.'

'But I want Buckie to look after me.'

'Does he not do that now?'

'Well, yes,' Susanne admitted, 'but . . .'

'Buckie, my friend, you should be flattered,' Mr Greenbaum said.

'I am,' Buckie said. 'However, the vexed question isn't whether the girl needs a guardian or whether I'm fit for the role, but—'

'No,' Mr Greenbaum put in, 'the vexed question is what becomes of her inheritance now that Mrs Hollander's gone. I assume it's locked up safe and sound with this London fellow, Spencer Reeve, through whose offices she received the quarterly payments and to whom she made the annual accounting.'

'I'm not sure she made any accounting,' said Buckie.

'Did Reeve not demand it?'

'I don't believe he did,' said Buckie.

Mr Greenbaum slid from the table and toddled about the room, hands clasped behind his back. He paused at the tall window and peered out at the view for a moment, then returned to his perch on the table.

'How long have you been in Fife, Miss Hollander?'

'Four years come March.'

'In that time you've had no connection with Mr Reeve.'

'Oh yes,' said Susanne. 'I've written to him and requested that he send small sums on my behalf to my cousin Louis.'

'Why did you do that?' said Mr Greenbaum.

'Louis needed cash and I was not unwilling to give it to him.'

'Uh!' Mr Greenbaum exclaimed. 'I take it your aunt used a bit of persuasion to induce you to help Louis out?'

'My aunt knew nothing of the arrangement.'

'How much did Louis make – I mean, how much did you send him?'

'Ten pounds now and then.'

'And Reeve stumped up without a murmur?' said Mr Greenbaum.

'He did,' said Susanne.

'This Reeve fellow asked no questions of Bette?'

'None that I know of,' said Susanne.

'How was the money paid to Louis?'

'By banker's draft.'

'And the bank?'

'The Union Caledonian in Edinburgh, I think,' said Susanne.

'You didn't tell me about this, Buckie,' said Mr Greenbaum.

'I didn't know about it,' Buckie answered. 'I was under the impression that Bette was supporting Louis from Susanne's payments into the Merchants and Traders here in Dundee. Nothing wrong in that, since Susanne wasn't being deprived of her rightful.'

'I earn fourteen pounds a year as a teacher,' Susanne put in, proudly.

Mr Greenbaum raised his hands above his head and muttered a few words in a language that may, or may not, have been Hebrew. 'This inheritance of yours, young lady, by which I mean the sum that your father left in trust for you – how much does the capital amount to?'

'Do you know,' Susanne said, 'I've no idea.'

Mr Greenbaum muttered again. He glared at the floor, at the window, at Buckie, and finally shook his head. 'High time you found out,' he said. 'Buckie, you've done the proper thing in bringing the young lady to seek my advice but I want you to understand that what may emerge from any enquiries I make on Miss Thorne's behalf might reflect badly on your wife and son.'

'I'm prepared for that. I just want the business cleared up,' said Buckie. 'Louis is married now and if he borrowed money from Susanne—'

'He didn't borrow it,' Susanne said. 'It was a gift.'

'A gift!' said Mr Greenbaum. 'Some gift, I'd say. By the by, who did Louis marry if it wasn't Miss Thorne?'

'Darsie Coburn,' Buckie said.

'Harry Coburn's youngest?' Mr Greenbaum asked.

'His one and only,' Buckie answered.

Mr Greenbaum blew out his cheeks once more, then, easing himself from the table top again, said, very, very quietly, 'I'll write to Spencer Reeve tonight – with your permission, of course, Miss Thorne?'

'My permission?' Susanne said.

'It's no longer necessary for you to have a guardian to act for you. You're now of a legal age to execute the terms of your father's will without consultation. It's well within your power to appoint a person other than Spencer Reeve to examine and, if necessary, alter the nature of your capital investments. In other words, you're a woman in your own right, Miss Thorne, and must make your own decisions.'

'Therefore,' said Susanne, 'I may appoint you to act on my behalf.'

'Employ might be a better way of putting it,' Buckie said.

'Yes, of course; employ,' said Susanne. 'Is that what you think I should do, Uncle? Employ Mr Greenbaum as my legal agent?'

'It's your decision, sweetheart,' Buckie said. 'You've more sense than I had at your age, or than I have now, come to think of it.'

'But what if Louis . . .' Susanne began.

Her uncle massaged his kneecap while Mr Greenbaum, whistling soundlessly, decanted warm water from one pot into another.

Buckie had brought her here because he believed that Louis had let her down. In the cries of the street vendors and the rattle of carts rolling down towards the docks, she could almost hear her cousin's voice pleading with her not to make trouble. She felt so young and volatile, yet Mr Greenbaum expected her to separate love from duty, forgiveness from stupidity. She gripped the arm of the chair tightly.

'If I grant you permission to act on my behalf, Mr Greenbaum,' she heard herself say, 'precisely how will you go about it?'

'For a start, I'll write to Mr Reeve requesting sight of all documents relating to your inheritance.'

'And then?'

'That remains to be seen,' the lawyer answered, cautiously.

'Do it,' Susanne said. 'Yes, do it.'

'Sweetheart, are you sure?' Buckie said.

'As sure as I'll ever be,' said Susanne.

Nancy had lugged hot water up to the bedroom to wash Darsie's hair. When it was almost dry she had helped the girl screw in curling papers and then to dress. When that was done she returned to the kitchen to prepare breakfast for the little mistress. It was, by then, approaching noon but over the years Nancy had grown used to Louis's idle habits and was reconciled to looking after his wife on the same terms.

Darsie thumped downstairs. There was little to show of her condition as yet and it was weariness not weight that made her heavy. She seated herself at the table, dabbled a spoon in her porridge plate, rested her cheek on her hand, and sighed. 'Where is my husband?'

'Gone into the town, I think,' said Nancy.

'Is he drinking again?'

'I doubt if he has the money to buy drink.'

'Oh,' said Darsie, 'he always has money to drink. He never has money to buy me a new gown, though I am so swollen that nothing fits me now. He wouldn't care if I went about clad in an old sack.'

'Perhaps he's gone to look for work,' said Nancy, not seriously.

'Work!' said Darsie. 'What sort of work will Louis find in Strayhorn that will accommodate his talents? He'll sit about waiting for someone to give him enough to buy drink with – and she will, you know.'

'Eat up your porridge,' Nancy said, gently.

'She gives him everything he asks for. All he has to do is talk sweet to her and she dips into her purse and pulls out guineas by the handful.'

'Will I fetch in the coffee?' said Nancy.

'Oh, is there coffee? I thought we were too poor to afford coffee?'

'There's coffee,' Nancy said. 'Are you wantin' some?'

Darsie did not answer. Head on hand, she spooned up a mouthful of porridge and swallowed without chewing. She looked, Nancy thought, like a witch's doll with her hair screwed up in paper and her eyes huge as crab shells.

'Where *has* he gone?' said Darsie, wailing a little.

'He took Ajax with him,' said Nancy.

'Well, yes, of course he would take Ajax. Ajax follows him around devotedly – just like that girl.' Darsie sat up, her eyes larger than ever. 'Perhaps he's gone to buy us a gig and pair.'

'I ha'e my doubts about that,' said Nancy.

Darsie gave herself a little slap on the forehead and her mouth became an oval of dismay. 'Oh no! He's gone to meet *her*. He's gone out to meet *her* and bring her back with him. He can't wait to see her again and has ridden out with the carter to the railway halt.' She spun round and pleaded with Nancy to confirm her suspicions. 'I mean, it is today that she's due home?'

'Aye,' Nancy said, nodding. 'Her, an' the captain.'

'The captain?'

'Mr Hollander, your father-in-law.'

'Why do you call him the captain?'

'Because that's what he was, an' what he'll always be.'

'I wonder' – Darsie returned her head to her hand – 'if Buckie will bring me a gift from Dundee, something nice to wear, perhaps, or a brooch, or a silver clasp for my hair. He's very fond of me, you know.'

'Aye,' said Nancy. 'I'm sure he is,' and stepped back into the kitchen and quietly closed the door.

In recent weeks Louis had lost all taste for ale, and for company. He stood on the brown rocks beneath the stunted headland and peered down into the deep water that lay beneath the skirts of weed. He hated the sea's changing moods and the ebb and flow of its tides by which his father set so much store. What was the song Pappy had crooned to him when he was a little boy? *The tide comes up and the tide goes down, and my wee darlin' wears a frown.* He could see Pappy's whiskery face looking at him, upside-down. *The tide goes down and the tide comes up* . . . The verse was lost for ever unless Pappy brought it out of hiding to sing to the child in Darsie's belly.

He stepped closer to the edge, slithering a little. He wondered if one careless step had caused Mama to fall or if she too had been in despair. No, he told himself; Mama was too strong a person, too sure of herself to flirt with death. If there was a heaven she would surely be looking down on him now, calling to him not to make the fatal step that would plunge him into deep water. If he slipped, though, he would not be responsible, would not be held to blame. Better to do it before Pappy returned from Dundee, before his crimes came to light and he had to answer for them. The weight of his coat would drag him to the bottom, to crouch like a foetus until his lungs split and he was born into the glory of the life hereafter where Mama would be waiting to forgive him.

He sweated inside his reefer jacket, though his lips and ears were cold. Drowning would be a very uncomfortable way to die, he thought, and inched away from the edge.

Ajax lay in the grass on the breast of the hill; Ajax who would have followed him to hell itself a year or two ago. The dog, like everyone else, seemed to have turned against him. Louis clambered over the rocks, away from temptation, and, with the dog mooching behind him, set off home to pick up the morning's mail.

If Sandy Raiker knew what had happened at Macklin House he kept it to himself. During the drive back from the railway halt, he was unusually quiet but Buckie was too exhausted to notice and Susanne too distracted by other things.

Darsie was in the doorway, a wispy figure in a pale silk robe, her hair spiked with curling papers, Louis waiting on the porch. As soon as the cart drew up, he grabbed the check-rein, and shouted, 'Has he gone, Sandy? Has Harry Coburn gone?'

'How would I know a thing like that?' Sandy said.

'Don't lip me,' Louis snarled. He waved a sheet of paper in the air so violently that the pony shied. 'Has Coburn gone off and left us in the lurch?'

Sandy said, 'Aye, so it seems, Louis, so it seems.'

'Dear God!' Louis yelled. 'Dear God! What has he done to me?' Before Susanne could step from the cart Louis caught her by the arm. 'Did you know of Coburn's intentions? Is that why you went to Dundee?'

'Louis, control yourself,' Buckie said. 'How can you be sure that Coburn's gone for good?'

'He sent me a letter, this letter,' Louis said.

Leaning on Susanne's shoulder, Buckie lowered himself to the ground. He took the letter from Louis and scanned it, nodding.

'You're not surprised he's done a bunk, are you, Pappy?'

'No,' Buckie said. 'I can't say I am. Sandy, drive Louis and Miss Thorne to Macklin House straight away. I haven't the strength to accompany you. Besides, somebody had better stay with Darsie.'

'No, Louis, I'm going with you,' Darsie cried, darting forward. 'I don't believe Papa's left me. It's a misunderstanding, a hideous mistake.'

'Aye,' Buckie said, grimly. 'It's all that, lass.'

The curricle was drawn up on the gravel at the front of the house. Benbow was seated on the board, nibbling a piece of cheese and staring disconsolately at the space between the shafts where the thoroughbreds should have been but were not. Nothing, Susanne thought, had ever looked so fixed and stationary as that high-sprung vehicle trapped in a pool of afternoon sunlight.

'Where is he, Benbow? Where is my Papa?'

Though she had ridden on the front board beside Sandy, Darsie looked so ill and shaken that Susanne thought she might spill her baby on the ground there and then.

The tiger stared at her, unblinking. 'You tell me that, Miss Darsie.'

'Where's Samson, then?' said Louis.

'Gone to Anstruther. He has a sister there.'

'And the other servants?' said Susanne.

'There's only me left,' Benbow said. 'Mr Jenks from Hask is expected tonight or tomorrow. He's promised to give me something for the curricle. My wage. Could have done worse, I reckon, since there's fifteen or twenty quid in it for me. Cook an' the girls got nothin' but a guinea an' all the clothes they could carry off.'

'Clothes?' Darsie cried. 'My clothes?'

'What about the silver?' said Louis.

'The master took the silver with him. Hawked by now, I reckon.'

Darsie fled through the open door into the house, calling for her father.

'Go with her, you fool,' Susanne said, 'lest she does herself a mischief.'

'Oh! Yes, yes, of course,' Louis said and, reluctantly, climbed the shallow stone steps and vanished into the house.

Benbow remained seated in the curricle, which was all he had to show for twelve years of service to Flash Harry Coburn.

'When did Mr Coburn leave?' Susanne asked him.

'First thing this mornin'. Right after breakfast, he calls us all round, tells us he's let the lease go an' we're all free to find other masters. All rattled he was, an' urgent, with three bags, strapped an' ready to go. He gave us some cash, not much, told us to take what we could carry from the house then went off over the field, headin', I think, for the railway halt.' Benbow put his head in his hands. 'I always thought he was a good man an' I was sorry to see him go. But then Samson cries out an' when I go into the gun-room, I found them all lyin' in a bloody heap.'

'Bloody heap?' said Susanne. 'What are you talking about?'

'The dogs,' said Benbow. 'He'd shot the blessed dogs.

Why'd he have to do that, miss, why'd he have to shoot the blessed dogs?'

'I don't know, Billy,' Susanne admitted.

'To tell you he ain't comin' back,' Sandy Raiker said and, nudging Susanne aside, climbed in to the curricle to comfort his unfortunate friend.

She lay like a slut in his armchair, skirts hitched up over her shins, calves and ankles exposed. He had often wondered what it would be like to enter his study late one night and find a woman sprawled in his chair, but the woman he'd dreamed of had not been his daughter.

'What do you think you're doing, Zena?'

'It's very comfortable here, isn't it?'

'Go to bed. I have work to do.'

'Work?' Zena slid down in the leather chair. 'What sort of work?'

'Do not be impertinent. I've a praise to write for Sunday service, if you must know.'

'A praise?' said Zena. 'What are you praising, Dad? The beauty of the lilies, or the beauty of Gillian Primrose?'

He set the lamp upon the table and showed her his fist.

'I'm warning you, Zena . . .'

He had been relieved when Gregor and Freddie had left home, for he could no longer control them. He would encourage Roland and Waylie to leave too, before they became old enough to challenge him. His daughters were another matter. He had failed to appreciate how dangerous daughters could be.

'Are you going to hit me?' said Zena. 'Or haven't you had enough to drink to forget that I'm the ugly lump you gave birth to?'

'Give me my chair and let me get on with God's work.'

'If you think what you're doing is God's work, Papa, then I pity you.'

'*You* pity *me*?' He felt his temper strain against the leash. 'What right have you, a chit of a girl, to pity a minister ordained by God?'

'Ordained by God,' said Zena, 'but licensed by the Presbytery.'

'What's this about the Presbytery? Have you been talking to Gamrie?'

'That boy, Brogan McQueen, is yours, isn't he?' Zena went on. 'Dear God, Papa, you just have to look at him to know he's my half-brother.'

'Coincidence.'

'Was it coincidence that Bette Hollander fell off the cliff when you owed her a large sum of money?'

'No, my dear,' Tom said, 'that was luck.'

'Was it luck kept Prim's mouth shut?'

'If you care to study the facts, Zena, you may conclude that Alan Redpath's departure and the schoolteacher's misfortune are connected.'

'Why have you stopped visiting the school?'

'Because Miss Primrose does not like my preaching.'

'Did you borrow money from her, too?'

'How could I? She's a pauper. Now, Zena,' Tom said, 'if you've finished cataloguing my sins, would you care to tell me what you really want?'

'I want to get away from this place – and away from you.'

'Then go,' Tom said. 'I won't stop you. However, you've missed one important item from your list, my dear. I invested every last penny we possess in railway shares that aren't worth the paper they're printed on. I'm the fool in this pantomime, not the villain. We are, in a word, broke.'

'There is nothing new in that.'

'True,' Tom said. 'What is new in our situation, however, is that I'm stuck, stuck in this parish, in this manse with you and your sisters and brothers, just as you are stuck with me. There is no hope for any of us now. So who am I to deny you the opportunity to make a better life for yourself? You may pack your bag at any time and set out in search of – what? Fame and fortune? A husband? A lover? If that's your objective, then go with my blessing.'

'I thought you wanted me to stay here for ever?'

'I've changed my mind.'

'Because I know too much?' said Zena.

'Because you are bitter, and bitterness has no place in my house.'

Flustered and unsure, Zena got to her feet. 'What if I decide to marry a fisherman, a common sailor like, say, Peter Macfarlane? Won't you stop me?'

'If he'll take you, he may have you,' Tom said, 'but once you've made your bed, you must lie on it. Do not come whining to me with your tail between your legs when it all goes wrong.'

'Is that your final word?'

'It is,' Tom said.

'Thank heaven for that,' said Zena.

Darsie, hysterical and retching, was put to bed with a hot pig at her feet, a basin balanced on her chest, and a glass of hot toddy in her hand. The doctor in Caddis was not known to the Hollanders and it was left to Nancy to unearth two laudanum pills that had mysteriously found their way into the cupboard above her cot and feed them to the master to give him respite not only from the pain in his legs but from the screeching that came from upstairs where Louis was vainly trying to placate his wife.

Sandy Raiker and Billy Benbow had dragged the dogs out of Harry Coburn's gun-room and buried them in a shallow grave in the pasture. Louis had been more upset by the fate of the dogs than by Darsie's frenzy when she'd discovered that every stitch of clothing, every pair of shoes, every bonnet and trinket that she had left in her papa's house had been looted. Blankets, sheets, bolsters had also been taken by the servants and in the kitchens there wasn't a pan, pot or kettle left, let alone a crust of bread or a pinch of salt.

On the way home from Macklin, at the crossroads that led to Hask, they had stumbled on Mr Bagshott's excavator drawn in for the night. Eight or ten diggers were camped under it, ready to make an early start on the long haul down to Kirkcaldy where a boat would be found to take the machine back by the sea route to Newcastle. Mr Bagshott and the horses had, it seemed, already left. By morning the encampment on the Fisherfield acres would be deserted once more and the dream of a railway link with the world at large extinguished once and for all.

Once Buckie had been helped to bed, Nancy went upstairs to sit with Darsie, leaving Susanne to serve Louis's supper.

Louis and she were alone at table, the same neatly set, gloomy table at which they had eaten the evening meal for what seemed like for ever. Ajax was prowling about and begging for scraps, and Thimble, more easily satisfied, soon fell asleep on Buckie's chair. It all seemed very cosy and comfortable, and dull. Indeed, if it hadn't been for Darsie sobbing upstairs, Susanne might have imagined that she was married to Louis and settled into peaceful monotony. She knew that he was weak and too impulsive to be a good husband, but she clung still to the remnant of her promise and a belief that her first love must somehow be her last love.

Louis, too, seemed empty of all concerns. He ate hungrily, without manners, and said nothing.

All too soon he would have to go upstairs again, to the ugly new bed in the cluttered room where his wife waited, to lend her a measure of his strength of which, heaven knows, there was precious little to spare. It would be cruel to leave him now,

Susanne told herself, to abandon Louis as Harry Coburn had abandoned Darsie and Alan Redpath had deserted Primrose, yet there was a small, eager part of her that envied men their selfishness and their callous indifference to anyone's wellbeing but their own.

She brushed the crumbs from the table, spread out the heavy red cloth in place of the white one and served tea without delay, for it was late and she was eager to get to bed. She watched Louis perform the familiar tea ceremony, a series of banal little actions that his mama had taught him or that he had acquired by emulation; Bette's clever boy, the would-be genius, reduced to a hang-dog husband dourly stirring his tea.

'Do you hate me, Susanne?' Louis said out of the blue.

'No, of course I don't hate you.'

'You should,' he said, 'after all I've done to you. Did you meet with Papa's friend, Greenbaum?'

'I did,' said Susanne. 'He has advised me to demand an accounting and will write to Mr Reeve on my behalf request-ing one.'

Louis sighed. 'I've no great liking for Jews, but I have to admit that Greenbaum is an admirable exponent of the law. Does he suspect that Reeve may not be straight?'

'I think it's in his mind that there may be irregularities.'

'I'll be very surprised if there aren't,' Louis said. 'Why do you suppose Harry Coburn's done a bunk? He and Spencer Reeve have been robbing you blind for years. Now, thanks to Pappy's interference, they're about to be exposed.'

'If you knew this, Louis, why didn't you tell me before now?'

'Because I'm in on it too.'

'The money I sent you was a gift,' said Susanne. 'You didn't steal it. Besides, it doesn't amount to very much.'

'Ah, but it does,' said Louis. 'It amounts, I think, to a very great deal. How much I can't say, for I was only the messenger boy. It wasn't your donations to my keep that were important: it was your letters.'

'My letters?'

'The letters you sent to Reeve were doctored to enable Harry Coburn to tap into your trust fund to finance the railway scheme,' Louis explained. 'My part in it was to purchase shares through an Edinburgh bank to provide Harry with working capital. Now, I fear, that money too will have gone south in Harry Coburn's pocket.'

'Surely you must have realised that I'd find out sooner or later?'

'The intention,' Louis said, 'was that I would marry you. Then, when the accounts came forward from Reeve I would take charge of them on your behalf, as is a husband's right and duty.'

'And would you not have questioned them?'

'No. I was taken in by Harry Coburn's promises too, you see,' Louis said. 'I thought the branch line would be a money-spinner and we would all be rich.'

'And all your promises were as fraudulent as Harry Coburn's shares?'

'I do not love Darsie.'

'What you did with her . . .'

'Was a mistake, a dreadful mistake,' Louis said. 'I am stuck with her, though. I'm her husband! Is that not punishment enough?'

'Do you expect forgiveness, Louis? Do you expect me to ignore the fact that not only have you deceived me you've robbed me as well?'

'I'll pay for my misdeeds. I am prepared for it. I'm just thankful that my mother didn't live to witness my shame,' Louis said. 'It would have broken her heart to see me sent to prison.'

'Prison?'

'Fraud and forgery are serious crimes. I may be transported instead. Yes, on the whole, I think I'd prefer to be transported.'

'Transported? What *are* you talking about?'

'Greenbaum will insist that I'm brought to book, together with Reeve and Coburn,' Lewis said. 'I know little about how such matters progress but it's my guess that Reeve will display your doctored letters and claim that he lacked the expertise to recognise them as forgeries.'

'Surely he will be charged with negligence, at the least.'

'Negligence?' said Louis. 'Hah! I doubt that Greenbaum, wily though he is, will pit himself against the Chancery Division which will, I fear, close ranks to protect its own reputation. With Harry Coburn missing, and most of the money gone with him, I'll be left to shoulder the blame.'

'That isn't fair.'

'None of it is fair, Susanne,' Louis said. 'I ask nothing for myself, only that you won't see my wife and child reduced to poverty and that you'll look after my father while I'm serving my sentence, however long it may be. I think you owe Pappy that much, since he was my conscience and the instrument of my downfall.'

Had he rehearsed the speech, Susanne wondered, or had the spate of recent disasters matured him?

It was quiet upstairs now, for Nancy had worked her gruff magic on Darsie, and the girl, if not asleep, was resting: all so quiet, so peaceful, so comfortable alone with Louis in the living-room.

'You must take me for a fool, Louis,' she said, 'to suppose I can be talked into making any sort of promise. I loved you once, and would love you still if I were still a child. But I'm not a child and I've been too long without you to believe that you are my one true love.'

'What do you mean?'

'I mean,' Susanne said, 'that I'll do nothing that will commit me to helping you or your family until I hear from Mr Greenbaum.' She tapped a finger against his lips to silence him. 'Not another word, Louis, not until I learn the truth of the matter.'

'I've told you the truth, Susanne,' Louis said. 'What reason do you have to doubt me?'

'Every reason,' Susanne said and, gathering herself, went off into the kitchen to scrub the pots and pans.

22

Rain moved in from the west, great squally showers that swooped over the moors, drenched the backside of Strayhorn and swiftly filled the trenches on the Fisherfield with milky brown water. High tides, rising against offshore winds, swamped the butt of the old harbour wall and slithered like silky fingers along the cobbles to poke and pry at the hole that Mr Bagshott's masons had left unfaced. It was a pretty sight at first but by noon on the second day it had become nothing but a trash-pit, heaving with weed and flotsam.

'It's only a matter of time,' said Zena, 'till somebody drowns in it.'

'A petition's being raised to have an iron grid made to cover it,' said Susanne. 'There's a public meeting in the Dalriada tomorrow evening to discuss who will pay for the grid.'

'In that case,' Zena said, 'there'll never be a cover and they'll still be discussing it in ten years' time. It won't matter to you, of course.'

They had walked from the schoolhouse in Susanne's dinner break to inspect the watery phenomenon.

'Why won't it matter to me?' Susanne said.

'You'll be gone, won't you? You can't stay in High Cross with a man who betrayed you. If I was in your shoes, and had some cash, I'd be off tomorrow.'

'I may not have any cash at all, you know.'

'What? Do you think he took the lot?'

'That remains to be seen,' said Susanne. 'But I've no

intention of being rushed into anything. High Cross is still my home.'

Zena spun away in mock disgust, slapping her hand to her brow. 'God in heaven, Susanne, what does he have to do to turn you against him? He and that precious mother of his were out to rook you from the first. And when that silly creature from Macklin threw her skirts over her head he didn't even have the gumption to resist. How does he intend to keep her, by the way?'

'Buckie has some income, I believe; not much but a little.'

'Don't tell me you're going to forgive him and remain in that house for the rest of your life, supporting a man who should be in jail?'

'I haven't decided yet,' Susanne said.

'Take yourself to Edinburgh,' Zena suggested.

'Edinburgh? What would I do in Edinburgh?'

'Call on Dr Redpath, for a beginning.'

'I've heard nothing from Alan since he left. Clearly he wants no more to do with us. Besides, he never loved me; he loved Prim.'

'I wonder if he still thinks of her,' said Zena.

The watery pool had lost its interest. Arm-in-arm, the young women set off for the Old Kirk road. 'Do you still think of your navigator?'

Zena laughed. 'Heavens, no!'

'Is there no one for you now, Zena?'

'Well,' said Zena, cautiously, 'there might be.'

'Is it Peter Macfarlane?'

'Not saying.'

'It is. It's Gregor's friend. Has he declared his intentions?'

'Don't be daft. Peter's only a boy. Boys do not have "intentions".'

'He won't be a boy much longer. He's been to Greenland.'

392   *Jessica Stirling*

'Aye, that's true,' Zena agreed. 'Three or four winters on the Greenland run will make a man of just about anyone.'

'Greg's friend,' said Susanne, wistfully. 'How nice!'

'He's not good enough for the likes of you. Besides, you have to take care of Louis,' Zena said and before Susanne could respond, punched her friend lightly on the arm and set off at a gallop for the manse.

In spite of the recent reverses in his private life Thomas Oakley was too conscientious to neglect his duty to the infant community for long. Spruce and spry, his hair sleek with pomade, his chin shaved smooth as a curling stone and his minister's stock starched stiff as a walrus tusk, he strode unannounced into the classroom at twenty minutes to nine o'clock on a bright spring morning and bestowed on Miss Gillian Primrose a knowing smile.

Susanne was handing out chalk to the infants when the minister appeared. As soon as the children caught sight of the man a groan went up and two or three of the smallest hid their faces behind their slates.

'Good morning, Mr Oakley,' said Prim. 'We've missed your instructive lectures of late. I trust that you are well.'

'Full of vim and vigour, thank you,' the minister said.

'Oh!' said Prim, with a chuckle. 'But then you always are.'

Tom Oakley seemed surprised by the response. He moved around the teacher like a large cat, while Prim preened and blushed, then, just when it seemed that decency was about to be challenged, flirted up the aisle between the benches and left the way clear for the minister to begin.

Puzzled, Susanne sat at the back of the class and listened to Mr Oakley intercede with God on behalf of the little sinners of Strayhorn before launching into a vivid account of the apostasy of Jezebel, princess of Tyre, who, for her sins, was thrown from a window by her servants and eaten by dogs. The tale was sufficiently violent to hold attention and only Mr Oakley's little acorns seemed bored, for they, no doubt, had heard it often before. Miss Primrose stood by the wall, arms folded under her bosom, and nodded gravely as if she agreed that the wicked queen had got no more than she deserved.

Another prayer, a blessing of sorts, and Mr Oakley's contribution to infant education was over for the day.

'Will you call again tomorrow?' Prim asked.

'Tomorrow and every day, if you wish it.'

'I do wish it,' said Prim.

'In that case I'll bid you a temporary farewell.'

Prim caught at his sleeve. 'Wait.'

The class were restless. One of the smaller children was crying. Prim, it seemed, was too preoccupied to notice.

'May I have a private word, Mr Oakley?'

'Of course.'

'Shall we step outside for a moment?'

'By all means.'

Then, to Susanne's astonishment, Prim led the minister out of the schoolhouse and not only closed the door but locked it, shutting them all inside.

She drew him away from the windows, along the path to the door of the cottage and, resting her shoulders against the doorpost, pulled him to her. 'Where have you been, Tom? Why haven't you visited me again?'

'Again?'

She took his hand and pressed it to her breast. For a moment, he was startled and mistrustful, then, opening his fingers he cupped her through the taut fabric. 'Don't pretend,' Prim said, 'that you've forgotten the way.'

'The way?'

'I've waited so long for you, Tom. I need a friend, a comforter, someone more – more . . .' He slipped his hand down and she closed her knees on his fingers. 'Not here,' she said. 'Not now.'

'When?'

'When you can,' she said. 'Soon.'

'Tonight?'

'Yes, come exactly as you did before. How did you come before?'

'Via the window,' Tom said.

'Come by the window, then and amaze me.'

He laughed softly, a thick little *huh-huh-huh*, too smug to be theatrical. 'Oh, I'll amaze you, Gillian dear. I promise you'll be thoroughly amazed.'

Prim giggled, pushed him coyly away and, with one last glance over her shoulder, scampered along the path to unlock the classroom door and slip inside, before he could detect the hatred in her eyes.

Business had been brisk in the Inns of Court and Neville Spencer Reeve had recovered a little from the downturns of the preceding year. He had earned a healthy fee from the Duke of Goodward's divorce case and had extracted a modicum of profit by arbitrating for a pretty little vixen in a case of neglect against her husband. Bits and bobs of this and that, and a brief but delectable passage of arms with the aforementioned pretty little vixen, had put Susanne Thorne into the shade. He had dealt perfunctorily with letters from Fife and as the months went by had all but forgotten about Flash Harry Coburn and his promise of railway returns.

News of Bette Hollander's death gave him pause. He considered sending a letter of condolence to the widower and another to the Merchants and Traders Bank requesting them to alter the payee's name on the account but had never quite got around to it. Winter slipped into spring and spring into early summer and life in the Staple Inn went on at its usual casual pace.

Returning from court late one afternoon, Mr Reeve was surprised to discover in his post a desperate letter from Henry Coburn suggesting that he beat a hasty retreat to the Continent before the law came down on him, too.

The letter, posted in Calais, had taken five days to reach London. Mr Reeve removed his wig, scratched his head and, unperturbed by Coburn's lunatic suggestion, put the letter to one side. The post also contained a letter from a legal agent in Dundee, however, a certain Abraham Greenbaum. He, it seemed, had been hired to enquire into the state of Miss Susanne Thorne's trust fund and inaugurate proceedings necessary to retrieval of said fund, together with interest accrued and, on instruction of the executrix, to arrange transfer of all holdings of all stocks, shares and capital assets into her name.

Mr Reeve removed his gown, poured himself a glass of sherry, lit a small cigar, and, seated at the table by the window, read through both letters very carefully indeed.

He had no intention of making a run for it, of course, and no reason to do so. He had never quite trusted Harry Coburn and had made provision for the Scotsman's hare-brained little scheme expiring through lack of financial oxygen. The fact that Coburn had succeeded in extracting some thirteen thousand pounds from the Thorne estate was neither here nor there. The fact that two thousand pounds, in addition to fees, had found its way into Neville Spencer Reeve's pocket caused the legal gentleman no distress at all. Now some Hebrew lawyer from – where was it? – Dundee had put himself in the way of cutting a slice of pie for himself and who was he, Neville Spencer Reeve, to grudge the fellow his share?

Mr Reeve calmly finished his sherry and cigar, after which he tore Coburn's letter into small pieces and burned them in the grate. He went next to his enormous safe, fished out the bundle of documents labelled with the name of Thorne, spread the contents upon the table top and systematically began sorting share certificates and bonds from bills and letters. That done, he lit the lamp, filled the inkwell, fitted a new steel nib into a pen-holder and, with a patient sigh, set out to write to the Hebrew lawyer in far-off, fair-minded Dundee.

Night crept stealthily over mountain, moor and manse. Tom padded restlessly from study to supper table and back again, pausing only to inform Effie that he did not wish to be disturbed under any circumstances.

Stretched in his armchair he watched the spring night grow dark and the great stabbing shadows of the trees rear up against the faint shimmer of McKinnon's barley field and the pale strip of starlit sky that linked him, magically, to his new-found love. He purred with satisfaction at the realisation that he had roused in the modest schoolteacher a passion to match his own, had punched into her, as it were, the hallmark of his authority. He might be nothing but a poor parish minister with a squabbling family and no prospects of advancement, might have been taken for a fool by the sharpster from Macklin, but, by God, he was man enough, in spite of all, to impound a lady and make her his devoted slave.

He lay for an hour, watching it grow dark and planning what he would do to Gillian Primrose, how many ways he would take her, how often he would make her cry out, and how, now that the callow young doctor had fled, she would be his and his alone. Then, at half past ten, with the family all in bed, the minister of Strayhorn parish clambered from the window of his study and set off across the barley field, heading for Rose Cottage.

She sponged herself with warm water, put on a freshly laundered shift, let down her hair and brushed it until it shone, then, seated in an upright chair, the knife in her lap, she waited as dusk deepened into darkness and the breeze through the half-open window grew chill. She had no idea how long she had been in the chair facing the window before the wicket gate clicked and, a moment later, Tom appeared outside. She got to her feet, the knife held down by her side.

'Is it you, Tom?' she said.

'Yes. Open the door.'

'No,' she said. 'Come as you came before.'

She saw his hands on the sill, lit by the candlelight.

'I expected you to be in bed,' he said.

'I will be soon.' She stepped into the shadows. 'Come just as you came last time, Tom.'

He clenched his fists on the sill and prepared to hoist himself through the half-open window. He had slender fingers, the nails clean and unbitten, and bony wrists, downed with reddish-brown hair. Prim raised the knife, slashed the cord and brought the window thudding down upon his hands. He roared and cried out to her to help him, then, when she did not, struggled to shoulder up the window, his black cloth coat slipping against the glass.

She stooped before him, her face and his separated by an inch of glass.

'Come to me now, Tom Oakley,' she hissed. 'Come to me now, you pig.'

She placed the knife across his knuckles as if she intended to slice off his fingers, one by one. He ripped his hands from under the frame and staggered back from the window. He stuffed his fists into his mouth, sucking on broken flesh, his face screwed up in fear and agony.

Prim pressed her lips to the glass in a lover's kiss, and saw him wheel and, crouched over like a cripple, hobble off into the darkness. Then, dropping the knife, she fell to her knees on the cold stone floor, and cried.

★   ★   ★

The three little acorns were late for school. Their papa, it seemed, had had an accident with the window of his study and had hurt his fingers. Mama had sent Zena to fetch Mr Raiker's cart to take Papa to St Andrews to find a doctor who could sort broken bones. The little acorns were remarkably unaffected by their father's misfortune and were soon engaged in solving the arithmetical puzzles that Miss Primrose had chalked on the board, and the school day went on quite merrily, without a hitch.

At the dinner hour Prim took herself off to the cottage to write a letter.

Susanne sat alone on the wall, ate her bread and cheese and wondered why Prim had been so nice to Mr Oakley yesterday and why she seemed so unperturbed by Petal's news. She must wait for Zena's return to find out what had happened to the minister, and how long he would take to mend.

On Sunday morning the assistant minister from Hask conducted the service and in the evening Mr Ellis did the honours. Bible Class and Sunday schools were organised by the elders for, so it was announced, Mr Oakley had sustained serious injuries to his hands and was in great pain and requiring of bed rest.

'Bed rest,' Zena said. 'Hah! He's never at rest. He's up and down and round about the house all hours of the day and night.'

'He's obviously suffering,' said Susanne.

'It would be surprising if he wasn't suffering,' Zena said, 'since he has eight broken knuckle bones. His hands are swollen up to three times their size and it was all the doctor we saw in St Andrews could do to bind them and put them in a basket.'

'A basket?'

'A wicker basket to keep the pressure off an' let the bones

knit.' She laughed. 'He's a sorry sight, though, and he can't do a thing for himself. Can't cut his meat or lift a spoon to his mouth, can't put on his clothes or unbutton himself to answer a call of nature. It puts a fair burden on Mama and me, for he would have us with him constantly, and cries when we won't give him attention.'

'When will he be ready to preach again?'

'Heaven knows!' said Zena. 'When he can write, I suppose, or turn the pages in the Bible.' She paused. 'He'll be more careful in future, I'm thinking.'

'With windows, do you mean?'

'With everything,' said Zena.

There was barely enough work in the district to support two carriers but with Alan Redpath's gig to add to his collection of vehicles, Sandy Raiker took the plunge and offered Billy Benbow both employment and a roof over his head. The two rubbed along well enough and the carter's cottage, though small, had a corner big enough to accommodate the tiger and, as each kept reminding the other, it was no more than a temporary arrangement.

It was Benbow who was manning the gig at the railway halt at Caddis in the hope of picking up a casual fare when Mr Abraham Greenbaum climbed from a first-class carriage and, with a snap of the fingers, summoned the bored little tiger and, once he was seated, told him to drive to High Cross where, so he said, his friend Buckie Hollander lived.

The Hebrew gentleman seemed to know a great deal about what was going on in Strayhorn and when he unearthed the fact that Billy had been groom to Harry Coburn he interrogated the tiger with considerable persistence and extracted as much information as Billy was willing to give, on the promise of an extra half-crown on top of the fare.

From Mr Greenbaum's point of view it was a half-crown

well spent. Harry Coburn's former groom was a mine of the
sort of information that might prove useful if charges were
brought. Mr Greenbaum considered it a favourable sign that
luck had put Benbow in his way and, in spite of the sober
nature of his business, was in excellent spirits when he arrived
at Buckie's little stone house on the edge of the sea.

Louis lay full-length on the floor, ear pressed to the boards.

Darsie, fully dressed, was seated on the bed.

'What on earth do you think you're doing, Louis?'

'Be quiet.'

'Don't tell me to be quiet. I'm not your little slave. It's bad
enough being ordered to stay in my room without you snapping at me. Why are we shut in here? Why can't we take tea
with Buckie's visitor? Why—'

'Darsie, will you please be quiet. I'm trying to hear what's
being said downstairs,' said Louis. 'Don't you understand
how important it is?'

'No,' Darsie said. 'I *don't* understand. But then I'm not
clever like you. Does this have to do with Papa's disappear-
ance?'

Louis could distinguish one voice from another but could
not pick up the gist of the conversation from the room below.
He'd met Abraham Greenbaum a long time ago when they'd
lived in Dundee.

Mama hadn't liked Mr Greenbaum and Pappy had been
prohibited from inviting him to the house. Mr Greenbaum
was one of a handful of his father's cronies who met in
Morren's Inn, the others, for the most part, being oil merchants, sea captains and ship-owners. Louis had never found
out what his mother had against Mr Greenbaum but, loyally
following Mama's lead, had nursed a vague dislike of the
lawyer for the best part of fifteen years.

'Louis, I'm speaking to you.'

He hoisted himself up on his forearms. 'Yes, dearest?'

'Does this have to do with—'

'Of course it does. Can't I get it into your . . . Look, I've told you a dozen times, Darsie, Greenbaum is the lawyer Susanne's hired to enquire into your father's affairs.'

'Papa took all our money, didn't he?'

'He took Susanne's money. That,' said Louis, 'is what the fuss is about.'

'I'm certain Papa didn't mean to,' Darsie said. 'I'm sure he'll return every penny. He's only borrowed it, you know. He's always borrowing money from people.'

Louis placed a finger to his lips. 'Can you pretend you're a little mouse, darling, just for a minute or two, please? Quiet as a little mouse.'

She nodded, pouting.

He lowered himself to the floor again and tried to catch a snatch of conversation from the living-room. Susanne's voice was raised. She seemed to be asking a question. Mr Greenbaum answered. Then, quite distinctly, he heard his father cry out, '*What?*'

'Louis,' Darsie said. 'Louis, I'm hungry.'

'For God's sake, Darsie, can't you shut up?' he snarled, and, when she began to cry, scrambled to his feet and hastened to the bedside to apologise for his rudeness and, if ever it were possible, make amends.

'What?' Buckie cried. 'Nine thousand pounds?'

'In round figures,' Mr Greenbaum said.

'An' the blackguard makes no bones about it?'

'He knows he has little or nothing to fear.'

'Nothing to fear! We'll sue him in every court in the land. We'll have the shirt off his back,' Buckie raged. 'Does he think us Scots are too stupid to recognise fraud when we see it?'

'Embezzlement,' said Mr Greenbaum.

'Forgery,' Buckie went on. 'Each and every letter is a fake, and by the look of them not very good fakes.' He speared one of the letters on the dining table and whisked it round to face Susanne. 'Now, tell me, sweetheart, does that look anythin' like your handwriting?'

'Well,' Susanne said, 'it does, a little.'

'How many of these damned letters are there?' Buckie said.

'According to Reeve, he has fifteen in his files,' Mr Greenbaum replied. 'He isn't going to surrender any more just in case we do take him to court. I think, Buckie, old friend, that the forgeries are rather good ones. It would require an expert to tell—'

'An expert!' Buckie would not be placated. 'An expert! Anyone with half an eye can see that my niece didn't write them. Even if she did, why didn't Reeve query her requests for such large sums?'

'Because he knew she was purchasing railway shares,' said Greenbaum. 'Someone – presumably Harry Coburn – twigged that Reeve was holding half Susanne's trust in floating capital, and persuaded Reeve to nod approval to any scheme that Susanne came up with. Tell me, young lady, how often did you ask Reeve to send five or ten pounds to Louis?'

'I'm not sure,' Susanne said. 'A dozen times or more.'

'Fifteen times, would you say?'

'Fifteen would be close to accurate.'

'Reeve acknowledged each one, did he?'

'Yes,' said Susanne. 'I have the letters in a drawer upstairs.'

'We'll examine them shortly,' Mr Greenbaum said. 'It's my guess, however, that the letters from Reeve don't mention specific sums and he hasn't committed himself, in writing, to any aspect of fraud.'

'Do you mean he wasn't party to it?' said Susanne.

'Of course he was party to it,' Mr Greenbaum said. 'He helped Harry Coburn milk your trust fund to float Coburn's

railway company. Everything went off the rails when Coburn's daughter and Louis . . . well, I need not elaborate.
What I can't deduce is when Susanne's letters to Reeve were
replaced by others requesting far larger sums.'

'Louis!' Buckie said. 'Damned if it isn't Louis.'

'No, Coburn and Reeve were in cahoots, so it was probably
Reeve who arranged to have the letters doctored. I fear we'll
never know the truth unless Coburn is laid by the heels.'

'Is that likely?' Susanne asked.

'Possible, not probable,' said Mr Greenbaum. 'If a warrant
is issued for his arrest in Scotland it will, with time, be lost in
the files of the English system. Meanwhile, unless I miss my
guess, Mr Coburn is sojourning in Italy or en route to
America. The Strayhorn railway account in the United Caledonian has been closed, so I fancy Mr Coburn made off with
a profit of not far short of ten thousand pounds, including the
sums he extracted from gullible local investors.'

'You mean Bette, don't you?' said Buckie.

'I'm afraid I do.'

'She gave money to Oakley and he gave it to Coburn;
money we could ill afford.' Buckie sighed. 'It hardly matters
now Bette's gone, does it? We can't prove anything against
Oakley.'

'How much remains of my father's legacy?' Susanne asked.

'The invested amount – which not even Reeve had the gall
to touch – amounts to seven thousand, two hundred and
twenty-eight pounds. The interest on this sum was paid to
your aunt in quarterly instalments, to the tune of three
hundred and ninety-one pounds per annum. Reeve's fee
for acting as trustee was ten per cent of the interest per
annum, deducted in advance. He earned you no money,
Susanne, not one penny over and above that sum.'

'But that sum is intact, isn't it?'

'It had better be,' said Mr Greenbaum. 'If it isn't, then we'll certainly apply for a warrant against Reeve as well as Harry Coburn and' – he glanced across the table at Buckie – 'against Louis.'

Her uncle slumped back in his chair. He pushed his tongue against his teeth and screwed his eyes tight shut for a moment before he spoke. 'Aye, Louis must be made to pay for his folly.'

'Even if it means imprisonment?' said Mr Greenbaum.

'Even if it means imprisonment,' Buckie confirmed.

And Susanne, very firmly, said, 'No.'

All the offices that Angus Gamrie had vacated had been filled and, somewhat to his chagrin, the Mortcloth and Benefit Society, the Sea Box Society, and the Poor House Trust all seemed to be sailing merrily along without his hand on the tiller. The Presbytery had appointed an ex officio school inspector in the shape of Peter Macfarlane's father, Donald, who made sure that the church's contribution to education was being prudently spent. The fact that the elder's son was courting the minister's daughter by letter from the Greenland seas was not lost on the kirk session. Donald relished the irony, though, and, chuckling heartily, relayed the news to Angus along with all the other gossip that Tom Oakley managed to generate, even with his hands encased in 'lobster creels', and his spirit dimmed.

It wasn't Donald Macfarlane who turned up at Angus's door that evening, however, but the minister's good lady wife.

'Effie?' Angus said. 'What brings you here? Is Tom worse?'

'It is Tom,' Effie Oakley said, 'but he isn't worse.'

'Come awa' in,' Angus said, opening the door wide.

'Is she here, that woman?'

'If you mean Annabel, aye she's here. Where else would she be?' said Angus. 'I hope you haven't come to bring trouble to my house, Effie? We're very settled an' content now, you know.'

Effie stepped into the tiny hall and peered curiously into the kitchen where Annabel was blacking Angus's boots for the following day, and Brogan, well aware of the visitor, peeped out from behind an armchair.

'I can see that,' Effie said.

'Come in, come in. Annabel will make us tea.'

'I'll not stop for tea, Angus, thank you all the same,' said Effie.

The servant girl was good-looking in a large kind of way. When she got up from her place by the hearth, with a boot still stuck on her fist, she towered over both Angus and Effie. It was only when she smiled that Effie saw how fey she was and that her size and full figure weren't mated to much intelligence. She waved the boot in Effie's direction and said over and over again, 'Pleased t'meetcha, pleased t'meetcha, pleased t'meetcha,' until Angus, very gently, told her to stop, which she did at once.

The little red-haired boy was more astute than his mother. Detecting no threat in Effie Oakley, he tugged out a chair for her to sit on, then went and stood by Angus's side and held on to his trouser leg.

'Is that him?' Effie said.

'Aye, that's him.'

Effie's expression softened. 'Tom's spit,' she said. 'No doubt about it.'

'I take it,' Angus said, 'Tom hasn't sent you here to claim him?'

'Nah, nah,' Effie said. 'If it was asked of me I'd take him in, but it will never be asked. Besides, he seems very fond of you, Mr Gamrie.'

'We rub along well enough.' Angus tapped Brogan's crown lightly with his knuckle. 'Don't we, son?'

'Aye,' Brogan answered in a gruff little voice.

The girl remained standing, with the boot on her fist. She

seemed, Effie thought, to be in a state of torpor as if she could only rouse herself when Angus gave her permission to do so. Effie couldn't believe that her husband had lain with this girl and taken advantage of her primitive innocence to pleasure himself, and, thereafter, had cast off all responsibility for her and for his child.

'Why are you here, Effie?' Angus said.

Effie gave herself a shake, like a hen in a dust bath.

'Pleased t'meetcha, please t'meet . . .'

'No, Annabel,' Angus said, and the girl fell silent once more.

He detached Brogan's hand from his trouser leg and, taking Effie by the elbow, accompanied her to the door.

'I had to see him properly for myself,' Effie said. 'I had to be sure.'

'Did you doubt that I'd look after him?' said Angus.

It was evening now, shadows spreading out across the water, the sea like ruffled velvet, while along at the quay the fishermen prepared their boats to sail out with the tide at dawn.

'I wish someone would look after me half as well.' Effie turned and touched his cheek. 'You won't bring Tom down, Angus, will you? I mean, he's all we have, the children and me.'

'No, I won't bring him down.'

'Isn't that why you took her in, to bring him down?'

'Yes,' Angus said, 'but it wasn't the only reason.'

'I know,' Effie said. 'Kindness, not malice. That's what you are, Mr Gamrie, a kind man with too much charity in him for his own good.'

'Is Tom bad?' Angus said.

'Bad?'

'Hurt bad, I mean?'

'Bad enough,' said Effie. 'I doubt he'll ever be the man he was.'

'No bad thing, perhaps,' said Angus. 'No bad thing.'

'Will you be here?' Effie Oakley asked.

'Be here?' said Angus, puzzled.

'If ever I need a helping hand?'

'I'll be here,' Angus promised.

And, having got her answer, Effie walked off through the gloaming, back along the quays to her children and her husband in the manse on the headland behind the hill.

'No,' Susanne said, firmly, 'I won't do anything to harm Louis.'

Mr Greenbaum nodded, as if he had expected as much.

'And Coburn?' he asked. 'What about Coburn?'

'He's beyond our reach, is he not?'

'Come now, Susanne,' Buckie said. 'You must do something. You can't allow Coburn and Reeve to rob you of half your fortune without—'

'I'm not thinking of Harry Coburn. I'm thinking of Darsie,' Susanne said. 'In any case, I'll still have an income of over three hundred pounds a year. Prim survives on a tenth of that amount. We will be comfortable on what's left. However, Mr Greenbaum, I'll be obliged if you dismiss Spencer Reeve as trustee forthwith and take possession of all the stocks and securities that he manages on my behalf, together with all and any interest payments that have accrued.'

'Screw him,' Buckie said. 'Screw him for every penny you can, Greenbaum. He'll consider himself lucky not to find himself in court.'

'My father worked hard,' Susanne said. 'He earned his wealth honestly. But his legacy has become a burden to me. Indeed, the only good that's come out of it was that it brought me here to High Cross. I'm not cut out for idleness, however. I'll continue to teach at school until I find a husband who will love me because of who I am and not for what I own.'

Buckie and Mr Greenbaum exchanged a glance that had in it a hint of doubt, as if they suspected that no such man existed.

'Yes, I know you think I'm foolish,' Susanne continued. 'Perhaps it is a mistake on my part to write off such a very large sum of money and let two rogues go unpunished, but think what it would cost us to pursue Harry Coburn and Spencer Reeve, and how we would ruin Louis's life in the process. Is that worth several thousand pounds that, in a sense, I've never had? I think not.'

'I'll manage the matter as you suggest, Miss Thorne,' Mr Greenbaum said. 'Transfer of all stocks, bonds and securities; interest to be paid in your name into a drawing account in the Merchants and Traders Bank, Dundee branch. Will that be satisfactory?'

'Most satisfactory, thank you.' Susanne looked up at the ceiling. 'Now, I think we should call Louis down and tell him what's been decided, before he does himself an injury by lying on the floorboards.'

'Lying on the floorboards?' said Mr Greenbaum.

'Eavesdropping,' Susanne said. 'Would you not be eavesdropping, Mr Greenbaum, if your future depended on it?'

Mr Greenbaum laughed. 'Indeed, lass, indeed I would.'

And Buckie, roaring, ordered Louis to come downstairs at once.

He snuggled up to his pretty little wife, one hand about her waist, the other upon her breast. She did not draw away. Her nightgown slipped and slithered between them as he pressed himself against her. Her petulance, he knew, was part of a regime to excite him. Soon there would be giggling and panting and a fair bit of noise to entertain his cousin in her bed across the passageway. He insinuated his hand on to Darsie's swollen belly and stroked her. When she began to murmur and purr he placed his mouth close to her ear and whispered, 'Your papa was right, dearest; she is an awfully easy mark.'

'Did you have to embrace her quite so tightly, though?'

'I was grateful. I am grateful.'

'And all that weeping, Louis. Most unbecoming.'

'A few tears go a long way. Even Greenbaum was moved by my show of remorse.'

'Now, now, naughty boy,' Darsie said, cupping her hand over his, 'you were very upset, and behaved abominably. Kissing her on the lips and rubbing against her as if you were about to . . .'

'What? About to what?'

'I am too much of a lady to say.'

'Oh, you're a lady all right,' said Louis. 'I can tell.'

'How? How can you tell?'

'Gentlemen do not have this sweet little hideaway, do they?'

Darsie moaned, then, twisting, kissed him on the mouth.

'Don't you wish she was here with you, instead of me?'

'Of course I don't,' said Louis.

'Such an easy mark, hmm? Such a little mark for you to aim at?'

'Susanne would not be so easy as you, my love.'

'Oh! And what does *that* mean?'

'Hush,' he said. 'Hush. She wouldn't have been right for me, not nearly as fitting as you are.'

'Fitting? Am I fitting?'

'Perfectly,' Louis said.

'What about her money, the money Papa borrowed?'

'Gone for good, I fancy,' Louis said. 'She seems, as you heard, quite willing to forgive us. At least your papa will benefit, as was his intention. Susanne has plenty of money left, however, and she will be our mainstay. Believe me, darling, as long as she stays here we will do very well out of her.'

'Why would she want to stay here now you are married?'

'Because she adores me,' Louis said.

'And will she look after me, and baby too?'

'Of course, she will,' said Louis.

Darsie giggled. 'Would you like me to turn over now?'

'If it isn't too much trouble, dear,' said Louis.

23

In fair weather and foul each day at noon Prim went out, alone, to the oak on the Old Kirk road to observe the traffic that trickled into town. She was pinched and drawn, and less patient with the children now, and it gradually dawned on Susanne that her colleague was pining for Alan Redpath and hoped that one day he would come riding over the hill, like the prince in a fairy story.

When Susanne thought of Alan, however, she imagined him living in a grand house in Edinburgh New Town – a house very much like the Thorne mansion in London – riding to the infirmary every afternoon to work miraculous cures upon the poor and needy and be duly worshipped, like a hero or a saint. The reality, she suspected, would be much more mundane; almost everything was these days.

'I think Prim's lost her reason,' Zena said. 'Don't you?'

'No,' said Susanne, staunchly. 'I think she's just melancholy.'

'Surely you can be melancholy,' said Zena, 'without standing about for three-quarters of the hour under a tree in pouring rain. How long is she going to keep it up?'

'Ask her.'

'Not I,' said Zena. 'She not over-fond of me as it is, and I might need her approval if I ever want to become a teacher here.'

'Must it be here?' said Susanne.

Zena glanced at her friend, and blinked. 'Pardon?'

'Why must it be in Strayhorn?' Susanne said. 'There are plenty of other school boards to whom you could apply for a teaching post.'

'You know,' said Zena, 'I never thought of that.'

'Unless,' Susanne said, 'you prefer to stay close to your family?'

'Hah!' Zena said.

'Or to be on hand when Peter comes in search of you.'

'Peter?' said Zena. 'Now which Peter would that be?'

'Do not be coy,' Susanne said. 'At least you can be sure that Peter Macfarlane *will* come back to you?'

'What about Gregor?'

'What about him?'

'Do you think he'll come back to you?'

'Perhaps,' Susanne said.

'That isn't very positive, is it?' Zena said.

'I'm not a positive person.'

'Well, at least you're not daft enough to squander your dinner time loitering on the Old Kirk road looking out for a man who's long gone away.'

'Do you think he'll ever come back here?' Susanne asked.

'He'd be a fool if he did,' said Zena.

The gravestone was a good deal smaller than the coffin and had cost a great deal less money; a fact that Louis was at pains to point out. Of late, her cousin had become quite an amateur economist, as if he, not Susanne, was the breadwinner and he, not Buckie, head of the house of Hollander. He had examined the bill for his mother's coffin and had queried every screw and sheet of varnish, and, to his father's annoyance, had taken it upon himself to select a gravestone and commission the inscription from a monument-maker in Pittenweem.

Louis's dictatorial penny-pinching also extended into the kitchen and Nancy suddenly found herself having to account for every tea leaf and fish head, a situation that led to several blazing rows. Only Darsie's interventions saved the day, for Darsie, it seemed, had the knack of placating not only her husband but also the servant by feigning a sweet sort of helplessness that, in Susanne's opinion, was no more than skin deep.

At last Bette's monument was delivered to Strayhorn cemetery and erected above the grave and Muckle Tam was despatched to High Cross to inform the Hollanders that the stone was ready for inspection. It was too late in the evening for the Hollanders to trail out to do the honours but Muckle Tam was instructed to order a gig from Sandy Raiker for half past ten the following morning, Saturday, to convey the family to the cemetery, and bring them back again.

At supper that night Darsie declared that she had been far too fond of 'Aunt' Bette to endure a visit to the graveside and Nancy, smelling trouble, volunteered to stay behind with the mother-to-be, and grumbled enough to make her offer sound convincing.

Saturday dawned red and raw with a froth of black cloud along the horizon and a bite to the wind more suited to November than May.

Deprived of laudanum, Buckie drank brandy with his breakfast to dull the ache in his legs, before Nancy helped him into his serge trousers and high boots and strapped him into the unfashionable greatcoat with the sealskin collar that he'd had since his whaling days. Then, with kisses and tears from Darsie to cheer them on their way, Buckie, Louis and Susanne set off to inspect the stone that Louis had picked to mark his mama's grave.

'Is that it?' Buckie said, aghast. 'Look at the size of it. Dear God, Louis, you need a glass to read the writing on it. What does it say? I can't get down far enough to see it. Susanne, what does it say?'

'Not very much, Uncle,' Susanne told him.

She knelt on the damp grass before the stone, which was hardly taller than her kneecap, and peered at the cheap gilt lettering that had already begun to peel. Buckie leaned on her shoulder while Louis, whistling soundlessly, stared off into grey space.

'"Elizabeth Garrett Hollander",' Susanne read aloud. '"Eighteen hundred and six to eighteen hundred and fifty-four".'

'Is that all?' said Buckie.

'No, it says . . .' Susanne paused. '"Sadly, Remembered".' She frowned at her cousin. 'The comma, Louis, the comma?'

'What about the comma?'

'Nothing about Bette being my wife and Louis's mother?' said Buckie.

Susanne shook her head. 'Nothing.'

'Louis, what possessed you?' Buckie said.

'It's immaterial,' Louis said. 'I mean irrelevant. I mean, you'll be buried next to Mama on one side and I'll be on the other and any passer-by who expresses the slightest interest in our history can guess—'

'Guess?' Buckie snapped. 'I'll not have anyone guessin' anythin' about my Bette. And what's this – this "Sadly Remembered" nonsense? Was there not a poem or biblical quotation you could have picked instead?'

'They charge by the letter, don't you know?' said Louis.

'By God in heaven!' Buckie said. 'You skinflint, you un-grateful dog, doing your poor mama's marker on the cheap. If I were younger, by Gum, I'd thrash you for this, Louis.'

'It has the virtue of being succinct, does it not?' Louis said. 'What's the point in raising some enormous monument with angels and crosses for the gulls to shit on and the weather to erode. It makes no difference to Mama now. She was never a great believer in wasting money on fripperies.'

'Fripperies!' Buckie raised his stick. 'I'll give you fripperies, you – you . . .'

Susanne scrambled to her feet. 'Stop it,' she said. 'Stop it this instant. We are being observed.'

Buckie grunted and swung round. 'Observed? Observed by whom?'

'She means Benbow,' Louis said, with a sigh. 'He's a half-mile away, for heaven's sake.'

'No,' said Susanne. 'There, by the shed: a man.'

All three stared in the direction of the man half hidden by the wall of the potting shed. He looked like a tinker or tramp, all dressed in black, a scarf wrapped raggedly about his jaws to hold on his chimneypot hat.

'Good God!' said Buckie. 'It's Oakley.'

'Come to pay his respects, no doubt,' said Louis. 'What's wrong with the man, why don't he come forward? You,' he shouted. 'You, show yourself. We know who you are, sir, and wish a word with you.' But when Louis started towards him, Tom Oakley skiddled off around the buttress out of sight.

'Odd!' said Buckie.

'Damned odd,' Louis agreed. 'Have you seen enough here, Pappy?'

'I've seen all there is to see. It isn't much, is it?' He reached out and took his son's arm. 'I'm disappointed in you, Louis, very disappointed. I thought you had more respect. If your mama's looking down on us now, she'll be annoyed with you, too.'

'She isn't looking down on us,' Louis said. 'Pappy, she's dead.'

'Aye, she's in heaven.'

'There is no heaven,' Louis said.

'Is that what you think?'

'Yes, that's what I think.'

Father and son strolled away from the stone on the rim of

the churchyard, each leaning on the other, arguing in hectoring tones.

Susanne had brought no flowers, no green wreath but she promised herself that she would come again soon to dress her aunt's grave and add a little colour to the corner. At no great pace, she trailed her uncle and cousin along the path that skirted the manse, heading for the gig that Benbow had parked at the end of the Old Kirk road.

Then a voice said, '*Psssssst.*'

When Susanne glanced round, Zena rose from behind the hedge.

'Here, I'm over here.'

Louis and Buckie were already boarding the gig, still, as far as Susanne could make out, arguing. She peered over the hedge that bounded the lawn.

'He told me it was you,' Zena said. 'But I didn't believe him.'

'Oh, it was your father then? He hurried off before we could speak.'

'He's shy these days, aren't you, Dad?' Zena said. 'Now, come along, stop hiding and say good-day to Susanne. She's not going to eat you. She's been to look at Mrs Hollander's marker and needs a few words of spiritual comfort, I expect. Don't you, Susanne?'

'Well, I . . .'

Zena reached down and, as if pulling a rabbit from a hat, hoisted her father up by the black wool scarf. 'Say good morning to Miss Hollander, Dad. Surely you haven't forgotten all your manners.'

'Good morning, Miss Hollander,' Thomas Oakley whispered.

It had been weeks since Susanne had seen the minister, not since the night of his accident, in fact. She was shocked by the change in him. He was unshaven and his bristles looked spiky, like bits of broken shell. His hair had turned rusty white, and his cheeks were so sunken that his teeth seemed huge, his once charming smile a parody of itself.

'Spiritual comfort, Dad,' Zena reminded him.

'I find gardening impossible,' Thomas Oakley stated. 'It is the bane and bugbear of my life not to be able to wield a spade and dig in the rich and fertile soil with which God in his goodness has supplied us.'

'Oh!' Susanne said, softly.

'Can't pot, you see.' With the bony grin still fixed on his face, he brought his hands from under the line of the hedge and held them aloft. 'Can't even pish properly, to tell you the truth. Does that shock you, Miss Hollander? Susanne, is it not?'

'Yes, Susanne.'

'He's been down to look at the stone, haven't you, Dad?'

'Not,' Tom said, 'awfully impressive, is it?'

'No.' Susanne glanced at Zena, questioningly. 'No, Mr Oakley, it's not.'

'Bette deserved better.'

'I agree,' Susanne said.

'She was a good woman, a sound woman. I knew her well.'

'Zena, is . . .'

'Nah, he's fine. He rambles a lot but he's not gone west by south, not completely. He'll come round when he gets the baskets off. Won't you, Dad?'

The hands, still held aloft, displayed clumsy gloves woven out of slender withy, like miniature cages, his fingers and wrists bound in grubby linen strips.

'When will that be?' Susanne asked.

'Monday week,' said Thomas Oakley. 'Monday week, Monday week.'

Susanne, brows raised, looked to Zena for confirmation.

'Yes, Monday week it is,' Zena said. 'However, we've had news this morning, very exciting news. Haven't we, Dad?'

'Very exciting, yes, a treat, a fair treat.'

'We're having an assistant,' Zena said. 'Apparently Mr Arbuthnot wrote to the Presbytery, and the Presbytery are sending us an assistant minister to help out until Dad is back on his feet again. Isn't that right, Daddy? His name's Mr Henceforth, and he's young,' Zena went on in a rush. 'Trained at the University of St Andrews, no less. Mr Arbuthnot picked him from a list. Mr Arbuthnot says once he's fully ordained and earns his licence, he'll go far.'

'Where will he stay?' Susanne asked.

'He'll stay with us,' Zena said. 'Mama will make up a bed in the study 'cause Papa doesn't use the study now. Mr Arbuthnot's factor has already delivered a nice wee chest of drawers for his clothes an' things.'

'Well, that is good news,' said Susanne, uncertainly.

'Good news! It's wonderful news,' said Zena, leaping up and down. 'Just think, Susanne, an assistant minister of my very own. Oh, I tell you, I can hardly wait to meet him.'

'When do you expect him to arrive?'

'Monday week,' said Tom.

It was over in a matter of minutes. There was no warning, no time to prepare. The schoolroom droned with arithmetical recitations and the scratching of chalk on slate. Prim was at the rear of the class, helping the youngest Macfarlane fathom the mysteries of one of Robert Burns' more respectable poems. Seated on the little teaching stool, Susanne was coaxing the difficult nine-times table from the infants when Matthew Brown, whose seat was by the window, suddenly shot to his feet, and shouted, 'Miss, Miss, there's a cuddy in the yard.'

'It's just MacKinnon's donkey again,' Susanne said.

'Nah, Miss Thorne. It's a big grey, wi' a man on its back.'

Susanne looked towards the rear of the classroom, straight

at Miss Primrose who, as if she had been lifted by a sea wave, rose from among the desks and floated towards the door. Lost to all sense, she tugged open the door and wafted like thistle seed into the school yard where a man had just dismounted from a huge dappled grey stallion.

He held the horse by the check-rein and stalked across the yard.

'Open the window, Matt,' Susanne said and, pushing the children to one side, leaned over the sill and peered out.

Dr Redpath looked much the same. He wore a bottle-green coat, a wide-brimmed hat and riding-boots that came up to mid-thigh.

He advanced, angrily, on Miss Primrose.

'What,' he cried, 'is the meaning of this?'

'The meaning of what?' said Prim.

'This idiotic letter you sent me?'

'What can't you understand about two words in plain English?'

Alan put the thick leather rein into his mouth and bit down on it, as a patient in pain might do. He dug into his coat pocket and produced a crumpled piece of paper that he proceeded to wave in Gillian's face. He took the leather from his mouth and shouted, '*Think again?* That's all, not even a signature?'

'I didn't think a signature was necessary.'

'Not necessary?' Alan spluttered. 'Good God, Prim, it could have been from any one of a dozen people.'

'In that case why are you here?'

'Pardon?'

'How could you be sure it was me?'

'Because I know of no other person, man or woman, who would be so stupid as to send an unsigned letter of just two words, and expect a reply.'

'Is this your reply?' said Prim.

'Is what my reply?'

'Riding all the way from Edinburgh . . .'

'If you must know, I came by railway to Leven and hired the horse there.'

'. . . all the way from Edinburgh to bellow at me in front of my class.'

Alan raised his shoulders and tipped back his hat; his hair was longer, Susanne noticed. 'I knew it was you for the simple reason that I've been incapable of putting you out of my mind since the day I left. Damn it all, Gillian, did you have to be quite so enigmatic?'

'It brought you here, didn't it?'

'I'm not so impetuous as a rule, you know, not so bold,' Alan said.

'You were bold enough when you rescued Zena from the navigators.'

'Aye, but I didn't have to keep her afterwards.'

'Well,' Prim said, 'you will have to keep me.'

'That's what I'm afraid of,' Alan said. 'Look, there's a train due at Hask at half past two and I wish to be on it. Are you coming, or not?'

'I'm coming,' Prim said.

'Just as you are?'

'Take it, or leave it,' Prim said.

'I'll take it,' Alan Redpath said.

Hands clasped about her waist, he hoisted Prim on to the horse and surged into the saddle behind her. He noticed Susanne in the window and, laughing now, raised his hand and Prim, laughing too, called out, 'Take care of them for me. Take care, Susanne.' And then she was gone through the gap in the school yard wall and galloping away down the long road to Hask with the doctor's arms about her, and never a backward glance.

⋆   ⋆   ⋆

Though the hour was late, she had too much on her mind to go to bed. She lingered in the living-room, staring into the embers of the fire, Ajax snoring on the rug at her feet, the cat on the armchair.

It had fallen on Susanne to explain to the children why Prim had left so abruptly, after which she'd sent Jenny to the manse to summon Zena. The minister's daughter had arrived, breathless and excited, and for an ecstatic quarter of an hour the pair of them had danced gleefully about the classroom, stirred by the promise that if such a wonderful and unexpected thing could happen to poor Miss Primrose it might also happen to them.

In the afternoon, while Zena took charge of the class, Susanne wrote to Mr Arbuthnot and to Mr Macfarlane to inform them of the change of circumstances and suggest that Miss Oakley be employed in a temporary capacity and that she, Susanne Thorne, be elevated to the position of principal until a suitable replacement could be found; then, with Jenny's help, she cleaned Rose Cottage and stored Prim's few possessions in a chest to keep them safe. After the children were released, she locked the doors and, with Zena by her side, walked on to the Old Kirk road and lingered by the oak, chatting to her friend for an hour or more before she went home.

She was confident that Mr Arbuthnot would accept her offer to conduct classes for the rest of the summer term, that Mr Macfarlane would put a favourable case to the Presbytery and that, if she wanted it, the post of teacher was hers for the asking: the trouble was that she was no longer sure she wanted it.

She did not hear her uncle enter the living-room and jumped a little when he said, 'What's wrong, sweetheart, can't you find your way to bed?'

'I've too much on my mind to sleep. Are you in pain?'

'No more than usual,' Buckie said.

He lifted Thimble, held her suspended in his hand for a moment, then, seating himself, placed her on his lap and stroked her ruff soothingly. His robe, like everything else in High Cross, had seen better days. It was patterned with faded whorls of a colour that had once been sea green and had a rope-like tie about the middle. His feet were encased in woollen socks and worn slippers and he had shuffled through the hall without his stick. Thimble purred, lazily washed her whiskers with one paw and burrowed deeper into Buckie's lap.

'Up and gone, just like that, eh?' Buckie said. 'I'd thought at one time the doctor might be the one for you, Susanne.'

'I liked Alan well enough but I did not love him,' Susanne said. 'Besides, I would never have dared declare myself the way Miss Primrose did. It was very immodest of her, in my opinion.'

'"Think again".' Buckie shook his head. 'What sort of a proposal is that, I ask you? Still, it seems to have had the right effect. I imagine our friend Alan didn't know how much he loved the lady until she reminded him – and coming for her on horseback in the middle of a school day: my, my!'

'He hired the horse in Leven. It was probably the only one in the livery stable. He travelled from Edinburgh by train.'

Buckie smiled. 'I see.'

For a minute or more there was no sound in the living-room save the ticking of the clock and the purring of the cat. Then her uncle said, 'It was never a horse with me. It was always a whaling ship. She would be waitin' for me along with the other wives and sweethearts on St Nicholas Craig. I'd spot her from the deck of the *Walrus* or the *Gypsy* or, once, from the *Polar Star*. After three seasons, it was Bette I longed to see in the crowd, waving her braw parasol as the ship passed into harbour.'

'You must have loved her very much,' Susanne said.

'I did not love her at all,' said Buckie. 'She loved me from the very first, though. To be honest when I was out on the ice I loved her more than I did when I sat with her in the parlour in her father's house on the High Street. Bette had a fiery nature, though, and once we came together . . .' He shrugged. 'He was a coppersmith, her father. He dealt in other metals too. He died of a diseased heart some months after we married. We took her old mother in, for there were no other children but Bette. We kept the old wife with us for a good six years, until she died too. I was out in the Davis Strait at the time and it was hard for Bette. He left us some money, her father did, not a great deal but enough to see me started and in the year Louis was born I bought a quarter share in the *Merrilyn*, and never went to sea thereafter.'

'Do you miss her?' Susanne asked.

'Aye,' Buckie said. 'She was a fine, fine ship – and is still.'

'I meant . . .'

'I know what you meant,' said Buckie.

He put the cat behind him, and eased himself upright. He spread his bent legs under the dressing-robe, braced himself, carefully lifted the model ship from its place on the mantelpiece and studied it for half a minute or so.

Susanne watched the miniature longboats swing on their tiny chains and thought of Gregor Oakley far away in Greenland bending to the oars; so small the model was compared to the real thing, a toy, really, in spite of its detail. Much as she loved him, she realised that her uncle's memories were too clean and polished to be entirely trustworthy.

'I noticed an interesting thing in the *Courier* the other day.' Buckie replaced the model on to the mantelpiece. 'The *Catherine* is up for sale. I sailed in her, too, many years back. She's not half the vessel the *Merrilyn* is, but for a barque of her vintage the owners are askin' a very fair price.'

'What constitutes a fair price, Uncle?'

'Forty pounds per part. Sixty-four parts total are on offer.'

'With all her gear and stores?' said Susanne.

'Aye, as she stands in the water.'

'So, it would cost three thousand pounds to buy her outright?'

'Close to.' Buckie clicked his tongue. 'It's a risky business, though, tying up all your money in one vessel.'

'What would it cost, say, to buy the *Merrilyn*?'

'These days, four and a half thousand.'

'I could afford to buy the *Merrilyn*, if she came up for sale.'

'Aye,' said Buckie, innocently. 'I suppose you could at that.'

'And I'd put you in charge of her, to be her captain?'

Her uncle laughed. 'Nah, nah, lass,' he said. 'You need sound legs and a young head to captain a whaler.' He leaned his hand upon the table, pressing into it. 'It's a teacher you'll be, a job as safe and dependable as a bank, with your money snug in Mr Greenbaum's care to keep you in comfort. What reason could you have for investing in whale fishing with all its risks and hazards? No reason at all, Susanne; no possible reason, at all.'

'When I am twenty-one,' Susanne said, 'I may do as I like.'

'You may do as you like now,' said Buckie.

'In that case, I'd like to go to bed.'

'Aye, dearest, off you go to bed,' Buckie said. 'I've bored you enough with all this prattle about ships and whaling.'

'Oh, no, Uncle,' Susanne said. 'I'm not bored at all. Far from it.'

Then she kissed him on the brow and, leaving him to make his own way through the hall, went thoughtfully upstairs to bed.

The study had been scrubbed to within an inch of its life and the brandy bottle removed from the cupboard under the desk, for, Effie said, there was no sense in putting temptation in a young man's way.

Monday week came round at last and Zena sent in a note with Petal to explain to Susanne that she had a chesty cold and would not be able to teach that day, which piece of news did not surprise Susanne in the least. Zena had sniffed and coughed pointedly throughout Sunday morning's service. She had also uttered a low but audible moan when it was announced that as from Monday Mr William Henceforth would be conducting services until such time as Mr Oakley was fully recovered in health and strength and able to resume his duties.

'He may be a horrid little chap, you know,' Susanne reminded her friend.

'Nonsense! He'll be tall and dark and dashing, and as handsome as a town hall clock, you'll see,' Zena said. 'He'll take one look at me an' fall madly in love.'

'What about Peter?'

'Peter? Who's Peter?' said Zena.

The table had been moved into a corner and the bed erected beneath the window where the light of heaven would bathe Mr Henceforth each and every day at dawn. The dressing-table, retrieved from the Arbuthnots' cellar, had been waxed and polished and the drawers lined with clean newspaper. Papa's books had all been put back on the shelf and his sermon notes bundled up and stored in the cupboard where the brandy bottle had once been hidden.

By midday, when Mr Henceforth was expected to arrive, Zena had worked herself up into a high old state.

Effie was busy in the kitchen, eking out the iron rations to ensure that the young, and presumably hungry, assistant would be satisfied. Tom, surly and sulking, had gone off early to St Andrews to keep his appointment with the doctor who would remove the wicker protection and examine his hands for permanent damage. Zena, her chores completed, had vanished into Mama's room to change into her very best frock and pull and tug, muttering, at her tangle of red hair in an attempt to make it neat.

She was at the study window by noon, Roland hanging on to her skirt and bouncing up and down to see what so intrigued his sister.

Noon came and went and Roland, bored, wandered off into the kitchen. As one o'clock approached, Zena's excitement also waned and she was almost on the point of giving up her vigil when the gig jogged into view on the Old Kirk road. 'Oh, oh, oh!' she cried. 'Mama, Mama, he's here.'

'Well, wait behind the door to let him in,' Effie called out.

Zena stood in the hall, tipping her curls, smoothing her skirt, her eyes closed in what may or may not have been prayer until, after what seemed an age, a gentle tap upon the door had her reaching for the handle.

She opened the door, smiling, and looked up.

To her astonishment, Mr Henceforth was exactly as she had pictured him: very tall, very dark, *and* as handsome as a town hall clock, the most handsome man she had ever seen, in fact, the regularity of his features, the manly jut of his jaw knocking even Louis Hollander's good looks into a cocked hat.

'Are – are you . . .' Zena gasped.

'William Henceforth, ma'am,' he said, taking off his little black hat and bowing from his narrow waist. 'If it's not too bold of me on so short an acquaintance, you may call me Willy.'

'Willy?' Zena said.

'I take it this *is* the Strayhorn manse and you *are* Mr Oakley's daughter?'

'Yes, yes,' said Zena, still gawping. 'You've come to the right place. I'm Zena, by the way.'

'The guardian of the keep?' young Mr Henceforth said.

'What? Oh! Aye! Yes! Pardon. Do step inside,' said Zena, blushing, then, remembering her manners, allowed the answer to every maiden's prayer to cross the threshold at last.

24

The hay was in, the wheat stacked and the barley crops were ripening in the fields when an August heatwave descended on the coast, a humid, sweltering tract of weather that drove poor Darsie Hollander, big with child, half mad.

An elderly doctor from Hask purged and bled her but failed to give her relief from toothache, headache and heartburn. Bella McCall, a local midwife, was dragged from the gutting tables to cast an eye over the mother-to-be. When Bella suggested that the lady should get up off her backside and walk on the beach now and then to tighten the child-bearing vessels, Darsie was disinclined to listen. She demanded an instant cure for her all maladies and when Bella pointed out that her business was delivering babies not pandering to spoiled wives, Darsie ordered Louis to throw the wretch out of the house, which Louis, albeit diplomatically, did.

Nancy provided the patient with a cooling diet of clear broth, cold rice puddings, milk jellies and thin oatmeal gruel. Darsie, however, craved meat, strong tea and sherry wine. Louis saw to it that she got what she wanted, but received no thanks for his kindness. In the middle of the month, when the heat was at its peak, he was unceremoniously expelled from the marital bed to sleep on a hammock on the porch. It was left to Susanne to dance attendance on the restless young wife by running forth and back throughout the night with cordials, chamber pots, paper fans and general reassurances that she, Darsie, was not about to die, at least not before morning.

School closed for the summer. Susanne saw little of Zena after that. Tom Oakley's daughter had fallen under the spell of the assistant minister, Mr Henceforth, and seldom left his side. Though undoubtedly handsome, Willy Henceforth had a sly and sinuous streak in his character that Susanne found irksome. In July Susanne received a cheerful letter from Prim, giving news of her marriage to Alan Redpath, and in early August two out-of-date letters from Gregor, but never a word from Harry Coburn who, it appeared, had vanished off the face of the earth.

Letters by the shoal passed between Mr Greenbaum and Neville Spencer Reeve until, in exasperation, Mr Reeve offered Miss Thorne the sum of four hundred guineas in compensation for negligence, while in no manner admitting to said negligence, and agreed to expedite the transfer of all stocks, bonds, shares and securities into the nominee's account in the Merchants and Traders Bank in Dundee. The transfer was duly accomplished and Mr Reeve, heaving a sigh of relief, severed all connection with Susanne Thorne, Flash Harry Coburn and the inhabitants of that benighted land far to the north of St Albans.

With seven thousand pounds in the bank, an annual income of over three hundred pounds and the reliable Mr Greenbaum to manage her financial affairs, Susanne had much to be grateful for. But happiness, like love, was proving elusive and, as the days grew shorter, she became lonely, bored and dispirited. She tried, vainly, to amuse herself by bathing but even the sea was still and sluggish and did not refresh her and being alone on the beach, without Louis to tease, or Buckie to talk to, only increased her depression.

Then, one sultry afternoon, a cart arrived at the house, two burly young men climbed out, had a few words with Louis, clumped upstairs to the big room and carried down, between them, the harmonium.

'What is this? Louis, what are they doing?' Susanne asked.

'Taking away the Seraphine,' Louis answered.

'But why?'

'Because I've sold it,' Louis said. 'I'll never play it again. All that musical nonsense is behind me. Darsie needs more space. And the money will come in useful. I've sold my books, too; no time for reading now.'

In the coppery light of an August afternoon, the parlour organ seemed small and fragile as the men hoisted it on to the cart and roped it down.

'Louis, if you need money . . .'

He held up his hand, pompously. 'No, Susanne. I cannot expect you to support us indefinitely. After the baby comes along I'll search for employment of a suitable nature, or, perhaps, embark on a course of study that will lead to a promising position.'

The men had gone upstairs once more and were lugging down Louis's battered library, armful by armful. Susanne did not dare ask what pitifully small sum the organ, let alone the books, had fetched. She felt a sudden welling of resentment at the realisation that Louis had all but thrown out the instrument simply because Darsie needed space.

'What will you turn your hand to now, Louis? I doubt if you'll ever find an occupation in which your "genius" can profitably flourish. I fear you'll go to your grave promising more than you are ever able to deliver,' Susanne said, waspishly. 'If you'd asked me I'd have bought the organ.'

'Dearest, dearest, don't you see, it's only a gee-gaw, a piece of cheap claptrap that Mama bought to amuse me?' Louis said. 'If you desperately want an organ why don't you buy a proper one, though where you'll keep it and when you'll find peace to play upon it, once the baby comes, I cannot imagine. Ten pounds, I thought, was a very fair price, and I do not have to pay for carriage.'

Hanging on Nancy's arm, Buckie appeared in the doorway.

'What's goin' on here, Louis?' he asked. 'I come in from the closet to find strangers trampin' all over the house.'

'He's sold our harmonium,' Susanne said.

'Who bought it, son?' Buckie said.

'Malone, in Anstruther.'

'Give you a price, did he?'

'He did, Pappy. Pretty fair. It'll buy a crib and small clothes for the baby – and a new dress for Darsie to wear when she has her figure back.'

'A new dress for . . .' Susanne said.

The carriers brushed past her and dumped the last of the books into the cart. One man hopped on to the board behind the pony and took the reins while the other mounted the flat-bed.

'Thank you, gentlemen.'

Louis slipped sixpence into the driver's hand and stepped back as the driver cracked the whip and the cart rolled away with the Seraphine lurching and creaking against the ropes.

'Well, that's a job well done.' Louis turned. 'What do you say, Pappy?'

'I say you're a fool, Louis,' Buckie told him and pointed his stick at Susanne who had started off, alone, towards the rank and stagnant sea.

For much of the spring and early summer Zena clung to the impression that Willy Henceforth was, indeed, courting her and would soon ask Papa for her hand in marriage. As summer deepened, though, Mr Henceforth's attentions became less respectful and it eventually dawned on the girl that the handsome young assistant was bent on attaining entry to parts of her body a good deal less accessible than her hand, and that, by means stealthy and profane, courtship had become seduction.

If lust had been the only blemish on Mr Henceforth's character Zena might have yielded to his blandishments and allowed him to introduce her to the mysteries of sexual intercourse. But Mr Henceforth had other faults too blatant to ignore and in the war with her father he was certainly not her ally.

She continued to wash his shirts, starch his collars, brush his coat, polish his dainty black shoes and sew up the frayed pocket of his trousers. She made his bed, swept his room, emptied the chamber pot, and, at meal times, made sure that he was served with the best of everything. She was as meek and subservient, as doting and devoted, as any aspiring wife and Mr Henceforth was grateful. He expressed his gratitude quite often, in fact, by patting her bottom, tickling her earlobe, stroking her thigh and, on more than one occasion, kissing the nape of her neck in a very polite and tender manner while politely and tenderly squeezing her breasts with both his hands.

'Oh, Mr Henceforth, you shouldn't be doing . . .'

'You are my cross, Zena, my Eve, my temptation.'

'Am I? Am I, really?'

'I simply cannot resist you. If you are ever generous enough to surrender to me, I will happily serve penance with ashes and sackcloth. It's all God's fault, you see, directing me here to do His great work then placing the most desirable woman I have ever seen upon my path. How cruel of Him, do you not think?'

'Oh aye,' Zena would say, breathlessly. 'Cruel.'

Which was all very fine and dandy: Zena was no shrinking violet like her friend Susanne. In different circumstances she might even have been willing to throw herself uninhibitedly into Mr Henceforth's arms.

Circumstances, however, were not as conducive to romance as she had hoped, nor was she quite such a wild and wilful girl as she had imagined herself to be. To add to her woes, her father was making rapid strides on the road to recovery. Once free of the wicker cages he had rallied very quickly and was soon debating all manner of subjects with his young assistant, for it seemed that in Willy he had found not just a willing helper but an echo of himself when young.

As spring stole into summer and the days became longer than the nights, Zena found herself becoming increasingly resentful of the bond that the man she was prepared to love had forged with the man she had learned to hate. She was also aware that come September Mr Henceforth would be called to a charge of his own in some far-off parish, and, in all likelihood, she would never see him again. He would become, like Danny, a ship that had passed in the night, another lost opportunity that she would rue in the evening of her life which, given the way things were going, would be upon her before she could say 'knife'.

All day long cloud gathered along the horizon and humidity increased. Buckie spent the afternoon on the porch, spy-glass in hand. The first of the whalers had returned from Greenland and he was eager for a glimpse of any large ship that might stray round the point. So far, though, he had spotted only fishing vessels and the dumpy hulls of coastal traders and, rocking listlessly in the chair that Nancy had carried from the living-room, spent more time asleep than awake.

Louis too had settled on the porch. There was little by the way of sunshine and, in consequence, little by the way of shade but he, and the dog, sought whatever faint breeze the turn of the tide might bring. His lethargy was excusable, for Darsie had been up half the night, complaining of an ache in her belly and Susanne, at her wits' end, had finally summoned Louis in the hope that his presence might bring some comfort to his wife.

By Louis's calculation Darsie was twenty days shy of

delivery. According to Darsie, though, she had been in labour for weeks and every gaseous eructation, every episode of cramp was a signal that she was about to drop. No amount of telling by Nancy, who seemed curiously well versed in such matters, would convince Darsie that labour was – well, laborious, and that bairns did not leap gladly from the womb at a snap of the fingers.

'Nature,' said Nancy, 'takes her own sweet time about these things. Nature knows what tae do for the best an' Nature'll tell us when the bairn's ready to come out.'

'Now,' Darsie cried. 'Now, it's happening now,' and, with a look of startled bewilderment, loudly broke wind.

On Susanne's instruction a crib, carved not with doves and snowdrops but with tiny sailing ships, had been purchased by Mr Greenbaum in Dundee and despatched to High Cross. Small clothes had been stitched and stored, dusty corners, once piled with books, had been sprinkled with sand and rosewater and scrubbed until the boards shone. For all that, the house reeked of Darsie, a sour, unwholesome odour that trailed from room to room, for she, in her misery, had become careless in her habits and, as her time drew near, became more careless still. No peal of thunder, no streak of lightning, no rushing wind announced the advent of Louis Hollander's son: an interminable evening of sullen, sweating heat faded into oblivion when Darsie finally ploughed her way from the supper table and, about half past nine, panted upstairs to bed.

Nancy cleared the dining table and seated herself on the step by the kitchen door to eat her supper, fan herself with a week-old copy of the *Courier* and watch Thimble, motionless as a statue, crouch by a hole in the hen-house, waiting for a mouse that refused to appear.

On the porch Buckie and Louis sipped wine and soda water and, in blessed silence, watched stars appear and disappear in scarves of cloud.

Exhausted by Darsie, and the heat, Susanne reclined against a cushion, thinking of Gregor Oakley's letters in which he described great cold sheets of ice and, in passing, mentioned that he missed her very much indeed. She had just closed her eyes on a vision of clear blue skies and white ice, when a series of piercing screams from the room upstairs brought her scrambling to her feet.

'Oh, God!' Louis exclaimed. 'What is it now?'

'Where's Ajax?' Buckie asked, looking round.

'Under the porch.' Louis hoisted up the jar of soda water and casually topped up his glass. 'Ajax knows better than to venture upstairs. Heaven knows, he's been cuffed for it often enough.'

Susanne said, 'I'd better go up and see what's bothering her.'

'Let Nancy do it,' Louis said. 'It won't be anything important.'

'No,' Susanne said. 'I'll go.'

She stepped wearily through the wide-open door into the hall only to discover that Nancy was already on the stairs. She followed the servant's broad bottom upstairs into Louis's room where Darsie, all dignity shed, squatted unsteadily on a chamber pot, screaming at the pitch of her voice, '*I wet myself. I wet myself. I wet . . .*'

Nancy put the candle-holder on the floor and, kneeling, wrapped an arm about the hysterical girl. 'There, there,' she said, soothingly, 'accidents do happen,' then, glancing towards the bed, saw that the sheets were stained not just with water but with blood and mucus too. She stiffened and, lifting Darsie bodily from the pot, sat her spread-legged upon the floor.

'Susanne,' Nancy said, evenly. 'Send Louis to fetch the midwife.'

Wide-awake now, Susanne said, 'Has her labour started?'

'Started?' Nancy answered. 'Damned near finished, more like.'

'Do you like that?' Mr Henceforth said. 'Does it give you pleasure?'

'I wouldn't say pleasure, no,' Zena replied.

'What would you say?'

'I – I don't know.'

'You're such an innocent, Zena, such a lamb.'

'That's as may be, Willy,' Zena said, 'but I'm not quite ready for the slaughter yet.'

Mr Henceforth laughed, trailed his lips across her bare shoulder and lightly licked the pulsing vein on her throat.

The touch of his tongue affected Zena in ways that might broadly be described as stimulating. Much as she enjoyed being kissed, she had reached the conclusion that she was no more in love with Willy Henceforth than he was with her. Even so, she was willing to play the game, to skate on the thin ice of desire in the hope that something approximating true love might come out of it.

They were on the drying lawn by the wall of the house. The manse was in darkness, the fire smoored, the last candle snuffed out. Papa was snoring by Mama's side upstairs, all the little acorns lost in dreamland.

It had been no easy matter to slip from her bed, though, and, throwing a cape over her nightdress, steal out of the house. Now the cape lay on the grass and her nightdress, damp with perspiration, clung to her like a second skin. Mr Henceforth had already brushed the nightdress from her shoulder and she knew that when he had finished with her neck, he would slide the garment down to expose her breast, would put his lips to her breast and . . .

'Ah, Willy, there you are.'

Mr Henceforth instantly removed his hands from Zena's soft flesh.

'Who said that?' he asked.

'I did,' Tom Oakley answered.

The minister stood by the corner of the house. He wore his long black preaching coat over a nightshirt, his legs and feet bare, his bandaged hands tucked into his coat pockets.

Zena said, 'Papa, I can explain.'

'I would, on balance, prefer to hear from Mr Henceforth,' Tom told her. 'So, now, William, am I to assume that you stumbled upon my daughter taking the air and seized the opportunity to instruct her in the Theory of Moral Sentiments, the subject of our discourse before supper?'

'No, sir, I cannot in honesty claim that to be the case.'

'You hoped to mow her then?' said Tom, and before the young man could bolt, clapped an arm across his shoulder. 'It'll serve you ill to lie to me, Willy. When it comes to the folly, infamy and misery of unlawful pleasure I am, as Zena will attest, more expert than you will ever be. Birds of a feather, are we, Willy? Of course we are.'

'Mr Oakley, it's not what you suppose it to be. Zena . . .'

'Zena, like Barkis, is willing; is that what you're telling me?'

'Pardon?' said Mr Henceforth, whose reading did not extend to Dickens.

'In other words, you blame my daughter for arranging this assignation.'

'I – no, my intentions . . .'

'Your intentions, sir?' Papa Oakley said. 'Do you expect me to believe that your intentions are honourable?'

The heat of the night was no less oppressive than the heat of the day and in the faint sheen of starlight and the fall of light from the August moon, Zena could make out the sweat on Willy's brow.

He no longer reminded her of Louis Hollander, or, for that matter of Papa. He was neither sufficiently stupid nor sufficiently heartless to be compared to either one. He was nothing but a handsome jellyfish who had learned to speak the language of his betters.

'Papa . . .' Zena began.

'Keep out of it, Zena,' Tom told her. 'I'm here to get you what you want.'

'What I want?' said Zena. 'What *do* I want?'

Tom ignored her. 'Now, Mr Henceforth, let me ask you once more; are your intentions honourable?'

'Well – well, yes, of course,' Willy said.

'Good,' said Tom. 'May I take it that you intend to marry my daughter?'

'*Papa!*' Zena cried. '*No!*'

'It will give me great pleasure to call the first banns on Sunday to herald my return to the pulpit,' Tom Oakley said, adding, 'The wedding? September, shall we say?'

Zena threw herself upon him. '*No, Papa, no.*'

'Do you not want to be married, Zena?'

'Not – not to this chap.'

'Nonsense!' Tom Oakley said. 'How many opportunities do you suppose you'll have to meet an educated gentleman of the cloth who not only loves you but, apparently, desires you? Few, my dear, precious few. Have you not told me often enough that you want released from my care? Marriage is the answer, the only answer. Mr Henceforth is the answer, in fact. He'll make you a fine, loyal, loving husband. Won't you, Willy? Well, won't you?'

'Yes,' Willy said: then, 'No.'

'No?' Tom said.

'No?' said Zena.

'I'd be only too pleased to marry your daughter, Mr Oakley.' Willy Henceforth paused. 'But I fear that my wife would not approve.'

'Your wife?' Tom said.

'Your wife?' said Zena.

'I've a wife and child lying in wait in Dumfries.'

'You said nothing to me about a wife,' Tom said.

'My marital state seemed of no consequence, not worth the mention.'

'You despicable coward.' Tom Oakley raised his fist, then thought better of it. 'You'd have taken my daughter under false pretences, would you, and left her to bear the consequences? I'll have you struck from the list for ordination. By God, Henceforth, you'll never darken my pulpit, or any other pulpit, again.'

'Why?'

'Because your behaviour has been contemptible.'

'Why?'

'Because you have broken my daughter's heart.'

'Have I?' Willy Henceforth said and, stepping to one side, nodded at the minister's daughter, who lay gasping with helpless laughter on the grass.

Louis's insistent knocking drew Bella McCall from her bed. She was bundled into Sandy Raiker's cart, brought at the gallop to High Cross and arrived not a moment too soon.

Bella was a large, stout woman, strong as a ploughman's horse. She had delivered many of the children who roamed the streets of Strayhorn, and a fair number of foals and calves besides. She had learned the craft of birthing from her mother and had attended so many ugly presentations that one glance at Darsie Hollander – spread-eagled on the tangled sheets with her feet braced against the board – informed her that labour was well advanced.

Nancy had lighted a fire in the old grate and the air was wreathed with coal smoke and steam from pots of boiling water toted up from the kitchen. Darsie had been sponged clean of the mess discharged from her bowels but, not unnaturally, was drenched in sweat and red as a beetroot with the pain of contractions that appeared to be coming without respite. In spite of her animosity towards the Hollander girl, who was too spoiled and spongy for Bella's taste, the midwife was neither slack nor clumsy in her ministrations, for a live birth was worth an extra guinea, as well as a good drink from the father's bottle, and Bella could make good use of both.

She hesitated for a few seconds, then, rolling up her sleeves, pounced on poor Darsie and, holding the girl down with her forearm, licked two big fingers and inserted the tips, quite gently, to test the width and thickness of the orifice.

Darsie, who hadn't drawn breath for what seemed like half an hour, shrieked at the pitch of her voice: '*Papa, Papa. I – want – my – papa.*'

Bella glanced over her shoulder. 'Where is her papa, then?'

'Only Satan can tell you that,' said Nancy.

Louis fitted the glass into his father's hand and said, 'Try not to spill it, Pappy. You know what brandy costs these days.'

'I should, since I'm paying for it.' Buckie gripped the glass firmly. 'Is it hard, son, to listen to your wife in pain?'

'I just wish she wouldn't keep calling for Harry.'

'Be thankful,' Buckie said, 'she isn't calling for you. Your mother was at it for twenty hours while I tramped the carpet and wished I was back at sea.'

'Twenty hours! Ye gods!' said Louis. 'Do we have to put up with this racket for another twenty hours?'

'Bella will see it through, however long it takes. She's a good woman with the hooks and the gutting knife, so I'm told, and a safer pair of hands for a birthing isn't to be found in the Kingdom of Fife.'

'Does she charge by the hour?' Darsie's shrieks rose in an ear-splitting crescendo. 'I mean, is there a tariff for this sort of thing?'

'She's a midwife, Louis, not a lawyer,' Buckie said.

'What did you pay to have me delivered?'

'Six guineas, I think,' Buckie said. 'I was so relieved that Bette came through her ordeal unscathed, and so pleased and proud to have a healthy son at the end of it that I never thought twice about cost.'

'I don't suppose you're so proud of me now?' said Louis.

It had been an hour since Bella McCall had gone upstairs, an hour of listening to Darsie scream for her father. Some time ago Nancy had thumped downstairs to fill another pot, though what phase of the process of giving birth required such quantities of boiling water neither man could imagine. Nancy was sweating and red-faced, as if she, not Darsie, was in the final stages of labour. In answer to Buckie's anxious enquiry all she would say was, 'Soon, soon,' before she hurried off upstairs again.

The dog and cat had been put out on to the porch. Ajax had scratched forlornly at the door for a while but had gone quiet now and, Louis suspected, had gone off to find a spot of peace in the yard. He envied the dog, that big, shaggy, soft-eyed beast that loved everyone indiscriminately, and had not a care in the world. He glanced at his father, a once hardy soul, shrivelled now by age and illness, and wondered if one day his son would experience the same feeling of disgust that he felt for his father now.

He paced about the living-room, inspected the model of the *Merrilyn* as if it were an object in a museum, peered at the spy-glass hanging from its thong, and tidied the curtain that in an hour or so would be tinted by dawn light. He yawned, sipped brandy, and wandered out into the hallway, his back to the dark ramp of the staircase. He tapped the barometer and adjusted the hands of the grandfather clock, then, just as he'd turned to return to the living-room, heard a cry, faint at first, but growing louder and more fractious by the second.

All dishevelled, her dress stained with blood, Susanne

appeared at the top of the stairs and, stooping, called out, 'It's a boy, Louis, a fine, big healthy boy.'

'And Darsie?' he said, thickly. 'How's Darsie?'

But Susanne did not reply.

The baby was long-bodied, with a lick of dark Hollander hair plastered to his soft scalp. He did not feel weightless, as Susanne had supposed he would, nor was he limp and passive in her arms. He wriggled his tiny unblemished legs, curled his miniature fingers into fists, and bawled fit to burst.

She held him as firmly as she dared, the woollen blanket slipping to expose the blue-black remnant of the cord that had attached him to Darsie, the little wound that Bella said must be bound to prevent infection.

Nancy, cooing, had washed him with a sponge and dabbed him dry with a towel while Bella awaited the expulsion of the placenta, which was supposed to be a painless, if bloody, process. The joy that Susanne had experienced on first holding Louis's child faded swiftly, for the midwife was busy again, working over the limp figure on the bed. She had watched in wonder as Darsie's parts had spread and, head first, the baby had appeared and Darsie with one last agonising thrust had pushed him out into Bella's safe hands and, that done, had fallen back insensible. She was still insensible and shivering now with a rigor that resembled the rigor of death. The cord had been tied but there was still blood. Susanne hid the child's eyes from the sight, turning away, but watched over her shoulder as Bella mopped and swabbed.

'Is she dying?' Susanne asked, in a whisper.

'Aye,' Bella rasped, 'she's fair wore out, though I canna think why since it was such a quick birth. She's coolin' down an' the blood's comin' in quantity but there's a wheen o' stuff to come yet, I'm thinkin'. I'll give her a bit rub soon if it won't expel of its own volition.'

'Will I fetch Louis?' Susanne asked.

'What use can he be to her now?' said Nancy.

Then Darsie shuddered, her belly quivered like the flesh of a horse bothered by flies, she let out a sigh that lingered in her throat, and was suddenly, shockingly, still.

'Oh, God, dear God!' Susanne murmured, and pressed Louis's lovely new-born son even closer to her chest.

25

For four days Darsie lingered in the vicinity of death's door, though the doctor from Hask could find little wrong with her once the bleeding had stopped. To be on the safe side, he administered a small dose of ergot and quinine and left a bottle of infant wine that he claimed would purge the baby's tubes and provide nourishment until a wet nurse could be found or Darsie persuaded to suckle the infant herself. Given that Darsie could hardly bear to look at her son, the possibility of her agreeing to attach him to her teat seemed remote. Water-pap mixed with small quantities of cow's milk kept young Hollander alive until Bella McCall found a farmer's wife whose baby had just been weaned but who still had milk enough to nurse the new arrival.

Louis wept a great deal at his wife's bedside and begged her not to leave him while, downstairs, Mrs McCorkindale, the farmer's wife, cradled Adam to her ample bosom and coaxed him to accept her milk.

Adam was a name chosen by popular vote; Darsie's suggestion that he be christened Henry Coburn Hollander had been rejected out of hand. Darsie was in no fit state to argue now and had so little interest in the creature who had given her so much pain that the Hollanders might have named him Lucifer for all she cared.

'If he goes off to sea,' Nancy said, 'he'll be called High Cross; that's no fit name for a boy tae be saddled with.'

'By the look of him,' Susanne said, 'he might be called the Dribbler.'

'The Dribbler, hah!' Buckie exclaimed. 'Now there's an apposite handle for him. Look how his toes curl when he sucks. Still, Adam is best, since he's the first man born since my Bette passed away.'

Entranced by the noisy pink bundle, Ajax would have washed Adam's face with a long pink tongue if Nancy hadn't pushed him off. Thimble, small, furry and greedy for milk, was also chased away from the crib and, after a day or so, fell into a sulk and ignored the small intruder.

Louis's attitude to his son was more difficult to determine. One minute he was all that a proud father should be, laughing and jolly, lifting a glass to toast the wee chap's safe arrival and bestow hearty blessings on his head. Next minute he would be sunk in melancholy, convinced that God had given him a child only to take him away again. When not wetting Darsie's sheets with his tears, he lounged outside on the porch, staring morosely at the sea, until, on the afternoon of the fourth day after delivery, Darsie sat up, demanded beef stew and a glass of sherry and complained that her nightgown needed changed.

Susanne carried the baby upstairs to encourage Darsie to feed him. Darsie would have none of it. She whipped her head away as if the smell, let alone the sight, of her first-born offended her. Bathed and dressed in his prettiest gown and bonnet, he seemed too perfect to ignore, but somehow Darsie managed it. She fussed with her cap and her bed-jacket, and enquired just when she might expect her supper brought up, and a glass of sherry too, if you please.

'Oh, Darsie, look at him. Is he not beautiful?'

'Not to me he's not,' Darsie said.

'He's hungry, you know.'

'Take him back to that woman downstairs,' Darsie said.

'Darsie, he's your flesh and blood.'

'He's Louis Hollander's son, not mine. If you want him,

Susanne, you may have him. I do not care if I never see him again.'

'What an awful thing to say!'

'Awful or not, take him away.'

Shaking off the responsibilities of motherhood was no simple matter, however. To Darsie's disgust, she was obliged to express milk from her swollen breasts two or three times a day, a humiliating ritual that, coupled with sordid changes in her shape, kept her skulking in her room and no amount of coaxing would bring her downstairs to join the family.

As soon as it became clear that Darsie was not about to depart for the great hereafter, Louis rapidly regained his equilibrium. He seemed quite willing to spend the rest of his married life sleeping in a hammock on the porch, or in his mama's bed in his mama's bedroom, while waiting for something that would engage his interest and restore his fortunes to turn up.

The hot August days were marked by the arrival and departure of Mrs McCorkindale in Sandy Raiker's gig at a fee that had Louis muttering, though it was Susanne and Buckie, between them, who footed the bill. The house in High Cross bay had never seen so much hustle and bustle. While Mrs McCorkindale did her duty, Sandy or, more often, Billy Benbow exchanged gossip with Nancy in the kitchen and enquired now and then if anything had been heard from Mr Coburn or, for that matter, from Dr Redpath and his teacher bride.

Languishing upstairs, Darsie heard laughter in the rooms below and, convinced that they were laughing at her, would swing herself from bed and drum her heels upon the boards until someone, usually Susanne, appeared to ask, rather crossly, what she wanted now and could it not wait until baby had been fed or changed or, like a little parcel, passed about to be played with and admired?

Then, one evening, a Tuesday, Darsie insisted that Louis attend her, only to be informed that Louis had gone off in the gig with Benbow and Mrs McCorkindale and would probably stop off at the Dalriada to partake of a refreshment and enquire if any clerking work was on offer in the neighbourhood and, if so, what did it pay.

The following evening, Wednesday, as soon as the door had closed on the wet-nurse and the gig had gone trundling off into the twilight, Darsie appeared in the living-room: Darsie washed, combed and painted, looking garish and ghastly in a lemon-yellow dress and the frilly lace pantalettes that had seen better days. She pushed open the door from the hall and entered, hesitantly.

The table was set for three. Nancy, in the kitchen, was wreathed in clouds of steam. Buckie had already taken his place at the table, Louis by the fireplace, an elbow on the mantelshelf, sipping something from a glass, as if, Darsie thought, he were the lord of a manor house and not an out-of-work good-for-nothing. He was looking down at Susanne who was seated in Buckie's big armchair with the baby in her lap, looking down with a warm smile as if he were proud not just of the little boy but of the young woman too; as if, indeed, Susanne Thorne was his good wife and she, Darsie Coburn Hollander, naught but a ghost or a memory.

'What's going on here?' Darsie said.

'Nothing's going on.' Louis broke the silence that had greeted his wife's appearance. 'We're just about to have supper. Is there something you want, dear, something we can do for you?'

'I'm hungry.'

'Well, that's a good sign,' said Buckie.

'Nancy will bring you a tray shortly,' said Louis.

'I don't want a tray,' said Darsie. 'I want a proper supper.'

'Are you sure you're strong enough?' said Louis.

'Of course she's strong enough,' said Buckie. 'Nancy, set another place.'

She wasn't strong enough, not quite. Her legs trembled and her back ached but she refused the chair that Louis pulled out and remained on her feet, staring down at Susanne and the baby who wore such a smug, self-satisfied expression that she was tempted to reach down and pinch his cheek, to force him to acknowledge her presence.

She gripped the chair-back, and said, 'Is it beef tonight?'

'Mutton,' Louis told her.

So far Susanne had uttered neither greeting nor reprimand but she altered her position and drew the baby closer to her, as if to protect him.

'Has it been fed?' Darsie asked.

'Who?' said Louis.

'It,' said Darsie. 'Him.'

'Yes,' Susanne answered. 'Adam has been fed.'

'Is he clean?'

'Clean and fresh,' said Buckie. 'Of course, he is.'

'Give him to me,' said Darsie.

Susanne glanced up at Louis, who shrugged.

Darsie stalked forward, arms thrust out before her as if she were sleep-walking. 'I said, give him to me.'

'He's asleep,' Susanne said.

'I don't care.'

'Darsie, my dear,' said Buckie. 'Have your supper first, then, if you're still of a mind . . .'

'Is it not mine? Am I not its mother?'

Susanne clung to Adam for a long moment before she transferred him not to Darsie but to Louis who in turn cautiously handed him over to his wife.

Darsie stiffened when the child was placed in her arms.

She held him awkwardly, arms extended, fingers digging into the shawl, and stared at Susanne with an intensity that hinted at achievement. Buckie flexed his fists as if he might be called upon to catch his grandson in mid-air, and they waited, all three, for some unassailable force to take hold of Darsie, sweep away her indifference and bring a tender smile to her painted face. With the instinct that infants share with animals, however, Adam Hollander sensed that he was no longer secure and, opening his eyes, squinted into the pastel haze that represented his version of the world and let out a yell so loud that Darsie would have dropped him if Louis hadn't plucked him from her arms.

'What is it? What's wrong with him?' Darsie cried.

'He doesn't know who you are, my dear,' said Buckie.

'Here,' Louis said, and passed the wailing infant to Susanne who cradled him against her shoulder and carried him off into the kitchen out of harm's way.

Two letters for Susanne arrived on Friday morning and when Mrs McCorkindale arrived to feed Adam, she went up to her room to read them.

The letter from Gregor was six weeks old. It had been sent back with the *Maiden of the Seas*, which ship, her holds full, had been first to turn for home. The *Merrilyn* had not yet attained capacity, however, and Gregor reckoned it might be September before he set foot on the cobbles of Dundee again. He requested Susanne's permission to call upon her as soon as he was discharged, for, he said, he had a great desire to see her again. He signed himself, *Sincerely and Affectionately, Your Servant and Pupil, Gregor Oakley.*

Susanne laughed and, hugging herself with delight, lay on her back on the bed and read the letter again, weighing every word that might indicate just how sincere and affectionate Gregor's feelings for her really were and how much of his 'desire' stemmed from having been too long at sea with nothing but seals and rough sailors for company.

Darsie sidled into the room. 'What are you doing?'

'None of your blessed business, Darsie.'

'I heard you laughing. Are you laughing at me?'

'Of course I'm not laughing at you.'

Darsie tugged the floral robe about her and combed her hair with her fingertips. 'Is that letter from my papa?'

'No.'

'Let me see it.'

'I'll do no such thing.' Susanne tucked Gregor's letter under her pillow. 'Take my word, it's not from your father.'

'Who is it from, then?'

Susanne lied without a qualm. 'Mr Greenbaum, my agent.'

'I don't believe you. I think you have a sweetheart and you're afraid Louis will find out.'

'Darsie, have you been drinking?'

'Not that I'd mind if you ran off,' Darsie went on, 'but Louis would be most annoyed. He wants you to stay here.'

'Does he?' Susanne said.

Darsie sighed. 'He thinks he's still in love with you.'

'I see,' Susanne said, evenly. 'Do *you* think he's still in love with me?'

'If only I'd died in childbed you'd have him all to yourself.'

'You have been drinking, haven't you?' Susanne said.

'Is that another letter I see there? Is that one from my father?'

'No, Darsie, it's from someone in St Andrews.'

'Who?'

'I won't know until I've opened it, will I?'

'Open it now.'

'No.'

Susanne planted both feet on the floor in the hope that Darsie would take the hint and leave but Darsie retreated only as far as the doorway.

She wondered if Darsie had told the truth, if Louis *was* still in love with her – if he had ever been in love with her – and, if so, what sort of love could accommodate two young women and a child.

Darsie said, 'I wish Papa would tell me where he is so that I might write and ask him for money.'

'Money for another new dress?' Susanne said.

'Money for my fare, to take me to be with him.'

'Leave High Cross?' said Susanne. 'Leave Louis?'

'Better off without me,' Darsie said, with a simpering smile. 'All of you, better off without me, don't you think?'

Susanne paused. 'He needs you, Darsie.'

'Louis? No, he . . .'

'Adam, I mean.'

'Oh, him!' Darsie said and, with a curious twitch of the head, drifted back across the passageway and shut herself up in her room.

It seemed odd to be heading for the church on a weekday afternoon. Susanne approached the manse warily. There were no signs of the minister or the handsome assistant but the sound of singing led her to the lawn behind the house where Zena was draping sheets across the privet hedge.

'Oh! It's you, is it?' Zena said, cheerfully. 'You got one too, I take it?'

'I did,' Susanne said.

'Are you pleased?' Zena asked.

'I am, I suppose,' Susanne answered. 'What terms has the school board offered you?'

'The post of assistant at fourteen pounds a year.'

'And the cottage, Rose Cottage?'

'Didn't they offer you the cottage?' Zena said.

'In fact, they did,' Susanne said. 'I shan't take it, of course.'

'What – the cottage, or the job?'

'The cottage,' Susanne said.

Zena wore a plain cotton dress and a skirt apron. She had
rolled up her sleeves and looked golden in the afternoon
sunlight. She unfurled the final sheet, flung it over the hedge,
then, holding the empty clothes basket above her head, joined
Susanne on the path. She dropped the basket, kicked it upside
down, sat on it and looked up at Susanne, ruefully.

'He's gone, you know,' she said. 'Willy Henceforth didn't
want to marry me. Turns out he already has a wife and child
hidden away in the Borders. My father and he had a frightful
row and Willy went off with his tail between his legs first thing
next morning.'

'Aren't you heartbroken?'

Zena stretched out her legs, rubbed her sturdy knees and
grinned.

'Not I! He was a cheesy sort of suitor in any case. All he
wanted was – well, a bit of diversion, shall we say? I'm more
relieved than heartbroken, 'specially since my daddy had us
levelled off as a matched pair. I couldn't help but laugh when
Willy broke the bad news. You should have seen the expression on my daddy's face when the word "wife" cropped up.'
She patted the top of the basket and invited Susanne to sit by
her. 'Now, tell me your news. Tell me all about Louis and
Darsie and the new baby.'

For ten minutes the young women chatted about all the things
that had happened to them in the weeks since their friendship
had fallen into disrepair, and then, affinity restored, fell to
discussing the Presbytery's offers of employment that were
dependent only upon passing certain tests in English reading,
history, geography, arithmetic and the shorter Catechism.

'The tests won't trouble me,' Zena said. 'Mr Arbuthnot will
confirm the school board's recommendation and my father
won't stand in my way this time. I've become too saucy for his
liking. He'll be relieved to see the back of me. That's why he
wanted to marry me off to Mr Henceforth.'

'You will have Rose Cottage for your own, then?'

'Aye,' Zena said, 'even with my father dropping in every day, my sisters and brothers to look out for, and my mother on the doorstep, at least I'll have a measure of independence and a bit of peace and quiet.'

'Until Peter Macfarlane comes to fetch you,' Susanne said.

'If he comes to fetch me,' Zena said. 'In any case, my daddy may be right. Perhaps I am better off waiting for the right man to come along. If you take on the wrong sort of man, like my mam did, you risk losing your self and your soul. No, Susanne, I've no wish to leap out of the frying-pan into the fire.'

'So you'll accept the Presbytery's offer?'

'Oh, yes,' Zena said. 'I'll grab it with both hands before I'm totally smothered by my family. Some good desperate soul is bound to want me sooner or later, I suppose. Until then I'll have a place and an income of my own; how many girls of our age can say that?'

'Not many,' Susanne agreed. 'Have you heard from Peter lately?'

'Aye, I had a letter just this morning. Weeks and weeks old, it was. He seems well enough, if a bit wearied with the weather, and the scarcity of blubber. He wants to call on me as soon as he gets home.'

'I hope you'll make him welcome,' Susanne said.

'Peter's only a boy, a daft boy. You know what they're like. He's been at sea for months – and who'd want to marry a whaler, anyhow?'

'True,' Susanne said. 'Who'd want to marry a whaler?'

Adam was small and helpless but not without power. He was a noisy baby, already quite wilful and demanding, but full of fleeting smiles, and as his strength grew, he clung to Susanne with his tiny pink fists as if he intended to hold on to her for ever. She knew that she must make her decision before Adam

Hollander, like his father before him, became so much part of her life that she would be unable to shake him off.

On Monday the Presbytery would send two representatives to Strayhorn to test the new teachers. If she met the required standard, she would take up her post in a fortnight's time with Zena as her assistant. Two young women in charge of Strayhorn school would set some tongues wagging but Susanne found that she no longer cared what folk thought of her. Unlike Zena, she was not entirely at ease with the notion of being a schoolteacher. By mid-winter her life would have taken on a new pattern, one pinned at each corner by things familiar and humdrum. But with August drawing to a close and autumn hanging on every bush and tree, she experienced a vague discontent with the responsibilities that she had put upon herself and a sense that she too might soon be smothered by circumstances.

At night, after everyone, including Adam, was asleep, she would slip Gregor's letter from the drawer, read it over and wonder what effect he would have on her future, or if Gregor, like Louis, wanted her only for the ease that the remnant of her father's fortune would bring.

She had come to Strayhorn as a child, uncertain, impressionable and afraid, but by some mysterious progression the balance had shifted and those folk upon whom she had once depended, depended now upon her. All too soon she would be absorbed into their story and would have no story of her own. Adam would watch her root and age and when his time came to go out into the wide world would allot her no more than a footnote in his own small history. Then she would be left with Louis and Darsie, with no virtues to record save that of indispensability, an epitaph as cheap as poor Aunt Bette's headstone. *Think again*, Miss Primrose had written to Alan Redpath: no wasted words, no despair, no plea for sympathy, just *Think again*.

Susanne rested Gregor's letter against her nose.

She listened to Buckie coughing in the room below, Adam whimpering in his sleep, Louis snoring in his mama's bed now that he had abandoned the hammock on the porch; to Darsie tossing restlessly across the passageway, and to the steady, solemn rhythm of the sea beating upon the beach, a sound she had always found comforting.

Soon, soon she must make her decision.

But not just yet.

It was a bright, frothy morning with an offshore breeze. Beyond the rocks, the sea ran deep, deep blue with creamy breakers rolling off towards the Isle of May and the faint, fretted headlands south of the Forth.

It was the first Friday in September; one step closer to the day when she must commit herself to teaching the sons and daughters of fisher folk and farmers, to digging in for winter on the lonely shore, to waiting modestly and patiently for Gregor to call; another promise that might or might not be kept. She was suddenly tired of patience and modesty, of being at everyone's beck and call, and of knowing in advance what each day would bring.

Breakfast was over. Darsie had wandered downstairs to eat porridge, sip a glass of sherry and, through the closed door of his mama's bedroom, nag at Louis to rouse himself and find something for her to do. The wet-nurse had come and gone, hurrying off to buy fish fresh from Strayhorn quay before the curers could snaffle the best of it. Nancy had gone into town with Mrs McCorkindale, cadging a ride on the gig in the hope that Benbow, out of the goodness of his heart, might drive her home again. Buckie had hobbled out on to the porch with his stick and his spy-glass. Ajax had followed him, while Thimble remained curled up, half asleep, beneath the dining table.

There was no sound but that of Darsie's cawing to disturb the smothering stillness. The fire had been lighted but the wind was too flirtatious to give it proper draught and little puffs of smoke blew out now and then from the throat of the chimney above the sluggish coals.

The baby lay kicking and gurgling in a fine wool shawl on Susanne's knee and only her duty to the child kept her from nodding off in her uncle's comfortable armchair.

Then Buckie shouted, 'Sail. Big sail.'

Susanne raised her head, scooped Adam into her arms and hurried outside. Bristling with excitement, Buckie had discarded his stick and was braced against the rail, the glass held to his eye. The glass was not required: the ship was close to shore, so close that she seemed to scrape the rocks at the base of High Cross hill, so huge and thrilling that the sight of her made Susanne gasp. Her sails were full of the offshore breeze, big and billowing, and white water streamed from her bow as she scudded past the lip of the bay then slewed away into the dark blue current and, within minutes, passed out of sight, heading for the mouth of the Tay.

'The *Merrilyn*?' Susanne cried. 'Is it the *Merrilyn*?'

'No, lass, she's the *New Resolution*,' Buckie said. 'Four hundred tons, packed with oil and bone by the set of her. I can't understand what she's doing so far south. She's part of the Greenland fleet, though, and sleek enough to make port before the rest of the stragglers.'

'Are they coming home?' Susanne said. 'Is Gregor coming home?'

Before her uncle could answer, she stepped off the porch and set off across the shingle with Adam cradled in her arms.

Gulls squawked overhead. The sea broke against the rocks at the base of the cliff and away to her left she could just make out the sails of the *New Resolution* dipping and swaying, and far off, beyond the point, other big sails, other big ships coming home on the rising tide.

She had spoken without thinking, from the heart not the

head. It hadn't dawned on her until that moment that her restless dissatisfaction had been so wrapped up with Gregor Oakley's return.

She reached the sea's edge and felt the wavelets break over her shoes. Kicking off her shoes, she stepped into the tongue of water that licked the clean brown sand, and, on impulse, lifted little Adam Hollander up so that he might experience the kiss of the salt sea breeze and taste the element that, if luck were on his side, would be his inheritance.

She stood stock still, the baby held up like a doll, her cheek pressed reassuringly against his cheek, ready at the first sign of fear or alarm to draw him down into her arms. But he did not cry out, did not squirm, for, it seemed, he was no more afraid of the sea than she was.

'*No*,' Darsie screamed. '*No*.'

The figures on the beach seemed small and inconsequential against the lift of the land: Darsie racing towards her across the sand, Ajax hot on her heels, Buckie hobbling far behind, and Louis, in his nightshirt, gingerly picking his way over the shingle, bewildered and half asleep. Then Darsie was upon her, splashing into the sea. Reaching out, she snatched at the baby with fierce passion, crying, 'Don't drown him. Don't you dare drown him. He's mine, Susanne. He's mine. He's mine.'

'Drown him? No!' Susanne said. 'I was just . . .'

She released the baby at once, easing him into Darsie's arms and watched the young woman clasp him to her breast and spin round and round in a mad dance of surrender and relief, chanting, 'You shan't have him. He isn't yours. You can't do what you like with him. I didn't mean it. He's mine, aren't you, dearest, aren't you mine?'

'Of course he is,' Susanne said and, picking up her shoes, walked off across the sand, leaving Buckie and Louis to escort Darsie and her son safely back to the house.

*   *   *

She was packed and ready when the gig returned from Stray-horn. Dressed in her Sunday-best day-dress and a loose-sleeved mantlet, she waited on the porch with the travelling bag by her side.

Nancy had gone indoors to attend to Darsie and the baby and she was left alone with Louis and Buckie while Benbow watered the pony in the yard. She couldn't make them under-stand that she was not offended, that Darsie's panic had been perfectly understandable under the circumstances and that she was leaving simply because she had better things to do than wait on the Hollanders. It would not be a final parting, far from it. She would return to High Cross often in the weeks ahead, attached, she hoped, to young Mr Oakley's arm. But she would not become a teacher. She would turn down the post of principal and leave the welfare of Strayhorn's sons and daughters in Zena's capable hands.

'There's a train through Hask at half past two,' Susanne said. 'I intend to be on it.'

'What will you do, where will you stay?' said Louis. 'You can't travel alone, Susanne. It isn't the done thing. What will folk think of you?'

'I don't care what folk think of me,' Susanne told him. 'Besides, I won't be alone, not for long.'

'Do you have enough money?' Buckie asked.

'I'll draw from my account,' Susanne said, 'and Mr Green-baum will help me find a suitable accommodation if I require it.'

'Why are you doing this now?' Louis said. 'What have we done to send you chasing off to Dundee on the spur of the moment?'

She glanced at him from the corner of her eye, more rueful than annoyed. Louis had not been man enough to hold her and had lost her long since but, his genius notwithstanding, had been too stupid to realise it. She had loved him when she was too young to know better and all she felt for him now was a wistful residue of affection, and a degree of pity. He had chosen his course by default and would muddle through without her, or her money, to lean on. He had Darsie, and Nancy, and a child to look after and to look after him, and would go dithering to his grave, eventually, still seeking approval and admiration. She would not, could not, wait for habit to bring her happiness.

On seeing the bag and the travelling dress, Buckie had said nothing. He had nodded once, quite gently, when she'd told him of her plans, then, leaning his forearms on the rail, had looked out to sea for sight of another ship returning from the ice-fields, another tall ship like the *Merrilyn* that would bring back memories of his youth and young manhood. There was nothing pretentious or effete about Buckie Hollander, nothing sly or demanding. Her uncle, like her father, was an honest man, a modest man, a man of strong appetites and firm convictions; that was what she longed to find, a man whose sterling and dependable qualities would sustain an enduring love, a love that, with luck and fortitude, would last a lifetime.

'Is it what Darsie said?' Louis went on. 'She meant no harm by it, you know. She hasn't been herself since . . .' He shrugged. 'At least she's taken to Adam. I suppose we've you to thank for that. When will we see you again?'

'Quite soon,' Susanne said, as Benbow nosed the pony around the corner from the yard and brought the gig up to the step. 'Now, however, I must go, Louis, for I've something very important to do in Dundee. Something that won't wait a moment longer.'

'What?' Louis snapped, desperately. 'For God's sake, what?'

If he had been awake, if he had been out of bed, if he had seen the whaling ship beating hard against the current, he might have deduced what business had summoned her to the port on the Tay; she had just enough of the devil in her still to keep him guessing.

Benbow lifted her bag and put it in the gig.

She tightened the strings of her bonnet and stepped down off the porch.

She looked up at her uncle, leaning on the rail, at Louis looming, and glowering, behind him. Then, stirring himself, Buckie said, 'Hold on, sweetheart. Hold on one second,' and limped off indoors.

He returned a minute later, carrying a faded, furled old parasol in one gnarled hand. He reached out, without ceremony, and gave it to her.

'Ah!' Susanne said. 'Aunt Bette's, I assume?'

'Aye,' Buckie said. 'My Bette's,' and with a wink by way of blessing, let Benbow drive his niece away to welcome her true love home.